Be careful what you wish for

Sue Nicholls

'Every normal person in fact, is only normal on the average. His ego approximates to that of the psychotic in some part or other and to a greater or lesser extent.'

Sigmund Freud

This book is dedicated to my long-suffering family, who endured late laundry, burnt dinners and missed appointments in sacrifice to my writing.

THE
MEETING

Chapter 1

The broad staircase of the small theatre is purple-shabby. Fee's footsteps are hushed by the fading carpet, and she glides her fingers along a hand-rail polished smooth by countless others before her. She is trying to suppress anxiety about her small daughter. Kitty has just waved goodbye from among several other little ones, variously sucking thumbs, hopping, and looking expectant. There is no indication that Kitty is worried by the bossy woman running the drama class so Fee decides to focus on the benefits of this new activity.

She sweeps her eyes over the muted foyer. There are people, but not many for a Saturday. Through a smoked glass wall to her left are spectral outlines of diners and drinkers in the cafe-cum-restaurant where she's decided to pass this forty minutes of Kitty's absence. She heads for the scent of coffee.

Waiting for a skinny cappuccino she scans the busy room for a vacant table, and spots one on the far side, next to a couple of women, chatting amid a tumble of squashy bags and folded coats. She fixes her eyes on the spot, hoping nobody will grab it before her order is ready. Coffee takes so long to make, these days. From the corner table a boy-child makes a tottering bid for freedom. One of the two women reaches out and grabs him by the arm. Her flossy locks bounce in the soft light. The other girl, Mediterranean in colouring, sips from a thick, white cup, and pushes a buggy back and forth.

Fee weaves between diners to bag her spot and drapes her jacket over the back of a chair. The two women at the next table are worrying about the officious drama teacher and It's hard not to eavesdrop.

There's a muffled squawk from the buggy and the petite and appealing, olive skinned girl bends to the small hollow of the pram and extracts a tiny, lolling infant with cappuccino coloured skin and a dandelion clock of black hair. She places the infant on her shoulder and rocks her body, patting its back. The new-born raises its wobbly head, belches and ejects a glob of creamy white liquid before subsiding again onto the sweet and slippery shoulder. Fee grabs the napkin from her saucer. 'Here, let me,' she offers, and soaks up what she can from the coat. 'Thanks very much.' The young woman screws her head in Fee's direction. 'If you could take Lucas a moment I'll get this thing off.' Fee accepts the child, and as the girl shrugs off her pea jacket, regrets wearing her Burberry sweater.

A familiar aroma of milk and lotion rises from the tiny bundle, and Fee finds herself enveloping him in her arms, and staring, fascinated, into the tiny face with its curdled-milky chin.

The flossy mother sits passively on the opposite side of the table with a small boy on her lap. His eyelids droop, and chubby digits twist and tug at a lock of the straw coloured hair draped over her slender shoulders. 'I'd forgotten how that happens,' Fee remarks. 'At the time, you think you'll never forget but you do.'

'He's so sicky. I should have learned by now.' The girl smiles a huge and open grin. 'Thanks so much for your help.' She holds out her arms for the child and Fee passes him back.

'I'm Millie.' She proffers a small hand under her son and they shake fingers. Millie indicates the other mother with a small movement of her head as she shifts the baby and sits back down.

'Twitch and I are waiting for our older children; they're upstairs doing a drama class with a terrifying lady.' She makes a comical face.

Fee remains standing looking down at her. 'Me too. She was pretty terrible, wasn't she? I hope they're OK.'

Across the table, Twitch, her young son dozing on her lap, regards Fee comfortably - not 'Nervous Twitch' then. 'Come and join us?' Her voice is deeper than her wraithlike features suggest. Fee slides into a seat.

Huddled in her corner, dark haired Millie breast feeds, and tells with engaging openness of her family. She has two mixed race offspring, Olivia upstairs, and the pukey baby. Her husband, Mick, is from Ghana. She drapes a terry nappy over her shoulder and winds Lucas without mishap then gathers him to her.

'So, what about you, Fee?' She asks as she buttons her shirt. 'Do you only have your little girl or is there a *New Man* at home with a brood of others?' She pronounces the words New Man, like the MC at a function.

'There's just Kitty. She's plenty for me – us. I work full time so having another baby would be a strain.' She avoids tackling the New Man reference. 'How about you, Twitch?'

'I've got the two. I'm just beginning to raise my eyes towards the future again, I feel as if I've been surrounded by nappies and feeding routines forever!'

'What might you do?' Millie gazes at the translucent eyelids of her son.

'Oh, I don't know. Escape.' Millie looks up and she and Fee regard Twitch in silence. Twitch looks at them both with a hopeless expression. 'Sorry. I can't think about anything else. I shouldn't have said that. You hardly know me – I hardly know you.' She shrugs her shoulders. 'I hardly know anyone!'

Fee leans on the table with both arms, and bends towards her new acquaintance but Twitch is backing off.

'It's just the usual stuff: boredom, inattentive husband, abandoned career.' She flaps a hand in the air as though batting at a wasp.

'Well, if you ever need a shoulder…' Millie smiles.

'Thanks.' Twitch gives a forlorn smile and picks up her cup.

The remaining forty minutes pass in small talk then Millie, with Lucas on her shoulder, drags her buggy to a space beside the bottom step, and they make their way up the stairway, hoping the lesson has been a success.

A crowd of boys and girls muddle out of the room, full of excitement, and Fee forgives the teacher. She's human after all.

They retrace their steps passing portraits and landscapes by local artists, on the walls of the corridor. The older children dance ahead, already friends, and the women, less impetuous, agree to meet again next week, then part, each in a different direction.

Fee grasps Kitty's hand, and heads for the underground car park. When she glances back through the glass entrance doors, Twitch's straw-coloured hair and ochre skirt catch her eye, swinging from side to side like pampas grass.

The parking floor is gloomy, and their footsteps echo off concrete walls.

'What did you do today, my poppet?'

'Well, we had to be tiny.' Kitty releases Fee's hand and stops to crouch into a ball. 'Then we had to be tall.' She takes a few steps and throws her arms into the air. 'Then we made ourselves as wide as a tree.' Her arms fly out to become branches, 'and really, really thin like a pencil.' This calls them to a complete stop as Kitty holds her breath and stands to attention, her whole being focused on narrowness. Fee needs to get on, there is a mound of work to do, but first, Kitty has a swimming lesson.

'Show me when we get home Kitty.' She opens the car door.

Has Paul started the chores? She suspects he's still in bed, and sighs as she settles in the driver's seat.

During the short journey to the sports centre Fee worries about what will greet her at home, while Kitty chirrups away in the back seat.

Chapter 2

Paul slumbers in the empty double bed, luxuriating in his solitude, half wondering what time it is. Today he plans to acquaint himself with his recent acquisition, an old, *Matchless* motorcycle.

There's a clatter from downstairs, and the front door bangs. His eyelids flick open. Christ. Fee's home. She wanted him to do something or other, he riffles through his memory, oh yes, wash up the breakfast stuff. Paul screws his head round at the clock on his bedside table. Its digital figures glare 11:30. He leaps from his cocoon and dashes naked to the bathroom, locking the door behind him. Twisting the knob of the shower he climbs into the not-yet-warm water, singing enthusiastically and scrubbing himself in the manner of a man who has been up for ages. When he's finished he towels himself with vigour. On the wide landing, he pauses and casts his eyes to the bottom of the stairs, meeting the accusing gaze of his wife.

'I'm on my way down.' Paul's eyebrows lift and his chin juts and shakes. Fee turns away towards the kitchen in silence. Cursing, he rubs the towel over his bushy chest and pads into the bedroom.

The solid, fitted wardrobes and quality curtains in this spacious room always please him, less so its unfortunate pink colour. All credit to Fee's father, he came up trumps when he bought this house five years ago for their wedding present. Fee had accepted the gift with reluctance but Paul, who came from humble beginnings, was overwhelmed.

The clattering of dishes floats up from the kitchen. Well, if she's doing the washing up, he can get straight out to the bike. He drags on grimy clothing and stuffs a battered cigarette packet into a pocket. Leaving the bed unmade and the bedroom in curtained darkness he gallops, whistling, downstairs to make a cuppa.

Fee stands at the sink with her back to him. As he steps into the kitchen Kitty, his inconvenient little monkey, throws herself at his legs, wrapping her arms round his knees then releasing him.

'Daddy. Have you just got up?' Without waiting for an answer, she rushes on. 'Guess where we've been?'

'I give in.' He crouches to squint into her mischievous eyes. 'Where have you been?'

'Swimming, silly. Can't you see my hair is wet and my eyes are red?' She opens her eyes wide, looking demented.

'Well,' Paul moves his head at an angle and concentrates. 'Ye-e-s, I see what you mean, but they're not red, they're bright green. I think you must have turned into an alien!'

Kitty giggles, and tries to hug him.

'Careful you little monster, you'll have me over.' He shoots out a hand to avoid landing on his backside.

With a grin Kitty lifts her hands and pushes his shoulders until they are both rolling on the kitchen floor behind Fee.

'Next week I'm doing swimming on Tuesday evenings 'cos I'm doing drama on Saturdays. Can you take me sometimes Daddy?' Paul gives a bear growl and pins Kitty to his chest.

'I expect so,' he says absent mindedly, and blows a raspberry into her ear.

Outside, someone is practising on a trumpet, its honking notes sound worse than a cow in labour.

Fee continues with the washing up, ignoring the noise, and her family writhing behind her.

'Kitty sweetheart, would you get your swimming things out of the bag and put them in the basket by the washing machine please?'

Kitty's face still beams as she scrambles up and goes back into the hall. Paul leaps to his feet and grabs the handle of the back door.

'I'll be in the garage, give me a shout when lunch is ready.' He opens the door and hops onto the path, his tea forgotten. The trumpet reaches an agonising crescendo.

***

He extracts dripping pieces of engine from a bowl of detergent and lays them on newspaper then takes a swig from an old bottle of Coke, wondering if he could put the carburettors in the dishwasher.

Through the window he sees a small figure with faltering steps approaching along the path and bearing a plate of sandwiches. Paul smiles. When Fee is out, he and Kitty have huge amounts of fun. Recently they've been practising on Kitty's new bicycle. Together they career across the lawn, plunging occasionally into the pond, then slopping through the house leaving muddy puddles for Fee to clean up. Paul applies an old toothbrush to bits of metal and his thoughts move to Fee. She seems to have lost her libido, and her sense of humour. He can cope though, he still has the fundamentals: his bike, his garage, his fags, his daughter, and not too much domestic hassle.

Kitty reaches the side door and he sweeps it open.

'Ah,' he makes a dashing bow, 'thank you waitress.' Kitty reaches to tilt the platter onto the bench and when it's safe, he spins her round to face the bike and lifts her by her armpits.

'What do you think of Daddy's other baby?' They study the skeleton that is his motor bike.

'Does it go?' Kitty sounds dubious.

'Well not yet, but wait 'til it's finished then it'll go like a rocket. I might take you for a ride if I can find a helmet to fit you.'

'Mummy says I'm not big enough to go on the back of a bike.'

Paul dangles her feet back to the ground. 'Well we'll keep it a secret from Mummy.

'How about giving me a hand?'

The little girl turns a worried face up to him. 'Won't I get dirty?'

Paul wiggles his fingertips in her armpits,

'You're already grubby, look.' She giggles.

He takes a grimy bite of his sandwich. Cheese and pickle, his favourite. His woman knows how to please him. Perhaps he'll have a try in the sex department tonight, after a beer or two in the pub.

***

It's later than he'd planned. Paul waves his key round the lock until it finds its home. The door gives under his weight and he stumbles into the hall. Throwing his keys on the table with a jangle he negotiates the stairs on all fours and staggers into the dark warmth of the bedroom.

14

The shadowy outline of Fee's slumbering body under the duvet entices him and he fumbles to remove his trousers. In his desperation, he over-balances and falls with a grunt onto the bed. Fee stirs and moans. 'What time is it?'

Far away, on this cusp between today and tomorrow, someone is having a party. Faint rock music floats through the night air.

'About 11,' he lies, and slides under the covers. Reaching out a hand, he lands it determinedly on Fee's warm breast. She yelps and rolls away.

'You're freezing. And you reek of cigarettes.'

'Aw, come on love, you're awake now, and we don't need to get up in the morning.' Fee groans and turns to him.

Chapter 3

Lucas is asleep and Millie rocks his buggy and talks. Twitch's Josh is between table legs with a pile of plastic dinosaurs, chuntering to himself in triceratops language.

As ever the table is cluttered with debris, although there is a small oasis of space in front of Fee. She and Twitch, shoulder to shoulder, are showing Millie their full attention.

'It's his mum who's the problem. Well there's nothing wrong with her per se, she's been good to Mick - brought him up on her own after his dad died.' She pauses and drops her chin into a palm braced on her elbow. 'The trouble is, Mick thinks she's right about everything.

'That must be hard.' Twitch puts a hand to her son's silky head but keeps her gaze on Millie as he walks a dinosaur up her thigh.

'It's difficult because I want to go back to work. Mick's mum says my place is with the kids. She wants me to stay at home, as she never could.'

Fee leans towards her new friend, and the sharp edge of the table digs into her breasts.

'Do you have something in mind?'

'Well, it's stupid I suppose.' Millie's brimming eyes scan Fee's face. 'Mick's a chef. He's been teaching me to cook. I think he hoped an interest in food would make me more content to stay at home.' She switches her eyes to Twitch, 'Don't get me wrong, I love my kids. It just didn't occur to me I wouldn't go out to work. The more they try to stop me, the more frustrated I get. Now I hate everything about being at home.'

16

Fee nods her comprehension.

'So now I can cook, the thing I'd really love to do is open my own restaurant. I don't suppose Mick meant *that* to happen!' Despite her tears Millie smiles. 'Ironic, isn't it?'

'Have you told him?'

'There's no point. I know what he'll say' She gazes down at the baby it his carry-cot. 'Do you think a woman should sacrifice her ambition for her children?'

Twitch's responds with uncharacteristic vehemence, 'No. You *must* do what's right for you. It's a big mistake to give up your dreams. Postpone them OK, but don't ever give them up.' She gathers her hair in both slender hands and flings it behind her. Millie looks at her. 'You sound very sure.'

'I *am* sure. I didn't realise it when I first married Maurice but I'm positive about it now. Every person has a right to fulfilment.' She takes a slopping gulp of her coffee and shakes her head at them. 'I don't mean neglect your children, but you know, this kind of thing should be talked about when you both set out in life together. Part of the deal. It needs compromise and determination. No person should make all the sacrifices in a marriage.'

The other two stare at her. She's never said so much before. Twitch prevents further comment by asking, 'how did you and Mick meet?'

'At a party. Mick towered above everyone else. I'm so little,' she wrinkles her nose. 'I noticed him straight away. He looked so...', she pauses, 'noble. Like some kind of African prince.'

Twitch leans on her elbows and her shoulder brushes against Fee's. Fee, leans away but Twitch doesn't seem to notice.

'You know that song?' Millie starts to croon. 'Some enchanted evening, you may see a stranger, you may see a stranger, across a crowded room.' Her eyes glow. 'My dad used to sing that. My childhood was joyous. I'm lucky.' Her face droops again. 'But sad.'

'It may pass.' Fee has her own story.

'What happened next?' Twitch leans closer.

'Our eyes met.' Millie presses her heart with both hands and looks lovesick. 'I knew he'd come over, and he did - not straight away. Suddenly he was beside me, offering me a glass of red wine. We talked all evening. The party went on around us but we were oblivious. He invited me out. We kissed but nothing more. He's always been incredibly romantic...'

'But?' Twitch asks.

But his mother disapproves of me. We don't talk about it, but in a good relationship you should be able to discuss your differences, don't you think?'

Fee shrugs. Discussion doesn't happen between herself and Paul. Their marriage is built on accusation and defence.

Twitch keeps her eyes on her cup.

'We found we shared a love of eating - we both adore spicy food. On our third date Mick took me for a curry.' Millie stops, her nose raised as if she is sniffing that long-ago Biryani, and her eyes stare into the past. It was a good meal.' She gives an apologetic laugh. 'We're both a bit obsessed.'

Fee, wonders if anyone could be less like herself.

'Mick told me about his childhood. He arrived in England with his parents at the age of two, but his dad died - knocked over by a car almost as soon as they got here. Mick's mum was left to bring him up alone.'

Millie's face takes on an impish mien. 'I asked Mick if his mum spoke English when they first arrived here, and Mick said *Yes and No.*'

'I didn't understand until he explained that she could only say *Yes* and *No*. He makes me laugh.'

'It sounds as though you love him,' observes Twitch.

'That's the problem, I do, but I feel imprisoned and I can't make him see. It's a cultural thing. My parents tried to warn me when Mick and I first got together, but I stormed off accusing them of racism.'

Fee pulls back her sleeve to uncover a gold watch - a gilt guilt present from her father, Clive.

'We should go.'

Back in the car, with Kitty fastened into her seat at the back, Fee contemplates the synchronicity of her meeting with Twitch and Millie. She points the car towards home, following the rural road's twists and slopes, half aware that Kitty is talking.

At home, she is amazed to find Paul standing at the sink with his hands plunged in a soapy washing up bowl. She's on the brink of expressing her gratitude, when she realises that the contents of the foamy water are not pots and pans. Projecting from the suds are the metallic edges of engine parts, and the floor is awash with oily water.

'Paul! How could you? Look at this mess.'

Paul takes in the puddle, and a sodden and grimy area round the sink.

18

'Don't get your knickers in a twist. I'll clean up afterwards.'
He might, but she'll have to do it again.

Chapter 4

At the work-bench Paul hums under his breath. This is what he loves most – after Kitty of course - and Fee. He pauses in his task. Hmm, if he had to choose between his motor bike and his wife, he's undecided which he would pick? He takes a long drag of his cigarette, and blows a stream of smoke from his nose.

Things are changing in their marriage. He's doing his utmost under very difficult circumstances. Hasn't he found another job after getting the push from the last one? And Kitty, he plays with her -that's important. Left to Fee, Kitty would be polite, tight-arsed and bored. He stops thinking about Fee and Kitty to administer some loving care to his bike, enjoying the simple rituals of filing and brushing, shining and buffing. He tightens a screw, and stands back to admire his handy work, then pats his mistress and leaves her alone in the middle of the garage.

In the silent house, he removes his shoes at the back door, congratulating himself on being such a thoughtful fellow, then, after removing the oil from his fingers, pads up to the bedroom. The weighty wardrobe door opens smoothly at his pull, and he runs a hand along the sleeves of shirts and jackets to the stiff brown and slightly flaky arm of a World War I flying jacket. Its bulbous arm looks as though the pilot might still occupy it. Using both hands he pulls the coat from its slot and lies it on the bed, then donning leather trousers, boots and sweater, he lifts the garment from its hanger, pokes his hands into the tubular sheepskin sleeves and shrugs himself into its snug interior. In the mirror, his stocky body stands like a small boy in a snow suit but this does not dampen his admiration. He decides that a scarf would complete the effect.

Sweat breaks out under his layers, so grabbing his helmet from the bottom of a cupboard, he squeaks down the stairs.

The stage is set, and swinging open the doors of the garage he gives a silent 'Tad*aa*.' The bike glints in the Super Trouper autumn sunlight, and he cocks his leg ready to mount it. The sound of grinding grit interrupts him, and Fee's car pulls into the driveway. He watches her elegant ankle extend below the edge of the door.

'The car's playing up. It keeps hesitating.'

Kitty bounces up.

'Ooh Daddy, she's beautiful. Can we go for a ride?' Paul lowers his poised leg, and smiles in approval of Kitty's use of the personal pronoun. Fee pauses in the porch.

'Certainly not. You're not big enough.' She stares hard at Paul, who was going to make a more optimistic reply.

'Go on in with Mummy.' He puts on a wonky face, wrinkling his nose and pushing his chin sideways in Fee's direction. Kitty squeals with laughter and runs off.

'We'll go to the park later,' he calls, 'when I've given this beauty her maiden voyage.' He settles into the saddle and stands on the kick start. The roar of the motor prevents him from answering the question Kitty is taking a breath to ask.

'What's a…?'

The bike reverberates between his thighs, and with a wave of his stiff arm and a twist of the throttle grip, he roars off down the road.

Chapter 5

'I hope you don't mind my asking…' Fee wonders if this is too personal? 'Twitch… is a very unusual name. Is it short for anything?'
'Sabrina.' Twitch smiles.
'Sabrina?'
'Yes, it's short for Sabrina.'
Fee spends a moment thinking before the penny drops. 'The Teenage Witch'
Millie laughs. 'That was quick. I hadn't heard of *Sabrina the Teenage Witch* so I didn't know what she was talking about.'
'My parents must have been out of their minds with a surname of Hazel.' Twitch gives a rare smile.
A loud guffaw explodes from Millie.
'What's your married name?'
'Roman. I suppose I should be grateful. There was a teacher at school called Miss Craft. Imagine if I'd wed a Mr Craft, I'd have been in the national papers. She punches splayed hands at an imaginary, headline. 'Twitch Hazel becomes Twitch Craft.'
Millie puts her chin in her palm and leans her elbow on the table.
'Are you ready to tell us about your life now, Twitch?'
'*Millie.*' Fee reproves.
'It's OK, I don't mind, but it's not very exciting.' Twitch pulls a long face. 'Sex got between us.' She stoops to check on Josh, leaning against her leg and playing with his dinosaurs, then lowers her voice. 'Not Maurice's and mine, but his with some girl at the office.'

There's a crash from across the room, and Fee slops her drink. For a brief time the camouflaging hubbub drops and Twitch falls silent. Her eyes travel to a waitress dropping to her knees between tables to gather white shards and crescents of broken crockery. The silenced diners lose interest and return to their conversations, and Twitch turns back to Fee and Millie.

'I got pregnant at Art College. We didn't plan it, obviously, but Maurice and I were in love so finishing my art degree wasn't a priority. We got married and moved to a grotty little terrace and Sam came along. Maurice finished his exams and found a job. After a couple of years, we could afford our own house – Maurice was working for a chain of estate agents so we were given the best choice of properties, and good deals on the mortgage and surveys and so on.'

She gazes at her coffee cup and after a few seconds picks up a snowy paper napkin and pulls at one corner. A slender strip of tissue wafts to the table and lies like a shredded promise.

Millie nods, her eyebrows high and her pupils shining like the eyes of a blackbird.

'We moved, then moved again. Maurice was doing well so we had Josh,' she jerks her thumb at the little boy beneath the table. 'I had two rowdy boys and a big house to manage. There wasn't time to think.' She strips strand after strand from the napkin making a feathery pile that shifts in the current of air. 'Sex was non-existent. Maurice put on weight and lost interest in the family. He watched TV every Saturday and ignored us.' Twitch covers the delicate heap of paper with long bony fingers, and crushes it into a sweaty bundle. 'Aren't men supposed to *play* football with their sons, not watch it on television, complaining if they interrupt?' She stuffs the shreds into her cup where it sucks slowly on the dregs of her cold coffee.

'Our relationship was going downhill, and then one night he came home looking more unhappy than usual. I thought: this is it, he wants to split up, but he broke down and apologised for the way he'd behaved. I didn't understand what he meant. I imagined he was bored – I know I was. But he was confessing to an affair. It was over, and had never been important because he loved me.' Twitch throws her eyes towards the ceiling.

'My first reaction was, I couldn't believe anyone would fancy him.' She blinks at Fee and Millie. 'I couldn't see the attraction at all.'

'You drifted out of love. It happens.' Fee leans back against the metal bars of the chair and folds her arms across her breast as Twitch continues.

'When I'd had time to take in what Maurice had told me, I was angry. I kept thinking about everything I'd given up: my career, my friends. I felt stupid. Duped. I moved into the spare bedroom and that's where I am now.' Twitch shuffles in the chair and shakes her hair. 'Maurice says I'm trying to make him suffer, but I'm not. I simply want to be away from him and the spare room is as far as I can get. I don't work, so I can't support the boys, and I won't leave them with a man who can't even boil an egg.'

Twitch drops her face into her hands and hunches over her elbows. The others reach out uselessly.

Chapter 6

Paul has bought a side car; it is a thing of beauty. He and Kitty are roaring along 'A' roads towards Alton Towers. As the road twists between hedges and through villages, Kitty shrieks with delight, her small features grinning under a lopsided red helmet.

They have left pan-faced Fee at home. She disapproves of the trip. Paul expected that when he announced it, intentionally late, over dinner last night.

They queue for tickets. They queue for rides. They scream on sweeping curves and dips and they line up for hot dogs.

'Can we have chips Daddy?'

'Sure. You can't have a hot dog without chips.' Paul adds mustard, ketchup and mayonnaise to his meal. Kitty adds ketchup, twice.

Kitty is too small for many of the attractions.

'We'll come back next year,' says Paul.

'Shall we come back every year?'

'Until we're old.'

When they have been on every possible ride and thrown quoits and steered boats, Paul drags his stumbling daughter through the October darkness. They cross car park after car park on throbbing feet.

At the corner of a distant field Paul lifts his daughter into the sidecar. He straps her in with the non-authentic seat belt, insisted upon by Fee. Kitty's neck flops like a tulip stem under the heavy helmet.

'Did you have a good time Pops?' Paul smiles down at Kitty. In the distance, they can still hear music from the merry-go-round.

The helmet nods.

Paul tucks a rug around his daughter.

***

The head-light streaks past silver tree trunks, through a lamp-lit village where some houses already have Christmas trees. Ridiculous.

Kitty's head is motionless inside the rug.

A sudden movement to Paul's left makes him swerve, too late. The creature skitters under the wheels and Paul yanks on the brakes. They bump to a halt and Kitty's helmet bobs up.

'What's happened?'

'Nothing Pops. Go back to sleep.' Paul climbs off the *Matchless* and squats in the road to look beneath the fuselage. In her seat, Kitty cranes her neck so that her helmet clonks on the plastic side-screen.

A cat. Stone dead and bloody.

Kitty struggles with her straps and fumbles with the door of the sidecar, then falls head first onto the pavement and remains on the ground, twisting her protective hat to look between the wheels and across the motionless feline to Paul's face.

'The poor thing! Why did you run it over?'

'I didn't mean to, it ran straight into the road before I could avoid it.'

'You were going too fast Daddy.' She sounds like her fucking mother.

Paul reaches out to extricate the warm, lifeless creature. It looks loved. Apart from a gash to its head and a tax-disc sized patch of blood matting the fur on its back, it seems undamaged, but it is unquestionably dead. A tiny bell hangs limp from a sea-green collar around its neck but there is no means of identification. Paul looks around at the nearby houses.

Kitty stands up on the tarmac. 'Here. It came from here.' she points to a cottage, set back from the road. Its path through a narrow hedge-lined front garden, leads to a faintly lit door. At the foot of the door he can make out the shadowy rectangle of a cat flap.

'Go and see. Go and tell them!' Kitty pummels his leather-clad leg.

The metal knocker echoes in a hallway then they hear the slow shuffle of feet approaching. The door opens.

'Yes?' The old man's speech is querulous. An odour of decay mixed with cat pee floats out into the chill darkness. A grey sock peeps through a hole in his slipper.

'Have you got a cat with a greeny collar?' Kitty squints up at him.

'Trixi?' The parchment face pokes at them, crumpled in expectation of unwelcome news. 'Is she alright?'

26

Paul shakes his head. 'I'm sorry. She just ran out under my wheels.' The rheumy eyes fill.

'She was only young.' He turns away as if to shut the door, but after reaching for something beyond their view, turns back and thrusts a carrier bag at them with an age spotted hand. 'Put her in here. I'll get my neighbour to stick her in the incinerator in the morning.'

'What's an...?'

'Come on Kitty, back into your seat.'

'But what is an incinimater?'

'Ask Mummy.'

'Can we have a cat Daddy?'

'It wouldn't be fair to have a pet Pops. You know what Mummy says: animals make work, and need company during the day.'

'Mummy is mean!'

'Don't say that about Mummy, Kitty. She loves you.'

Chapter 7

The children burst from their drama class clutching pieces of paper.
Kitty doesn't wait to be asked for news of her morning.
'Mummy, we're going to do a ferformance.'
'That's very exciting.'
Kitty shoves a mangled leaflet at Fee.
'It's in three weeks' time. You will come, won't you - and Daddy?'
'Definitely, and Daddy wouldn't miss it for anything.'
Fee's phone trembles in her bag. The others are moving away.
'Hello, darling.' Her mother's words have an unaccustomed quake.
'Mummy, are you OK? Are you hurt?'
I'm fine. It's not that, but can I see you.'
'I'll come straight over. Kitty and I are just leaving the theatre.'
'Take Kitty home first.'

***

In the open driveway Mummy's car stands alone - Father must be
playing golf. Fee slams her door and teeters across the gravel in her
heels. Joy waits at the open door, her hand resting on the catch, her
eyes ruddy. They embrace, and stroll hand in hand to the stone flagged
kitchen.
The older woman scrapes out a chair from the heavy oak table and
makes Fee sit, then she sits next to Fee so that their shoulders touch.
She takes one of Fee's hands in both of hers, and Fee's stomach twists.
'I've been to the hospital.'

***

Millie looks across at Fee's drawn face and glances at Twitch.

'It's terrible out there today.' Twitch nods her head upwards at the battering of hailstones on the roof of the restaurant.

'Yes, we're in the best place here,' Millie replies, lightly.

Fee stares at her spoon until Millie can no longer resist.

'Fee. What's happened? Are you alright?'

Fee raises her eyes and slips the spoon into her saucer.

'Not great. My mother has cancer.' Her face crumples.

Millie and Twitch wrap Fee in their arms while she weeps.

'Is it bad?' Asks Millie.

Fee picks up the teaspoon again, and winds it through her coffee.

'Weeks, possibly months. She won't accept treatment or come to me. She's going to stay with that… my father. I can't help her.' Fee throws the spoon into her saucer and it clatters onto the table leaving beads of coffee in its wake.

'If you need me to have Kitty or,' Millie's lips skew, 'come and thump your dad, just ask.'

'Anything you want,' Twitch interjects, 'we'll be here.'

'Thanks.'

'Is she managing?' Twitch returns to her seat.

'She seems OK at the moment. She doesn't want me to put myself out but I think she understands my need to visit.'

They drift into silence. Sipping from cups, even after they are empty. While Millie threads her way to the bar to order more drinks, Twitch leans towards Fee.

'Has the doctor put you in touch with a hospice?'

He may have. Fee hadn't taken much in. 'I think so.' She rakes her hair back until it stands up in a dishevelled mane.

When Millie returns they discuss the forthcoming performance. It's a variety show and Kitty is singing a solo.

'Your mum will enjoy that Fee. Bring her along.'

'That's a good idea, Twitch.'

What about your dad?' Millie cocks her head.

'He won't be coming.' Fee's tone brooks no discussion, and Millie moves on.

'My parents are on holiday for the next month. They won't be here either.'

'Mine live in Australia.' Twitch tells them, 'It's a long way to come.' Millie's lashes almost touch her eyebrows.

'We know so little about each other, and yet so much.'

'When all this is over,' Fee wafts her hand through the air, 'we'll have to spend more time together. Maybe take the children for a day out.'

'Yes. Let's.'

'That would be good.'

***

At home, Mick is padding around the kitchen in the shorts and baggy tee shirt he slept in. The hailstorm has abated but it's still icy outside. The heat from the kitchen welcomes Millie and the children.

'Hi guys. Had a good time?' His palm rasps across Saturday morning stubble.

'Not bad. Livvie had a lovely time at drama, didn't you Liv.'

'I'm gonna be a flower, and sing a song, and dance.' The child beams.

'Well, I need to see that.' He winks, and Olivia screws her face in an attempt to wink back.

'I think you'll be working.' Millie pulls Olivia towards her and unzips her padded coat.

Mick rubs the little girl's coarse curls.

'Sorry Babes, I'll have to come to the next one.'

Olivia shrugs and dances off and Mick lowers his large body onto a kitchen chair. 'I wish I could be there more.'

'Well, you could cut down your hours. If I went out to work too we could share the childcare.'

Mick waves a finger at her. 'Don't start, Millie. You know how I feel about that.'

'I do.' Millie sighs and pulls Lucas from his romper-suit.

'Fee's mum's got cancer.'

'God, that's terrible. Poor Fee. Can you do anything to help?'

'No doubt *we* can help some time.' She flings the romper suit into the laundry basket.

Mick stares out of the window then rises and reaches for Millie. When he wraps her in his big arms the lingering odour of bed rises from the warmth of his chest.

'Millie. Give me a break. I only want to look after you. Is that so bad?'

She stiffens in his embrace. 'I appreciate the sentiment but I wish you wanted to keep me *happy* instead of safe?'

'We need you at home babes.' He squeezes her then releases her.

She is a caged panther.

Chapter 8

'We'll do what we can to maintain your mother's comfort.' The
doctor's raspberry tinted eyelids droop over pale blue eyes and his
hand trembles in Fee's grip.

She's dragged a bedside table from the master bedroom and piled it
with books and magazines to make the small, spare bedroom more
homely, but it's hard to ignore the metal morphine driver attached to
Mummy by a plastic tube. The nurse smiles efficiently and indicates the
cannula protruding from Joy's arm. 'If she feels any pain she just needs
to press this.'

'I am here,' Joy protests from the pillows.

'Yes dear, I'm just putting your daughter's mind at rest. She's going
home now. You wouldn't want her to worry, would you?' The nurse,
with the doctor, leaves the room. Fee can hear their lowered voices on
the landing then the doctor's feet creaking away.

Mummy is fading. Each day her face is drawn more tightly, and her
voice is weaker, meanwhile her volatile father is downstairs, his
demeanour sad, almost kind.

Fee visits as often as she can, fitting in the odd half hour after work.
Today, her mother looks sicker than ever. The skin on her face and
arms are papery. When Fee bends to kiss the fragile cheek, a veiny
claw-hand shoots out and grips her by the wrist.

'When I die,'

Fee frowns, but Joy looks hard at her, then loosens her grip. Fee sits
down on a chair beside the bed.

'It's going to happen, Fifi, and quite rapidly. We can't ignore it.' Her face pleads. 'We *can* talk about this, can't we?' She lifts her eyes to Fee, who nods once. 'I can't thank you enough, darling girl, for everything you've done for me. I appreciate your visits when I know how busy you must be.

The hot room is suffocating, and Fee heaves her chest to draw a breath.

'I loved seeing Kitty in the show, and meeting your friends. You need girlfriends in life, Fifi. You and I have always had each other, but now…' The words are jagged in the soft, bedroom stillness.

'Mummy.' Fee's voice cracks.

Joy closes her eyes and lapses into silence, while Fee sits, frozen. Her mother doesn't move and a moment of panic sends Fee to thrust her face close to her mother's. Soft breath kisses her cheek then Joy's eyes jerk open revealing pale rivers of blood-vessels crawling across yellowing sclera. Fee drops back onto the chair, and takes her mother's hand.

'Fifi, I want to ask you a big favour.' The wispy skull stretches towards Fee, neck sinews tautly strung. 'When I go.' She shakes her head to silence Fee's objections. 'I hope you understand sweet girl, I can only think of it as freedom.' Her grip tightens on Fee's hand. 'I don't want to be revived. I'm begging you. Please.' Her mouth is straight and sure. 'I have no desire to live any longer my dear. I've had enough.'

She collapses onto the pillow her eyes still on her daughter.

'Darling Fee, you're the most precious thing in my world. I've never asked you for anything before but this…'

Dropping to her knees beside the bed Fee wraps her mother in her arms. Aromas of talcum powder, medication and putrefaction, rise from the bed. They embrace in silence until Fee makes the requested promise. If it is in her power she will not break it.

***

Paul is home from work. He's picked up Kitty from the child-minder and they are playing their favourite game, Bucking Bronco. This involves a lot of springing on hands and knees by Paul and shrieks and bumps from his mount.

To Fee they may as well be screaming. Their enjoyment brings her almost physical pain. She creeps upstairs and lowers herself onto the bed with her head bowed, longing for someone to remove the overabundance of jobs still to be done. She wants only to curl up somewhere like a dead leaf. Two pairs of feet, and possibly some hands, paddle up the stairs, and two vivacious faces breeze into the room. She rubs her palms over her eyes, holding them there for a few extra seconds, then removes them in time to see Paul's cheerful expression extinguishing.

'Kitty, go and play for a while.'

'But...'

'I said go.'

Kitty's bottom jaw shoots out, and she turns and wiggles her small behind from the room.

'How was she?' He stuffs his hands into his pockets and leans on the door frame.

'Not good - I don't think she's got much longer. There's a nurse. She knows to ring if anything happens.' Fee doesn't meet his eyes. 'Paul, I haven't organised any food. Can you manage dinner?'

'No worries.' He leans into the landing. 'Kitty. Come on. We're going for fish and chips.'

'Yippee. Is it a special occasion?'

'No, but Mummy's tired.'

Kitty maintains an excited prattle as they descend to the hall. Her trills are muffled as she rummages for a coat, then the front door slams and the house is still.

***

Fee gropes her way out of a dream. She was beating someone with a mallet. Who? It couldn't have been Kitty. The shrill of the telephone stabs the stillness and Paul moans beside her,

'Get that bloody thing before I throw it across the room.'

She leaps into wakefulness and out of bed.

'Hello.'

'Mrs Thomas?' The voice is too kind.

***

Still in in her night clothes, a coat and boots pulled over the top, Fee holds Mummy's hand and listens to the labouring breath, and watches the impassive face, as pale as the pillow.

Clive, lurks at the door like The Grim Reaper.

Despite her efforts, and that man hovering nearby, Fee's memories creep up and pounce.

> *Her name was Priscilla but they all called her Silly, and she took it in good part. She was everything Fee wasn't: noisy, open and fearless. In*

*class, whether right or wrong she would stick up her arm. When she spoke
her mind, she managed to do so with charm. Fee never understood why
Silly had chosen her for a friend. She must have discerned something
behind Fee's raised shield.*

*The summer term was over. Fee and Silly were walking home from school,
arm in arm. Heat rippled from the paving slabs and sparrows chirruped
in the suburban hedges. Silly was chattering about plans for the long
break. Fee dreaded the holidays, knowing that she would find herself more
in the company of Clive.*

*They approached the corner where usually they headed their separate ways.
Sometimes at this point they would rest their bottoms on top of the road
sign to talk and giggle, and make themselves late for tea, but today Silly
stood, tense and silent.*

'Fee?'

Fee glanced at her.

'Can I come to your house for a while?'

*Fee's stomach jolted, even though Clive wasn't usually home at this time
of day. She considered Silly's troubled face.*

'What's wrong?'

*The girl's shoulders lifted. 'My mum's got a boyfriend. He's OK, Dan,
but he's there all the time. Mum's different around him. They keep
kissing, and looking into one another's eyes as if the rest of us don't exist.
I'm scared Fee. He might move in with us. He's all sort of friendly, tries
to talk to me. I suppose he wants me to trust him but I don't.' Silly
released a long breath. 'I like things the way they are.'*

*Fee stared. Silly seemed to have such an uncomplicated home life, and her
house was an easy to reach bolt-hole for Fee.*

*'Of course. Come back. Mummy would love to meet you. I'm sorry I
haven't invited you before but I love your house, and your mum, and
Caroline and Stuart.'*

*Caroline and Stuart were Silly's siblings. Squashed into their tiny
Victorian terrace the four formed a joyous and noisy unit.*

*The girls walked on towards Fee's house and were crunching across the
gravel on the drive when a bellow cut through the baking air, bringing Fee
to a standstill. She clutched Silly's arm. 'Silly. Wait.' But to Fee's utter
horror, Silly prised off the fingers and scampered up the drive to fling open
the heavy wooden gate. Fee rushed up, and over her friend's shoulder
beheld an unsurprising scene. Her father, his face suffused and angry,
knelt by the swimming pool with one knee on the tiles and the other*

digging into Mummy's back. Joy's head and shoulders hung over the water and rivulets streamed from straggling hair and the end of her nose as it skimmed the blue surface. Pale arms flapped on the meniscus like an exhausted albatross. As they gazed, Fee's father rammed Joy's face into the pool and held it there, while her legs thrashed behind, her toes churning the edge of the lawn.

Silly screamed and Clive's head shot up. He bounded to his feet making Joy grunt, and began stumbling towards the two girls. Silly must have panicked. She shoved Fee to the ground and bolted, as Joy tumbled forwards into the swimming pool with a splash.

Clive lumbered up to Fee and gripped her arm, digging in his fingertips until she yelped. He dragged her to her feet and yanked her into the garden, kicking the gate shut. Fee's slender limb contorted and twisted in his fist and she was forced to her knees and then flat to the ground. Face pressing on the hard ground, and grass entering her ears and eyes, she made her body limp, the best defence, and waited for the first blow, but instead there was a loud thunk. With her eyes squeezed tight Fee tensed in anticipation, but Clive's grip loosened, and there was a heavy thud on the ground beside her.

'It's OK Fifi, you can open your eyes.' Her mother's voice had an unusual strength, and Fee relaxed her eyelids to be confronted by her father's ruddy nose, millimetres away from her own. She leapt into a sitting position, massaging her aching shoulder. Above her stood Joy, a sodden gladiator, dripping pool water and brandishing a garden spade.

Sirens wailed from the road but Fee and Joy remained still. A freeze frame for the approaching officers.

They travelled by car to the police station, but thanks to a statement from Silly, whose mother had dialled 999, were soon back at home.

Clive stayed overnight in the hospital, then came home, chastened but free, as Mummy refused to bring charges against him.

A gurgle comes from the bed, then a gentle exhalation of breath like a sigh of relief. Clive comes to stand beside her.

'She's gone, Fifi.'

'Don't ever call me that.' Fee turns and stalks from the room.

THE
LEAVING

Chapter 9

Millie squints into the low sun, and hangs onto a felt beret and a canvas
bag of picnic food.

Ahead, on the bright and blustery esplanade, Fee pushes pukey Lucas
in a buggy, with Kitty holding on to the side. Beside Fee, Josh perches
aloft on Twitch's shoulders, while the other two children, Twitch's
Sam, and Millie's Olivia, prance about. The gritty beach is divided into
ballroom sized sections by thick groynes. Beyond the beach, a few
yards away, the ocean slops against the steep slope of the shore.

'Here.' Fee halts in front of a faded, primrose beach hut, raised at the
front on legs, to compensate for the bank. The three older children
rush up the few wooden steps and dance on the veranda.

'Open the door, Aunty Fee.'

'Come on Mummy. Hurry.'

Millie dumps the heavy bag on the floor, and surveys the pastel hut.

'Gorgeous. You lucky thing.'

'It's been in my mother's family for years.' Fee appraises the miniature
building. 'I haven't been to Tankerton since I was a child.' She pulls a
heavy key from the pocket of her windcheater, a crumpled luggage
label is attached to it by a piece of coarse string.

'Let's go in.'

Inside, the brine-scent of sea mingles with a powerful fug of mildew. Fee hooks back the double doors to let in light and fresh air. The hut's fittings are of sun-bleached wood, apart from a diminutive, cream-coloured electric stove, and what could be a refrigerator. On one side is a sort of day-bed-cum-settee, with canvas cushions that were once red but are now a faded cherry. Propped against its side are folding chairs and a bamboo gate-legged table.

'This is quite a bolt hole.' Twitch gapes.

Fee drags the table to the veranda, beside the buggy containing a sleeping Lucas, and Twitch brings seats.

Millie, still inside, peers at the kitchen area.

'We should have brought cleaning materials, it's very dusty.' She opens a cupboard.' And spidery.'

With yells of pleasure the children find ancient buckets and a holey fishing net under the settle.

'There's not much sand but there may be rock pools, and we can certainly look for shells.' Fee grins. 'Let's walk into town later.'

Without a thought for the grime Twitch drops onto a seat outside. Fee dusts the seat of another chair with a tissue, and sits beside her. She gazes at the waves, breathing the salt air. 'It's good to be here.' Her eyes move to Twitch. 'This *was* a bolt hole. Mummy and I often came here when I was a young.'

'What were you bolting from?' Millie emerges into the sunshine.

Fee looks at Millie, her knuckles on seated hips in mock accusation.

'I may tell one day, Millie.'

'Sorry. I'm being nosey.'

'You wouldn't be Millie if you weren't.' Fee lobs a smile.

The key to the hut pokes from the lock, with the buff luggage label flapping and smacking in the breeze.

Kitty climbs onto Fee's lap and rests her head on her mother's shoulder.

'It makes me think of Granny.' The golden hair nuzzles closer. Fee squeezes the little girl, and bends to look into her face.

'We'll think of Granny watching over us whenever we come here.'

Kitty's mind trips to more important matters. 'Can we have ice-cream?' Fee waits. 'Please?'

The women laugh. 'That's a brilliant idea,' says Millie, 'but let's do it later. I've got drinks and cake here.' She begins unloading the bag and a greedy riot of seagulls materialises in the air round them, screeching and whining, and landing on the deck with brash determination. Twitch waves her arms and shouts, and the enormous birds rise into the air, and land a few feet away, strutting back and forth, with blackcurrant eyes fixed sidelong on the group.

Fee has brought chalks, and after the food is cleared away they teach the children to play hopscotch on the esplanade. Everyone plays for a while, then Lucas wakes for milk and the women return to the veranda, leaving the young ones playing some chalk and pebble game of their own devising.

Millie, with Lucas clamped to a nipple, looks across at Fee, who is fiddling with the clasp on her bag.'

'You OK, Fee?'

'Not bad.' She appraises Millie and Twitch, then says, 'I've made a decision. I'm leaving Paul.'

'Oh Fee.' Millie moves her body, thinking to hug Fee, which is impossible with Lucas sucking.

Twitch is near to tears.

'I didn't realise.'

'Well, I've been moving towards it for a while. Since Kitty arrived I suppose. Mummy's death brought home how short life is. She,' Fee hesitates, 'had an unpleasant marriage. '

'Where will you go?' Twitch shuffles her chair closer to Fee. The children are now drawing chalky faces on the ground, turning it into a horizontal graffiti wall.

'I'll rent to start with. Mummy bequeathed me enough money for a deposit and furniture.'

Without thinking Millie blurts out,

'Well, make sure there's a spare room. I might need refuge too.'

'Me too,' pipes Twitch, and they stare at each other, then Millie bursts out laughing.

'What a hoot. Three women and five children under one roof.'

'It would be difficult,' Fee nods. 'I plan to have an extra bedroom though. In case of guests.'

'Let us know if you need help when the time comes.' Millie fastens her blouse, and rises to joggle Lucas.

Twitch turns her head and studies the beach hut.

'I think I'll move in here. It's so peaceful. I could paint the sea in all its moods.'

'I don't suppose the children would think much of that.' Fee nudges her, and she sighs.

'In another life.' Twitch stands up. 'Come on. Let's get those ice creams.'

Chapter 10

Fee stands on the suburban pavement before a large, Georgian, semi-detached house with a generous frontage. The threatening sky is markedly different from the wild, blue and white one of that lovely day at Tankerton. She turns up the collar of her coat and bends her left arm to check her watch. The tiny hands show a quarter to one, he should be here in five minutes.

The tree-lined street is bordered by a haphazard diversity of old and new houses. Over the road the tops of swings and slides peep above a line of grey, swaying bushes. A park could be noisy but what a lovely place to bring Kitty.

A red saloon pulls up next to her own, and a fresh-faced estate agent springs out, teeming with energy and salesmanship.

'Mrs Thomas?' Fee nods.

'Darren Cooper.' He gives her hand a confident shake then squints up at the slate grey clouds. 'Let's take cover.'

Fee trips after him as he strides up the path through a generous, well established garden.

'Did I mention that this property is vacant?' He calls back. 'The owners have emigrated.' He stops in the porch and pats his pockets.

'Somewhere warm if they have any sense.' He grins and his shiny black shoes squeak on dull red tiles as he inserts the key. A wide staircase faces them, and along the hall Fee glimpses a room with windows looking out onto a back garden.

The agent begins his spiel.

'The main reception room is through there. He indicates a closed door to the right. Down at the end is a separate dining-room-stroke-morning-room, and this is the kitchen'

As she follows him round the deserted house, Fee becomes increasingly excited. It's too large, but she adores the high ceilings and original features. The shabby walls only need a lick of emulsion. Upstairs: three bedrooms. There's only one bathroom but that shouldn't be a problem. If guests stay, someone can use the little cloakroom off the hall, downstairs. She walks to the window of the largest bedroom and stares at a long, narrow plot. According to Darren there's a vegetable patch at the bottom. Selions of neighbouring gardens stretch to left and right. Next door a trampoline slopes on undulating scrub.

The agent leaves her to wander round the house alone, and she walks from room to room imagining pieces of furniture from home, and deciding what else might be needed. By the time she clops back down the stairs she has made up her mind, but she says goodbye to Darren without giving him any hint.

As they leave the house, dark blemishes of rain pepper the pavement, but before diving into her motor, Fee peeps through the gate of the house next door. The front is overgrown but not neglected, and there's a car in the driveway, shabby like the grass.

***

Street-lights cast a golden confetti of rain onto the wet pavement. Fee dashes up the path and into the shadowy shelter of the porch. She applies her thumb to the circular button and hears a faint shrill, deep inside.

Above her head a bulb glimmers to life, bringing into relief a blistered ceiling. The door opens a crack, then further, and a woman of about Fee's age stands inside, one hand cupped and glistening with soap-suds.

'Oh,' Fee takes in the dripping fingers, 'I'm so sorry, I didn't mean to disturb you. I came to introduce myself. I'm thinking of renting the house next door.'

A broad smile transforms the woman's plump face.

'Come in.' She opens the chipped front door with an elbow. 'Excuse the mess. If you're going to live there,' she nods towards the other house, 'you'll get used to my chaos.'

42

The layout is a reverse of the adjoining property, but where next door there is space, here clutter sprawls across carpets and clambers up corners. From the lounge a television bellows over the arguing voices of children.

Fee follows the dumpy figure into the kitchen, and waits as the woman unloads a pile of papers from a chair. 'Have a seat.' She wipes her hands on a tea towel, and offers Fee a drink.

The kitchen is like a production line. Potatoes, peeled and partly sliced are growing orange-brown on a chopping board, and beside them lie several carrots and a head of broccoli. A saucepan fizzes on a glowing electric ring. At the end of the table where Fee sits, an open laptop is half swamped under a heap of drab, red exercise books.

'No, really, I won't stay. I can see you're busy.'

'It's not a problem.' The girl beams and catches hold of the kettle. 'As I say, it's always like this. No husband to help out. Three kids and a full time career.' She flips the switch on the kettle and turns off the cooker. 'I'm Nicola, by the way.' Her hand in Fee's is still damp.

The noise from the front room reaches a crescendo and Nicola makes a droll face.

'Sorry about this.' She shouts through the door, 'Charlie, it's Finn's turn to choose what to watch today. Now be quiet. I'm trying to talk.' She plonks onto a chair, and a boy, presumably Charlie, flounces from the room opposite and up the stairs.

'Please, don't stop cooking for me,' says Fee.

'Oh, they can wait a few minutes. I've just picked them up from the child minder. They need time to unwind.'

'How old are they?' Fee releases herself from her coat as the steamy kitchen warms her face.

'Charlie's nine, Finn's seven and Annie's five.'

'Oh, that's lovely. My daughter Kitty's five.'

'Annie will be pleased. She's always complaining there are no girls to play with. I expect the boys will be glad to get shot of her once in a while. When are you planning to move in?'

Fee answers vaguely.

The kettle boils and clicks off, and Nicola stands to shovel granules of instant coffee into mugs. She hands one to Fee. It is emblazoned with the instructions KEEP CALM I'M A TEACHING ASSISTANT.

'Is this your job?'

'It was. I'm a teacher now. As soon as I qualified, Steve got ill. He died a couple of years ago.' The smile does not mask her sadness.

Fee takes a tentative sip of the brown liquid in her cup. 'I'm so sorry. What a good thing you managed to qualify, though.'

'I suppose so but teaching is heavy going with these three, and marking and preparation.'

Fee puts down her unfinished drink and rises. 'I must go.'

Oh. I didn't mean…'

She shakes her head. 'I know that, but I also work full time and have things to do.' She fastens her coat. 'It's been lovely. I hope we see each other again.'

'Me too. And I'll tell Annie about Kitty.'

As she dashes across Nicola's pock marked drive, rain slops into the sides of Fee's court shoes. If her mother's advice is to be believed, and girlfriends are to be desired as support, then a good relationship with Nicola, a fellow singleton, could benefit them both.

Chapter 11

Something is jamming the lounge door. Fee pushes harder on its glossy surface and reaches in to feel a soft doll's head pleated beneath the wood. She drags it out and the door swings free. Hugging the toy, she surveys the room. Several gummy circles, a half-eaten biscuit and a cup of orange juice decorate the coffee table in a scatter of crumbs. The sofa, is a tumble of cushions, and on the muted television a rabble of cartoon mice bounce on a distressed cat. Silence informs her that she is alone in the house.

She cocks her foot over two more naked dolls and turns off the TV, then begins to restore order. In the kitchen, she wipes a final smear and hears the back gate clink. Kitty flings open the door and flies in, followed by an ebullient Paul. Folding up the dishcloth Fee bends nylon clad knees to hug her child.

'Hello Poppet, have you been having fun?'

'We bought fireworks,' pipes Kitty. 'Daddy says we can have them tonight, and a bonfire, and sausages, and Emily is coming round, and her mummy and daddy.'

Fee wills her body and face to remain motionless.

'That's nice, and has Daddy bought the sausages?' She lifts her eyes to her husband.

'Course I haven't, not my department. Why keep a dog and bark yourself?'

Fee gives Kitty a squeeze, then aims a chilly look at Paul as she rises. 'I'll see to it later.

'Come along Kitty, you're going to need warm clothes.' She stretches out a hand and starts for the hall. Kitty, after a moment's hesitation, runs to take it.

While her daughter describes the different fireworks she and Paul have chosen, Fee's mind is on an approaching conversation with her husband. His whistling rises from the kitchen as he makes barbecue preparations, and at the back of her mind lurks the irritating knowledge that the tiles will be muddy again.

Leaving Kitty to struggle into tights and trousers. Fee marches off in search of rudimentary food. She's fishing frozen chicken from the freezer when the side gate bangs for a second time, and she looks up into three faces, beaming at her in the doorway. Her face bends into a welcoming look.

Soon, with a beer in his hand, Paul applies his lighter to the taper of a rocket that stands in a jam-jar on the lawn. The rest watch and wait. Kitty hangs onto Fee's hand and Fee can feel her quivering. The rocket shoots into the night sky with a loud shriek and bursts into a crackling flower. With terrified wails, Emily and Kitty dive inside. Fee follows them, and drags toys from the sideboard for them to play with, amongst them the doll with the pleated head. Back in the garden the adults knock back beers, a bottle of wine and set off the remaining fireworks.

***

At the end of the evening, with the kitchen cleared and the floor mopped, Fee watches her husband head for the fridge, humming.
'That was good fun.' Paul lights a cigarette and, holding it between his lips, flips the cap from his beer, his eyes like slits behind the smoke.
She doesn't reply. Her hands are fixed to the back of a chair. There is only one matter on her mind, and she takes a breath.
'Paul, I'm leaving.' Her hands cling to the slick metal as though her life hinges on it.
Paul's head shoots up, his eyes searing like a roman candle. The beer bottle in his fist slams onto the work top with a crack, and Fee flinches.
'Leaving?'
She nods her head to avoid his eyes and fixes her eyes on his bottle.
'We're going - Kitty and I. I've found a house.'
His eyes drill into her, and in the threatening silence she turns, a pulse throbbing in her shoulder, and forces both feet to tread calmly from the room and mount the stairs. In the spare bedroom, she wedges a

waiting chair under the door handle and lies, fully clothed on the bed, straining for sounds. Across the landing Kitty curls puppy-like beneath the covers. Paul has never used violence towards Fee but in the past, she has sensed his suppressed anger. Kitty's sleeping presence should control his behaviour tonight.

After a few minutes the back-door slams and the house shakes, then she hears the groaning of the garage door and Paul's motorbike roars into life. Furious engine notes crescendo then fade into the distance and Fee's taut body subsides into the mattress. Tomorrow she will have to tell Kitty that her world has collapsed. Her thoughts whirl in a disorganised vortex until sleep engulfs them.

***

He shouldn't be driving - too many beers. Paul opens up the throttle, not knowing where he is going, not caring. He needs to think, no, to stop thinking. He increases his speed until fear gives him no choice but to focus on survival. Tarmac looms in his headlight, and corners whip into view. No time to take in sign posts, he flies between hedgerows, seeing but at the same time blind.

Without warning headlights are rushing towards him - a juggernaut, too wide for this narrow lane. Air brakes hiss. Paul throttles back and skitters between the monstrous vehicle and the bare hedge. Branches whip his goggles and cheeks and the bike bounces over the uneven verge.

The lorry drives on, honking its horn. Paul judders to a stop and dismounts, the heavy motorcycle in danger of falling from his shaking hands. He raises his face to the sky and vents his anguish into the night.

By the time his heart has slowed and sobs abated, his hands and arms ache with the exertion of supporting his bike. He lifts a weary leg across the saddle, and points the machine towards what he hopes is home. The implications of Fee's revelation begin to dawn on him and he pictures his future, without Kitty, without his perfect garage, without his pink bedroom and his impromptu barbecues. A black tar of anger begins to drip into his breast.

At a little after three the garage is silent. He leaves the bike cooling amid his ranks of tools, and lets himself in. He wants to rush straight upstairs and confront Fee but instead, squirts water into the kettle and switches it on, barely aware of its crescendo. While it boils, he goes to the cloakroom to pee. Bladder emptied, he considers the lifted seat and decides to leave it vertical. His face in the mirror is slashed with red wheals from the whipping branches. He splashes them with cold water and dabs them dry with toilet paper. They sting. He drops the paper into the toilet bowl and returns to the kitchen. With a steaming mug of coffee and a lit cigarette, he sits in the deserted kitchen to wait.

***

Six o'clock. Sounds of movement. Fee is showering while Kitty sleeps on. It is, what day? Saturday. No work for Fee, but some activity for Kitty.

Fee enters, and halts in the middle of the floor looking calm and immaculate. The chair grinds against the flooring as Paul rises.

'So, are we going to talk?' His accusing face and aggressive stance contradict his implied negotiation.

'We need to,' Fee sits down at the other end of the table. 'I'll leave you our address and telephone number. You can see Kitty whenever you want, within reason. She has a right to that.'

'*She* has a right! What about my fucking rights, have you thought of those?' He glares over at her - it would be so easy to punch that frosty face.

'I *have* thought of you although I don't expect you to believe me. You are Kitty's dad and that will never change, but Paul, you can't think that you have made me happy.' She avoids his face. 'Do you think I enjoyed waiting on you, taking Kitty to *all* her activities, doing *all* the housework, cooking *all* the meals, paying all the bills?'

'You could have asked for help.'

'You mean like on Saturday mornings when I asked you to clear the breakfast dishes?'

'Well, you should have been more insistent!' Paul's voice rises.

'That's right Paul, it's my fault. I should have begged you to help then stood over you to make sure you did. Is that what you're saying?' Fee's eyes meet her husband's, but her tone remains irritatingly level. Paul's anger is driven higher. He takes a breath to make some explosive retort, when there's movement by the door and Kitty, bleary eyed and disheveled, totters in.

'Why are you shouting? Don't Daddy. I don't like it.'

Paul's body deflates and he sits, his anger transmuting to despair as he reaches out for Kitty. The little girl patters to him on bare feet, and he draws her sleep-warm body onto his knee. Tiny toes dangle from his thigh and the sight lacerates his heart. In a moment of panic he considers grabbing Kitty and making a run for it, but rejects the impulse. He may be angry but he's not mad. Oh, but he hurts.

'Fee's eyes fix on Kitty and her mouth opens. Paul watches this final scene play out.

'Kitty, darling, Daddy and I are shouting because we are unhappy. It's nothing to do with you, we both love you very much but,' she glances at Paul, 'we don't love each other anymore.'

On his lap, Kitty start to tremble, and he hugs her to him. She digs her fingers into his arm, her face, like his, fixed on Fee's.

'Mummy, are you getting a divorce? Jack's mummy and daddy got a divorce and it made him cry. Mrs Pryce asked me to look after him but he wouldn't talk to me. He wouldn't talk to anybody.'

And so it goes on, reassurances, inducements, explanations, all is planned, nothing will stop them.

Chapter 12

Erect on the landing Twitch regards her reflection with little interest. She's wearing a soft green evening dress, and her hair is caught up in a gold clasp. Escaped strands tumble at her temples. She practises smiling and each muscle strains in effort as if her cheeks have been painted with rubber.

Maurice emerges from his bedroom and stands at her back. He puts his hands on her waist and pulls her to him.

'You look lovely.'

She jerks her body away, grabs her clutch bag from the window-sill and hurries downstairs.

The two children are snuggled up with their teenage babysitter. As it's near to bedtime, they are quietly watching Ben 10 on the television.

They drive in silence towards Maurice's office Christmas party. The firm is not large, with some 20 employees. Most are young men and women, brash and hungry for house sales, others, rather like Maurice, are paunchy, married men.

They park in the street and Twitch pulls her flimsy wrap round her shoulders Inside, the restaurant is bright with fairy lights and hanging baubles. Maurice is hailed by a crowd of male and female colleagues at the bar and he and Twitch join them. Soon Maurice is knocking back a pint. Standing beside him Twitch sips sparkling water and studies the females in the group, wondering which one could have fancied her husband. After deciding that none of these women would be so stupid, she raises her eyes to her surroundings. At a dining table nearby she recognises a group of wives and strolls to join them, wishing the night were over.

The women chat and husbands turn up occasionally to offer more beverages. At the bar the noise is rising, and Maurice is getting drunk. Eventually the men come over, and Maurice slumps into a seat on Twitch's right.

'How is my *loving* wife?' He leers at her and flaps his fingers either side of his head like quotation marks. Twitch stares at him coldly and turns to the man sitting on her left, and asks about his plans for Christmas. Maurice mauls at her arm. 'Won't talk to your own husband then. Rather chat up someone else's, huh?'

'Steady on Maurice, mate.' The fellow stretches across Twitch, and places a hand on Maurice's arm.

'Fancy her then do you, Sebastian? Well don't expect any *rumpy pumpy*.'
Enough. Twitch launches herself upright and her chair topples to the carpet behind her. At neighbouring tables the Christmas revelry subdues. Ignoring everyone else, Twitch looks down at Maurice.
'I'm going home. Come if you want a lift.'

He grimaces and flaps her away. 'Naah. I'll gedda taxi. You bugger off, you're no fun anyway.'

Twitch stalks between diners, her eyes straight ahead. Shiny decorations wave and weave as she pulls open the doors and emerges into the icy darkness.

In the sanctuary of the car she rocks and weeps until she is emptied of shame and fury, then rams the vehicle into gear and drives home. According to the clock on the dashboard it's 9:30, at least the children will be in bed.

In the driveway, red, swollen eyes stare at her from the mirror. Her cheeks are streaked with Mascara. Because she can't think of a plausible explanation for her appearance she decides to give Mia a condensed version of the truth.

Letting herself into the hall she calls, 'Don't worry, it's only me.' and pokes her puffed face round the lounge door. 'Had a bit of a disagreement with Maurice, I'm afraid.'

The girl looks embarrassed. 'Oh dear.'

Twitch doesn't want to prolong the conversation any more than is necessary.

'I'll pay you for the full four hours. Lucky you, you get a night off with full pay.' She raises her hand to prevent further conversation. 'Would you mind finding your own way home, Mia. I'm a bit tired.'

'Of course not Mrs Roman. Are you sure you'll be alright?'

'I'll be fine. I just need a good night's sleep.'

The girl gathers her belongings. 'Bye then – hope it's all OK.'

Twitch pours a large gin, and falls into an armchair. She gazes round her arty and eclectic lounge with new eyes. She's put her soul into this house but it is no longer home. She envies Fee her career. Something outside the home to focus on, a passport to another life. There must be an occupation for Twitch somewhere. She rises from the chair and fetches her laptop.

Scrolling through vacancies, dipping in and out of possible opportunities, she is distressed to find the job descriptions and application forms so daunting. Her mind weaves around, looking for an escape route, and finally she puts the P.C. aside and picks up her mobile. Listening to the burr burr of Fee's phone, she takes a deep, shuddering breath.

'Hi' Her voice sounds strange.

'Is that you, Twitch?'

'Yes.'

'What is it? What's the matter?

'I can't talk now, and I can't come over because Maurice is out and the babysitter's gone home.' She looks at the gin. 'And I've had too much to drink.' A sob escapes her and Fee's concern pours from the ear piece.

'How about tomorrow?' Fee offers, 'Could we get together when the children are at school? I'll ring work and tell them I'll be in late.'

Twitch tries to control her mouth.

'Would you mind? I'm at my wit's end.'

When she's ended the call she flops back into her chair. During the short conversation she's made a decision.

***

Fee greets her with a hug, and leads the way into the living room. Twitch observes the shabby walls and lofty ceilings.

'It'll perk up when I've put a coat of paint on it.' Fee's face is apologetic.

'It's got lots of potential.' Twitch studies the room.

'I could do with a decorator. Work's manic at the moment and I'm dashing here, there and everywhere. '

'You need help.' Twitch fixes her eyes on Fee. 'I could do all that for you. The decorating, dealing with Kitty, cleaning, weeding. Then you could concentrate on work.'

Fee stares at her friend in silence, and Twitch shrugs her shoulders. 'I've decided…' She hesitates. 'I'm going to leave Maurice. I'm not qualified to do anything and you need a housekeeper. You could pay me a wage and I could find somewhere to live or,' she takes a breath, 'I could move in here rent free and keep house for you. I'd have to bring the children of course.' She stops herself from adding that it will be a squash.

Fee drops into an arm-chair and stares up at Twitch, then shakes herself.

'Sit down Twitch. Sorry to hesitate it's just that I'm finally alone after so long and I'm still licking my wounds a bit.' She stands again. 'Let me make us a drink.' She holds up her hand as Twitch starts to rise, 'No. You stay here, I won't be long.'

Twitch subsides again and watches Fee's back. This was a daft idea. Of course Fee won't want another person under her newly acquired roof.

***

In the kitchen Fee fills the kettle and opens cupboards and drawers, thinking about Twitch's proposal. In all honesty, after their fantasy at the beach-hut, the idea of the others moving in with her has been at the back of her mind. Also, although she was desperate to leave Paul, now that she is here she finds herself lonely. And she's frustrated that she has no time to work on the house and garden.

As she drops two teabags into mugs and pours on boiling water she weighs the advantages of Twitch's proposal, against its potential problems. Although they are good friends - very close companions by now - living together is quite a different prospect from sharing confidences across a table.

She wonders how the children will get on, and it dawns on her that she should consult Kitty before making a firm decision. She drops the sodden teabags into the bin and with the two china mugs in her hand, returns to the lounge with a smile on her face. Twitch is still crumpled in the chair but now her face is in her hands, and her shoulders are shaking.

Putting down the cups Fee crosses the room and props a hip onto the arm of the chair, wrapping an arm round her friend's shoulders.

Twitch's body heaves as they sit quietly listening to children's shouts from the park opposite. At last Twitch fumbles in her sleeve for a scrubby tissue, and straightens her body to blow her nose.

'I'm sorry. I shouldn't have asked. It's too much to demand of anyone.' She wipes under her eyes with her fingers to clean up smudged mascara.

'I'm glad you asked me dear friend. It just took me a bit by surprise.' Fee pokes out her bottom lip. 'You know me, I need to think things through, I'm not good at knee-jerk decisions.' Twitch lifts her face and meet's Fee's wry expression, and Fee squeezes her shoulders. 'I can't say yes or no. I need to talk to Kitty. You need to think about Sam and Josh, too. How will they react? It's not just about us, is it?

'Well whatever I do will be hard on them. I just thought we'd muddle through really. They're young enough to adapt.' Twitch stuffs the tissue back into her sleeve.

'They will adjust, but I know from my experience with Kitty that it will affect them in ways you can't predict. Their confidence will be knocked and they might have problems with friendships, school, sleeping, I don't know what else.'

She slips her arm from behind Twitch and rises to fetch her drink. 'Here, have some tea, it's good for the nerves.'

Twitch takes the cup and sips, holding the mug in two shaky hands to stop it from slopping.

Fee sits opposite and rewards her with a smile.

'My first instinct was to say yes to you; I hope you believe me. I need help and I'd love some company. I find I'm not very good on my own. But we need to discuss how we'd make it work. Who would sleep where, what we do with the children, what jobs you'd be prepared to take on, and access for our husbands.'

Twitch smiles and gives a small nod. 'You're right. I was so desperate to escape that I haven't thought it through properly. I just want to run away with the children under my arms. I suppose that's not fair on anyone.'

'Well that's more or less what I did, but no, it wasn't fair. And if you move in, which would be lovely I think, we need to make sure it works. One broken home for the children is a problem, but two would be disastrous.

54

They grin across the room, and then Twitch appraises the walls.
'I can see this room in a soft sea green,' she says.

***

Downstairs the front door opens and closes. Twitch pictures Maurice taking in the pile of cases in the hall. Footsteps creak on treads but she continues with her task of wiping out drawers. He stops at the open door to the spare room but she doesn't yet look up.

Shutting the last drawer she rises from her knees and turns to see his expressionless face.

'I'll leave my new address on the kitchen table. I've told the children I'll pick them up from school, but we'll be back with a van at the weekend to collect the rest of our stuff.' She clamps her jaws to control the tremble of her lips, and after a tense moment, Maurice turns away and goes into the bedroom next door.

Chapter 13

'It's going to be very snug for all of you,' grunts Millie. Standing on one leg she waves her foot behind her to locate the threshold, while her hands clutch one end of Twitch's chest of drawers.

Twitch hefts the other side and they dump the piece of furniture in the hall.

A Luton box van stands at the curb, its rear shutter rolled up. It's not full but it was the only transport Twitch could find.

'Thanks for helping me Millie. I was wondering how I'd manage without Fee.'

'Where is she?' Millie plops her buttocks onto the bottom stair and massages her fingers.

'In Bath. She'd organised a work thing ages ago. Bonding? Something like that.'

The sound of the back door interrupts them and five children troop through kitchen towards them. Kitty leads Lucas and Olivia and they are followed by Sam and Josh. All the children look disorientated.

'I'll make drinks… and biscuits?' Twitch is upbeat. Sam nods and for once, she doesn't remind him of his manners.

While Twitch pours apple juice, Millie looks around. The place has a rented air.

Movement outside attracts her attention and she lifts her eyes to a meet those of a round, even-featured face grinning in the porch. She scrambles to her feet and dusts her palms on her behind.

'Hi.' The woman takes a step onto the mat. 'I'm Nicola.' She gestures to her right. 'From next door. I thought I'd come and see how you're getting on. '

She cranes her head towards the kitchen where the children grasp tumblers and regard her balefully.

'Hello, hello. Which one of you is Kitty? Let me guess.' She directs her index finger to one side of the group of children and moves it past each one until it points at tiny Josh. 'Is it you?'

Kitty smiles at Nicola. 'No. That's Josh. He's a boy. Try again.' Nicola indicates Olivia's dark face and tight curls.' It must be you then.

Kitty squeals with laughter, 'No, it's *me*.'

Nicola puts on an amazed expression 'Oh, so *you're* Kitty. Your mum told me about you because we thought you and my Annie could be friends. In fact I wonder if all you children would like to meet mine now. They're hoping you'll have a picnic with them in our house, if that's OK with your mums.' She raises her eyebrows at Millie and Twitch.

'Fine by me,' says Millie.

Twitch nods. 'Thank you.'

They troop off, and Twitch gives Millie an anguished look. 'This is so difficult. I didn't think they'd mind so much. Maurice ignored them most of the time but they seem to want him with them.'

'Children don't like change, but they'll adapt. Look at Kitty, she's recovering already, and they've only been here a short while.

Twitch nods.

'I hope you're right. Let's get this thing upstairs.'

***

The van is empty and they sit on the newly erected bed, their limbs aching. Millie can't dispel a pang of envy. Tomorrow, Mick's mother arrives to stay with her for a few days. Gloria and Mick have arranged the visit without consultation, although Millie would not have objected. This morning, Mick had wanted Millie to stay at home to make sure the house was up to his mother's exacting standards. They'd argued, but Millie had already promised Twitch, so after a few choice words she raged out of the house, her left arm clutching a squawking Lucas, and her right hand clamped round Olivia's reluctant fingers. The children bawled as she forced them into seats, and drove too fast to Fee's. Now she feels guilty. Furthermore she is uncomfortable that they are still next door.

'Can you manage now?' She asks. Twitch, also seems pensive.

'Yes. I was thinking that we should rescue poor Nicola from our children. I'll have to invite her round for a drink one evening, to say thank you'.

During Millie's drive home, the back seat is silent. She squints through her rear-view mirror.

'Did you have a good time?' Lucas has his thumb in his mouth, his lids are drooping, but Olivia's bright, brown eyes sparkle back.

'We had a picnic on the carpet then we played on the 'puter, then we went on the trampoline. Mummy, can we live there?'

Millie's eyes shoot back to the glass.

'What do you mean Livvie?'

''You and me and Lucas and Daddy, we could live in a house there. Then we could play with Kitty and Sam, and Josh, and Annie, and ...'

'I don't think Daddy would be keen on moving, Lovey. He's got so much to do at work. Moving house is hard you know?'

'Well, Aunty Twitch did it.'

'Mm.' Millie turns her eyes back to the road. They are almost home.

***

'What you got all this stuff in here for?' Gloria waves a handful of string, pens, batteries and other detritus from a kitchen drawer, at Millie.

'Oh, I don't know.' Millie tries to sound unconcerned. 'It's things we don't need every day but it's handy to have nearby.'

'Well, you could organize it a bit better than this,' Gloria says. 'You got some bags or boxes or somethin'?'

'Sorry. No. I haven't.'

Gloria tuts, and rattles in the drawer trying to sort it out. 'You could save some margarine tubs and put the batteries in one, and these elastic bands in another.' Millie ignores her and concentrates on the soapy breakfast bowls.

Gloria's voice at her shoulder makes her jump.

'You got too much washin' up liquid there,' she peers into the washing up bowl, 'an' if you wait until the bowl's full of water before you put it in, you won't get all them bubbles.

'Where's a tea towel?' Gloria opens and closes drawers, exclaiming at their shameful state. When she finds them she unfurls a linen rectangle 'Don't you iron these?'

Millie sighs.

'They could do with a soak in biological powder. I'll do that next.' Gloria goes on.

'Whatever you think, Gloria.' Millie uses a corner of Gloria's tea towel to dab her fingers.

'*Hand towel*,' exclaims Gloria. 'Don't dry your hands on *this*.'

For goodness sake. Millie stalks into the garden to calm down. Gloria's been here less than one day and already she's intolerable. Millie considers going away for the week and leaving Gloria and Mick to it. She'd do it if she were a different person. She would stroll through the kitchen, smiling sweetly. Go to her room and pack a bag, leave a note on the hall table and walk out of the door. It's tempting. When the Pankhursts tried to free women from oppression, it was the dominance of men they were fighting. Would they have foreseen women dominating each other?

The garden is cold and she hugs her arms against the wind. Her mind goes, as it has often done of late, to Fee and Twitch, snuggled into their little house with nobody telling them what to do. She pulls out her phone.

'Hi Millie.' Fee's voice lifts in enquiry.

'Hi Fee. Are you in?' She hears traffic rumbling in the background, and knows the answer.

'I'm in town. I'll be home in about half an hour. Is everything OK?'

'I need to escape for a while.' Millie stamps her feet on the icy ground.

'Twitch is home if you need a friend.'

Millie looks over her shoulder at Gloria, stretching up to cupboards and bending to the washing machine.

'I'll be round shortly.' She hangs up and stalks past her mother-in-law to the end of the hall. Her jacket, the one Lucas was sick on, is hanging from a hook, and she lifts it down and opens the door.

'Where are you …?' The end of Gloria's question is cut off by the slam.

***

'You should have told Mum where you were going.' Mick pulls his shirt over his head and drops it on the floor by the bed. 'What if there'd been an emergency?

'I had my phone. Anyway, don't you know, your mother's better than me at everything? Emergencies? Huh. She wouldn't need me to help.' Millie glares. 'I can't do anything right.'

'Keep your voice down, she'll hear you.'

'And you think that worries me?' Millie turns from Mick, drops onto the side of the bed, to take off her shoes. 'She's your mother Mick - your guest. You spend time with her. Don't bugger off for a whole day and leave her with me.'

Mick's apologetic voice reaches her.

'I couldn't help that. Barry was in a car accident for goodness sake. I couldn't have known I'd be needed.'

Barry was supposed to have been yesterday's duty chef, but instead is in hospital after he and his car connected with a lorry on the road to Chelterton.

'That's right. Work must come first. Never mind your poor wife left to cope with a pair of demanding children, and an incredibly bossy mother in law.' Millie grasps her shoes and throws them at the wardrobe. They bounce off and roll to the floor.

'*Millie*. Calm down.'

Millie rests her elbows on her knees and drops her head onto her hands, digging hot fingers into her curls.

The bed sags as Mick sits beside her. His big arm lands on her shoulder, and he pulls her into his armpit.

She holds her body stiff, keeping her head in her hands.

'I'm telling you Mick. If you ever do that again I won't come back until she's gone.'

'OK, OK. I'm home now.'

They sit for a while in silence, and Millie thinks back to her visit to Twitch, and later Fee. She had poured out her frustrations, ending up in tears, as usual. She gives herself a mental shake and straightens up, patting Micks brown knee.

'Come on, it's getting late. Let's get some sleep.'

Later, when Mick reaches for her, she pretends to be asleep. The crumpled pillow presses its creases into her cheek and her mind ranges, searching for a way out. Mick might die - instantly she feels guilty for letting the thought enter her head. Perhaps she will win the lottery. Gloria could die – if she carries on as she did today, Millie might murder her.

She gives a mental shrug. None of this will happen so she needs to get on with things.

***

A few weeks later she stands at the sink, gazing out of the window. The garden needs weeding again, and the children need new shoes. At her feet, the kitchen floor is scuffed with muddy footprints and the beds upstairs have yet to be made. Millie's hands hang motionless in deep suds, and she dreams of a buzzing restaurant. Happy customers raising forks of spicy deliciousness to their lips, and raising their eyes to the ceiling in ecstasy. Bustling waiters and waitresses carrying bottles of wine and plates, and Millie, in the kitchen conducting events, a taste here, an instruction there.

The post drops through the letter box behind her with a clatter and a flop, and pulls her back to the present, but a decision has been made.

CONSEQUENCES

Chapter 14

Paul licks his lips and his tongue rasps past teeth coated with flock. He shifts his aching body, opens one eye to look at the ceiling, and lies still, waiting for his sleep-fog to clear. His bladder begins to nag so he forces open the other eye and swings stiff legs from the sofa.

The television is on standby, its light, redly accusing. On the coffee table lie discarded foil take-away containers, scabbed with the congealed remains, some stabbed with the ends of doused cigarettes, others with the first mycelia of mould creeping across their surfaces. He stretches his back, and rises with a hammering head. Kicking beer cans and a pizza box out of the way he crosses the room. In the toilet he stares at his foaming urine as it plunges into the water. Splashes of ochre, spray the rim, and small drops burst out and settle in a jaundiced sweat on the surrounding tiles.

In the kitchen he throws three Paracetamol to the back of his throat and gulps a pint of water then, waiting for the kettle to boil, passes an eye round the kitchen, where he's been working on the bike again, aggressively cleaning wire wheels on the kitchen table and willing Fee to come back and witness the desecration. A thought winkles its way into his head. A woman is coming at eleven, from Green and Roe, the estate agents. He squints at his watch. 10.30, already. Tea forgotten he takes the stairs two at a time, pulling off yesterday's shirt as he goes. Fee is arranging for the house to go on the market. This woman is the first of three Estate Agents, booked in over the next couple of days. No doubt they'll report back that the house is a refuse tip and then, he grins to himself, the shit will hit the fan.

While he massages his body with a musty smelling towel, he enjoys the sight of the ring of scum round the sink, and the pattern of curly hairs on the sides and bottom of the bath.

The bell rings while he's applying deodorant, and after sniffing a few shirts draped round the bedroom, he dons one and gallops downstairs. A strong smell of make-up and powder rises up his newly cleared nostrils, from a scarlet haired apparition in a fur coat. The woman's shrinking red lips are warped into a professional smile, while arched eyebrows that could have been drawn on with a marker pen, are raised in confident expectation of a warm welcome.

'Mr Thomas?' She extends a gloved hand, and meets his startled gaze. Her nose screws up in a brief expression of distaste as she steps into the hall, and Paul smirks.

Viv-ee-anne (don't call me Viv) says she'll explore on her own, 'Don't even think of putting yourself out, Mr T.'

So he doesn't. He retreats to the kitchen to finish making breakfast, and listens to footsteps above his head. He pictures Viv-ee-anne's face as she takes in the squalor. The footsteps descend and doors open and close in the hall, then she clops into the kitchen. Paul is rescuing two slices of toast from a stream of smoke issuing from the toaster, and observes the woman through a floating, black fog.

'Thank you Mr Thomas.' The agent keeps her distance and gives a wave with her glove. 'I'll send a report to Ms Thomas. I'm sure she'll be in touch.' The felt tip lines shoot into her ruby fringe then, like a disapproving drag queen, her seamed stockings and patent leather stilettoes stalk elegantly down the hallway and out of the house.

The carbon flying from the toast, coats the sink in a black scum, while a burning cigarette balances next to him on the edge of the drainer. He contemplates the day ahead. Kitty's birthday party is this afternoon and he has yet to buy the present. Of one thing he is convinced though, it will be the biggest and best gift she's ever seen.

***

'Daddy!' Kitty ogles at Paul, who is hampered by a huge parcel, wrapped in mismatched paper.

'Happy birthday Pops.'

He dumps the parcel on the hall carpet, poking a poster sized envelope against the wall next to the familiar, old grandfather clock.

'Come and see everything.' Kitty grabs his hand. 'This is the lounge.'

Fee stands by the patio doors looking out into the night, and their eyes meet in the reflection.

'Hello Paul. I see you've found the birthday girl.'

'Yeah, well, it wasn't hard.'

The room smells of new paint. The greenish blue walls look cool and calm, as does his wife.

'Come on Daddy, come and see my room.' Kitty yanks him towards the stairs. 'The kitchen's through there.' Kitty indicates the room to their right, where Paul glimpses Millie placing snacks into small bowls. The smell of cake and crisps triggers memories of his own childhood parties.

Upstairs he follows his daughter along the narrow landing.

'That's Aunty Twitch's room, that's Auntie Millie's.' She pushes a door on the right. 'Tadaa.' The compact room houses a double bed, a wardrobe and a chest of drawers.

'Where's your bed Pops?'

'It's coming tomorrow. Then I'll stop sleeping in with Mummy because I'm a big girl of five.' Kitty's face begins to fall and Paul drops to his knees to hug her.

'You are such brave girl.'

He fumes silently. 'And you're going to have a terrific time today.'

'I know.' She pauses. 'Daddy?'

'Yeah?'

'Don't you miss me?'

Paul squeezes tighter and blinks his eyes.

'Of course I do Pops. Of course.' They cuddle for a few minutes until the door-bell interrupts. Paul forces a smile. 'Sounds like someone's arrived.' His voice conveys unconvincing optimism. 'Come on birthday girl, let's go and open your presents.'

'Present opening is at the end, after everyone's gone.'

'Oh. OK. Well let's play games then.' He pushes Kitty gently through the door. 'When I was your age I used to have parties in the garden.'

'I know. You told me before.' Kitty's spirits seem to be rising again.

At the top of the staircase they look down upon several yummy mummies, and one or two gym-sculpted dads shaking hands and clapping arms. Millie ushers the adults into the kitchen, while the children, including little Sophie from bonfire night, are sent to the lounge. Paul's parcel has vanished.

Paul bobs through the kitchen door in search of beer and sensible conversation with Sophie's dad. Parents mill round a table bearing filled wine glasses and bowls of nibbles, but no ale. Oh well. He lifts a glass of red and drains it then picks up a second. Sophie's parents seem to have left. Damn.

'I hope you've eaten.' A voice at his ear jolts him, and he grips his glass to prevent it plummeting to the floor. A plump, vivacious woman with an impish smile is wagging a finger at him.

'I think there are sandwiches under there. They'll soak it up.' She points at four covered plates balanced on the cooker hob. 'I'm Nicola, from next door.' Her handshake is firm and warm.

'Paul, Fee's ex.'

'I guessed that when I saw you struggling up the path with that *huge* parcel.' She grins. 'That must be the biggest bear I've ever seen.'

'It's an elephant actually.' Paul smiles back. 'The trunk was a bugger to wrap.'

'Well,' she puts her empty glass on the table, 'I must go. Marking to do. Can't let that empty house go to waste.' She nods. 'Nice to meet you. See you again I expect.' And she's gone, squeezing through the crowd. Children's voices reach him over the hubbub. Nobody seems to be paying them much attention in the other room. No party games? No music? Paul knocks back the glass of wine, picks up a third and weaves through the melee to the lounge.

The children become quiet when he stumbles in, and Kitty's eyebrows crinkle into a wave of worry.

'Come on kids, time to have fun. Where's the music in this place?' Soon Abba is blaring from the I-pod, and the children are dancing wildly for musical statues. The music stops.

'You're out, and you.' Come and stand at the side. 'OK now - dance!' *Voulez v...*

A small boy wavers.

'Out, fella.'

The child's face takes on an aubergine hue.

'I AM NOT OUT.'.

'Sorry mate, I'm the judge and you are well and truly out. Come here with the others and stop being a berk.'

'I AM NOT A BERK. WHAT'S A BERK?'

'*You* are. Now stop that.'

'MUMMY.' The child rushes out.

Paul starts the music again but the game has lost its appeal and the participants shuffle from foot to foot without enthusiasm.

'Come on kids, let me see you dance.' Paul wiggles his hips and grins but the room has become still and the children's faces are fixed on something behind him. He turns in a drunken skew, to find Fee leaning on the door-frame with folded arms. Behind her the astounded faces of other parents jostle for a view.

'Paul. What happened?'

'Happened?' Paul looks innocent. 'Oh, the kid. Well he wouldn't accept that he was out - musical statues you know?'

'Yes, I know. What I don't understand is why you decided to interfere in our arrangements.'

'Well excuse me if was trying to help at my own daughter's party. Someone had to give these poor kids some fun.'

Fee shakes her head in slow disapproval.

'There are games organised, and we're about to start. We delayed because one or two children had activities this afternoon.'

Paul hides his humiliation with bluster. 'Well you should have told me!'

'Right. My fault again.' Fee is infuriatingly calm and Paul becomes aware that he is standing in the spotlight of everyone's deep disapproval.

He pushes past Fee, ignoring the undisguised glee of the small crowd, and hisses, 'You know what you can do? Stuff your stupid party up your arse.'

There's a childish gasp behind him and a gloating murmur of censure in front.

As he powers from the house, Fee is calling the children to play Pass the Parcel.

Chapter 15

Fucking photocopier's packed up again. Give him a motorbike any time, at least if you fix a bike it stays fixed for longer than a bleeding week.

Paul's head throbs with another hang-over, and he needs coffee. He stalks to the small kitchen to find a few lonely granules lurking in the bottom of the jar, and an unpleasant sticky mass adhering to the rim. The sink is full of dirty mugs, and the milk - he sniffs it warily - is sour. Kayleigh, *bloody stupid name, bloody stupid tart*, sits at her desk with a telephone scrunched between chin and shoulder. She is writing on a shorthand notebook.

'Of course Mrs Jackson... Oh, OK - Jackie'

Jackie Jackson. Christ.

The moment she replaces the telephone on the littered surface, it delivers another plaintive cry.

'Brown and Martin, how may I help you?' Her tone drops and rises. Paul waves a post-it note under her nose and a furrow digs in between her eyebrows as she tries to read it. Capital letters gouge the paper: BUY SOME COFFEE! WHAT THE HELL DO WE PAY YOU FOR? Smacking it on the desk he strides off.

At the water cooler, plump, middle aged Iris joins him.

'How's it going Paul?'

'Crap.'

'Fancy a ciggy?'

Paul nods abruptly and makes for the door carrying his cone of chilled water.

Standing on the pavement they puff. Iris is quiet, and Paul is relieved to avoid small talk.

'Paul?' Her voice carries the gravel of a habitual smoker.

'What?'

Countless lines slice from the corners of Iris's eyes and her mouth is like the knotted end of a deflating balloon. A jet of white smoke funnels from her nose into the chilly air. Her pale lips suck again, and more smoke is whisked away.

'I've got a friend whose husband went off with a younger model. Gabby, her name was.' She takes another life-sucking lungful.

What the fuck is she going on about? Women are all the same, on about feelings, sympathy, empathy.

'Gabby got terribly angry and started hurting the people she loved: the kids, her parents and friends - me in fact.' She studies the glowing end of her fag.

'Can't think why.'

'Paul, I'm trying to tell you something.' She looks straight at him. 'I can't help you, none of us can, but if you want to keep your job and your friends then you need to take action.' She drops the dying cigarette on the paving and terminates it with a twist of her toe, then presses something into his palm.

'This man helped Gabby.' She turns away and goes inside.

Alone on the cold pavement Paul lifts a business card between thumb and forefinger. In plain black text he reads: Max Rutherford, Counsellor in relationship breakdown, bereavement and anger management, Marchmont House, Melmsbury.

Chapter 16

The room is airy with a tall bay window, underscored by a cream, painted seat, that looks onto a tufted lawn. The walls are hospital-coloured, but the ornate coving rescues them from the institutional. To his right, licks of flame insinuate themselves round nuggets of coal. A man, in his thirties with flopping, light brown hair, rises from a deep arm chair, set behind a low table.

'Mr Thomas, how do you do?' The man extends a hand across the coffee table. 'Max Rutherford.' Max sweeps an arm past an assortment of chairs from an upright club chair to a squashy, leather one. 'Take your pick.' Paul selects a wooden carver. Max picks up a clipboard and sits in an upright chair nearby, smiling pleasantly. 'Good to meet you,' he says. 'You need help with your marriage break up - is that right?'

Paul's mouth is welded shut. Over the last couple of days, he's been cursing himself for his behaviour at Kitty's party, and blaming Fee for his state of mind. Hardly a word has come from his lips, even at work. Staring at his interlaced fingers, he nods his head.

'How long ago was the break up?'

The counsellor stands to pick up a crystal glass and water jug from the low table. He places them beside Paul. Paul pours and gulps, then stares at the orange flames weaving in the bottom of the pitcher.

'Four months.'

Max nods, taking up a pen, and begins asking basic questions: work place, full name and address, contact numbers and age, then he straightens his back, and his voice becomes brisk.

'So Paul, tell me about your life. How are you getting on?'

Without warning Paul's whole body clenches, and a torrent of words breaches a barrier he hardly knew he'd built.

'Cross. No. Bloody furious. She took my life and screwed it up, threw it in the bin as if it didn't matter, then swanned off to a new life with my kid. I couldn't do a thing to change her mind, there wasn't time. She said they were leaving then they left. After she told me I nearly killed myself on the motorbike.' He is shouting and it feels good.

'Well, anger would be a natural response to an experience like that.' Max is calm.

'But I do things that make it worse.'

'For example?'

'For *example*, spoiling my daughter's birthday party, and banging around at work. It's Fee's fault.'

'Any friends you could talk to?'

Paul thinks of his old mates, Pete, Phil, Johnny. Good drinking partners but not the kind you'd share feelings with.

'We lost touch after Fee and I got married.'

'Any reason for that?' Max sweeps a flop of fringe from his eyes and grabs the clipboard again.

'Not sure. Fee wasn't keen on them. We used to see them but it stopped.' Paul is stunned to realise that he left his old life so completely behind.

The counsellor nods and waits. There's silence as he waits.

Paul glares at him.

'What do you want me to say? Fee's a scheming cow and I'm the gullible fool who's been taken for a ride. I feel a complete IDIOT!' The words echo in the room. 'And I want my kid!' He sounds like a small child whose ice cream has plopped into the gutter.

Max nods again, jots some private notes, and continues to wait.

Paul squirms between the wooden arms of the chair, and lapses into silence.

With gentle questioning Max extracts the whole story: the bonfire party and the revelation of Fee's departure. Her announcement, presented coolly and calmly once Kitty was tucked up in bed. The motor bike ride, and the morning-after exchange.

'Did she give her reasons for leaving?'

'Can't remember.' He's not ready to share the full conversation that morning.

Max nods again and although his face is passive, tense sinews in his neck hint at a clenched jaw.

'So what do you need from me?'

'I dunno. A woman at work thought you could help me.' He raises his eyes to meet Max's. 'Bollocks I expect.'

'Well, not necessarily, but it's up to you. We can talk in more detail about your childhood, your marriage and so on and perhaps you will make sense of why this has happened. I can't promise miracles but sometimes sharing can help put things into perspective. People discover things about themselves.'

'You saying I'm to blame?'

'It's not for me to judge who is to blame, if anyone. I'm simply stating that talking can untangle thoughts. Tidy minds are easier to manage, believe me.' His face is a picture of empathy. 'They flow in one direction instead of in circles and they point to the future. If ever you decide I'm not helping, then you are at liberty to stop coming. I won't criticise you, Paul. This is your life, your pain, I'm just here to help explore your feelings.'

'OK, I get it.' He should apologise but instead gives a grunt.

'In this room you can say what you wish, I'm quite robust. I know how you feel.' There is empathy. Max's eyes as he smiles. Paul's lips mirror Max's. He doesn't know what the bloody hell he's doing here but now he's made the appointment he'll give it a go.

The two men talk about Paul's childhood. His kindly but simple grandparents, who raised him, and the largely unexciting primary school days. Paul begins to squirm at the intensity of Max's attention.

'What are *your* parents like?' He throws out at Max.

Max's eyes shoot to the fireplace.

'We're here to talk about you, Paul.'

'Yeah, I know, but it's not easy to talk about this stuff. We could make it a bit more mutual.'

Max's fingers whiten on his pen for a moment, and he swallows.

'Sorry, Paul. That's not the way it works.'

An hour later Paul emerges, and looks left and right. A small group of students descend from a bus a hundred yards away, and opposite, a young couple with a huge brown dog on a lead, stride along the pavement, but there is nobody who would recognise him, and he slips down the steps.

***

7.00pm. Paul rubs his frozen hands together and looks carefully about. A wild night has descended and shadows shimmy and dive in the laurel bushes. He emerges silently from his hiding place and glides like a wraith, round the corner to his motor bike. The rumbling of his stomach brings fish and chips to mind.

The bike fires up beautifully. There's a chippy on the way home, run by a Chinese couple. Paul calls them Mr and Mrs Hun Po, because that's the name of the restaurant. He has no idea what Hun Po means, hopefully not Fat Pig or Shit Heap.

The Hun Po has been his regular stop since Fee left. Paul has become fond of the charming couple - the wide, welcoming smile of Mr Hun Po, and the shy one of his wife, nodding at Paul from the fryer, although Paul has spied her, not shy at all, at the back of the shop, chattering and laughing in a shrill, East Asian dialect.

The bike is parked, and he walks across the car park. The smell of chips and five spice float deliciously through the dark evening. Bodies move behind steamy glass and it soon becomes apparent that they belong to a group jostling lads, in high spirits, possibly the liquid variety. Paul's fuse begins to fizz.

In the tiled interior there is no welcoming smile from Mr Hun Po. He is writing in pencil on a small white order pad, his face grim. Lounging against the glass cabinet, a tall, shapeless youth in a flapping leather jacket, grins over at Mrs Hun Po.

'Come on darlin', I'm talking to yer. Bloody Chinky.'

Three other young men leer at the poor lady, who shakes her head in incomprehension.

The ring leader pokes out his acned chin and flicks back a greasy blond fringe.

'What yer doin' comin' over 'ere and takin' our jobs when yer can't even speak bloody English?'

Mr Hun Po interjects.

'Excuse me sir. Please be polite. My wife speaks poor English. She does not understand but she works hard and she taking lessons.'

'You wanna put 'er on the game mate. She don't need no English when she's flat on 'er back,'

The fuse burns out and Paul explodes.

'Oy! Wanker!'

Four dangerous faces revolve in his direction. In the corner of his eye, Mr Hun Po picks up the telephone.

Anger makes him brave. 'Leave them alone. These are good people. Pick on someone your own fucking size.'

The youth at the counter turns towards Paul, and his little gang part to let him through, falling in behind him and grinning. Paul sees the middle class parents in Fee's hall.

From behind the counter Mr Hun Po calls loudly,

'Police on way.'

'Still time for a small dust up,' the yob snarls, flexing his fingers.

Paul is powerful with adrenalin. He pulls back an arm, clenching his fist and steps forward before the youth has time to think, putting his weight behind a most satisfying punch. As his knuckles make contact with the yob's disintegrating nose, Paul shifts onto his left leg and jerks his right knee into a yielding crutch, then canons his shoe down the length of the fellow's shin and stomps viciously on his foot.

The youth screams and drops to the floor in a writhing ball, and Paul looks at his mates, beckoning with both sets of fingers.

'Anyone else?'

With looks of horror on their pasty faces they abandon their leader and make a run for it. They dodge past a pair of police officers leaping from a police car, who give chase. The siren of a second car wails balefully, in slow pursuit. Avoiding Paul, the injured yob staggers to his feet clutching his genitals, and limps out of the door.

Mr Hun Po puts both arms round his wife, and she cowers against his chest. He smiles warily at Paul.

Paul brushes his palms together in a mock dusting action.

'Well, that seems to have sorted that out.'

The proprietor beams in relief.

'Thank you. Thank you.'

Paul feels like The Terminator.

'Large cod and chips, please.'

'On the house,' grins Mr Hun Po.

The police car returns with three heads in the back. The two officers from the first car follow on foot, and before long, one comes inside. The blue serge is tight across his chest. A ruddy neck bulges over a crisp white shirt. It supports a weathered face that looks mildly at Paul.

'Good evening Sir.'

'Evening.' Paul unwraps his parcel of steaming food and pops a chip into his mouth.

'May I take a few particulars from you, sir?'

'Sure.' Paul plonks himself on a low window ledge, while the officer digs a pad and pen from the recesses of his uniform.

After noting contact details the policeman makes notes as Paul describes events, in between mouthfuls of supper. The meal finished he wipes his fingers on the paper and screws it into a ball.

'Thank you Mr Thomas.' The PC sounds satisfied. 'I have to arrest you now for causing actual bodily harm. You are not obliged....' Paul's mouth drops open, and behind the counter Mr Hun Po shouts, 'No, no, no.'

Before he can take in what's happening, Paul is being pressed into the back of the second police car, where he comes face to blotchy face, with the greasy haired recipient of his former attentions. A woman officer in the driving seat, speaks into her radio.

'Delta, Charlie 467, on way with five bodies, one injured, possibly a broken foot. Medic to attend.'

Paul groans.

Chapter 17

After a night in a cell Paul longs for a cup of tea, a shower and a kip. He wanders to the kitchen and fills the kettle, putting it on the crumb-scattered counter and flipping its switch.

A potential charge of ABH is so unreasonable. Without his heroic actions that poor couple's place might have been trashed. If he wasn't so tired he'd be more incensed.

There are no clean cups so he fishes one from brown water in the sink and rinses it under the hot tap. As he pours boiling water onto a tea bag his mouth distends into a yawn. Tea made, he starts up the stairs for the bathroom.

A long ringing stops him in his tracks. Bugger. If it's someone selling dusters he's not in the mood. Still clasping the mug he stomps back and flings open the door.

'Paul.' Fee looks agitated.

'Fee.'

'Can I come in?' She goes to step over the threshold, and Paul moves to block her way.

'This isn't a good time.' Fee folds her arms and stares at him, then sniffs, and crumples her nose.

'The house smells awful.' She leans towards him and sniffs again. 'And so do you.'

He looks at his wife. Her shining blond hair swings with every move of her head. Her crisp white shirt is tucked into light blue, belted jeans that skim her hips perfectly. Over the shirt she wears a tweed jacket, and round her neck, a skilfully tied, gold, paisley scarf. In comparison he is very aware of his crumpled clothes, sweating armpits and stubbled chin.

'Well, I've had a hard night.'

'I've had a hard night too, worrying how we're to get a decent price for this house if you can't manage to look after it.' Her head cranes past him and her eyes reach the kitchen. 'What's that?' Paul, I can't believe you've brought car parts into the kitchen.'

Fury rises Paul's breast.

'Just fuck off Fee. You left. It's my business how I choose to live.'

She recoils. 'If you don't take care of it, we'll all suffer. The value will be affected. The lower the price, the less your share will be and the less you'll have, to spend on your next house.' Fee takes a breath. 'And what will Kitty think when she sees the house in this state? I suggest you give that some thought.'

She spins round and stalks away down the path.

Under the steaming the shower at last, Paul scrubs at his body as if it were stained with Fee's remains.

Chapter 18

The room is peaceful with the usual bright fire crackling in the hearth. Between them on the table stand the two crystal tumblers with a water jug placed precisely half way between.

Max is languid in his chair. His left leg is loosely crossed over his right and a pen and pad rest on it.

'How was your week?'

Paul's shoulders are hunched in a straight backed wooden chair and one heel drums on the floor.

'How do you expect? I've been arrested, my wife's selling the house from under me, and my kid's growing up hardly knowing me.'

How did you get arrested?

Paul recounts the events in the fish and chip shop.

'Were you angry?'

'Course I was. *Anyone* would be.'

'True. Do you think *anyone* would have got into a fight?'

Paul is silent and Max seems to take this as *no*.

'Indeed. And you say the proprietor of the restaurant had a telephone.' Paul nods his head.

'Yeah, and I had my mobile.'

'Might a different course of action have been possible?' Max's expression is unfathomable.

'Well I suppose I could have dialled 999. But they were being complete arse-holes.' He looks at Max, who remains inscrutable. 'OK, yes, I should have walked away and called the police. I'm not sure how I could have told myself that at the time though.' Max smiles.

'That's why you're here Paul. Once you've acknowledged that change is possible, we can start to work on method.'

Max wants Paul to keep a diary. Not a journal of everything that happens, but the times when he loses his temper, the cause and the effect.

'Is that it?'

'To start with. If you do it for a few weeks we'll get a picture of your anger, and we can look at ways to manage it.'

Max throws his pen onto the clipboard.

'Let's take a break from you and your feelings this week. Tell me about Fee. What's she like?'

'More intelligent than me, too beautiful for me, and bloody middle class!' The words explode into the peaceful room and hover in the warm air.

Max pauses, then as levelly as always asks, 'What attracted you to her?'

'Her tits.' Despite his negative emotions he smirks as he thinks back to his first sight of the lovely girl, who walked past his office each morning. It was winter, and she was smartly muffled in a coat, fur hat, scarf and boots, only her pale, elegant face peeped out.

As spring and summer woke the drowsing neighbourhood gardens, Fee's layers of clothing were shed until she was revealed in all her glowing beauty. Long slender legs emerged from demure skirts, complemented by immaculately cut jackets. She had straw coloured hair, a palely freckled, aquiline face and those breasts, marching before her like majorettes leading a band.

Through the tall bay window of Max's room, Paul's eyes stare without seeing at budding branches stabbing a luminous sky. His eyes focus back on Max in time to catch a gleam that could have been empathy, in his eyes.

'How does she manage bringing up your daughter, um, Kitty isn't it?' Max's memory is impressive. Every tiny detail is filed in that intelligent head. Any inconsistency in Paul's responses is picked up.

'Oh she's got that sorted out!' Paul describes the arrangements between the three women, and as he speaks, the volume of his voice rises. 'They don't need bloody men to help them. We're surplus to requirements, redundant!'

Max is quiet for a moment while Paul's latest outburst joins his last. 'You could look at this as an opportunity.' He leans forward and takes a drink of water, replacing his glass in the centre of its coaster. 'There are plenty of men who would love to be in your shoes, to have a chance to do as they please. Come on now, think back; there must have been times during your marriage when you longed to escape, wished you'd never had kids, heard railway announcements and were tempted hop on a train to the coast without a care?'

Paul has to admit that life was far from perfect after the baby. Once upon a time Fee was available for all his needs. Her well paid career meant that Paul didn't need to put much effort into his own. Fee often found him listening to music and drinking lager when she got home from work.

Then Kitty arrived and she wanted him to help with everything. She was often too tired for sex, and the house was covered in baby clobber. 'Maybe,' is all he says.

Max pokes his lips out thoughtfully. 'You could get fit, learn to fly, buy a bachelor pad, date women, who knows? What do you fancy?'

For the first time Paul contemplates the advantages of a single life, with a fleet of classic cars and bikes. Showing them at motoring events, with admiring visitors examining their upholstery, paintwork and gleaming engines. Girls in tight jeans smiling at him as he cruises through towns, like James Bond, a blond in a flapping scarf at his side.

Max jolts him back to reality.

'Why do you think she's more intelligent than you?'

Paul's head flies up and his knee resumes its jumping and bumping. 'Well she programs computers for a living.' He ticks off his fingers as he speaks. 'She adds up figures before I've focussed on the page, and she can put up self-assembly furniture without reading the instructions.' He sounds more flippant than he feels.

'And what are you good at?'

Paul is still vibrating.

'Well, I suppose I can fix things, you know, the bike, the central heating, a broken chair. '

'Anything else?'

The knee becomes still.

'Geography. I was good at it at school: capitals of countries, rivers, climate, economy, that sort of thing. And I've got a good sense of direction.'

'That's excellent. Have you travelled much?'

'Not really, I'd have liked to but marriage and family got in the way. Fee never wanted to go anywhere after Kitty, not even the pub.' Paul ponders life before Fee, B.F. - bloody fool more like. He certainly spent a number of weekends in the pub with his mates. They're probably trapped in tedious marriages now, having to help with the nappies and the washing up, poor sods?

Max intercepts again. 'And middle class is bad is it?'

Paul glares. 'I don't get how she ticks. She makes stupid things important.'

'What sort of things?'

'Who Kitty is mixing with. Do they speak nicely? What school will she go to? Whether the table's laid properly - all sorts of crap.'

'How was your sex life?'

Paul narrows his eyes. 'Is that relevant?'

'Sexual frustration can certainly influence mood.'

'Maybe it can but it was fine. No problem. Well…'

Max cocks an eyebrow.

'We didn't have it as much after Kitty, but I suppose that's normal. Life gets in the way doesn't it? And if I was persuasive I could always bring her round.'

'Do you think she went off you?'

'I never considered it. I just thought she was tired. She got pretty off about everything. You know, hung up?'

'Hung up?'

Paul looks at the fire as if it might hold the words he seeks. Tense. Her humour became a thing of the past. The two of them had spent their first year laughing at nothing but as years passed, the jokes came only from him, and her response would be a narrowing of the lips or a brief glance at the ceiling as she flew round the kitchen or wielded a duster in the living room.

'We stopped having fun.'

Max sits with his chin propped. He looks interested, less neutral.

'Why do you think she got that way?'

Paul is not in the habit of analysing life.

'I don't bloody know Max. Busy. Demanding job. Big house and garden. New baby.'

'But you took the pressure off, right?'

Did he? Should he have?

'I know nothing about housework and cooking. Fee always did it, and she didn't ask for help.'

'But she was tired.'

Paul's voice rises. 'She might have been tired, but she *never* asked for *help*. Am I supposed to be psychic?'

Max is silent. Then, in his usual way, 'The other two women, Millie and Twitch, are they middle class too?'

'Shit yes. What do they call it?' He adopts a far back accent. *Received Pronunciation*, designer clothes, organic food, fine wines, table manners. I bet their meal times are spent sipping glasses of Tesco Finest Shiraz and telling the kids to sit up straight and not talk with their mouths full. Poor little buggers!'

'I expect they have plenty in common then?'

'S'pose so. I think Twitch stays at home and looks after the kids. She probably paints with them and that sort of thing - she's arty-farty. Fee will be the earner, and Millie, I'm not sure about her. I think from what Kitty says that she wants to open a restaurant.'

Max looks impressed.

'What's she like, this Millie?'

'Bit of a shrimp, dark curly hair, pretty in an Italian way.'

'And they all live together.'

Paul smiles a secretive smile.

'Yep. They don't always manage to be *terribly civilised*.' Paul uses a Fee-type accent 'Kitty told me there was a big row the other day.'

'And that makes you feel…?'

Paul shrugs his shoulders,

'I dunno.'

He does know. He feels triumphant. Relieved that he is not the only person to irritate Fee. He stares back at the fire and Max waits but Paul decides not to speak.

'When did you last see her?'

'Yesterday. She came to have a go at me over the house. My lifestyle doesn't meet with her approval.'

As usual Max is in no hurry to interrupt.

'She threatened to stop Kitty seeing me. *Cow.*' There's a pop from the grate and a small glare of flame leaps towards the chimney. 'She says if I don't clean up she won't let Kitty come round. She's my daughter. I have rights.'

Max shifts his eyes to meet Paul's.

'Tell me about your house.'

When Paul left this morning the bed was unmade and the bathroom even scummier than when Fee had called. The kitchen was moderately less oily, as the wheel has gone, but the floor is almost certainly grimy, although he hasn't looked at it.

'It's a mess. I'm not a housekeeper.'

'Do you want to stay in that house?'

'Well moving's such a hassle. I'm not bothered about the house.' Paul thinks of the rows of tools on pegboards in his garage, and the vice on the bench, the shelves, neatly organised with jam jars of nuts and bolts and boxes of parts. 'All I need is a workshop with a flat above.' He flicks Max a brief grin.

'And what does Kitty want?' Max leans forwards in the chair and rests his forearms on his knees, letting his hands dangle between.

'Are you trying to trick me?' Paul's chin juts at Max and he glares through half closed lids.

Max shakes his head. 'Not at all. Just trying to make you see it from the point of view of all parties. It seems to me, and I may be wrong, but from what you've told me Fee's not prone to knee-jerk reactions so she must feel quite strongly about this. What do you think Kitty's reaction will be to the mess?'

Paul tries to imagine his house through the eyes of his daughter. Kitty is not one for holding back. Paul almost hear her stunned voice quavering in disapproval.

'She'd tell me off. She's her bloody mother's daughter.'

'She's yours too. You've told me before about how you've influenced her.'

'Mm, yeah, but the house has always been clean and tidy.' He lapses into thought. He has let it get that way on purpose - to spite the obsessively neat Fee, but he hadn't thought that it might alienate Kitty. He pouts. 'I bloody hate cleaning!'

'There are firms that do it.'

'I s'pose.'

Max veers in a new direction. 'So they've had a row. What was that about?'

'Oh, something about mess. There's three of them in that small house now, with all the kids most of the time. I think Fee tripped over some shoes or something. I don't think she would have yelled or anything, that's not her way. She probably just made someone feel guilty - that would be more like it. Millie wouldn't have kept her mouth shut if she got annoyed. She's a fire ball when she gets going, well, so Kitty tells me.'

84

Max's eyes stray to the clock.

'What's Twitch like? You haven't mentioned her much.'

'Not sure. Quiet, sexy actually…' Paul stares at Max. 'Are you getting off on the idea of having three women at the same time?'

Max pulls himself up in the chair and shakes his head, his fringe flapping from side to side. For a moment he looks guilty, then he grins. 'Ha. Good try Mr Thomas.' He looks at the clock again. 'Time's up. See you in a week?'

As Paul leaves the office, shrugging on his leather motor cycling jacket, Max is writing intently, one elbow on his knee supporting his forehead, his fringe flopping between his splayed fingers. Paul wonders what he is writing: 'Miserable bastard? Complete bore? Poor man has been seriously damaged by his selfish ex-wife?'

Chapter 19

'I hate to pull this on you, but we have to do the childhood thing in more detail.'

'Childhood? Do me a favour Max. What the hell good is it going to do, finding out whether I pulled the legs off spiders or got bullied at school?'

'Did you?'

'No, to the spiders. The worst thing that happened to me when I was small, was my mum and dad dying when I was six. A rail disaster. They were coming home from a weekend in South End. I was staying with mum's parents, Nan and Grandad. I never left after that. It was hard at the time but I don't dwell on it. No point. I'm just a working class boy from a working class home. No complications, no hang ups.'

'Not even about the middle classes?'

'I'm not hung up about the middle classes but I don't want to be a member.'

'Why not?'

'Well, it's a club, isn't it? You have to send your kids to the best school, recycle your rubbish, clean the car on a Sunday wearing a lamb's wool sweater, keep the lawn nice, and,' Paul searches for a way to explain his antipathy, 'you have to own things: detached house, wide screen telly, four by four for the wife.'

'But you used to have all those things. Didn't you say you were pleased when Fee's father bought you that house?'

'Well,' he hesitates, 'I was wrong.' He had thought it was just a house but it wasn't, it was a way of life. He screws his face up and shakes his head. 'Look, I'm happy when I'm tinkering with my motorbike or having a pint. Not sitting round at bloody *dinner parties* making *small talk* with a load of *tossers*.' His head shakes at each word and Max scribbles a note or two.

'So, were you ill at ease with Fee's friends?'

Paul slumps in the chair.

'I embarrassed Fee,' he mutters.

The counsellor looks quizzical.

'Not sure if I did it on purpose,' he hesitates 'I wanted to shock them. I dunno why.' He pauses again. 'They made me feel stupid. I felt like saying fuck, cunt, and shit - wipe the smug looks of their faces.'

'Is that how your Grandparents would have felt in your shoes?'

'My Nan and Grandad wouldn't say 'Boo' to a pantomime goose. They thought those types were better than them. When I was nine there was a kid at school, James Whittaker. His dad was a doctor. I was quite small for my age, a late developer and he was built like brick shit-house.' Paul glowers. 'He had this la-de-dah accent, and he used to nick my crisps every play time. He didn't want them. He'd throw them on the playground and stamp on them then run away with his mates, laughing.

I told my Nan but she did fuck all. You didn't argue with a doctor.'

'Did you see Fee as a member of the Middle-Class Club when you met her?'

Paul had watched Fee going past his window for ages before managing to catch her eye. He'd played the fool, done a stupid dance close to the window, pulled faces and made her laugh. After that she'd looked in and waved every time she passed. One day he'd been at the door, waiting for her to come past and they'd had a conversation. He couldn't remember what it was about, but as for her accent, had he noticed it? He decides that he had but it hadn't mattered, she'd laughed at his antics, talked to him as an equal. He'd assumed that she would be like him with a posher voice.

'Naah, she was good fun in those days. We went out with my mates mainly, and she was one of the crowd. Everyone was envious of me having such a classy bird.'

He broods over the laughs they used to have. Fee began taking life seriously the day her job became more responsible.

'She got all upwardly mobile when she got promoted.'

'So you're better off without her then, if she wanted different things from you and,' Max flips back through his notes, 'you didn't have much sex and you couldn't go to the pub any longer?'

Paul feels wrong-footed. He has to agree that Fee and he are now different, so why is he upset that she left? He doesn't want to accept Max's analysis, he wants to blame Fee for not being the person he thought she would be. An uncomfortable thought bounces into his head, perhaps she had been surprised too, that he was not as she expected.

Max is watching him.

But Kitty. His baby.

'She stole my kid and left before I could even think.'

'Would you like to take Kitty back?'

'Of cour...' He hesitates. That would be a lot of work. 'I just want things the way they were.'

'And is that a possibility.'

'Not a fucking chance!'

'So?'

'No, I couldn't manage her full time.' He slumps his chin onto his chest.

'How are you getting on with the house?'

Paul frowns. 'The house?'

'Yes. You were putting it on the market.'

After their last session Paul went home alone and railed at Fee, and Max. He paced the floor in the lounge, stepping over the food cartons, then sat down and looked at his surroundings as if for the first time. Half an hour later he was scrolling through Google for cleaning companies.

'It's clean as a whistle. Fee's happy and Kitty has been over. Fee even let her stay overnight.'

'Are you pleased?'

Paul shrugs and looks away.

'Is it on the market?'

'Next week I think. I'm looking at rental properties. Not a great prospect but I suppose it's got to be done.'

'Anyway,' Max clears his throat, 'We were going to discuss your childhood.'

Paul submits to questioning about his grandfather, a maintenance man at a local hospital, and his grandmother, a sales assistant in the corner shop. He describes their home, a semi-detached house on a council estate, and their pride in him when he passed the eleven plus and got to the grammar school.

'I don't think they expected me to do it,' he spreads his palms. 'People like us didn't do exams, let alone further education. I think my Nan and Grandad are clever, but they're a different generation. They both came from huge families where everything they wore was a hand-me-down, and they had to go out to work as soon as they could, to help bring in money for the family. My Nan once told me that when she was 14 her teacher had tried to persuade her parents to let her stay on at school, but her dad said it couldn't be managed. I think Nan regretted that but she never complained.'

'So, is it possible that you think Fee is, not better than you, but more confident, that her expectations are higher?'

So many difficult questions. Paul's knee jiggles like a hammer drill, but deep inside there spreads a small pool of understanding. He went to clever kids' school, and college but he always felt an imposter. He'd slunk through school waiting for someone to stop him and say, 'Hey, you. Who said you could come here?'

Is Max trying to trick him into letting go of his beliefs? Paul returns to his well-rehearsed mantra: Fee left him. Fee took Kitty away. Fee made him look inferior. It's Fee's fault. It'll take a better person than Max to change his mind.

Chapter 20

The bathroom door is locked, at 6.30 in the morning! Fee always gets up now; everyone knows she has priority in the shower. The door flies open.

'Sorry,' sings Josh, 'needed a poo.'

Wrapped in a robe Fee returns to the bedroom, squeezing between beds to reach the wardrobe. She pauses to watch her daughter, deep in sleep, eyelashes splayed across soft cheeks, mouth lolling.

Outside the room Twitch and Millie are rousing the other children for school.

'Kitty, time to wake up Poppet.' Fee shakes the child by her shoulder, and Kitty moans and stirs.

'Come on, rise and shine, everyone's getting dressed.'

'I don't want to go to school.' Kitty's forehead corrugates and she slits her eyes apart to peer at Fee over her covers. 'I feel sick.'

Fee puts a hand on Kitty's head.

'You're fine. No temperature, and you haven't *been* sick.' She tilts her head to one side and looks kindly at Kitty. 'You need to go to school with the others.'

'I do feel sick Mummy. Really.'

Fee gives inward groan. This has been happening too much lately. She hardens her tone.

'Kitty. You have to go.' She sits on the bed and strokes hair from the little girl's eyes, feeling the warmth of the small body against her hip. Her voice softens. 'You like school, don't you?'

'Yes.' Kitty snuggles up to Fee, 'But everything's different now. Going to school with Aunty Twitch is funny.'

Josh's raised voice vibrates through the closed bedroom door.

'I didn't get it out, Olivia did. Make *her* put it away.'

Then Millie's quieter, firmer one,

'I'm asking you to help, Josh. Everyone needs to do things to keep this little house tidy, and you're nearer to that coat than Olivia is. Please pick it up and I promise you that Olivia will put away something of yours one day.'

Fee rises from the bed and pitches Kitty a brisk smile.

'You see? We're all finding it a bit strange. It'll get easier. I guarantee.'

Footsteps thump and doors slam on the landing. 'Come on Poppet. Get up now. You'll be fine.'

Kitty yawns and climbs to the floor. Fee struggles to dress in the tiny space then says, 'I'll see you downstairs, poppet. Don't be late or I won't get my goodbye kiss.'

The cramped hall is a mess of school bags and coats. In the kitchen Twitch pours milk onto bowls of cereal, while Sam, Olivia and Josh sit at the small table, leaving little room for anyone else. Fee pokes her head in through the door.

'Any tea in the pot?'

'I'll bring it through in a tick.' Twitch looks distracted.

Fee glances at her watch, it's ten to eight. She usually leaves the house at 8am to avoid the traffic and to prepare before the rest of her team arrive.

'OK. Thanks.' She hesitates, 'I'll get breakfast at work.' She crosses to the other room and joins Millie, sitting in the lounge browsing the local paper.

Twitch leans out of the kitchen and bellows up the stairs to the other two children to hurry or their cornflakes will be soggy.

Millie folds the newspaper, exposing snapshots and columns on the property pages.

'Moving out already?'

Millie smiles.

'No, I've found commercial premises to let, on the High Street, up by the church. I think I'll go and have a look.'

Fee looks distractedly at her watch.

'Great Idea.' She stands up and at the same time Twitch arrives in the doorway with the tea.

'Sorry, I haven't got time now.' Fee squeezes past her and picks her way to her coat.

'Well, you could have a sip…' Twitch looks put out.

'Sorry. Must go.'

As Fee pulls the door closed she can hear Twitch complaining to Millie, and as she reverses her car from the drive she realises that Kitty has missed her kiss.

***

Millie lays her newspaper on the arm of the chair and pounds upstairs.

'*Kitty. Lucas.* Breakfast time. What are you doing up here?'

The landing is silent. Cautiously she pushes Fee's door open. Kitty is sitting on the edge of the bed, her little body sagging over her knees and both hands over her face. Millie rushes to wrap the child in her arms, dropping her head onto the soft hair. Kitty's delicate shoulders shake and Millie croons, half of her mind wondering what Lucas is up to.

Kitty grows calmer and Twitch's impatient voice rises from below.

'Kitty. Lucas. Will you hurry up?'

Millie, still cuddling Kitty, shouts back, 'Twitch - Kitty and I'll be there in a minute. Do you think you could check on Lucas?'

Twitch bangs up the stairs, and the door of Millie's bedroom thuds open. There's a silence then they hear Twitch's voice.

'*Lucas.*'

'I'll be back shortly.' Millie squeezes Kitty and extricates herself. Along the short landing Twitch's hands grip the door frame. Millie peers fearfully over her shoulder. On the bed stands Lucas, stark naked and looking like the victim of an explosion in a dairy. Dotted over his body are thick blobs of face-cream and attached to each blob is an unfurled tampon. The bedcover is littered with empty cellophane tubes. The window is similarly embellished. Multiple Lillets with dangling strings, resemble a plague of tiny white mice scuttling up the glass.

'Oh my God!' Millie is so relieved that Lucas is alright, she can't suppress the guffaw that bursts from her belly.

Kitty thrusts a blotchy face under Twitch's arm with a shriek of delight, and they cling to one another, tears of mirth running down their faces. Lucas grins.

Millie ruffles Kitty's hair.

'At least you've cheered up.'

At last the house is silent; the children are at school or nursery and
Millie has gone to look at the property in Chelterton. Twitch stares
glumly at the cluttered kitchen.

Other people's children. Is that the title of a book?

Twitch wonders whether Fee and Millie feel as guilty as she does.
Possibly not as much because they are caught up in exciting projects.
She *is* glad for them, but at the moment she's feeling sorry for herself.
Nothing has changed. She's moved from one dogs body job to
another, and this one is even more demanding.

She has only herself to blame. Being Fee's housekeeper was her idea,
but with Millie on the scene, getting excited about opening a restaurant,
Twitch's resentment is growing.

She labours up the stairs to her rumpled bedroom and strips off her
clothes, folding them carefully, trying to enjoy the time alone.

Naked, she stands in the middle of the room, her toes wiggling in the
soft carpet. There is a full-length mirror on the wardrobe and she
regards her body. Not bad considering she's had two pregnancies.
Tumbling chestnut hair, gently curved hips offset by a slender waist,
and perky breasts, so far unaffected by gravity. She cups them in her
hands, and her long fingers rub the nipples making them hard. A flash
of desire shoots through the centre of her body, it has been a long time
since a man has seen her undressed. Will one ever do so? Is this her
life then, no career, no love and no sex?

She suddenly has the uncanny feeling that someone's looking at her.
Her eyes fly to the window. The curtains are open but nobody could
see in without the light on. Still, she wraps her body in a robe and jerks
the drapes shut.

In the shower she washes her hair, letting the water run along her spine
and between her buttocks, warm and delicious. She drips shower gel on
her palms and begins to caress her body. Her neck, nipples, even her
arms are charged with hidden electricity. With eyes closed she rotates
beneath the jets. The water strokes her skin, running over her
shoulders, between her throbbing breasts and into her slippery crotch.
Finally, she steps from the shower and wraps herself in the bath robe,
enjoying its roughness against the tips of her nipples.

In the bedroom, she lays her open robe on the bed and lies on top of
it. Her hands caress her body and she moans with pleasure. When she

climaxes, crying out to the empty house, she finds that there are tears in her eyes. She curls into a foetal ball and sobs.

Chapter 21

The leaves of the laurel rustle in front of his nose. At his feet, a dog turd lies on the rigid morning earth. Paul has been here for a couple of hours, smoking cigarettes and watching the various members of the household opposite, depart for their respective labours. His feet and back ache, and he needs a leak. He unzips his fly and pees surreptitiously into the roots. *Huh!*

Standing here, behind this hedge, he has seen his ex-wife leave for work in her Audi, so beautiful he can hardly look at her. He's seen his baby and her new 'brothers and sisters', heading on foot to school, holding on to Twitch, whose cheesecloth skirt flapped in the chilly morning air. Next, Millie emerged, pert in her short black skirt, dark woolen tights and flat boots. Carrying a rolled newspaper under her arm she climbed into her pink VW Beetle. Twitch returned an hour ago but Paul's still here, picturing her in their orderly hall, hooking her jacket by the grandfather clock and going into the kitchen to clear the breakfast things. He is suddenly overwhelmed with self-pity and, to his horror, tears fill his eyes.

That last session with Max has left him feeling unsettled. He has vacillated between wishing to change and fearing it. He is beginning to recognise the destructive effect of hanging on to his anger but has yet to start recording his feelings as Max suggested. As he stands, chilled and miserable behind the accursed bush, he decides. Tears blur the road as he crosses and stumbles up the steps. The bell rings faintly and soon the distorted outline of Twitch hovers in the bottle glass. The door opens.

'Paul.'

He can't speak.

'Come in, quickly, you poor thing.' Twitch pulls him into the warm hall and undoes his coat, dragging it from his shoulders, while he stands like a kid. He lets her push him across the poky living room to a leather sofa. Sitting beside his hunched body, her hip pressing against his own, she waits. The smell of shampoo rises from her, and the only sound apart from his snuffling is the slow tick of the grandfather clock. When at last he straightens, she slides a box of tissues along the low coffee table.

The settee lifts, and she leaves, returning with two steaming mugs. They sip, shoulder to shoulder, then he meets her sympathetic gaze. 'I don't know what I'm doing here. I need to talk to Fee. I saw her going out. She looked so happy.'

'She is happy,' says Twitch. 'They both are.' Her voice is wistful and Paul looks at her sharply, then leans forward for another sip of tea. When he speaks again his tone is firmer.

'Fee doesn't realise the damage she's done.' He remembers Kitty clinging onto Twitch's hand, and rounds on her. 'And you.' He glares. 'Don't think you're going to steal my daughter!'

Twitch's eyebrows shoot up and her mouth opens, then her lips skew and her chin retracts, and to Paul's dismay tears spring into her azure eyes. She shakes her coils of hair.

'I haven't stolen her.' She wails, 'She's yours and Fee's. I only provide a routine so she's not too upset by the changes in her life. You think I am happy? You're wrong.' Her voice rises to a shriek. 'I want a normal life with a good man and my own family. Not to be everyone's servant. They sail off to their exciting lives,' she punches her arm in the direction of the hall, 'leaving me here with their dirty laundry, their squabbling children and their mess. I do care about Kitty, but I'M NOT TRYING TO TAKE HER AWAY.'

They look at each other, each face twisted in pain, then, without thinking, Paul reaches out for her and pulls her into his arms. They hold each other for a long time, Twitch's grief gradually subsiding in the warm, ticking room.

He rubs her shoulder feeling the bra strap beneath her sweater, and strokes her arm and kisses the top of her head. To his disbelief she lifts her head he feels her lips on his.

His response is immediate, his need matching hers. Their lips part and her tongue slides tentatively from between her teeth, then they are kissing with urgency, their bodies pressed together. He grabs at her full skirt and struggles to find a way under the hem. She holds his face between her hands, weeping, and panting.

Her hands move to his fly and release his throbbing erection. He groans.

Then, she is gone.

He opens his eyes to see her standing, red faced and breathless a yard or so away with her skirt caught round her hips. His penis pokes ridiculously from his open fly as she shakes her head, staring wildly.

'We can't do this! You're Kitty's father, my best friend's ex-husband!'

Paul feels confused, then bereft and then the anger and frustration of the last months explodes from him. He leaps forwards and grabs her, throwing her onto the sofa

'Don't you dare stop. Don't you grab my cock and walk away.' He is blinded by fury. 'You're gonna do this you bitch!' He presses her chest into the settee while the other hand yanks up her skirt and tears at the button at his waist band. Releasing her briefly to grab both her knees, he drags her body forwards to the edge of the cushions and rams inside her.

'You can't do this on your own can you, prick teaser? You can't do this, this, this, this, this.' He pumps again and again, ignoring her pleas.

'Stop, please stop, Paul.'

It doesn't take long for him to finish. Anger spurs him on. He withdraws and stands, glancing at her with disdain while he wipes himself on a tissue, then without a word he stalks from the room, grabbing his coat and slamming the door on the silent house and the ticking clock.

Chapter 22

Rhododendron bushes outside the window, fade into the moist morning. It is 10.30 but the day will not get any lighter. Max's face is a steel mask and Paul drops his head.

'She led me on,' he says to his feet. 'She started things and changed her mind. I didn't mean it to happen but I'm only human.'

'I'm not here to lecture you.' Max's voice is brittle, and Paul's thoughts flick to something he heard on the radio: It is easier to detect a liar from the voice than the face. 'I'd like to know what you plan to do next, though.'

When he slammed the door on Twitch, adrenaline propelled Paul round the corner to his bike. Leaping on the kick-start he roared away with no destination in mind. As the bike carried him along the quiet daytime roads, the bleak countryside began to penetrate his consciousness, and the anger that drove him began to subside. Realisation of what he had done brought horror and self-loathing and he pulled into a lay-by. Propping the bike on its stand he dropped onto the kerb. How long he sat there with vehicles roaring past, whisking up grit and paper from the ground, he didn't know. When he rose, frigid and stiff, he flipped out his mobile phone. Max's secretary must have sensed the urgency and booked him in for this session.

In the warm room, Paul's thoughts rush and spin, seeking options. He should go back and see Twitch. What can he say? He won't be able to look at her. It won't achieve anything, anyway.

But Kitty lives there.

He wishes he hadn't lost his rag.

God he's a mess.

He struggles on, battling between conscience and fear. Max sits in his chair and watches.

Although Paul vacillates, in the depths of his mind the decision is made, and eventually he admits that there's only one road he can decently take.

'I'll go back.'

Max nods but shows neither approval nor disapproval.

***

Hoping she is out, he mounts the steps and waits at the door, puffing his cheeks and emitting small sighs. As before, footsteps approach the door and Twitch's head morphs across the glass. Then the sound of a chain being slotted into its mate on the door frame makes him quail. The door opens a crack and Twitch's face, hair tied back emphasising dark rings beneath her eyes, guards the narrow opening. She takes a sharp breath but says nothing.

'Hi.' He croaks.

She remains silent.

'May I come in? I promise I won't hurt you; I want to try to put things right.'

'Do you think I care what you want?' Tears begin to stream over her cheeks. This is not the way he had imagined their conversation, and he wonders if any Crispin Road curtains are quivering behind him. 'I'd like to explain,' he tries. 'I wish it hadn't happened; I know that's not much comfort but if I could undo what I did then I would.' He holds his hands towards her, palms upwards, as his words echo in the porch. It is hopeless of course.

'You needn't worry Paul, I'm not going to the police if that's what's worrying you.' Her voice is bitter.

He tries to deny this motive but she cuts him off.

'I won't tell because it would cause too much hurt.'

He searches his brain for the words to convince her she is misreading him, but Twitch's head shakes in dismissal. She straightens her body, lifts her chin, and takes a long breath, 'You will never enter this house again.'

Paul steps back before her rising cry.

'If you want to collect Kitty you'll have to do it when I'm not here.'

Shards of hatred fly from her eyes, then her energy seems to desert her and her face and body droop. 'Just keep away from me.' She turns to the hall muttering, 'go away before you do any more damage,' and closes the door quietly.

Paul stands on the chilly tiles, staring at the blank door. From the ceiling of the porch, cobwebs wave in the cold air, their silent spiders crouched in judgement.

When he's sure she isn't coming back, he trudges away. The gate swings open with a slight squeak and clatters shut behind him. He still needs someone to talk to but this time it won't be Max.

Chapter 23

Three eggs froth in the stainless-steel bowl and Mick's whisk gyrates and clacks in their golden slime. The hotel kitchen is silent, the staff finished for the night, the only clue they have been there, the faintest, lingering aroma of garlic and steak. Mick pours his seasoned mixture into the pan and it sputters quietly around the edges, turning glossy and mucus-like as he lifts the buttery base to let liquid egg glide underneath. When the omelet is cooked to his liking he flips it onto a plate, grabs a left-over lunch roll from the store room and eats, standing up.

Laughter and chatter from guests of a long-finished wedding, filter in from the lounge bar, where staff are in for a late night.

Mick washes his dishes and makes for a minor kitchen on the level below. This second kitchen operates until midnight to provide room-service. It's likely tonight that sandwiches and chips will be in demand.

'Everything OK, Steve?' The young sous-chef stretches from a dining chair, his long legs crossed at the ankles, and his checked chef's trousers, rucked up to expose pale shins and the tops of fluorescent-green socks. His hands grip an I-pad, thumbs occupied in a rhythmic dance.

'All quiet, Chef,' Steve replies, without looking up.

'Don't get back-ache, mate.'

Steve's eyes remain riveted on the tablet.

'See yer,' calls Mick.

'Yeah.'

The lamp-lit car park is quiet and the roads deserted on his drive home.

He moved into his flat a few days ago and unpacked a rudimentary selection of equipment to keep him afloat: toothbrush, razor, towel, kettle and bedding, and a few bits of clothing and underwear for work. The rest is still in boxes.

Work is demanding. His boss seems to be testing him. Mick is keen to make a good impression but with the kids expecting a visit, and his mother clucking at him about curtains and furniture, he's spread thinner than margarine on a poor man's doorstep.

In the flat boxes are stacked in every corner. Newspaper sheets, moulded in the shapes of their unpacked contents, litter the floor. He hobbles into the living room on aching feet and lifts a crate onto the coffee table. By half past one four more boxes lie flattened in the hall and Mick falls into bed.

***

'This is a very big house Daddy.' Olivia is full of wonder as she stares up at the Gothic Victorian mansion.

'I don't live in the whole building, Babes. Only that bit.' Mick points to an upstairs corner. Reflected in his sash windows, the tops of conifers wave before a pale sky. Down below, lawns edged by flower beds of budding daffodils, disappear on either side of the driveway, towards the rear of the property.

'Come on. Let's go in.' Mick lifts Lucas onto his thick shoulders. Inside, they mount the echoing staircase in silence. The children scan the curving banister and wide foyer with doubtful eyes.

Mick follows as they explore his new flat. Olivia crosses the tiny sitting room and pokes her head into the kitchen. 'This is the smallest kitchen I've ever seen, Daddy. How are you going to cook your curries and bread in this?'

'I don't suppose I will, babes. I'll have had enough of cooking when I get home from work.'

Olivia looks at him, her face a picture of sorrow. 'Will you be very sad, Daddy? You always used to make rolls and cakes for us.'

'I want cake,' announces Lucas and his face begins to crumple. Olivia rushes to his side and drops to her knees.

'It's OK Lukey, we can have cake when we get back to Crispin Road. Aunty Twitch made muffins yesterday.'

Mick wants to grip his chest in pain.

'Why don't we go out somewhere and have juice and cakes. How about the swings?'

102

'We've got swings in our park. Can we do something else?' Olivia looks at Mick expectantly.

Mick decides they'll go for a walk in the woods.

'We'll climb trees and hunt for bears.'

'I don't like bears.' Lucas looks ready to cry again.

'Pretend bears Sunshine, not real ones. Come on, it'll be fun, and there's a tea room.'

***

Dog walkers and families mill along the roadside as the car creeps through the forest towards the bumpy parking area.

'I wish we had a dog.' Olivia presses her nose to the window.

'Don't do that Livvie, you'll get it mucky.'

She wipes the glass with her sleeve.

'Here we are.' Mick pulls into a space in front of a sign reminding him to pay and display, and he remembers that he has only notes in the wallet that digs into his hip. They climb from the car and Mick scans the area for someone who might have change.

Three people have shaken their heads without concern, and the children are making anxious noises beside him, when a twittering woman smiles at them. She is glad to relieve the pressure in her purse, she tells them and fumbles clumsy fingers into stiff leather.

'Sorry, it's a new purse. I can't quite get to the coins.' She laughs, a silly self-deprecating sound. 'I bought shoes for my son and they'd run out of ten pound notes.' She drops nine pound coins and then one coin at a time, a pound's worth of small-change, into Micks cupped palms.

A broad footpath leads them between budding beeches and hazels. Under them the green tips of bluebells promise gorgeous treats to come. The children are wrapped against the gusting wind that seems to be a constant theme of this year. They kick up soggy leaves, and when Mick suggests hide and seek, rush away with glee. He takes a deep and relieved breath.

'Here I come,' he sings, and pretends not to hear their sniggers and rustles.

They walk further into the forest and Mick notices his shoe lace dangling in the dirt so he stops to tie it. The children run ahead, Lucas, still unsteady on small legs. Olivia, in front, spots a fallen tree and squeals. On his knees, Mick shouts at her to wait but the two are already scrambling over the thick branches that lie like huge arms across the earth. Mick yanks the laces tight and rushes towards them.

Lucas' clothing catches on a projection, and the little boy tips forwards with a cry, and drops between projecting spikes, his neck yanked by his winding scarf as he falls.

Mick throws himself onto his stomach. Among a tangle of branches his son is hooked by his scarf but the undergrowth has cushioned his fall. Mick's heart slows a tad and he hauls out his shaking boy. Lucas whimpers as Mick lies him on the ground to examine the damage. Thank God the neck seems unharmed, but the leg. He swallows, and his heart races as he pats his pockets for the tissues he knows he hasn't brought. Only the heavy load of coins clink at his touch.

Lucas sits up and looks at his thigh. He screams when he sees a jagged tear in his trousers, and a deep, dripping slice in his tender flesh.

Mick cradles his son in his arms. 'Alright Sunshine. Nothing to worry about. We'll get this cleaned up and you'll be fine.'

They hurry to the tea room, and in the lavatories, dab the sobbing boy's wound with damp napkins, borrowed from the café.

'It's OK Lukey. Don't cry,' Olivia croons like a little mother.

On the way home Mick leaves the children locked in the car, and watches them nervously through the window of the pharmacy, while he queues for sticking plasters. Lucas's pale face stares back at him from his car seat, and out of sight, Mick knows that he holds a moist serviette over his injury.

With medical purchases in a bag, Mick winks across the pavement at his son, and nips to a nearby bakery.

Back home in the flat Mick and Olivia apply steri-tabs, gauze, sticking plaster, and a bandage for good measure, to Lucas's leg. The boy tests it out, hobbling round the room and sniveling.

'There, that's better,' Mick insists, and fetches plates and knives, hoping sugar will distract Lucas from his troubles.

'Can I go home now?' Lucas looks tired.

'Of course, Sunshine. It wasn't a great day, was it? I'll do better next time.' He puts the cakes back in their boxes.

***

'Hi Ma.'

'Hello Son. How was your day?' Gloria's voice is comforting.

'Oh, you know, could have gone better.'

He pictures his mother's firm, portly figure, perched in a wing chair, her head cocked to one side, waiting to hear his news.

'Did the kiddies have fun?'

Mick goes over the day in his mind. *He* didn't have fun, worrying if the children were enjoying themselves. Of course the accident scuppered everything in the end.

'I hope so Ma. Lucas got upset. It's such a change for them.'

'They'll come round Son. Don't worry. You've all got settlin' in to do.'

Mick rubs his eyes with his spare hand, squeezing his eyeballs until he sees red blobs.

'Yeah, I guess so. I didn't know it would be so hard. They're my kids, we know each other, but today I felt like a stranger.'

'You'll be fine. Give it time. What did you do?'

Mick recounts their trip, glossing over Lucas's fall.

'I'm going to have to buy a TV, and get some things to keep them entertained here.'

'Good idea Son. You don't have to go out every time you see them.'

'I should have thought of that earlier though Mum. I should be better than this.'

'Don't be hard on yourself Mick. Men aren't designed to look after children. That's women's work.'

Gloria's indignation zings from the handset.

'No Ma, it's *my* fault. I didn't consider their needs. You're right, I'm not used to it, but that doesn't mean I can't do it. Millie's not coming back (*damn her*) so we've all got to be prepared for a different way of life. *All* of us Ma.'

Chapter 24

Paul rubs his thumb against the spine of a small book in his pocket. He bought it as a feeble gesture towards recording his anger, and he's angry now but he can't explain why. Does Max want him to write in it this minute, in this condition? Well he can forget that.

The Laurel bush has welcomed him like an old friend. The dog turd at its base is flattened into the earth as if some other person has passed through this leafy hiding place. Kids perhaps? The weather is warming up at last. In gardens opposite, tubs of daffodils and other unknown muted pink and blue blooms bring dancing colour to the neighbourhood.

A powerful looking, black-skinned man alights from a car, and as Paul watches, collects two small brown children from Millie at the open door. He walks back along the pathway with the kids clinging to his wrists. This must be Mick. Paul wonders how he's coping. He looks cheerful and confident with those kids.

He strains for a glimpse of Kitty or Fee inside but after Millie has stood on the step to wave them off, she closes the front door.

Paul sucks his cigarette and drops it onto the earth, then glares at the façade of the house and looks at his watch. Time for his weekly appointment with Max. He hasn't much to offer the man this week but at least he's bought the book.

He plunges deeper into the bushes, and squeezes along the metal railings to a hidden gate that opens into the park. The tufted grass is fragrant underfoot, and after a brief march past the playground, he exits through another gate into a side road. As he mounts his bike, he nods at a woman putting out her recycling and she nods back with a smile.

'Bit nicer today.'

'Yes. At least it's not raining.' Paul smiles at her without humour, and jumps on the pedal. With a twist of his wrist he takes off in the direction of Melmsbury.

***

'How's the flat?' They've been together about ten minutes and Max is beginning to probe.

'It's a flat. Over an estate agent's. Not much to write home about but it's home – as I now understand it.'

Max ignores Paul's sarcasm.

'Good. That's excellent.'

Paul seethes.

'If you say so.'

'Has Kitty seen it?'

'Yeah, she came on Thursday after school.'

'And what did you do?'

'Pizza, telly, there isn't a lot of time on a school night.'

'Did you listen to her read, anything like that?'

'Never even thought of it.' Paul remembers the thin blue bag, and lunch box that Kitty had carried out of school. He'd told her to leave them in the car. He thinks now that it might have been nice to listen to the child read, he's never done that. He wonders how Kitty does at school. It's a new thought.

'We did have a chat though, about life in Crispin Road.'

'Crispin Road?'

'Where they all live.'

'Oh, right, and how are things there?' Max picks up his pen.

'Well, chaotic from what Kitty says. It's crowded, and they're getting on each other's nerves. There have been a few rows, between the adults and among the children.'

Max makes a note and Paul wonders why.

'Are you worried?' Max asks.

'About what?'

'Well, the impact on Kitty.'

'Not really. Well, I get mad about it. She shouldn't have to listen to adults arguing.'

'Did she never hear you and Fee disagree?'

'No. Fee didn't argue. She had a look though, you know?' Paul adopts an expression of disdain. 'She could make you feel an inch tall. I bet it's the others that are bitching. Fee would just walk away.

'Millie's been looking at properties for her restaurant. Now that her house is sold she can afford to take a punt.' He catches interest in Max's face. 'You interested in food?'

'Yes.' Paul waits for more but Max doesn't oblige.

'I learned something else. My, soon-to-be-ex-wife, has inherited a beach hut near Whitstable.'

'Very nice. It's a lovely town.'

'I wouldn't know, mate.'

Paul can't believe it. A bloody beach hut, on top of all Fee's other advantages.

'Have you been recording your anger?'

He's been hoping to avoid this moment, and frowns, poking out his lips.

'It's hard - writing about your feelings,' then he brightens. 'I've got the book though. It's a start.'

Max smiles.

'You don't need to write while you're angry. Just be aware, and record afterwards, when you're calmer.'

Paul curls his hand into a fist and thumps it gently on the arm of the carver.

'Yeah but afterwards I don't want to think about it.'

'Look. Just rule three columns. Date and Time, Level of Anger on a scale of one to ten, and cause. You don't have to pull it apart and analyse it that can be done when we've got the data.'

Paul rubs his cheeks with the palms of his hands. When he looks up, Max is regarding him with a sympathetic expression.

'When did you last have a holiday, Paul?'

'A few years.' Paul contemplates the idea of a break. He doesn't fancy a fortnight on his own, or even a week, but maybe a weekend. A change of scenery could be pleasant. Whitstable for example.

'I might consider it.' He smiles.

Chapter 25

'Maurice. *Maurice.*'

Maurice grunts, groping for a route into reality, knowing who he'll see when he unsticks his eyes. In the glaring daylight he squints with an effort at the despairing face of his mum.

'Hello. What's the matter?'

'The children. You've fallen asleep while the children are here.'

Maurice struggles upright and blinks.

'Are they OK?'

'Yes they are. No thanks to you, lad. But your bathroom's a mess. They had a lovely time shredding the toilet roll and stuffing it in the pan.'

The smells and sounds of his surroundings begin to filter into his consciousness. The television, on which he'd been watching sport, has been switched off. Sam and Josh are chattering at the end of the room, dipping fingers of toast into soft boiled eggs. The smell of grilled bread mixes with furniture polish, and the room has a newly cleaned and plumped air. His mother, he notices, has her palm resting on the handle of his battered vacuum cleaner.

'I didn't know you were here. Why didn't you wake me?'

'I wanted to see how long you could sleep when you should be looking after your own children. Frankly Maurice, I'm disappointed.'

Familiar self-hatred overwhelms Maurice. Throughout his life his parents have pointed out his shortcomings rather than celebrating his small successes. He doesn't need anyone to tell him that he's an inadequate father, or that he was a useless husband. He's also fully aware that he's average at his job and socially inept.

The children are kneeling on rustic wooden chairs at his Mexican style table. The furniture, bought for his marital home, overfills the tiny dining space.

Maurice stands. 'Sorry kids. Daddy dropped off.'

'That's OK Dad,' Sam chuckles. 'We had fun without you. The toilet filled up with water, then we ran the bath. We were going to swim in it, but Grandma arrived and made us let the water out.'

Christ.

In the act of plugging in the Hoover, his mum raises her eyes to his, wearing a look of martyrdom.

'Bring them to us when you have them next. Your Dad will enjoy the company. He's fine by the way. Thanks for asking.'

Maurice is silent. Should he have asked after his father, whose legs are inflamed and senseless through diabetes? He sighs.

'That's good Mum. I'll call in and see him tomorrow after work.'

His mother nods.

'And thank you for the offer of help, and for doing this.' He sweeps his arm round the tidy room.

She puts her foot on the button, and the wailing of the machine prevents further conversation.

Chapter 26

Millie climbs into the driver's seat of her car and is soon zipping along the short dual carriage-way to Chelterton.

The car squeezes its way up the sloping High Street through morning traffic. Ahead, the church thrusts its long spire into the sky. The young agent stands on the pavement with his ear welded to a mobile phone. As Millie climbs from the car, she can't help noticing that he's pretty damn gorgeous.

'Gotta go.' The agent pockets his phone and approaches Millie with his hand extended. 'Mrs Sabatini?' She nods.

'Darren Rimmer.'

They shake hands and Millie doesn't correct his assumption that her maiden name is preceded by a married title.

She's already been to look at the outside of the premises, but to remind herself of just how perfect the position is, she takes another sweeping look up and down the street. No yellow lines, that's important. She reviews the frontage of the darkened premises. It is wide, with two bay windows made up of small, white-washed squares flanking glass doors. Above the panes a sign board declaims that this was once *Chez Ralph*. Darren, pulls a handful of keys from his pocket and starts trying them in the lock. They clatter against the glass as he fumbles.

'Sorry about this, I'm not sure which...' a key turns. 'Ah, there.' He holds back the door, and Millie steps over the threshold.

She stands in the gloom then the agent switches on the light and the room is washed in gold. A few feet in front of her, a black and chrome bar gleams in the glare. There's space either side for sixty, maybe eighty covers.

'Where's the kitchen?'

'Through here.' Darren starts towards a door to the left of the bar and they pass into a spacious but empty shell. The floor is tiled but the walls bear only jagged evidence that there were once waist-high fixtures and fittings.

'What happened to the equipment?'

'Let's say they sold it.' Darren looks at her meaningfully.

Went bust he means. Is she mad to consider this place? It's a good position. There's plenty of parking nearby, and a few bars and pubs.

'Storage?'

'Upstairs.'

They climb the bare stairs to the first floor. Another big, empty area. Storage at first then, maybe one day, more seating. Millie's pulse begins to speed.

***

She reverses into the drive next to Twitch's people-carrier. At four twenty, Fee will still be at work.

In the kitchen, five small heads are stooped over school books at the table. Twitch is tipping wholemeal pasta into a pan of boiling water. *Lovely home. Lovely life.*

'I've found it!'

'Found it?' Twitch sounds distant.

'Yes, my restaurant!' She waves the details, like a pennant.

The children drop pens and pencils, and thrust back their chairs, the legs scraping on the floor. Twitch lowers the heat under the saucepan and everyone crowds round Millie, at the breakfast bar.

'It's perfect.'

'It's cool!'

'Can we go and see it?'

'Millie meets Twitch's eyes over their young heads. I think it's the one but it's going to cost a fortune.'

'We'll find a way. It's your dream.'

Millie hugs Twitch. 'I'm so lucky to have you.'

Chapter 27

'Cheers Mate.' Paul takes possession of a pint of bitter and gulps down the top two inches before putting it down.

The pub is treacle-brown and sticky. It serves real ale and boasts an 'authentic' atmosphere. At one end of the bar a crowd from a local office is loud, with eruptions of laughter and fluttering eyelashes.

'Cheers,' returns Mick. They look at each other with interest.

'Good idea this - getting together.'

Fee hadn't been at all keen to give him their details, but when Millie and Twitch could think of no reason to refuse, she had handed over a Post-it note with their mobile numbers.

Paul glances at his watch, wondering if Maurice will show up. When Paul rang, the man had, in a pathetic tone, expressed reluctance, then skepticism. Mick had accepted straight away.

'Yeah,' Paul grins, 'I suddenly realised that I haven't been down the pub since, you know, since the girls went. That's months.'

Maurice appears from the direction of the bar, carrying a glass of Coke. Paul studies the drink. 'You on the wagon?'

Maurice sits, nodding a greeting to Mick, then shakes his head.

'No, just driving, and I've got an early start tomorrow: work.' He raises his drink and they all swig.

'What's the work?' Queries Mick.

'I'm designing an extension up the road.'

'You could have a few pints and leave the car here,' says Paul. 'Pick it up tomorrow after you've seen your bods.'

'I think not.' Maurice's face is as disapproving. 'I can't afford to throw money away on taxis, not with a mortgage to pay on my own, and having the children for weekends. It costs a fortune, doesn't it?'

Gloomy nods.

'Well the girls seem OK don't they?' Says Paul.

'You're not kidding,' Mick exclaims in his deep, rich voice, 'They've really got things sewn up.'

'Stitched up, more like.' Paul glares.

Maurice is still morose. 'I couldn't believe it when Twitch said she was leaving. I still don't understand where she got the idea from.'

'They encouraged each other and made prats out of us.' Paul suppresses his rage and makes a mental note to record it later. He raises his glass, forcing a smile.

'To prats!'

'Prats.'

After going to Max a few times, Paul feels more comfortable than he did about opening up. With care he ventures, 'I've been totally pissed off.'

More nods and gloom from round the table.

You guys OK?'

Opposite Paul, imposing in his leather bomber jacket, Mick seems at home with his new single state.

'Work keeps me going, catering's long hours, and I've got other interests. I'm not so good with the kids though.' He looks at the others for corroboration.

'Yeah, it's hard.' Paul nods.

He tries to imagine Mick in his kitchen at the hotel. He must make an imposing figure in his Chef's whites, a tall hat standing firm on his well boned head.

'My mum's fuming.' Mick smiles and raises his voice an octave, swaggering his torso and wiggling his head. 'That girl should take her responsibilities more seriously, she's had things easy her whole life. Where would we be now if I had rushed off to follow my dreams when your father was killed?'

Paul gives a clipped laugh.

In contrast to Mick, awkward Maurice with his flabby body and pale complexion, reminds Paul of a hamster. Conversation with him is stilted. Moan-y Mo with baggy trousers, his waist band supporting the beginnings of a pot belly.

'I'm totally pissed off,' Maurice states and takes a gulp of coke, belching into his curled fist.

Paul thinks of Max and wonders how he can drive the conversation on, then Maurice, who has been glowering at Mick's pint, bursts out, 'I can't do anything.'

Paul is quick to question, 'What do you mean?'

'My mum looks after me, like I was still a bloody kid.'

'You want cookery lessons?' asks Mick.

'No thanks mate.'

'You don't want to be running to mummy all the time, do you?' Mick persists. 'Come on man.'

'I suppose you've got everything worked out.' Maurice looks like a cross child.

'Well I haven't' interrupts Paul. 'Want to know what I feel? Fucking furious.' His voice is rising, and one or two drinkers turn worried faces towards the table.

'Calm down man.'

'I have calmed down, Mick. You should have seen me last week.' Paul lowers his voice. 'That's why I rang, I wondered if we could, you know…'

There's an awkward silence.

'What we need is another beer.' Mick tilts his wrist to and fro to indicate an empty glass.

'I'll get these.' Paul jumps to his feet. 'Mick?'

'Pint of the same, thanks.'

'Maurice?'

'Oh, go on then, one pint won't hurt, I suppose.'

Several rounds later while indulging in Vindaloo, they agree to make this a regular event.

Maurice leaves his car at the pub, and a passing taxi gets a long and complicated fare, delivering Paul locally, Maurice to his tiny semi, down the road from his parents, and a bleary, beery Mick to his flat. A generous tip from Mick dispatches the obliging driver happily about his further business.

At home Paul downs a long glass of water. Tomorrow he has an 'appointment' with his daughter so he mustn't have a hangover.

Chapter 28

'Hi Paul?' Fee's voice is metallic through his phone.

'Hi, I'm outside. Could you send Kitty out?'

Her tone becomes baffled.

'OK, but why don't you ring the doorbell?'

'Do I need a reason?' He touches the note book.

'Okay.' She doesn't sound impressed, but the front door swings open and Kitty runs down the path into his arms.

'What are we doing today?'

'We-e-ll,' Paul pauses for dramatic effect, 'I thought we could go and…'

'What? What?' Kitty's eyes are dancing.

'and buy… a puppy!' The last words rush out.

Kitty squeals and claps and dances a jig on the pavement.

'Where are we going? Have you found one? Where will it live? What shall we call it?'

Ha. One to Paul, nil to Fee.

'Woah. Slow down. We're going to a dogs' home. That's a place where dogs with no owners live, waiting to find someone to love them.' He takes her hand.

'I'll love them, I really will. Have you already been there?'

'Yep, I've got my eye on one special puppy, but I wanted to get the OK from you before I bought it.'

Paul is using the car today, there's no way for a puppy to travel on a motorbike - yet. Paul pictures the adult dog in a natty pair of goggles. Why not?

As they leave suburbia for the countryside, Kitty is silent for a change, her small hands gripping the seat-belt in excitement.

They turn onto a piece of scrubland. Barks and yaps greet them as they climb from the car and cross the pot-holed car park to a ramshackle hut. They are greeted by a beaming elderly woman behind a wooden counter. She sports a plaid shirt bursting at the bust exposing her grey bra and wrinkly cleavage.

'Hello. Back again are yer? Brought a friend I see.' Her puffy visage splits into a grin and she winks at Kitty, who screws up her face, failing to reciprocate.

'Carol.' She thumbs her chest and lifts a flap in the desk to reveal stocky legs which, to Kitty's evident astonishment, are clad in a pair of yellow Hawaiian-print shorts with below them, long, thick, woollen socks and workman's boots.

'Come on then, let's go and get the little blighter.' She grabs a set of keys from a hook by the door.

They wait while Carol unlocks a wire covered gate, and lets them into an enclosure. On either side of them caged canines leap hopefully at the bars or lie defeated in boxes.

Kitty pulls a face. 'It smells.'

'Well lovey, there's too many dogs and not enough help so they get smelly. Still, they're better off 'ere with me than roaming the streets. That's what I always say.' Her large back side blocks their view into a cage as she stoops to insert a key in the padlock. ''Ere she is.' She darts her hands out to catch a scrap of wriggling fur. 'I've 'ad a few folk after 'er but I kept to me word. She's yours if you want 'er.'

The tiny brindled pup has silken, drooping ears, and enormous feet. Paul asks about the 'provenance' of the pot-bellied creature but Carol can't say.

'Couple of kids brought 'er up 'ere. Found 'er in a plastic bag by the canal.' She shrugs.

Kitty is enchanted.

'Oh. So sweet.'

It's love at first sight.

'You're sure? We could look for another one if you want to.'

'No, I want her. She's called Topsy, OK?'

'Whatever you think, Pops.'

He's already purchased a crate for the return journey, and a collar and lead, and at home in his compact kitchen, two bowls and a plastic bed take up half the floor.

Topsy howls all the way back and Kitty croons through the metal bars of the carrier. By the time they arrive the puppy is sliding in a pool of pee, and has puked through the grill onto one of the seats.

'Oh, poor baby. Poor Topsy.'

Poor bloody car.

Paul propels Topsy into the flat at arms-length demanding a towel, and Kitty rushes to the bathroom. They dab off the worst of the muck, with Topsy attempting to murder the towel in her needle-sharp teeth. Once clean, the little dog takes a few sloppy laps of water and collapses into the bed. Kitty strokes her as she whimpers and twitches in her sleep, and Paul fumigates his car.

***

'Mummy, guess what we did?'

'Er, you went to the park?'

'No.'

'To Alton Towers?'

''course not. There wasn't time.'

'I give in.'

'We bought a puppy. She's at Daddy's flat and she's so-o-o sweet.'

Fee turns towards the kettle and with her back to her small daughter, manages to sound enthusiastic.

'How lovely! What has he called her?' She spoons coffee grounds into the cafetiere and pours on water.

'She's mine too Mummy. Mine and Daddy's, and she's called Topsy. I named her. She's sort of browny coloured.'

'Daddy's going to have a sleepless night tonight.'

Fee feels outdone. Still the boring parent. She puts a smile on her face as she comes back with the coffee. 'Puppies are hard work Kitty-mitten. They need walks every day, and training, and they often chew things. Has Daddy made plans for that?'

'Of course Mummy, we've got everything worked out, and I'm going to help. I'll take her to the park and throw balls for her, and we're going to dog disobedience classes starting next Saturday morning.'

Fee hides a smile, 'Dog Obedience, Kitty, obedience means doing as your told.'

'Oh, right. Well that's what we're doing.

'Mummy, why didn't Daddy bring me to the door?'

'I'm not sure Poppet.'

Kitty rushes upstairs to tell the others and Fee perches on a chair wondering if they could get a pet. She rejects the idea. It's not a competition. If Paul wants a dog for Kitty then good. She's glad they can have fun together.

***

By 2am the pitiful sound of howling and yelping has stopped. The duvet is mangled from Paul's twisting and fretting. He's tempted to have a peek into the closed kitchen to check on the damage, but decides against it. It should be OK. He bought a couple of newspapers to put on the floor (best place for them).

He flops the pillow over, and his thoughts zig zag about.

Kitty, the light in his darkness, was so excited today. He relives the events, and smiles at himself. One minute he wants to hit someone and the next he's waxing poetic about his kid.

Sunday tomorrow – no, today. They have an appointment at the vet's for Topsy's second set of injections. In a fortnight he'll be able to walk her along the canal.

A yelp comes from the kitchen and he pulls the pillow over his head.

Chapter 29

The hedgerows beside the towpath are beginning to come alive. Insects hover over daisies and dandelions, and Blackthorn, heavy with flowers gives off its sickly aroma. Paul's spirits lift, the scent evokes memories of long ago spring evenings on the bike, heading off to a party, with a girl on the pillion.

At the beginning of their walk Topsy didn't understand the lead and kept biting and pulling it until Paul was compelled to dispense a sharp tap on her nose and a stern 'No.' She got the message but then entertained herself by running between his feet and tripping him. Now they've reached an understanding, but the unfamiliar exertion has taken its toll on the puppy.

They are, as planned, approaching The Barge so Paul picks Topsy up and strokes her head. 'Come on girl, it's time you went to your first pub.'

The beer garden runs alongside the towpath, and as he enters the garden, the wicket gate snags on tall grass at the base of the hedge. With the puppy under his arm he crosses a patch of lawn and a paved rectangle dotted with wooden picnic benches. From the back door, they make their way along a well-used passage to the public bar.

At 11.30, an aperitif seems in order, and he leans his forearms on the smooth black wood with Topsy under his arm. Her small nose quivers at the unfamiliar smells of beer and kippery smoke.

A barmaid approaches and stretches across to pat Topsy. 'He's gorgeous.'

'She. Topsy.'

'Hello Topsykins.' The girl leans across the bar exposing a generous eyeful of cleavage and fondles the dog's silky ears.

A babe magnet, nice one Topsy. Paul winks at the girl and orders a pint. He finds a seat on the patio. A young couple sit on the grass drinking lager, and watching their small son and daughter showing off their skills on the apparatus. Kitty would enjoy it here, it could be a regular jaunt. He puts Topsy between his feet as a man with an enormously fat Golden Labrador, goes past. The dog shambles loose, and as it passes, lowers its huge head to sniff Topsy. Her small bottom quivers and her ears lay backwards, then she rolls onto her back, exposing her round, little tummy.

'Come Major,' the man commands, and Major, after administering a slobbery lick, lumbers inside.

Paul sits for a while sipping his beer, then tips his head to drain the last quarter pint.

'Right pup. Let's go see Maurice.'

***

Mick is already here, his car parked against the curb.

Maurice's front gate like the one at the pub, is rickety. A narrow concrete path leads to a double glazed front door, then along the front of the house to a side gate. Topsy sniffs at a straggly rose bush and squats to pee. Good. One less accident on the carpet. They take the side way to the back garden.

Through the kitchen window, Mick is pointing at kitchen tools and knives on the worktop, and Maurice is nodding in concentration. Both men look up when Paul taps the glass.

'You've arrived just in time. I'm cooking lunch.' Maurice stoops to pat Topsy. 'Hello dog. Nice to meet you.'

'I'm not sure I should let her in.'

'Well she won't be safe out there, the garden isn't dog proof. Bring her through and I'll find an old blanket or something. She'll be fine.'

In all honesty there isn't much to spoil in Mo's house. Curtains droop like loose washing, onto a swirly, umber carpet. A smell of stale towels and unwashed bedding pervades the air, and despite the fine day, the air is clammy.

Mick opens cupboards, spotted with mildew, and peeps into an ancient fridge.

'Hey man, don't you even have milk? I could murder a cup of tea.'

'Sorry. Mum hasn't been this week. Dad's been in hospital so she hasn't been able to do my shopping.'

Mick looks at Paul and shakes his head.

'We'll go into town, then.' He pulls a pen from his shirt pocket, and grabs an old envelope from a heap of opened post. 'OK: milk, tea, coffee…' Mick's face shows that this is an important business.

A slight sound attracts Paul's attention, and he turns his head in time to see Topsy squatting in the middle of the kitchen floor.

***

It is Easter holiday time, and tourists have flocked to the little town of Chelterton. Families walk along the canal to The Barge, visit the gift shop, and search for bargains on market stalls. Women gaze at displays of exclusive clothes, and a rotating stand in front of the Post Office spins with picture postcards of the High Street with its bow-windows, walls of Wisteria and sagging roofs.

They've left Topsy in Maurice's kitchen, and Paul is already worrying. Mick's car crawls through pelican crossings and traffic-lights. The supermarket car park is full, and hopeful drivers loiter for spaces. The car continues up the High Street towards the church. People bulge into the road from the narrow pavement as Mick manoeuvres into an awkward spot behind the graveyard, hoping the vicar's driving skills are equal to squeezing through the slender gap they leave between the car and lichgate. On their way back down the hill they pass an empty shop with an estate agent's board declaring the premises sold.

In the middle of town, the delicatessen stands at a cross roads. Its lovely old curved glass front displays exotic tins and packages nestled in a bed of straw. Beyond the window display, salamis hang from hooks in the ceiling, and golden and speckled drums of cheese are heaped behind glass in a chilled counter. The pungent smell of Parmigiano and spices, is overbearing.

'Ah Mick.' A bulky man in a green and white, striped apron greets them with a grin, while forcing the neck of a plastic bag into a slot to seal it. He hands it to a waiting lady. 'There you go Mrs Shaw. Make sure you eat it at room temperature.'

Mrs Shaw squeezes past Mick, Paul and Maurice to escape into the fresh air.

The interior is deceptively roomy. Past the refrigerated counters is a higgledy-piggledy arrangement of rooms, where fruit and vegetables, and labelled stretches of shelving can be glimpsed.

Mick approaches the counter and shakes the proprietor's hand. 'How's things Malcolm?'

'Can't grumble Mick. If we can't make a living at this time of year then we may as well give up.'

Mick and Malcolm exchange pleasantries, while the other two men hover, then Mick commences the important task of choosing cheese; tasting carefully and offering pieces, and advice, to his companions. 'This Stilton is absolutely as it should be. Look at the creamy colour going right up to the crust, and the blue, not too much, not too little.' Paul and Maurice nod and observe. Next the apprentices follow Mick deeper into the shop, to the vegetables. He cups tomatoes in his pink palms to sniff for freshness, and pinches the ends of avocados. Paul senses someone's eyes on him and raises his own to see Max smiling back from a short distance away. Mick glances up. 'Mate of yours?'

'Naah, just a neighbour.' Paul looks towards the exit. 'I'll see you in a bit, I need to go to the chemist.' Just what he needs, to bump into his bloody therapist while he's with his mates!

By the time Mick and Maurice struggle back through the narrow door of the shop, their hands dangling lumpy bags, Max has vanished. Paul is waiting on the pavement trying not to look agitated.

Many of their needs have been satisfied in the deli, but they pick up a joint of beef from the butcher (look at the marbled fat in that meat) on the way to the small supermarket, for basics.

Back at the church Mick is relieved to find the car unharmed, and their spirits lift as they squeeze out of the churchyard and Mick announces his intention to cook them all a meal on this rare Saturday off. 'Just to get over Maurice's lunch.'

'Haw haw.' Maurice responds and thumps Mick's arm.

Back at the house Maurice goes ahead to open the door, leaving Paul and Mick to gather the shopping. The two men stride up the narrow pathway with Mick in front, and as they near the door Maurice, emits a disgusted expletive from the kitchen: *'Bloody Hell.* At the same time Topsy belts towards them and swerves past Mick, making a bid for the gate. Still on the path, Paul drops his bags into the flower bed, and throws himself at Topsy's squirming body, capturing her with some difficulty and clamping his fingers to the scruff of her neck. With the puppy in one hand and an awkward tangle of carrier bags in the other, he struggles over the threshold and slams the front door shut with his foot. His pet writhes in his grasp and unpleasant odour rises from her clinging fur and wet feet. Paul holds his face away as he carries her in an outstretched hand towards Maurice and Mick.

Standing at the kitchen doorway the three men contemplate the kitchen floor. Pleated sheets of newspaper lie like a wrinkled skin in puddles of urine. Partially dissolved in the liquid, a brown and smelly substance is streaked across the floor.

Chapter 30

It's still a bolt hole.

Fee and Kitty have dragged everything they can from the beach hut onto the veranda, and swept, wiped and sterilised the interior. Now Fee is cleaning and returning selected items, while Kitty takes pebbles and shells from a bucket they found under the bed, and arranges them in a pattern on the table. Beside Kitty in the spring sunlight, lumps comprising broken spades, rusting pans and gnawed cushions, protrude from a growing mound of black plastic sacks.

'Why couldn't the others come Mummy? I want someone to play with.' She doesn't sound in the least bored. In front of her, a spiral of shells and stones is growing into an ornamental ammonite.

'They can come another time Poppet. I think it's lovely to be just us. I don't have much time with you at home.

'You're making a lovely pattern there.'

To be alone is balm to her soul. Here in the beach hut, Fee has control of her surroundings. A place for each thing and nobody to move it. She thinks of her mother. If she is looking down on the, she'll be saying, 'You're doing fine darling. Just relax.'

Fee sits beside Kitty and adds a cockle shell to the pattern. 'I expect I collected these shells when I was a child.' She picks up a broken snail shell and rubs the exposed corkscrew with her thumb. 'Shall we go and paddle?'

Despite the finer weather, there is still a cool breeze coming off the sea. Kitty shakes her head. 'It's too cold.'

'Well I brought wellies. We can look for more shells.'

They trudge along the shale beside the slapping, sucking water, keeping to the wet edge. Occasionally a stray trickle of scummy foam slides over their gleaming toes making Kitty squeal. Fee breathes in the briny air, her head flung back to look at the sky, where grey gulls mass and screech. To their right the esplanade is empty. Fee's thoughts move to a boy she played with here, all those years ago. What was his name? Michael. His family owned one of the other beach huts. She scans the rows of pastel coloured shacks trying to spot which had been theirs. Michael's mother used to chat to Joyce while the two children larked around, just as Kitty and the rest did a few weeks ago, at hop scotch and chase, and treasure hunting on the beach, hauling bits of wood and rocks to be stashed under the day bed. Fee never mentioned her monster of a father to Michael. She wonders now if Joyce confided in the boy's mother.

Kitty is roaring out a song from school, shouting it over the wave-noise, *How high does a fly fly when a fly flies ever so high?* Flanagan and Allan. It's a long way from Fee's school renditions of *Jesus bids us shine with a pure clear light*.

Every now and again they stoop to pick up a treasure for their pail, and before long they reach the groyne, and follow it back up the beach towards the huts. The pair turn right again and back to their hut to dump the bucket of shells and pebbles onto the wooden deck.

'Let's go and find lunch.' Fee grabs her purse and secures the door, stashing the key and money in a large pocket in her coat then, still in boots, they strike out, uphill to Marine Parade. They follow Tower Hill and Harbour Street round the coast and into town. By the time they get to the High Street, Kitty is whining that her feet hurt, and Fee is regretting that they didn't take the trouble to change into shoes. She was trying to be spontaneous. Oh well, mustn't give up now.

'Come on. We'll have a rest.' She pulls Kitty into a café.

Sausage and chips, tomato ketchup, lemonade, Kitty's eyes open wide as her mother agrees to every request.

'Now, we need a knickerbocker Glory.'

'What's that?'

'You'll see. You have to have one when you come to the seaside. We'll share it.'

When the lurid confection arrives, Kitty laughs in delight over a billow of whipped cream. They eat with matching spoons, clicking the long handles together like swords as they battle for the last of the strawberry sauce at the bottom.

Hunger satisfied, they meander through the small town exploring the quaint gift and food shops. Fee buys apples and Kitty chooses a kite in the shape of an eagle, then they re-trace their footsteps, weary but happy.

Fee holds Kitty's hand, and half listens to her chatter. When the little girl asks if there's time to try out the kite before they go home, Fee opens her mouth to concur when she spots a pair of eyes, staring intently at them from the reflection in a shop window on the opposite side of the road. She looks away quickly then looks up again. The eyes are still fixed on hers.

'I don't think there'll be time Poppet. We'll leave it at the beach hut and you and the others can try it out next time we're here.'

Kitty starts to argue but Fee, with uncharacteristic sharpness, snaps, 'No arguments Kitty, we've had a lot of fun but it's time to go home.' She increases her pace until Kitty is trotting along behind, at arms-length. Fee's neck tingles and a cold shiver passes between her shoulder blades.

Chapter 31

Footsteps thunder on the stairs and the kitchen fills with a ravenous mob of children, their arms stretching to reach and grab slices of toast, brioche, croissant, butter, jam. Fee reaches among them to land glasses of fruit juice on coasters, and shakes her head in disapproval.
'Will you get Mummy from the garden please, Sam?'
The boy scrapes back his chair and flies out of the back door to bellow at the vegetable patch, 'Muuummeee, breakfast's ready.' Fee shudders. Sam charges back, and plunges across the table between Lucas and Josh to grab a croissant. Bronze flakes float in his wake as he makes a break for the stairs.
'Come back Sam. Where are your manners?'
The boy flounces back and glares a Fee. 'Why do I have to eat here? I'm in the middle of a game. You're not my mum, anyway, you can't tell me what to do.'
Fee looks the boy in the eyes until he drops them. 'The rule is: No food upstairs.'
Twitch stomps in. 'What's the face for Sam?'
'Nothing.'
'OK well try another face please,' and she turns briefly from her place at the sink to watch her son leave the room, still chewing. With clamped lips, she flutters her earth-caked nails in the stream of tap water, watching rivulets of earth-slurry trickle into the drain. The other children demolish the remaining food and lurch, a joyous rabble, into the sunshine.

'Sam's young to be a teenager, isn't he?' Twitch scrubs her hands on a tea towel, leaving a smudge of mud on the gingham linen, and throws it at the washing machine. Fee stoops to throw it into the drum. 'I think he wants a dog.'

The gardener slumps onto a chair at the table. 'I'm not having a bloody dog. There's enough to do round here as...'

'Oh, no. I didn't mean we should have one. I just wanted you to know that it's not something to do with you, or me.' Fee wipes the jam-sticky table and stacks discarded dishes, before putting a plate of mangled biscuits in front of the sagging Twitch. 'Are you tired Twitch?'

'I'm *fine*.' There is pain behind the words and Twitch's tight-strung body jerks and snaps like a brittle twig in a winter storm.

'I've made tea, and the children made these,' she indicates the grey offerings and pulls out a chair beside her house-mate.

'Great,' says Twitch without enthusiasm.

Fee blows on her tea and takes a sip. 'Paul's being weird. He wouldn't come to the house to collect Kitty so I had to send her to the gate.'

Twitch's back rises, javelin straight.

'Oh?'

'Mm. I couldn't understand why, but when I asked he got shirty.' Fee ignores Twitch's lurching and fidgeting, and keeps her eyes on the children, playing chase among the bushes.

'Where's Millie?' Twitch changes the subject abruptly.

'Still in bed. Busy time yesterday.' Fee looks at her watch. 'It's late though, I'll take her tea up or she'll have no day left.'

In her bedroom Millie is staring at the ceiling with her hands deep in a mound of pillows, behind her dishevelled head.

'Hi. Tea.' Fee crosses the room and pushes books and papers aside to make space for the cup on the bedside table. 'What are you day-dreaming about?'

'Christmas.'

'Christmas? The restaurant's not even open yet.'

Millie looks at Fee, her face alight with the thrill of the unknown.

'I've no idea how much food to order, how many staff to take on, that sort of thing.'

'I should think you'll have more idea once you've started trading. How are things going with the launch?'

Millie humps herself upright in the covers, and wraps her arms round the duvet-peak of her knees.

'Ready I think - I hope.'

'Well it's only a party, and we'll all be there to help.' Fee's eyes range round the room. A heap of clothing swamps the back of a chair, and two shoes lie where they were dropped, one pointing at Fee, while the toe of its mate pokes from under a chest of drawers. On the dressing table a flotsam of makeup and used cotton wool is scattered with abandon.

Gripping her fingertips in her palms to keep them from tidying, Fee turns away. 'I'll see you in a while.'

***

Butter slicks from Fee's knife onto seeded bread, while at the table Millie communes with her lap top. Fee's attention is taken up with Twitch, whose gaunt frame rises and falls outside, doing battle with weeds.

A quiet bong sounds from Millie's computer and after a brief pause she says, 'Mick's been promoted. Oh, that's so great.' Leaning towards the screen she reads more. 'He's going to be in charge of new business for the whole hotel chain.' The dark head nods at Fee. 'You remember? The hotel was taken over by Waterford Hotels last year.'

Fee pretends to remember.

'The job will involve a lot of travelling.' Millie holds the edge of her hand against the screen to shade it from the low sun. 'But he won't start until January. Phew, that's a relief; I can get Christmas sorted before he goes for training.'

'Send my congratulations. Why don't you ask his advice about Christmas?'

'Not going to happen.' Millie's eyes harden and she presses her lips against each other.

'Millie?'

'Mm?' Millie's small fingers tap out a literary polka.

'Have you noticed a change in Twitch?'

Millie lifts her hands to hover above the keyboard. 'Change? No, not really. What do you mean?'

'It's as though a switch has been flipped and Twitch has gone from happy to sad.'

Millie frowns and drops her hands into her lap.

'I've been so wrapped up in my own little life I haven't noticed. Has something happened?'

Fee slides onto a chair beside her.

'No idea. I've tried to find out but I don't want to press her.'

'I feel terrible now.' Millie pulls a face, 'You and I are so lucky. Maybe we've taken Twitch for granted.'

Fee puts her elbows on the table and rests her chin on the backs of her interlaced fingers.

'And what's the matter with Sam suddenly? I thought he wanted a dog but perhaps it's something else.'

***

Slumped on the sofa, Twitch is staring mindlessly at the television that none of them are watching. Fee wishes they could turn it off and sort out this latest problem.

She takes a breath. 'The house is looking lovely Twitch, I don't know how we'd manage without you.'

Twitch's gaze doesn't shift. Her hair is draped heavily over the back of the settee, and under her skirt, bony legs flop in front of her. At either side of her hips, her hands rub the seat, backwards and forwards.

Opposite Twitch, Millie curls in an armchair, her eyes staring at the sit-com.

'It's my job,' Twitch says in a flat voice. 'We all do what we're best at and I can't earn enough money to pay the bills. What else would I do?'

Millie turns her head and stares, baffled, at Fee.

Twitch catches the movement and her hands become still. 'Do you miss having a man around?' She asks, out of the blue.

'Well, I wouldn't mind a cuddle now and again,' Fee gives a short laugh, 'but I certainly don't miss the dirty floors, the upright toilet seat and so on.'

The clock ticks a calm rhythm in the hall and laughter dips and swoops from the set. Twitch's face blanks and she resumes her cushion massaging.

Millie joins the conversation. 'Have you met anyone friendly outside the school gates, Twitch?'

'Nobody I've clicked with. They're friendly enough but you know women, all gaggle and gossip. I prefer my own company, wish I had more of it.'

'What do you mean?' Fee's head snaps round.

'Well, time to paint.' Suddenly Twitch bursts out, 'to go to Art College. I want to live my dream the same as you!'

Fee fixes her eyes on Twitch.

'I didn't realise.'

'Well, there wasn't much point in mentioning it. I needed to get out of my marriage and I didn't have any earning skills. There's no point in whinging. I make my creativity match my life, hence,' she indicates the newly decorated room, with an angry sweep.

'What's happened, Twitch? You seem unhappy and we're worried about you.' Fee glances at Millie, who nods.

'Nothing, it's nothing.'

'I'm sorry but I don't believe you.' Mummy would be proud of her for being so forthright. 'You seemed fine when we moved in here.'

The silence from Twitch suggests she is not going to answer but finally she murmurs, so quietly they have to strain to hear, 'After I had the children I suffered with depression. I didn't tell you because I wasn't planning any more kids. I was just recovering when I met you in the theatre.' She looks away from the television at last, meeting Fee's gaze. 'I feel the same as I did then.' Her face twists.

Fee takes a deep breath and rises from her seat to kneel beside her friend. 'You poor thing.'

Millie crosses the room and sits on the arm of the chair.

Twitch weeps for a long time, and Millie and Fee don't budge from her side.

Chapter 32

'A toast: To success.' Millie stands behind the polished bar and raises a
shiny new champagne glass. Everyone she cares about stands before
her: proud parents, friends, children, neighbours and new employees.
'Success,' they intone, and point flutes of champagne or lemonade at
the ceiling.

This is the first time the others have met new recruits, Liz and Daisy.
Older than Millie by possibly ten years, Liz, with restaurant experience
gained before the birth of her grown-up children, will be invaluable.
She is a widow; her husband having suffered a heart attack three years
ago.

Sweet Daisy, a catering student, is as bubbly as her Bollinger. With
glossy, auburn hair cascading to her waist, and an engaging smile, she
has achieved something most of her college friends envy, a job in her
chosen trade.

Millie hopes business will soon allow her to employ more staff but she
thinks the three of them should be enough for now, and Fee will be on
hand to skivvy on the first night – tomorrow.

The little party admires the restaurant, laid up with white cloths and
immaculate cutlery, and smelling of furniture polish and paint. In the
kitchen, a pristine gas cooker is still partly coated in cellophane.
Smooth surfaces and shining pans and utensils, hanging from walls,
elicit exclamations of approval.

They wander to the store room, where shelves are arranged with dried
goods: rice, flour, dried fruit. They peep into chillers containing dull
red beef and chicken with pimply skin, admire racks of vegetables, and

fridges of butter and cream. Small, fingers are stayed before they touch the precious produce.

Twitch, looking faintly envious, manages small, occasional smiles; Fee, helped by Millie's mum and dad, watches the children, all excited, snotty and fiddling

Liz and Daisy are soon pals. They point, nod, plan. They will be good together the young one with the older one.

Millie looks at them all, then thinks ahead to the opening, and her insides lurch.

***

Liz and Fee are in the kitchen with Nicola from next door, whom Millie, in a last-minute panic has pressed into helping. Daisy, in black and white, smiles nervously from behind the bar. In the window a large, hand-written poster announces, *Opening night, 25ʰ May, 7pm. Full tasting menu. Sample our delicious fare, with a complimentary glass of sparkling wine. £35 per head.*

Twitch has been to the doctor and seems a little happier already. Tonight, she has agreed to stay at home and supervise all the children, including Nicola's.

Millie goes to the restaurant door, turns the hanging sign from 'closed' to 'open' and pulls the handle to greet her first customers. Behind them are more, and more. Millie gives silent thanks to the local paper. A scruffy reporter had shambled into the restaurant as the final workmen were clearing up their tools. Amidst their echoing chatter and clatter, Millie described her dreams to him. The article came out two days ago, with a striking picture of Millie gazing up at her new sign – the old *Chez Ralph*, now replaced by the single word *Feast*.

Arrivals are seated, and Daisy flits between tables, delivering flutes of Prosecco. Soon the room is murmuring and guests are perusing their menus.

In the furnace-hot kitchen Millie lifts carefully laid trays of food onto gleaming chrome oven shelves and sets the timer. Under her instructions, plates are laid along worktops, garnishes applied and soon the first hot samples are on the way to tables.

The evening is a roller coaster of mistakes and triumphs. In the kitchen voices rise, more in panic than anger, then Daisy's frightened face bursts in at the door.

'Help. I can't manage,' and Liz runs to help.

Guests smile - in the main, although some have waited longer than Millie had hoped.

At last desserts are served, and Millie emerges, red faced but triumphant, into the restaurant. The kitchen is piled with debris and Fee and Liz scuttle to and fro organising its clearance.

Wandering from table to table Millie asks, 'Did you enjoy your meal?'

'Fabulous.'

'Delicious.'

'Fantastic.'

With a huge smile Millie chirps, 'I'm so glad. I hope you'll come again.' One couple, somewhat blotto, insist she share their wine, and she sits for a while, high before taking a sip.

When the work is over and the last guests have departed, the women hug, and sit amid the tables with their shoeless feet on chairs, remembering significant moments and congratulating one another. Liz makes mugs of tea and they drink, lapsing into comfortable silence.

'Well, that's day one,' says Millie. 'Now the work begins.'

They look at her in horror.

'You need more staff.' Fee leans forward to massage an aching foot, and Millie nods.

'Yes, you're right. Daisy, have you got any friends who might be interested.'

Daisy grins.

'Definitely. No problem.'

'That's sorted then.' She arches her back in the chair. 'Let's go home.'

Chapter 33

Paul rubs a paper napkin across his lips and gathers the remains of his meal, stuffing them into a cardboard carton bearing the unmistakable *golden arches* logo. Opposite, at the high bar where they sit, Kitty is picking up fries, one at a time, and dipping them into her corrugated cup of ketchup. Beneath the table her legs swing backwards and forwards, while her eyes scan the rest of the diners.

'There are three families with only a daddy,' she says.

'It's quite common now for dads to be alone with their children.'

Kitty dips a chip into her ketchup. 'I miss our old house.'

'Me too, Pops, but we can't go back.' He makes his voice positive. 'Didn't you say you wanted a *Disney Dee*?'

Disney Dee has been the family name for a DVD since, as a toddler, Kitty, in her innocence, christened it so.

'And felt tips,' she looks expectantly at Paul, 'please?' She crumples her napkin and stuffs it, mimicking Paul, into the box of her Happy Meal, then the two of them head for the door leaving their tray where it lies.

Later, gripping shiny carrier-bags, they climb the bare stairs to Paul's flat. The loud thud, thud of hip hop, or garage (who knows the difference?), makes the stair treads vibrate. Topsy's yaps are just discernible over the racket. This is not the first time Paul's neighbour has demonstrated his indifference to the peace of the building. Paul has been forced to buy earplugs, and turn up the volume of his television on a couple of occasions.

On the landing, the noise is mind-numbing. Paul drops his bags to unlock the front door while Kitty screws up her face in disapproval.

They burst into the hall and shut the door to muffle the sound but the walls of the little flat are inadequate for such a purpose. Kitty presses her palm against the wall.

'I can feel the music.'

'Yeah, me too.' Paul's hands shake, and so does the floor.

'Poor Topsy.' Kitty stoops to stroke the cringing creature. 'Come on girl, this way.'

The pup follows as they take their shopping into the living room and dump it on a sofa then Kitty unpacks her treasures.

'Please may I watch this?' She waves the Disney Dee at Paul.

'I'm not sure you'll be able to hear it Pops.' He's controlling his face with difficulty. 'I'll go and have a word with the man next door. See if he'll turn his music off.'

He barrels out of the room, leaving Kitty standing in the middle of the carpet and Topsy cowering behind an armchair.

If this were a cartoon, the door opposite would bulge with each beat. Paul bashes the palm of his hand on the door and waits. The drumming drills on and he thumps again, this time with his fist. Still nothing. In fury, he steps back from the door and raises a foot, aiming its heel at the flimsy ply-wood. It flies open and hits the wall with a crash.

The smell of stale fat and unwashed clothes hits him. This stink, combined with the throbbing base notes blasting from a room ahead, confuse and blind him with fury. He leaps the couple of paces across a short hall and bursts into the front room. A youth leaps from a stained settee, another, pasty and dazed, remains slumped on greasy cushions. On a packing case in front of him lie tin foil and a candle.

Paul flies to the source of the music and pulls the plug from the wall.

'Hey! We were listening to that.'

'Yeah,' mutters the slumping youth. 'Yeah.' His eyelids droop.

'I don't give a fucking toss what you were listening to. My kid wants to watch a DVD and we can't hear a bloody thing.'

The youth holds up his palms, weakly.

'Calm down mate.'

Paul glares and stalks out.

Back in his flat, he watches as Kitty slots the shiny new disk into the machine then he takes the food shopping to the kitchen. Trailers for forthcoming Disney films drift in from the other room as he puts away their purchases, and soon he hears the familiar *When you wish upon a star* tune, announcing the start of the film.

Boom boom, boom. The racket starts again. Paul slams a cupboard door and marches past Kitty and out of the flat.

The door of the neighbouring apartment is still ajar, and at his entrance the youths repeat their former routine, one rises, and the other slumps. But this time Paul changes his part. With such speed that the befuddled lad in front of him has no time to react, he slams his knuckles into the pallid chin. The boy collapses backwards onto the seat beside his, now wide-eyed, companion. Once again Paul snatches the plug from the wall but this time he picks up the ghetto blaster and gives it a mighty lunge down the stairs. It cartwheels, exploding shards of black plastic, and crashes to the floor at the bottom.

Back in his living room Kitty hugs the puppy and looks fearfully at Paul. Her face brings him back from the blind, red room in his head. 'It's OK Kitty. Don't worry.' He sits wearily in an armchair and pulls the little girl and the dog onto his knee. Kitty clings to him, her body trembling. On the television screen, Tigger bounces with indecent enthusiasm.

In a small voice she says, 'I want to go home, Daddy.'

'Come on Baby, it's fine. I'm fine. Let's watch Tigger.'

'But the man. Did you hurt him?'

'I just stopped him making a noise. He'll be fine.'

'He won't come and get us?' Kitty's voice quivers.

'Don't worry, I'd never let that happen.'

They sit for a while, watching the DVD, then Paul stiffens. From the street, the wail of approaching police sirens infiltrates their hard-found tranquility. *OH God. Not again.* He extricates himself from Kitty.

'I think you're going to have to go home after all baby.'

They gather Kitty's belongings into a carrier bag. Heavy footsteps clump on the stairs and voices murmur on the landing then fade into the flat opposite. Nobody knocks on Paul's door so he pulls Kitty silently through the door and down the stairs. The smashed music player still lies in the middle of the foot well and they skirt round it to get to the street.

With Kitty bundled in her car-seat Paul starts the engine, just in time to glimpse the dark form of a policeman coming towards them across the pavement.

***

'So, you made a run for it?' The imperturbable Max looks almost impressed.

Paul takes a gulp from his tumbler.

'Not precisely a run for it. I just needed to get Kitty out of there before she got even more scared. I did report to the police station afterwards. Thought it might help my case.'

'How did Fee take it - when you told her what had happened?'

'I sent Kitty up the path on her own, what with Twitch being there. Fee came to the door and whipped Kitty inside.' Paul pictures Kitty sobbing out the details of this latest debacle to a stiff faced Fee. 'Once Kitty's had time to get over her shock it'll be an adventure.'

'So will you to be around to complete your course of anger management or should I visit you in prison?' Max raises his eyebrows and Paul shrugs.

'The solicitor says there are mitigating circumstances. He was impressed when I told him I was seeing you, said it showed the right attitude.'

'But it's the second incident of ABH in a few weeks, Paul. How do you view that?'

Paul raises his shoulders again. 'We'll have to wait and see.'

'Have you written in the book?'

Paul nods and passes the small pad to Max.

'Fee rang.' Max looks up. 'What did she say to make you angry?'

'Hello.' Paul gives a small smile.

'Have you looked at this, Paul?' Max flaps the little booklet at him like a fan.

Paul shakes his head.

'It looks clear cut, but tell me if I'm wrong. I'd say you're annoyed by two things: anti-social behaviour and your ex-wife. Would you agree?'

Paul shrugs again.

Max asks about the symptoms that preceded Paul's latest episodes.

'People tend to experience a rise in adrenalin.'

Paul can't remember his physical reactions, apart from the punches.

'Also, you can take avoiding action. Walk away from gangs of lads horsing around, before you have a chance to be annoyed,'

This makes sense.

'Let's imagine your next conversation with Fee.' Max watches him. 'What might occur?'

Paul's fists clench. 'She might tell me I can't see Kitty again.'

The counsellor's head tips to one side and his hair flops onto his brow. He sweeps his fingers backwards through the fringe. 'And what might you say and do in that circumstance?'

Paul's pulse throbs in his ears and his head is a red room. His hands begin to shake.

Max raises a palm. 'OK. Calm down. *Paul.*'

***

'She doesn't want to come.' Fee's voice is stony.

Paul stands in his hall with his eyes closed and the telephone pressed to the side of his head

The corner of the notebook in his pocket is worn to a flat stump by his thumb. He listens to the pounding in his ears and takes in air. *One elephant, two…*

'Can I speak to her?'

'She's not ready for that yet, Paul.'

He stops massaging the book and lets his back slide down the wall to the floor. His legs press against his chest and he wraps his arm round them to rest his head on top of his knees. A tear runs from the corner of his eye and onto his jeans. Another crosses the bridge of his nose. Topsy nuzzles her nose at his face, licking the tears that now flow, silent and unhindered. His knuckles ache from their slippery grip on the handset and he terminates the conversation with a thumb.

***

Paul cranes to see past the backs of Mick and Maurice, who stand side by side in Fee's porch.

The door opens to the extent of the chain, then wider and Twitch's smiling face comes into view. After a brief conversation the men turn, and with their attention focused on their children, lead them away.

The front door shuts and Paul stares at the stern façade of the house. His eyes strain to see inside the black windows, and he catches a small movement. An upstairs casement opens and a despondent face leans out, waving to the departing children. Unthinking, Paul bobs his head up above of the tops of the shrubs. Kitty spots his movement and turns her head and their eyes meet. Kitty's face crumples and she vanishes, slamming the window.

Bad to worse, bad to worse, the words repeat themselves in Paul's head as he drives home. White lines on the road blur past in his peripheral vision.

THE DYING

Chapter 34

As soon as she unlocks the door to *Feast* the familiar aroma of wine and spices fills Millie's head. It is still a thrill to walk into her own restaurant especially now that it has become so popular. She locks the door behind her and weaves between empty tables to the stairs, humming a song they listened to last night, *Jambalaya, crawfish pie and fillet gumbo, 'Cause tonight I'm gonna see my cher amio.* Hauling a sack of potatoes down from the stock-room, her notes become grunts as she hoists the half hundredweight bag from tread to tread.

'Need a hand there?' Millie jumps as a voice booms from the top of the stairs.

'I'd forgotten you were here,' she said to Paul, 'No, I'm fine, thanks.' She grips the corners of the bag and hefts it to the bottom. 'How have you got on up there?'

Paul takes the stairs two at a time and takes the bag.

'Not bad. I've been up in the attic sorting out the electrics. I think I've worked out which wires are which.'

Millie is beginning to convert part of her first floor to seating, and Paul has agreed to help when time permits. This was Kitty's idea. Neither Fee nor Millie were keen, but the child went ahead and asked him when he came to collect her, and when he said yes, rushed back up to the house dancing with pleasure that she had been able to contribute to the adult world of work.

'I appreciate your help Paul. It's good to know there's someone I can call on, who's not going to rip me off.'

'Well, I'll get back upstairs and take a few measurements. You sure it's OK for me to carry on while you're serving?'

'Of course. The only thing that worries me is if you need to come through the restaurant in your scruff.

Don't worry. I brought a change of clothes. Just knock on the bottom stair before you come up.' He grins, and she smiles back. He's a good bloke really. Not right for Fee – at all, but… She stops herself before contemplating an inappropriate thought about Paul, and scoots off to the kitchen.

Peeling the spuds she thinks again of the night before - more cooking but she doesn't mind that. Over dinner Fee had described a client whose nostrils kept flaring as he talked, distracting her so much that she frequently needed to ask him to repeat what he had said. To make matters worse she worried that he was going to ask her on a date, and was wondering how to turn him down without risking the contract. Of course Millie and Twitch had teased her madly. Helped by a bottle of Chianti, she and Twitch had screamed with laughter, flaring their nostrils and insisting she owed it to the company to go out with him. Millie smiles at the memory.

The complications of her divorce and setting up the business have kept her mind occupied, but that conversation, and the suggestion of dating, has made her skittish. She plops a potato into the pan and gives a mental shrug. Dating is out. She won't inflict a strange man on the children at the moment.

A key turns in the front door and Liz rushes in trailing the smell of sun cream and holidays. Millie glances at the clock, it's 4.03pm.

'Sorry I'm late, it's mad out there. I think the whole town has decided to go to the summer sales!'

She dumps her bags on the floor and her coat beside them on a stool, and bustles past Millie to wash her hands.

'How many in tonight?' She calls over her shoulder.

'Fifteen tables, mostly twos. There's a table for one, and a table of six - they're bringing in a birthday cake.'

The restaurant is open six nights a week, plus Friday and Saturday lunch times. She and Liz are considering opening on the other lunchtimes, including Sundays. They've had a few enquiries but it will be a major commitment: Extra staff, a new menu, and increased working hours for Millie, taking her away from Lucas and Olivia even more.

The two women work companionably, preparing food for the coming night's service. At 5pm front of house staff begin to arrive, then customers, and before long the restaurant is alive with clatter and chatter. The kitchen becomes a racket of activity.

By 9.30 most people are eating their main courses or desserts, and the kitchen is calmer. Leaving Liz in charge, Millie removes her hat and slips out in her chef's whites, to circulate.

An attractive and stylish man sits at a corner table. A good table she is pleased to note, she wouldn't want to seat a restaurant critic next to the loos. She glances at him, and intelligent eyes look back from behind gold rimmed glasses. Her gut gives a kick and she looks away.

She spends a while chatting to the birthday family, sharing a little wine in a toast, then she moves on, gradually closer to the man. Only when she reaches his table does she allow herself to meet his gaze.

'I hope you're enjoying your meal,' She eyes his plate, empty apart from the watercress garnish.

'How was the sea bass?'

'Excellent, thank you. You're busy tonight.' His voice is smooth, his accent refined.

'Yes, it's good for a Thursday. Have you been here before?'

'Quite a few times but I don't usually see *you*.'

Not a restaurant critic then.

'I only come out on busy nights. People aren't keen to have attention drawn to them when it's quiet so I stay in the kitchen - a woman's place.' Her eyes twinkle. He ignores her opening for banter so she rushes on, 'I'm glad you enjoyed your meal, I'll get someone to clear your table,' and tops up his wine. As she turns to leave he murmurs his thanks.

'It's my pleasure.' She smiles coquettishly over her shoulder then feels silly when he seems to be weighing her up.

The lights go out and Liz materialises from the kitchen carrying a large cake in the shape of a 60. *Happy Birthday to You* romps from the speakers, and sparklers on top of the cake send tiny shards of light into the gloom. Other diners turn to watch the spluttering concoction. Teeth, noses and chins turn a fleeting, flickering silver as it passes. The birthday family begins to sing and the others join them, *Happy birthday dear hmm hmm, happy birthday to you-oooo*. There are cheers and claps as the lights go up and the beaming middle-aged lady blows out her candles. Millie glances at the table for one and the handsome stranger smiles at her.

Later, after the diners have left and she is clearing tables, Paul stomps down the stairs looking tired and thoughtful.

'Anything wrong Paul. Would you like a drink?'

Paul's face brightens. 'A beer'd be great.'

'Just help yourself, would you? I'm afraid there's no draft but there are bottles or cans in the fridge or on the shelf.'

Paul potters behind the bar, exploring, and eventually flips the top from a bottle and tips back his head, letting the chilled liquid glug straight down his throat.

Chapter 35

'Why didn't you come today?' Olivia looks accusingly at Kitty. 'I was the only girl. It was boring.'

'I didn't *want* to.' Kitty hides her face in one of Fee's pillows. 'I hate my daddy and I don't want to see him.'

In the cramped bedroom, Olivia hauls herself onto the bed and gawks at the back of Kitty's head.

'You mustn't hate him. Why do you?'

Kitty's voice is muffled by the pillow. 'He gets angry and hits people.'

'Hits who?' Olivia takes a bounce closer to Kitty and lays her head beside Kitty's on the pillow.

'Nasty people.' Kitty turns her head, her nose inches from Olivia's.

Olivia frowns. 'That's not bad. Hitting nasty people.' She puts her arm round Kitty.

'But he was scary. He frightened me.'

'Well he's your dad. Why were you frightened?'

'He shouted.'

'At you?'

'No, at the men next door. I could hear him through the wall. Then we ran away.'

Olivia is quiet for a while. The situation Kitty describes is beyond her experience. She's always been envious of Kitty. Her dad bought her a puppy. He does exciting stuff, takes her for motorbike rides and gets on his hands and knees to give her rides on his back. To Olivia Paul is a swaggering hero, like a prince or a pirate. 'Do you miss your puppy?'

'Yes.' Kitty squeezes her eyelids together. 'And,' her voice is timid, 'I miss Daddy.'

Olivia sits up. 'Well that's alright then.' She thumps off the bed making bottles clink on the chest of drawers. 'Come on.'

Kitty pushes her body upright. 'Where are we going?'

'To tell Aunty Fee.'

***

Paul looks at the display on his phone. 'Hello Fee.'

'Paul. Hi.'

He waits, staring at his office wall. What now?

'I've got someone here who wants to talk to you.' There's a short pause.

'Daddy?'

He smiles at the wall and wipes a hand across his eyes. 'Hello Pops. How are you?'

'I'm OK. Can you come and see me?'

'Course I can. I'd love to. Does Mummy say it's OK?'

'Mummy doesn't mind but we have to stay here.'

His happy balloon springs a small leak. 'How about Aunty Twitch and Aunty Millie, are they OK for me to come over?'

'They're going out for a walk. Aunty Twitch thought we should have some time alone.'

'Put Mummy back on.'

Fee's voice is off hand but she is co-operative - she was always fair. They agree a time.

***

Paul sits on the bed beside Kitty and pulls her to him. 'I'm sorry Pops. I promise I'll never get angry like that again.'

'I was scared. You frightened me.' Kitty's voice is dampened by Paul's jacket.

He releases her and looks into her eyes. 'I know. I'm a bad dad, but it won't happen again.'

'Why were you hiding in the bushes?'

Paul's back stiffens but he keeps his tone light. 'I was missing you so much. I wanted to see you.' He gives the child a squeeze. 'What did Mummy think when you told her I was hiding?'

'I didn't tell her. I forgot.'

'Well, everything's fine now. No need to tell Mummy about it. She might not want you to see me if she knows.'

Kitty nods. 'OK.'

Chapter 36

Lunchtime service is coming to an end. Millie polishes a glass and places it carefully on a shelf. On the other side of the bar the restaurant is a half-set stage- some tables pristine with white cloths and shining cutlery, others littered with crumbs, and cluttered with used coffee cups, and glasses containing lemon slices or wine dregs.

A final group of diners, three middle aged ladies who have giggled guiltily while choosing the most extravagant and fattening meals, make moves to leave. They hug each other then turn, apologetic about the lateness of their departure, to thank Daisy, who is clearing their table. Millie looks up to call goodbye to them but stops, startled to see her elegant, gold rimmed stranger holding the door. The women twitter out, looking at him through the corners of their eyes, and he nods and flirts, then lets the door close behind them. Wearing a confident smile, he approaches the bar and slips off his coat, draping it over a stool and perching on another, at the same time ordering a gin and tonic.

'I'm terribly sorry,' Millie pulls an apologetic face, 'we're closed for lunch. You're welcome to a drink but I don't want to mislead you into thinking of it as an aperitif.'

'I know you're closed,' he replies with another grin 'I hope you don't mind if I sit and talk to you for a while?'

'Of course not.'

It would be a lie to say she hasn't thought about this man a few times since his visit. What girl wouldn't?

'Ice and lemon?'

'Lovely. Will you join me?'

'Well, just one, thank you. I have to drive later.' Her fingers shake as she pulls 2 hi-ball glasses from a shelf.

Liz is busy cleaning up in the kitchen and Daisy, after scanning Mr Gold Rim, passes through the connecting door to join her. She and Liz will no doubt enjoy a bit of speculation, while they complete the last jobs of the afternoon.

Millie clinks ice into glasses and adds slices of lemon. She measures in gin and opens a couple of tonic water bottles, placing one glass in front of each of them.

He introduces himself as James. Millie proffers a damp hand and they are soon discussing business in the restaurant, and James's own line, which is property development. He buys run down premises and modernises or rebuilds them as sleek apartments, travelling all over the country in search of the right opportunities. He has recently completed one in Lymchester, some 50 miles away. She must let him show her round. The way her business is growing she will soon be looking for an expensive 'pad'.

Millie finds herself leaning on the counter, gazing at him, talking too much and laughing at nothing. She explains her home arrangements, and he in turn reveals his own story. He's a divorcee, but happily so, with no wish to settle down. He's too busy enjoying his business and his independence.

After half an hour James looks at his watch, and knocking back the last dribble of liquid, says he must be somewhere. Millie too must get on and she bustles to the till to cash up, trying to look relaxed, while wondering if he will ask her for a date. He shrugs on his coat and then, instead of leaving, he comes behind the bar and stands close to her. She fumbles with a handful of coins as the rough material of his sleeve brushes against her bare arm. For a wild moment, she wonders if he is going to kiss her, or even rob her, but before she has time to deal with these possibilities, he leans forward and murmurs into her ear.

'You and I could be very good together. Two business people, independent, no strings.' He softens his voice. 'I could make you *very* happy.'

A shot of desire fires right to Millie's groin, and her cheeks sizzle like two embers.

James turns from her, and slips a business card from the top of the bar, into his pocket. He crosses to the door, and as he steps out into the night, he throws back a flirtatious look. 'I'll call you,' he says, and closes the door over a wink.

Millie drops her trembling body into a nearby seat. That is one sexy man. She thinks back over their meeting, knowing that she wants him to call.

No strings, he said.

Chapter 37

Three weeks pass before he calls. Now she is inside *Feast,* waiting for their first night out. Her mind is not on any task. Guilt and anticipation vie for supremacy.

Upstairs, work is progressing on the new restaurant space. Paul has been in and out, and when she let slip that she had a date he was all ears. She regretted speaking of it and didn't expand when he teased and probed. She has the feeling that Paul fancies her, but she's not interested. Too complicated. Still, it's nice to feel you're attractive.

The restaurant is empty, final tasks completed and staff dispatched to their own dramas. She glances at the door then goes to check the kitchen, a quick glance, not her usual tightening of water and gas taps and checking of doors. Back in the bar she resorts to polishing sparkling glasses and wiping immaculate shelves. A lorry rumbles past, blinking out the light from a street lamp opposite. Without aim she meanders among the tables, straightening a chair here and a napkin there.

When the knock finally comes she starts. James grins through the glass, his fist poised to knock again, then he is inside.

'I hope you don't mind a short walk, I've left the car round the corner in Watco's car park. I had to get a few bits and pieces, and it seemed silly to move it.'

Millie doesn't mind anything. She leaves him by the bar while she goes to the loo - again, and checks her make-up - again. With her coat over an arm she returns, to find him studying the menu.

'I thought we might eat in tonight.' he says, eyes on the open folder.

Could he mean here in her restaurant? Millie experiences a pang of disappointment, but he goes on, 'You know the development I mentioned, in Lymchester? I thought you might enjoy seeing it. There's a show flat I'm pretty proud of. Only if you're interested though.' His deep eyes lock onto hers and she is sucked in.

James's black BMW is at the end of the car park, nearest the road and furthest from the entrance to the supermarket. A few people have parked nearer the building, hardly surprising at this late hour.

He drives fast, a bit too fast but Millie is excited. Her nerves stretch, and each bump and twist of the road sends a hot flare through her body. She looks at his profile, jaw firm and eyes fixed on the road ahead, taking bends with deft confidence. He doesn't speak much, leaving her with little to do but wonder what's in the Watco bag between her knees.

After 40 minutes or so the car turns through tall, wrought iron gates, and James to the back of an impressive edifice.

With the Watco bag clutched in her fist, Millie stares through the darkness at an Edwardian block of three stories, restored to its former glory but with a modern twist. The pipe work and window frames, although traditional in design, are of ultra-modern steel that gleams in the low light of an outside lamp. James takes the bag from her and guides her round the building to a front door of light wood, embedded with steel bands that form the rectangular shapes found in a traditional Georgian door, but as smooth and cool as the surface of a table.

Inside an impressive curving stairway leads to a galleried landing, but they don't go up. James unlocks a door to the right of the entrance and holds it open. Her shoulder brushes against his chest as she passes through the doorway. Lofty ceilings and thick carpet meet her eyes but she isn't in any state to take them in.

James swings the shopping bag into the spartan but beautiful kitchen to the left of the hall, and calls back to her to take off her coat and dump it in the bedroom, 'It's at the end of the hall. Go on in.'

She slides her feet from her shoes, and thick tufts of carpet sprout between her toes as she walks between apricot coloured walls to the master bedroom. Wow! An enormous bed, and are those silk sheets? There's a jacuzzi and a double shower.

'Turn on the hot tub,' James calls, 'We can drink our Champagne in there.'

154

She fumbles with clumsy fingers and manages to get water to spring from little holes that puncture the surface of the deep tub.

Back in the kitchen James has placed cutlery, napkins and wine flutes on the table. A bottle of Champagne pokes from a glass wine-cooler beside the sink. 'I hope you don't mind eating in here. I'd like to keep the flat tidy. I'm expecting a viewer tomorrow and I don't want us to spend half the night cleaning before we leave. I can think of better things to do with our time, can't you?' He gives her the look again and she is a schoolgirl on a date with a film star.

'Did I hear you say Champagne?' Her voice sounds artificial.

'Mais oui.' He flourishes the bottle in front of her eyes. 'Will this be to Madame's taste?'

'Perfetto,' she replies in her mother's native tongue.

The cork makes a muffled pop inside a tea towel and James pours two glasses.

The oven light blinks off and he slides in foil containers, the contents of which, he tells her, have been created by an ex-girlfriend with an outside catering business.

While he works, Millie returns to the bathroom to check on the Jacuzzi, and soon there is a movement close behind her. James stands their glasses on the edge of the tub then pulls her towards him and methodically removes her clothing one item at a time until she stands, naked and quaking before him. He undoes his own shirt and throws it across the room, then pulls off his shoes, and lines them up side by side, never taking his eyes from her face. When he is undressed he stands, almost touching her. Millie waits for his lead but he does nothing, just looks at her body. She looks at his: smooth, muscular, flat stomach, huge erection.

He lifts his hand and places the tip of his index finger on her right nipple and an explosion of desire surges through her body, then he takes her hand, leads her to the Jacuzzi and switches on the bubbles. She climbs in and takes the glass he holds out.

He sits in the water beside her, his hip millimetres from hers.

Tiny jets pummel her naked skin and she is overwhelmed with lust but still he doesn't touch her. His arm drapes along the edge of bath behind her and he tilts his glass towards hers until the rims touch with a small tink. 'To a long and satisfying friendship.' He takes a gulp, and she raises her glass in response, then he removes the glass from her hand, puts both drinks on a ledge and lowers his cold lips to her left nipple.

She arches her body towards him but he presses her back. He works his mouth down her body, plunging his head into the water until she is nearly mad with lust then his head bursts to the surface and he shakes his hair like a dog and turns from her to take another sip of champagne. The pummelling in the tub has stopped and he stands, lifts her from the Jacuzzi and carries her, dripping, to the bed. Now she is allowed to touch him, now she can make him pant with the same lust she is feeling. She'll show him every trick she has and he'll be back for more.

Later they sit naked, eating braised pigeon and sipping more Champagne. Soon they are panting and throbbing again, first on the kitchen table, and then on the hall floor.

On the way home, every inch of Millie's skin tingles. James drives in silence, occasionally putting his hand on her thigh.

At 4am the street outside *Feast* is empty. She leans to him, and they share a deep kiss before she climbs onto the pavement feeling transparent, glad nobody can see her.

There's no need to go inside the restaurant so she follows the brickwork down the shadowy side passage, to her car. The Volkswagen crouches in its dark space, overshadowed by the locked kitchen door and two battered refuse bins with hinged lids, that smell of rotting vegetables. She opens the car door and is relieved when the interior light brightens the little area. When her car noses out of the alleyway James is at the roadside opposite. He flashes his lights, and rockets away.

At home, she creeps up the stairs and showers before sliding under her duvet. Her breasts still carry the memory of James's lips, and her mind sings.

An hour later she gives up trying to sleep and puts on clean clothes. 6am finds her back at the restaurant. It's still dark but there is some traffic. The curtains of the restaurant are drawn, and the inside is dark as she opens the door. Her hand goes automatically to the light switch – an instant before she smells gas.

156

Chapter 38

Twitch opens her eyes wondering what woke her. She hears only birds and the toot of a distant train. The clock says 6am, half an hour before the alarm is set to go off.

The bedroom handle moves downwards and the door opens a short distance. Two flattened, sleepy heads belonging to Lucas and Olivia, peep through the gap, and when they meet Twitch's eyes, their bodies follow.

'We heard a big bang, and we were scared.' Olivia's brown head nods as if to prove the truth of her statement.

Twitch sits up in bed. 'I think I heard it too, it must have woken me up, but I'm sure there's nothing to be scared about. Let's have a look.' She swings her legs out of bed and slips across the room to pull back the curtains. It is a fine morning and she puts her face to the pane. From here the roof tops of Chelterton's small town centre can be seen in the middle distance. The church spire at the brow of the High Street, stabs the early morning sky, but it is not this to which her eyes are drawn. She grips her right pyjama sleeve in her fist and wipes the glass with the heel of her hand to clear her breath. A pillar of smoke is pouring from somewhere in the area of the church. As if to confirm this, they hear sirens, their Doppler-distorted cries howling as they fly past the top of Crispin Road.

Twitch sends the children to get ready for school. Luke and Olivia are usually at Mick's on a Friday but he's swapped to Saturday this weekend, which means they have a houseful.

Still in her pyjamas, Twitch pads along the landing to Millie's room and knocks quietly. All is silence within, so after knocking again she opens the door. The room is empty. The bed looks as if it's been slept in, but Millie must have gone in to work early.

She pops her head round the girls' door to check they are doing as directed, then taps quietly on Fee's door. Fee's breezy shout invites her in. Her alarm went off ages ago and she is showered and dressed, and hunched over her chest of drawers applying mascara in front of a small mirror. Kitty is curled in a ball, her eyes still shut tight despite the disturbance going on around her.

Fee heard no noise at 6am - she was probably in the shower. She drops the mascara, adds shoes to her ensemble and runs downstairs to her car. As she reverses from the drive she lowers the window, 'I'll call you.' Her voice is hushed and Twitch, standing at the door, gripping her dressing gown around her body, nods.

Twitch shuts out the chilly air and goes to the kitchen, her feet slapping lightly on the bare floor as she fills the kettle and begins making a mug of tea. The routine of adding tea bags and getting milk from the fridge provides a distraction. While the water is still roaring, the telephone rings.

'It's me.' There is a silence on the line that tells Twitch all she needs to know.

'Oh God! What's happened to Millie?' She presses her palm to her mouth as she listens.

'I don't know. I'm up the road because there are fire engines outside but it doesn't look good. The roof of the restaurant's completely missing, and all the windows are smashed.' Fee's voice wavers. 'What if she was in there?'

The children are pounding down the stairs.

Twitch hisses quickly, 'Fee, what are we going to say to the children?'

'There's nothing to tell them - yet.'

'I'll send them to school then.' Twitch slams the phone down and organises her face.

***

It is midday before Fee pulls onto the drive. Twitch, who was sitting in the lounge, staring at nothing, dashes to the front door and watches Fee tumble from the driver's door.

'She was in there.' Tears cascade from Fee's eyes. 'She's dead, Twitch! I went to the police station, and they told me there was a gas explosion. She didn't have a chance.'

The two women cling to each other in the middle of the hall and weep, rocking their bodies and clutching one another like shipwreck victims.

***

Mick's knees buckle and he drops to the floor in front of the kitchen pass. It is the middle of lunch service and around him the crash of the sous chefs and serving staff comes gradually to silence, as he clamps both arms silently round his knees, still clasping his phone. A hand touches his shoulder and he flinches.

'Mick. *Mick.* What's happened?' Waitress, Mary, eases the phone from his hand. As she draws him out of the room, the kitchen accelerates back to life, pressure of orders taking priority over personal tragedy.

In the staff room Mick squeezes his body between the wooden arms of a low chair, and with his elbows resting on his knees puts his head in his hands. Across the room the kettle roars. Mary is making a cup of tea. She doesn't speak, and a minute or two later a mug emblazoned with the hotel name and rather overstated crest, appears on the table in front of him. He picks it up and gazes at its revolving surface, watching small bubbles cling to the glazed sides.

Mary sits down opposite him.

The sounds of service filter into the room, and Mick takes a sip of his tea. When he raises his head, he meets Mary's kindly eyes. 'It's Millie.' He can hardly say the words. 'She's been in a terrible accident.'

It is Mary who brings up the subject of his children.

The children. He hasn't thought of the children. He springs from the chair and blinks at his watch, shouting, 'When do they come out of school?' then runs at the door like a confused bullock. 'How am I going to tell them. God help me!'

'Any time you need to …' Mary begins, but he's gone.

***

The school is scruffy but alive. In the foyer, his children wait, puzzled. He looks at the receptionist and her eyes well with tears. His own are dry and sore.

As they walk towards the car, the children cling to his legs as though sensing trouble. Gently he disengages them and holding one in each hand, tries to prepare them. 'Something bad has happened.' The small faces look up with wide eyes and half-open mouths, and Mick wishes his mother was here.

He lets them into the car, and climbs into the back seat after them. The three sit, scrunched together, Mick's knees filling most of the foot well. He reaches round and puts his arm round them, pulling them close. When the words have been spoken, Lucas bursts into frightened tears but Olivia pulls out of his grasp and stares in disbelief.

'She can't be dead. I kissed her goodbye after breakfast.' She shakes her head. 'Not this morning, she wasn't there this morning…'

Mick can't find any more words so he watches as his daughter turns away and stares out of the car window. After a long time before she begins to sniff, then she yelps like a puppy in pain and throws herself onto Mick. They cling in a bundle, and the children's tears soak Mick's chest and shoulder as he glares at the roof lining.

After a while the pavement outside begins to fill with parents: whispering, serious. Mick disengages arms and persuades the children into their seat belts. No booster seats, how could he have forgotten? Millie would have remembered.

He wishes it was possible to manoeuvre his bulk into the front of the car without getting out, but he has to step into the road to duck in the driver's door. Twitch watches from the perimeter of a growing crowd of parents. Earlier, after more weeping, Mick, Fee and Twitch decided that Lucas and Olivia should come to the house but stay upstairs with Mick until the other children have been told. After that they'll play things by ear.

Mick makes a three-point turn and heads for Crispin Road.

Chapter 39

Lucas and Olivia lean against Mick's chest, their knees and heads touching, their legs dangling between his thighs. Lucas sucks his thumb and Olivia moves her fingers between her brother's cheek and Mick's hand, as it rests on her leg.

Sitting beside them, Paul's left arm presses against Mick's muscular suit sleeve. Maurice on Mick's other side, hangs his head and hands between his knees and stares at the parquet floor.

Coughs and shuffles disturb the relative peace of the place, and Paul screws his body round on the bone hard pew to study the mourners. There are a some with Millie's Mediterranean colouring, including Millie's mother Mimi, sitting behind Mick. Paul twists further to meet her red eyes as she clenches a tissue in her manicured hand. Mimi reaches out to squeeze Mick's shoulder, and Mick, his eyes staring ahead, tilts his head to press her fingers with his cheek.

Gloria, Mick's mother has put herself beside Mimi. She sits, spine erect, a black version of the Queen. Paul turns back. To his right is a lectern, and in the centre, a table. Above and around the table is a rail, from which hangs a muddy red, open curtain.

Kitty's stage whisper reaches them from the back of the chapel, and Paul swivels again. Fee and Twitch are coming in with the other children, shushing and tiptoeing along the aisle. A chute of indecently cheery sunshine follows them through the heavy door, and blinks across four expressionless pall bearers, following, with shuffling gait. Millie's coffin wallows on their mismatched shoulders.

The women and children hurry to slide into the front row of seats on the opposite side of the aisle, and the casket perambulates towards the table. Paul leans forward to wave at Kitty but she does not see him. She is watching the coffer being delivered, tipped like a ship on the tide, and her hand steals into Fee's.

The service is brief. A calm and sympathetic launching of their loved one into the next life (Paul wonders how much of Millie's body is left to be launched), then after a pathetic rendition of *The Lord is my Shepherd*, the curtain shimmies into life and crawls smoothly along its rails, to the sound of electronic organ music. Damp eyed mourners file into the warm daylight, nodding subdued greetings as they recognise old friends and distant relatives. Flowers must be admired in the porch before the funeral-goers are directed by Paul and Maurice to a local hotel where they can imbibe some stiff comfort.

***

Fee and Twitch sit at a table. Kneeling on a chair beside Fee, Kitty wields coloured pencils, her head bowed over the outlines of two hens and a cockerel in a cheap sugar-paper book. Josh is curled on Twitch's lap, twisting his favourite strands of hair. Sam stares moodily at the ingress of people, and kicks the table leg making their drinks wobble. The adults grab their wine glasses, and Kitty's coloured pencil shoots across the outline of her picture. She lowers her eyebrows in silent reproach and takes to her knees to continue her task on the wooden seat of her chair.

Guests surge in and make for the teak and brass bar, then drift down the room, settling like snow on seats and in spaces.

Along the wall to their left runs a table presenting a sepia, monochrome assortment of canapés. The murmuring guests clutch glasses of over-fruity wine and stuff mass-produced pastry into their mouths.

Paul and Maurice stand beside the bar, still flanking Mick like two minders. Nearby Millie's parents and Mick's mother try to absorb a proportion of sympathy from well-meaning guests. Mick, wearing a bleak up-turn to his lips, greets and nods, shakes hands and hugs, while Lucas and Olivia press against his legs, offering shy smiles when adults bend at them.

'Sam,' Fee says, touching the boy's arm, 'look, there are Lucas and Olivia. Why don't you go and see if they're all right?'

'Course they're not *all right*.' Sam scowls and kicks the table leg even harder. Twitch leans forward and presses her palm onto his knee.

Fee perseveres. 'That's true but you could help them feel better.'

Sam doesn't move. His hands form fists, and his toes swing close to the table leg, daring someone to scold him. Fee grips her glass, and refrains from uttering the curt warning that hovers at her lips.

162

'What's going to happen after this? Will they come back and live with us, or go to Mick's?' There is a threat of tears, a constriction of the throat, behind the fury in Sam's tone.

'Well, there's a lot to be sorted out. They'll be going home with Mick tonight, but we're not sure what will happen after that.' Sam's head flies up, and Fee hurries on. 'I hope they will. Mick still needs to work, and Crispin Road is Lucas and Olivia's home now, but they're bound to want to stay with their dad for a while.' She gives him an understanding smile. 'We'll have to wait and see.'

The level of noise in the room, rises as the alcohol does its work. Occasionally someone arrives at the table, offering condolences, smiling, apologising, awkward.

At last the food on the side tables is rendered to crumbs, and there is egress and diminuendo. Last mourners leave with sympathy painted on their faces. Millie's mother hugs Mick, and her father shakes his former son-in-law's hand, and administers a pat to his upper arm. Gloria links arms with her son, a tiny woman reaching only to his chest. She glares across the empty tables at Fee and Twitch.

They get the message and rise, gathering the children and their belongings, and head towards Mick and his minders. Luc and Livvie watch their approach in dismal silence, cowering beside their father and Grandmother. Paul and Maurice step back as Twitch approaches. Paul stares at his drink and doesn't see Kitty lift her face to greet him then frown when he keeps his eyes averted. She turns her attention to Lucas and Olivia and gives them both a cuddle and a loud kiss. Sam hangs back, glowering.

'How are you, Mick?' Fee stretches across Gloria, to embrace him. Twitch follows suit, and Maurice puts his hands in his pockets, pursing his lips in a silent whistle.

'I'll cope.' Mick drops his eyes to his children. 'We'll manage, won't we kids?'

Gloria presses closer to her boy. 'We'll all manage together.'

Twitch touches Mick's arm. 'Take your time and look after each other - we're here whenever you need us. I'll be at home if you'd like me to have the children - in fact we're both there at the moment.' She glances at Fee, who is on compassionate leave from work, then at Lucas and Olivia. 'We'll see you soon my darlings.' She bends to hug them and they wrap their arms round her neck as if they might lose her too.

'They'll be fine,' snaps Gloria.

Twitch wears a sympathetic face. 'When you're ready to discuss the future, let us know. There's no hurry. None.'

Mick nods, then Maurice hurries to interrupt. 'I think it's time to go.'

'Yes, of course; you're right. We need to get these children home.' Fee is quick to respond. 'Let us know if you'd like a contribution towards this.' She sweeps her arm round the room taking in the bar and the food.

'I can manage thank you.' Mick frowns at her.

Nothing they say is right so they herd Sam and the others out of the door, leaving the men with Gloria, to settle up. Kitty looks back at Paul. He is still contemplating his drink.

In the back of the car Sam's feet keep up their angry drumming.

'Stop it Sam.' Kitty has had enough. Her own father ignored her today, and she doesn't understand why. It must have been something to do with Aunty Millie dying, but he should at least have looked at her. She thumps Sam on his leg. 'You're annoying us.'

'Don't care.' Sam keeps on kicking the back of Fee's seat.

'It does make it difficult to concentrate, Sam.' Fee's tone is conciliatory.

'I DON'T CARE.' In a moment Sam is bawling; his tears undammed at last.

Kitty and Josh wrap him in an embrace, and as they pull into the drive at Crispin Road Sam is sobbing, 'it's never going to be the same again;' over and over.

***

Gloria, Mick and the children step from the wake onto a wide pavement. There is light traffic on the road, so Mick takes the curb side of the walkway, holding Lucas by the hand. Gloria is on the inside of the pavement, and Olivia trails along behind them.

Gloria mutters, 'That girl goes on hurtin' people even when she's dead. I knew she was trouble the first time I met her.'

'Ma, don't be like that. I wouldn't change anything, well, apart from this, he gestures behind him with his free hand. Millie made her own decision to follow her dreams. We should all do that if we can.' Mick releases Lucas's hand for a moment to pat his mother gently on the back. 'Don't get yourself upset. We're going to be fine.' He glances down at Lucas, whose expression offers little hope, and grabs hold of him again. Behind them Olivia stares at the ground. 'You OK Liv?'

'Yeah,' the little girl sighs.

Gloria blurts, 'Well I didn't follow my dreams when your father died. I had a sense of responsibility.'

'Please Mum, think of the children before you speak.'

Every moment since the birth of her handsome son, Gloria has watched over him, doing what any mother would to protect him from hurt. The day he brought Millie home to meet her she started to worry. 'She'll break your heart Son,' she had warned, but Mick said she was being racist. Well, she wasn't, she could just tell that Millie was going to run him a dance. She wished her husband had been alive, he'd have been able to talk sense into their boy, then none of this would have happened.

Gloria thinks back to her arrival in England, that dingy day when they set foot on the docks at Dover. No colour, and the weather chilled her bones. She wondered then what Albert had brought them to?

'You remember when we first came here, to the UK?'

'Vaguely.'

Robert, Albert's brother, suggested they come. Robert had a good job and said he could get one for Albert. Things were not good in Ghana, and Albert persuaded Gloria that the move would be best for three-year-old Mick. Albert was a good man, proud, and he wanted to work. He only had his family's interests at heart.

'You can live in a brick house with a kitchen and a bathroom and a garden, how about that?'

Gloria remembers his pleading face with affection.

Robert found them a flat in Watford, near to the new job. They took a train from Dover and struggled through St Pancras Station, hanging onto one another and marvelling at the high ceiling and rushing crowds. They found a taxi. It had cost a fortune. Gloria's English was not good then, but Albert told her later that he only just had enough money to pay the driver. When he counted out notes and coins, the man had raised his eyebrows in a disdain that could have expressed his opinion on Albert's colour, or on the lack of a tip.

From the pavement Gloria, holding the infant Mick tightly by the hand, stared at their new home. At the front, behind black metal railings with a matching gate, was a wide, shallow patch of scrubby lawn. Beyond the garden, rose a majestic if shabby, Victorian, red brick building, with a fading leaf-green front door and a symmetrical pattern of sash windows. They let themselves in through the low gate and struggled over a path of cobbles, with grass and moss growing between. A push on the door

*brought them into a narrow, lino floored hallway with doors to right and
left, and a staircase ahead.*

'Smile.' Albert held up a camera.

'Aw, Albert I look terrible.'

'Just smile woman, 'dis is an important day.'

*She stood obediently with Mick, by the newel post, and the instamatic
discharged a dazzling flash.*

'Now me. You take me.'

*She pulled Mick across the passage and let go of his hand to do as he
asked, trying not to complain about the soreness of her feet and her longing
to see their new home.*

*Albert took a set of keys from his pocket and studied the fob. 'It's
number 31.'*

*They toiled up three staircases heaving suitcases behind them, and once
inside, fell exhausted onto chairs in the living room, unable for a moment,
to take in their surroundings. Eventually Gloria looked around and
admitted that the flat was beyond her dreams. It did indeed have a fitted
kitchen and a bathroom, a matter of excitement for Gloria, who hadn't
had plumbing before. Her only complaint was the number of stairs.*

Gloria chortles to herself. That breathless climb, and the delight and
fear.

*Poor Albert never got a chance to take up his new job. She kissed him
goodbye, sending him off to his interview in his best clothes, with his shoes
conker-shiny. It was the last time she saw him alive. Witnesses said he'd
looked the wrong way at the main road. They'd just got used to cars
driving on the right back home and then there they were in the busy streets
of Watford with everything reversed again.*

*Gloria and little Mick waited, excited to know how Albert's first day at
work had been but when the doorbell rang, they opened it to Robert. The
police had found the interview letter in Albert's pocket and traced Robert
at work. He had been to identify the body and come straight over to break
the news.*

Gloria looks up at her son's hanging face and reflects that every life is
touched by sorrow.

'How much do you remember of your father?'

'A bit. Mostly I remember *you* being there for me. You were so strong.
Do you still miss him Ma?'

'I was just wishin' he was here,' Gloria admits, and nudges her son. 'To
make sure you don't do anythin' else stupid.' She grins up at him.

166

They've both come a long way since she opened the door to hear of her husband's death. That was the worst day of her life, but she didn't give in. How could you, with a three-year-old son?

Robert whisked Gloria and Mick back to his house that day, and she saw Alicia, Robert's wife for the first time in years, and met their three children. There was barely room for two extra in the tiny house, but Gloria was thankful for the bed and their support.

She and Mick began taking outings, to get out from under Alicia's feet. Gradually they found their way around Watford, then began to venture on the train into London. There they walked and walked, through the wet and gloomy streets of the capital, jostled among its pale inhabitants.

With the help of her in-laws, television, and friends at church, Gloria's English improved. She and Mick learned the history of the dirty capital with its rich, cruel royals and filthy residents.

It was on one of these trips to the capital that Gloria spotted an advert. CLEANER AND HOUSEKEEPER REQUIRED. It was a live-in job, space for herself and Mick, and money for food. She made a note of the number, and that evening rang it. In her best diction, she asked for details of the job, and to her utter amazement was invited for an interview.

The people were Arabs, and the flat was extensive, with floors deep with Chinese carpet, and bathrooms of marble and gold. Although Gloria was overwhelmed, she managed to keep her poise, and with the bearing of a woman used to such surroundings lied shamefully about her experience back home. No, she couldn't provide references but she was a poor widow with a son to bring up. She got the job.

She and Mick, to the unspoken relief of Robert and Alicia, left Watford to start the next stage of their lives, in Hampstead.

Gloria spent three years in the employ of the Arabs. By the time she left she had saved enough money to move to a small, rented flat.

She moved on to a job with a bookmaker nearby, running his office and managing the money. Her new boss was not always comfortable with the way she talked to his customers. While her fingers flew through piles of grimy notes and her portly body bowled between office and counter, her mouth berated the sinners who lost their precious incomes. 'How is your wife goin' to pay for the food on the table now?' She scolded as they departed with empty pockets. 'Ain't you got nowhere better to go than this?' But Gloria was a bundle of energy, and despite her nagging, the

punters seemed fond of her - a reliable and motherly figure in a less than
stable world.

They cross the road to the station. Gloria is to go home by train, and
Mick and the children will pick up a taxi. They all huddle into the small
entrance, and Gloria turns to her family, her eyes suddenly filling.
'Son.' Mick stoops to receive her hug and they hang together for a
minute, then she turns to embrace the children and tells them she loves
them, and will see them very soon. Backing through the ticket gate, she
waves and sniffs, watching her big, sad son turn away.

She finds a seat on her train and digs out her book. She is not going to
read it, but opens it to discourage chatty neighbours. Her mind returns
to the betting shop and those sorry men. She wonders what happened
to them, especially Jim.

Jim was a nice man with a decent job in a bank. Over the months Gloria
watched in horror and scolded mercilessly as he squandered thousands of
pounds.

At the end of each day, back in her cosy house she prayed for him, and
after hours on her knees, inspired if not instructed by the lord, she decided
on a plan. The next time Jim came in Gloria proposed a deal. She would
put £20 on his recommended horse, a significant sum in those days, and
when she lost it, Jim was to give up gambling. With distorted logic, she
hoped her uncharacteristic fling might demonstrate to Jim how much she
cared, and longed for him to put his home and career first. Jim listened to
her proposal, his clerk's hands resting on the counter and his wispy pate
tilted to one side, and she was delighted when he agreed, saying in a
resigned voice,

'Gimme £50 each way on Flaming Glory in the 2 O'clock, just for old
time's sake.' The odds were long.

Gloria took his bet, and after clearing it with her boss, put her own £20
on the same horse.

The train begins to fill up. Gloria squeezes herself into the corner of
her seat, gripping her book like a shield. A heavy, male body
compresses the springs, and brings with him a smell of fresh air and
aftershave.

In the bookmaker's, a dusty television blared from a high shelf. Gloria
and Jim watched the race, with Gloria expecting every moment for her
£20 to be lost forever. The horse however ran strongly, and gradually
pulled to the front. At the end of the race Gloria found herself clinging to
Jim in excitement as their runner finished in first place. To her chagrin, as

it crossed the line, she was leaping and cheering. Oh, she understood Jim's
addiction at that moment. Was that God's punishment?
Jim was financially set up, and as promised, after hugging her tight, he
walked from the shop and she never saw him again. She hoped he hadn't
taken his business elsewhere.
The win provided Gloria with enough money to buy the little terraced
house where she now lives, in Fulham. The real cost, though, was a
lifetime praying for forgiveness, for accepting the 'wagers' of sin. In her
shame, she has never shared this story.

The locomotive jerks to a start. In half an hour, she will be in Euston.
She stares sightlessly at the charcoal print on her page, and prays that
she has been a good mother. Mick is her reason for living - him and the
children. Millie had never been good enough for him. She stops and
chastises herself. *Mick's right. You don't speak ill of the dead.* After all Millie
gave them those lovely kiddies. Gloria loves Lucas and Olivia deeply,
and now she worries about their future, brought up by those women.
She'd like to get a toe in the door there.

Chapter 40

The fine weather that began on Millie's last day, has continued for two weeks now.

Mick sits, sandwiched once again between Paul and Mo, on a playground bench. A phalanx of green railings protects their rear, interrupted by a metal gate that allows access to and from a wide pavement. Beyond the slabs, a noisy road imposes pauses in their conversation as HGVs roar past trailing sooty exhaust fumes that pollute the crisp air.

Lucas and Olivia have been staying with Mick since the funeral. Like iron filings to a magnet, they have clung to him, whether it be squeezed into the kitchen during food preparation, or heaped on the couch with a book, or the television. Lately though, their cluster has loosened, as though the strength of the force has reduced.

'I need to get back to work.' Mick presses his lips together and frowns. 'The children have been asking when they can go home. *Home*.' He shakes his head then shrugs. 'Fee and Twitch seem keen to take them. It's good of them really.' He inhales deeply, expanding his chest and forcing his shoulder against Paul's.

'How *are* the nippers now?' Maurice has to raise his voice over a passing truck.

'I think they'll be OK. Thing is I haven't got a choice really. Work's been good to me but two weeks off - it's putting pressure on the rest of the team.'

'You can still see the kids, nobody's going to object to that,' observes Paul. 'It'll be easier for you than me and Maurice now. You can play the sympathy card.'

Mick nods without comment.

The three men fill the long, slatted seat. At their feet, the remains of a take-away and the discarded outer clothing of their young, overflow from cloth bags. Maurice is pushing and pulling a buggy in which Josh, too big for it now, lolls, his eyes closed. Their other three children, and a few other families, are dotted around the playground. Nearby, a boy-toddler supervised by his father, climbs a ladder with rungs as high as his shoulders. The dad offers gung-ho encouragement and the mother warns, 'Hold his hand, he's only small.'

The men lapse into quietude, listening to the rumble of the traffic, and to childish squeals. Mick looks for his kids, and spots Lucas pushed on a swing by Olivia, now even more motherly and grown up.

Kitty and Sam are at the top of the climbing frame, about 7ft from the ground.

'Look Daddy,' cries Kitty, in the way of children the world over: *Mira Mama. Regards Grand-pere.* Paul glances up and nods vaguely at her.

'No, keep looking, I'm going to do something amazing,' and when his eyes are focussed to her satisfaction, she throws herself from the top of the tower.

Paul leaps to his feet, fright choking his cry, and launches himself towards her.

She bounces to her feet. 'See, I told you I'm amazing!' She beams up at him, panting, and triumphant.

Paul's heart races and he grasps Kitty by her sleeve to swing her towards him. Seizing both her shoulders he pushes his face into hers, yelling, 'That was very silly. You could have hurt yourself.'

The child's pride transforms into astonishment, then her eyes brim with tears.

Immediately he smothers her in his chest. 'I'm sorry Pops. I shouldn't have shouted but you gave me a fright.' He drops down and hugs her. 'Look at me, I'm crying too, daft old Dad.' *What a bloody life.*

Behind Paul, Mick rises from the bench and begins gathering his things. He has made his decision and is going to take Lucas and Olivia back to Crispin Road. 'Come on man,' he calls 'we need to make a move.'

The group files through the gate and a passing refuse cart wafts its smells at them.

Chapter 41

Millie is gone forever. Fee, standing in the 'quick' queue at Watco, finds she must remind herself again and again.

This early evening is a lonely time to shop, there are no mothers with unruly children, no oblivious elderly couples, gossiping with unexpectedly met neighbours, the supermarket is quiet, occupied only by hurrying, suited women, and loose-tied men in shirt sleeves. Harsh lights make even the light evening outside look grim. People's baskets speak of evening plans: ready meals, bottles of wine or beer, loaves of bread and pints of milk.

Fee puts on her few items onto the conveyor belt: eggs, yoghurts and chocolate, then a red plastic strip to separate her goods from the next.

'Thank you,' says a warm male voice, and she looks behind her.

'My pleasure.'

'The queue for the lost and the lonely,' comments the man.

'Well, some of them,' she smiles briefly, 'I'm not as sad as you might imagine from my shopping. The eggs and yoghurts are for the children and the chocolate is for myself and my girlfriend.'

'Oh, I see.' He looks away, misunderstanding.

She rushes to put him right. 'I live with friends, we are divorced, with children.' Why is she explaining herself to a complete stranger?

'Oh, right' He gives an embarrassed chortle. 'That's a good arrangement.' He eyes her shopping as she puts it into a plastic bag. 'And do you live on eggs and chocolate?'

'Only if *I'm* cooking.' Her items have reached the till and are being passed across the bar code reader by a pair of pudgy hands.

'One pound, twenty eight please.' Fee looks into the round pasty face of the busty girl behind the till. She beams back from beneath a shock of candy pink hair. Her breasts strain at the buttons of staid blue overalls.

Fee rummages for her purse and pays for the goods then turns to the man. 'Goodbye, have a nice evening.' She looks at his basket, what tale does it tell? Something fish shaped in a white crispy bag, new potatoes, garlic, ginger and watercress, and a bottle of white wine, she can't see the label. Impressive. 'It doesn't look as though you'll starve.' She starts to move off.

'Would you like a coffee before you go?' Fee turns back to meet two enquiring faces: the man indicating the supermarket's café, and the sales assistant with her eyebrows raised in enquiry, clearly enjoying the exchange.

'I must get this stuff to the children but thank you for the invitation.' Her cheeks are warm as she appraises the man's friendly face with regret. *Oh, what the heck?* 'Actually, that would be lovely.'

There's an awkward moment when they both want to pay, but Fee allows herself to be treated.

'So - are you on your way home from work?' He asks when they have settled onto plastic seats.

'Not today.' She doesn't explain. 'I do work though - in Kingsthorpe. And you?'

'I'm an engineer. Will.' He holds out his hand and she takes it. It is warm and dry.

'Fee.'

He grins, and settles into his seat.

'I work on the oil rigs. I'm away for a few weeks and then home for a couple. I've just got back from Aberdeen, it's been a long drive. I'm not sure why I bought this fish, oven crispy stuff would have been much easier tonight, but you can't always get red mullet, can you?'

'No idea,' admits Fee, 'I don't normally cook, or shop, I do the washing up and help with the children. My kitchen speciality is goats' cheese salad, no cooking, no clearing up and ready in five minutes.'

'And it tastes delicious too,' he says, 'especially if you grill it and serve it with figs or fresh mango and watercress.'

Gosh, the man understands food, is good with his hands - presumably, and is away for weeks at a time. Has someone up there planted him to tempt her from celibacy?

'Do you live locally?' She asks, hoping she's not being nosey.

'I have a flat on Mill Road. It's neglected,' He raises his shoulders. 'I'm never there long enough to make it a proper home,' he leans back in the seat, 'but this leave I've promised myself I'm going to start decorating.'

Occasionally, if the traffic on the main street is too heavy, Fee takes a detour along Mill Road. It is a wide residential street, lined with trees and large mansions, most of which bear the tatty evidence, and zig-zag escape ladders, of apartment buildings.

'Oh, you should speak to my housemate, Twitch, she's very artistic.'

'To be honest, I fancy having a go at it myself,' he says. 'I have a good idea what I want, and I like the feeling that I've done a job totally by myself.'

As they chat, Fee scrutinises Will, and is mildly dismayed to find nothing she can criticise. He's striking in a dishevelled but stylish way, dishevelled mainly due to his habit of scraping his fingers through his longish, mid brown hair. Stylish because he is not dressed by a chain store. He models slim, well-fitting jeans, black V-necked sweater with a bare chest, not too hairy, and a soft grey casual jacket. This he manages to sling or drape from a finger, over his shoulder with casual indifference. Notwithstanding his looks, he is easy to talk to and seems bright.

'You said you were an engineer on the rigs?'

'I'm a diver, you know, scuba? I do under water safety checks.'

'That sounds dangerous. I've done a little of scuba diving on holiday. I love it. It's so beautiful under the sea.'

Will smiles. 'Not so much in the North Sea on a grey day.'

The cups are empty and Fee looks at her watch.

'I must go. They'll be worried at home. Thank you for the coffee.' She scrapes back her chair and picks up the shopping.

'May I see you again?' He asks.

She looks at him dubiously. She is tempted, although the timing couldn't be worse. She puts a hand in her pocket to find her car keys and touches a hard edge. Without over-thinking, she pulls the block out and slips a business card from the top. As she passes it to him, her hand brushes his surprisingly smooth skin.

'If you'd like to ring me at work in about a week, perhaps we can manage lunch.' He holds the small rectangle between is fingers, and studies it with interest.

'IT Director, wow, I didn't know I was talking to a business mogul.'
'Well, hardly that, it's the American type of Director, I'm not on the board. It's an overly grand title for a senior manager.' She starts to move away, conscious of the time. 'Thanks again for the coffee.'
'See you soon then.' He raises a hand as she leaves, she sees it reflected in the inky window, but doesn't wave back.

Chapter 42

The office seems alien after two weeks away. Fee goes to her desk, enclosed, as they all are, in a 'pod', a cubicle divided by screens with a gap at the bottom. The dividers are tall enough to see over if one is standing up but frustratingly high when seated. Colleagues, like the weather and traffic, are heard but not seen unless heads appear unexpectedly over the top, or in through the small entrance.

With anxiety born of experience she switches on her PC, and logs into her emails. Hundreds of unread messages meet her gaze.

'I couldn't deal with your mail. I didn't know your logon, and I didn't want to disturb you at home.'

Fee looks up at the sympathetic face of Nick, her young protégé, peering down at her over the divider.

'It's OK. I'll cope. Have you got time this morning to update me on what's been going on?'

''Course. Give me half an hour.'

'And will you organise a managers' meeting, for this afternoon, please Nick?'

'Consider it done. By the way, I think you have an admirer.'

Fee tenses. 'Oh?'

'Some guy's been ringing. He wanted your home number but of course I didn't give it to him.'

'Thanks.' Fee's mind springs to Will. 'I expect it's the man from Michael and Morris. He's trying to recruit me but I'm not interested - especially not now.' She looks straight into Nick's eyes. He nods and she nods back. 'I'll get my desk sorted out and be with you in half an hour or so.' She directs her eyes back to her screen, and Nick takes the hint.

Another head peers over the partition. 'Hi de hi.'

Fee breaths deeply. She will never get used to these continual interruptions. She smiles with what she hopes is sincerity. 'Lucy, hello. How are you?' The busty little admin clerk must be on tiptoe. 'Come round. How can I help you?' The girl comes in, her shirt snug across her breasts, and a short pencil skirt displaying strikingly shapely legs. Shirley reminds Fee of Dolly Parton in *9 to 5*.

The girl brandishes a brown envelope and a large greeting card.

'Sorry to trouble you when you've just got in Fee. I'm about to buy a present for Shirley, and I wondered if you wanted to contribute.'

'Shirley? Is it her birthday?'

Lucy shakes her blond curls. 'No, she's leaving.'

'Oh of course, I forgot.' Fee delves for her purse and adds a five pound note to the collection.

'That's generous Fee, thanks. We're all going to the pub next Friday to say farewell. I'm sure she'd love you to be there.'

Fee is non-committal, thinking that Shirley won't want to have her boss at the gathering. Anyway, she doesn't want to leave Twitch alone at present. She studies the card, browsing the messages and kisses that pepper it, and composing an appropriate message in her mind, distant but appreciative. Eventually she pens: *Wishing you every success in the future. Thank you for all your hard work and enthusiasm, Fee Thomas.* As soon as Lucy's curvaceous figure disappears round the partition she returns her thoughts to emails.

The latter part of her morning is spent with Nick, and when she tells him he's done an excellent job in her absence, is rewarded by his look of delight. The telephone has been ringing throughout the morning, but she's been letting the calls go to voicemail. There are two from Will, asking her to call him, and leaving his mobile number, which of course she knows.

At lunch time, she slips on a light jacket, and makes for a cake shop popular with staff at the office. She queues for a sandwich and a bottle of sparkling water, and stops at a small table in the window.

The little café is cool after the heat of her walk, and she unbuttons her jacket, in a hurry to satisfy her complaining stomach. With the bread held in in both hands she takes a couple of generous bites, then wipes her fingers and lips on a napkin, and pulls out her phone. Will's name

178

fills the screen, and Fee takes a swig of water as she calls him back. He doesn't answer and his voice tells her he is away, but that she should leave a message.

Of course, he's probably working. Fee speaks briefly and over-formally into the mouthpiece, leaving her number, then she clicks the red button, instantly regretting her message. She should just let things die between them. Twitch's mood is still fragile, especially since Millie. If Will rings back she'll tell him they can't meet again. She picks up a fallen prawn from her plate and bites it in two.

By four o'clock everything in Fee's department is under control. She tells Nick she is going to work from home and sets off with her laptop and handbag, driving through parched, sun-bathed residential roads with gardeners stooping to weed and water brimming tubs of flowers, and children skipping and skate-boarding on pavements.

Kitty's high-pitched yells, and angry shouts from Sam assault her ears as soon as she opens the front door. Fee lowers her bags to the floor and jogs up the stairs to find the two children facing one another on the landing. Kitty has her back to Fee, her body taut, her head thrust towards Sam. Sam's face is a mask of frustration and guilt.

'Why did you do that Sam? Shouts Kitty. I spent ages on it'

'It's a stupid picture.'

Fee's eyes move to the object of their argument, a juvenile scene of human figures, crumpled on the floor. 'Hey, you two, what's going on?' Kitty rushes to Fee and pitches her arms round her mother's waist. 'Sam spoiled my picture. I was drawing us - our family, I wanted to stick it on the fridge for Lucas and Olivia when they get home.'

Fee releases herself from her daughter's grasp and stoops to pick up Kitty's art work. She spreads it against her front to smooth it, before holding it up. In the middle of the page is a house, drawn in red pencil, with criss-crossed windows and floral curtains, and standing in a childish row in front, are the children with Fee and Twitch. Flying above the roof, resembling a curly headed crow, is the figure of Millie. Fee perches on the top stair and pulls Sam and Kitty to her sides. Together they stare at the picture.

'So, Kitty, Poppet, tell me what you have drawn.'

'Well that's us,' she jabs the stick like characters standing on the ground, 'and this is Millie.' Kitty's finger strokes the figure in the sky. 'She's watching us, caring for us. I wanted to do it to make Luc and Livvie feel safe when they get here.'

Fee pulls Sam closer, her arm round his middle, and gives him a squeeze. 'Sam, what's upset you about this?'

'I don't want to think of her any more. She's not here and we have to get used to that. Mummy says life goes on. Well let's get on with it then.'

Kitty looks at Sam with an expression of disbelief. 'We can't just forget her. We loved her. And for Luc and Livvie, well, she was their real mum. I did this picture for them, and you ruined it.'

Fee looks from one to the other wondering where Twitch and Josh are. 'You know we've all had a big shock, and we all miss Auntie Millie, but everyone has a different way of dealing with their feelings. Kitty, this is a lovely picture and I'm sure Lucas and Olivia will be happy you've done it for them. Sam, you are angry. Life doesn't always go the way we expect it to, does it?' Sam gives an affirmative grunt. 'But we've still got to live together. It's fine to disagree but not to hurt each other's feelings.'

The boy tries to pull from Fee's grasp, but she holds him tight.

'Kitty will just remind Luc and Livvie what's happened. Won't that hurt *their* feelings?' he mutters.

'I hope not. They won't want to forget their mother, and if Kitty explains why she drew this picture, I think they'll be comforted because they'll know how much she cares about them.'

Sam looks at Kitty and at the picture. 'Can we fix it? Could you iron it or something?'

Fee gives the boy a hug and stands up, pressing a kiss to his cheek. 'I expect we can do something. Where are Twitch and Josh?'

'In the garden.' Kitty is smiling again.

'The garden? It's a bit late.'

'Well, they're burning off some energy.'

Fee recognises Twitch's terminology. 'Come on then, let's go and *burn off some energy* with them. First one to the swing gets a biscuit.' She pauses. 'Have we got any biscuits?' But the two children have already disappeared.

When the doorbell rings they are playing French cricket, and Fee slips off her muddy court shoes and runs through to open the front door to Mick, Lucas and Olivia. When she has hugged each of them tightly she looks down at Mick's children.

'The others are in the garden you two. They'll be very pleased to see you. They've missed you.'

The two speed off.

'How are you, Mick?' Fee strokes her fingers up and down the outside of his sleeve, then Twitch runs up the hallway and embraces him.

'Not too bad. The kids are still cut up. I'm not that comfortable leaving them here so soon after Millie…' He glances at the wall with a look of pain then back at Fee. 'I need to get back to work though, and this is home to them.' He looks perplexed for a moment. 'Once I wouldn't have wanted to say that but now,' he pauses, 'well, it's reassuring.'

'Stay for something to eat, Mick.' Twitch takes his arm and pulls him towards the kitchen, 'It's only Spag. Bol. - not up to your standards – or Millie's.'

The women potter in the kitchen, laying the table, stirring, tasting, opening wine, and Mick stands in the doorway with his hands in the pockets of his trousers telling them about his new role at work.

'It's going to involve a fair amount of travel I'm afraid. I need to visit other hotels, in Europe.' Enthusiasm grows on his face, and his voice becomes animated. 'We need to standardise our dining identity. I want this chain to have a reputation for class eating. Most hotels don't realise that having fancy facilities but poor food just lets them down.' He jingles the loose change in his pockets and grins at the two women. 'It's a fantastic opportunity.'

Dinner is ready, and Fee calls the children, while Twitch lifts steaming spaghetti with a special tool, and drapes it into bowls. By the time she is spooning on the sauce, all the children are dragging out chairs to sit down.

'Well, good luck with your job. We'll see you as much as possible and in the meantime these two,' Twitch smiles at Mick's children, 'will be absolutely fine. We'll take good care of them.'

Fee's mobile rings in the hall, where it is charging. 'Excuse me; that might be important.'

Twitch raises her eyebrows. Answering the telephone in the middle of a meal is not what they do. Fee crinkles her eyes, and squeezes her mouth into a line of apology. 'Sorry, there's a lot going on at work and it might be urgent. Carry on without me - don't let yours get cold.

In the low light of the hallway Will's name glares from the screen of her phone. Fee unplugs it and runs up the stairs to her bedroom as she says 'Hello?'

'Fee, it's Will.'

'Oh, hi, Will.' She makes her tone casual although her hands are shaking.

They exchange pleasantries.

'I hope you don't mind but I'd like to see you again.' He sounds diffident, unsure of himself, and she warms to him. Despite her resolution in the café, she finds herself accepting a lunch invitation. After saying goodbye, she clicks the red phone symbol and looks at her face in the mirror. 'You,' she points at herself, 'are a very silly woman.' Then she skips back downstairs and plugs her phone back onto its lead before returning to the kitchen.

The others have all finished, and the children are waiting for ice cream. 'Sorry everyone.'

'Are things difficult at work?' Twitch looks at Fee with sympathy in her eyes.

'All sorted out now.' Fee picks up her cutlery and spins a deft reel of spaghetti onto her fork.

Chapter 43

Fee suggested ages ago that Twitch should have a day out, and today she is finally free. While Fee works from home, Twitch is heading for Oxford. Oxford Castle to be precise, to view an exhibition of aerial photographs.

Her GP has prescribed anti-depressants and today, for the first time in years she is up-beat, looking forward to this trip to Oxford, and planned lunch in one of the little restaurants described on the Oxford Castle website. She may even indulge in a glass of wine in the cool sunshine.

With her artistic eye, she enjoys the view of the winding country road curving through fields of green and brown, and between the gentle slopes of hills. Soon though, the road becomes clogged with cars and trucks. Industry and commerce line the thoroughfare and traffic bunches at countless signals and junctions. The car noses through side streets, guided by Fee's Satnav, and Twitch pounces on a parking space on the right-hand side of the road, facing the oncoming traffic, a short walk from her destination. A litter bin blocks the driver's door so she slides across and throws open the passenger door, and extends her leg towards the road. A yell and a crunch startle her and the door flies back at her, banging her hard on the ankle. She yelps and pulls her foot into the car, then presses her forehead to the window. On the road lies a man, very much tangled in a bicycle.

'Oh, my goodness.' Twitch winds down the window, and is horrified to see blood oozing from the man's knee through a tear in his worn and faded jeans. 'Let me help you! I'm so sorry. I wasn't thinking. Are you alright?'

The fellow looks up without moving. His fine features are drawn into an expression of shock and frustration. 'If you could give me a hand - I can't get my leg out.' His trainer has been forced into the triangle of tubes that form the main structure of the bike frame, and to makes matters even more difficult his jeans are trapped between the cogs at the centre of the rear wheel. The other leg is underneath the bike making escape impossible. Cars ease past them, their passengers craning to see.

Twitch manages to open her door and scrambles over the man and his bike. The dark green door of the MPV is scarred by a deep dent, and a white scratch describes the path of the bicycle as it crashed to the ground.

They wrestle with the jeans, the leg and the bicycle, inflicting more harm on all three, and eliciting whimpers from the cyclist, and anxious apologies from Twitch. When he is free they examine the damage. 'Your poor leg, I think it's going to need stitches. God, I'm so sorry!' She is repeating herself, babbling, while the white-faced man before her has hardly spoken a word. 'I'll take you to the hospital, I can find my way. I have my friend's Satnav - I'm Twitch.' She extends her hand to him feeling ridiculous.

'Luke.' He responds, and shakes it. 'Er, I think we should get out of the road.'

'Oh, gosh, yes. Here, let me help you.' She takes his arm but he gently withdraws it saying shyly, 'if you could take the bike?'

'Yes, good idea. Silly me.' What is the matter with her?

With a sense of relief, she remembers that the car has a first aid kit, and she rummages in the back until she unearths it from a cubby-hole over the wheel arch. Luke rips off the half-severed leg of his jeans, and Twitch does her best to stem the flow from his knee with bandages and wadding. He stands on the pavement like an unlikely freemason. By the time they have removed the front wheel from the bike and jammed it into the back of the car, blood is seeping through the bandage.

Setting the Satnav to find the hospital calms Twitch, and by the time they set off, she feels equal to the job of navigating them to the A & E, trying not to regret her thwarted attempt at culture.

They are silent for a while then Twitch says, 'I'll pay for the damage of course.'

'That's very kind; I've only just bought the bike, as a matter of fact.'

'I don't know much about bikes, was it very expensive?'

He looks embarrassed. 'Well, it was for me. I'm a social worker, so money's always a struggle.'

They discuss cycling and social work, and the pitfalls of both. How surreal, making small talk to a strange man, while driving through the Oxford streets at the instructions of a computerised woman. Blood trickles from the wound, staining Luke's sock. The wrecked bicycle rattles behind them.

They cruise round the hospital perimeter before giving up the idea of finding a parking place. Twitch drops Luke at the main doors and bounces the car up a curb onto an illegal grass verge a short walk away. As she marches back she hopes she won't get a ticket, this is proving to be an expensive day.

In the waiting area they settle, side by side on low, dun coloured plastic seats, not holding out much hope of the promised 'short wait'. Luke sticks his leg out in front of him to keep it straight and they stare straight ahead in awkward silence. To their relief a nurse with a comforting smile soon leads the limping Luke away.

Twitch flicks the pages of a dog-eared magazine. Around her, children play with grimy plastic toys, and men and women sit in resigned silence. Nearby, a group of elderly people wait for an ambulance, and their banter provides a little diversion.

Eventually she looks up from her magazine to see Luke hobbling towards her. His knee is swathed in a huge bandage, only slightly whiter than his face. Beneath the dressing, he reports, are four stitches. Thankfully the car has not been clamped, and Twitch collects Luke from the entrance.

'Where shall I take you now?'

'Could you drop me at the bike shop? I'll direct you. I don't live far from there. Honestly, I'll be fine.' This last remark is to block her attempted objection that he can't possibly walk anywhere. She relents only when he has accepted her contact details, and promised to ring if he needs her - and to call when he knows the repair cost of his bike. As she drives away from the bike shop she wonders where he lives. In the rear-view mirror, she sees him standing on the pavement, a buckled wheel in one hand and the rest of the bike supported by the other. He is staring at the back of her car, and continues to watch until she has turned the corner.

Chapter 44

From her desk Fee can hear car tyres swishing through the rain, and flurries of water slashing against the window panes. She puts her elbows on the desk and covers her ears with her palms, screwing her eyes to help with concentration. Not only is she trying to cut out the noise of the office and the weather, but more distracting thoughts of her forthcoming lunch date with Supermarket Man, as she has dubbed him, keep creeping through her mind.

Part of this document doesn't make sense, and she stands up to attract the attention of her assistant. 'Nick, can you spare me a moment?' The young man nods and stands up immediately.

By the time they have sorted out the report and decided how to make it clearer, it is twenty past one and she is late for her date. This does not stop her from ducking into the Ladies' to check her reflection, put a comb through her hair and apply a fresh coat of gloss to her lips. Swinging her head from side to side she watches her glossy locks lift and brush against her shoulders before falling back into place. The weather beyond the heavy glass doors in the foyer has not improved, summer is ending, so she turns up her collar and raises her umbrella before diving out into feverish rain. With the point of her brolly facing into the wind she struggles blindly along the pavement, wondering if she will recognise Will. She can picture his hands, and auburn hair, maybe.

At the entrance Fee reverses through the door, folding her umbrella and shaking droplets onto walls and floor. The temperature inside is steamy but as her eyes scan the noisy crowd, she notes with approval the scrubbed wooden tables and heavy square chairs on a stone flagged floor. Customers, young male and female office workers, stand shoulder to shoulder at the bar, sipping white wine spritzers or halves of lager. Diners devour artistically arranged salads, fishcakes and burgers from rectangular plates. In the midst of the diners, Supermarket Man rises from his chair with a welcoming smile, and beckons her to his table. Ah yes, she remembers him now, how could she not? The casual strength, the stylish posture. Fee pushes between laughing drinkers to reach him, dishevelled and flustered. Without artifice, he places a kiss on her cheek then takes her coat and pulls out her chair.

They face each other across the table and Will raises his voice to offer a drink. She chooses a house white, dry for preference. While he is at the bar she fiddles with her coaster. It's been a long time since she dated anyone. While Will tries to attract the attention of the busy staff behind the bar, her confidence plummets. What on earth is she doing here? Panic almost lifts her from her seat and back into the rain, but then Will is elbowing his way back with their two glasses, and it is too late. They pass the potentially awkward first few minutes discussing food and getting it ordered, and once the waiter has scuttled away, Will proves himself admirably equal to the task of entertaining her. After a brief time, and with the relaxing influence of her drink, Fee finds herself having to resist spilling out her whole life story, battering, screaming, the lot. Not advisable on a first date. *First date?*

He is talking about his flat but Fee is distracted from his words, watching in fascination as he runs his fingers through his hair, ruffling it carelessly in his enthusiasm so that it stands on end. She jerks her attention back to what he is saying.

'I've chosen the colour scheme. You'll have to come and see it when I've finished.'

She smiles, commenting that she is not very good with colours. Will looks crestfallen, and she changes the subject. 'Tell me more about your job.'

He explains that his work involves four weeks on the rig, and two weeks at home. He's responsible for the diving crews and the maintenance of their equipment in the exclusively male environment. 'The men relieve their boredom with stupidity.' He explains. 'I remember one time, a huge piece of machinery was delivered, wrapped in bubble wrap – masses of the stuff.' He sweeps his wine glass through the air. 'One of the engineers unwrapped it and ended up with a whole sheet spread across the floor. He couldn't resist trying to pop the bubbles with his toes. He was prancing all over it like a ballerina, and when he looked up there were three blokes watching him from the door.' Will shakes his head and guffaws. 'He didn't live it down for weeks. It's sometimes mentioned even now, and it must have been a couple of years ago.'

As Will describes life on the rig, the practical jokes and lewd humour, Fee wonders if this man is quite her type. He chats on, describing jocular punching and play fighting. 'I steer clear of it all. Give me an enjoyable book and some Pavarotti, any day.'

With a sense of relief Fee joins in a discussion about literature, and finds that they have a liking for many of the same authors, although when Will admits to hiding recipe books in his room she admits it would not be something she would ever do.

'I enjoy eating though. Millie cooks for us all the time at home – cooked.' Will doesn't notice her muttered amendment, and offers instead another parried invitation, to taste one of his culinary creations. He chats comfortably and she learns without needing to ask, that he has never been married although he is not averse to the institution 'Just never met the right person,' he shrugs. 'There have been women, you know, but nothing that's worked out. I'm not ready if I'm honest - working on the rigs isn't ideal for a relationship.

Fee stops herself from remarking that the shifts might not matter too much if he met the right person. A woman with her own life and career would be happy to have that kind of marriage. They chat around the usual first date subjects: homes, films, music: they are both tone deaf, work: they are each dedicated to their careers, and holidays. Fee reveals that she hasn't had a holiday for years as she's had 'personal' things to cope with.

'My work and my daughter take up most of my time, now. In fact, my passport expired nearly a year ago.'

They have hardly finished their meal when she needs to leave, unwilling to take more than her allotted hour. The pavements are still wet, but a dazzling sun now blinks between speeding clouds. She squints as she steps into the light, then turns to thank Will for lunch. He stands on the step looking down at her, one hand on the jamb and the other with its thumb stuck into the pocket of his jeans. His hair is everywhere. She smiles inwardly, ignoring an urge to go back and hug him.

Chapter 45

Embarrassment and curiosity over the incident with Luke keep sliding into Twitch's mind. It's been three weeks since it happened, and she wonders how his knee is.

After their encounter, she was struck by the idea of owning a bicycle of her own and, ignoring the risky nature of the pursuit, ventured one day into a local store to purchase a middle of the range road bike in a dashing electric blue.

She hadn't ridden a cycle since she was a teenager, but after rejecting her flowing skirts in favour of jeans, and wobbling round the block a few times, the skill returned and now she uses the bicycle for most local trips, loving the sense of freedom, of being in the open air, and the convenience of reaching her destination with speed.

The evenings are beginning to draw in, but tonight she's pedalling in daylight towards another new experience. It was Fee who spotted the advertisement for life classes in the local paper.

'Why don't you give it a try? It would do you so much good.'

Twitch rang the following morning and found herself carried along by the loud and enthusiastic voice of Anna, a retired teacher, who, she boomed down the line to Twitch, returned to the profession because she, 'missed the thrill of watching students grow and blossom.'

'Do come along,' Anna begged in her public-school accent, and Twitch found herself replying with an enthusiastic, 'I'd love to.'

The classes are held in a school. Twitch is amused to secure her bicycle to a bar in the bike shed, and wonders if she should have worn a navy-blue, pleated skirt. On her back, a rucksack containing paints and pencils, long unused, bounces loosely with her steps as she crosses the playground. A few other adults stroll towards the front of the school, in pairs or alone. As they too are carrying bags, and one man has what appears to be a drawing board under his arm, she assumes she is going the right way.

Inside an echoing foyer she spots a dayglo-orange poster, hastily scrawled with the words *Life Class*, subscribed with an arrow, pointing to a long corridor. Further posters direct her through heavy swing doors, then up several flights of stairs and along another passage. She halts at one of a rank of large gloss-grey doors on her left. Another eye-catching sheet informs her that she has, without the aid of a satnav, reached her destination.

A strident monologue comes from within, exhorting students to find a spot and set up. Twitch pushes the door into a room bustling with activity, and Anna waves her over from across the heads of several students of varying ages and genders and bellows cheerfully, 'Hello. You must be Stitch.'

Twitch eases her way between men and women, erecting easels, fixing on paper, and selecting brushes, pencils or pastels from their bags. 'Twitch.' she corrects, and Anna beams unapologetically, 'Sorry, useless with names. Bit of a problem when you're a teacher, eh?'

When Twitch had spoken to Anna on the telephone, she had pictured a stout, middle aged woman in tweeds - she sounded so very much like the iconic dog trainer Barbara Woodhouse. The person before her couldn't be further from that. Although definitely in her middle years, Anna is tall and angular. She is dressed in an Indian style skirt and shirt of a startling blue, printed with a gold and red paisley design. Round her neck are several garlands of beads, and many-coloured bangles encircle her wrists. Her shoulder length hair is rusty brown, wiry, and heavily woven with grey. As she speaks she drags it impatiently behind one ear or the other with bony fingers, causing the chains and bracelets to rattle.

Sitting to one side of the room, wearing a thin, pink satin dressing gown, an auburn haired, double-chinned young woman reads a paperback novel, ignoring the crowd gathering around her.

'That's Jess.' Anna nods in the direction of the girl. 'She'll be modelling for us when this lot get settled.' she raises her voice to chivvy some late arrivals. Twitch has been to life classes before, and knows that models are chosen more for their interesting features than their beauty. There will be plenty of opportunity to shadow and highlight Jess's generous curves.

Most students have adjusted their easels by now and are chatting to one another in low voices. Anna explains to Fee that paper, paints and so on can be supplied by her for a nominal sum, but that most people tend to bring their own. She can recommend a good shop if Twitch wishes. Twitch already knows where the art shop is. She needs paper for this evening and once she has paid for it, dropping a few coins into Anna's cupped and charcoal-blackened fingers, finds a space near the wall. It's not a great position, and she makes a mental note to arrive earlier the following week.

Anna 'arranges' Jess, on a bench draped in rose coloured velvet – probably an old curtain. Twitch lets her eyes roam around the room. There is a display of childish art work on the walls, and on a table near the window, some half-finished models made from papier-mâché balance in a crooked crowd.

Suddenly she senses someone watching her, and turns her head. A person she recognises smiles shyly back from a short distance away. For a moment she can't place him, then her attention darts to his knee, clad in a new-looking pair of jeans. She looks up at his face again and he nods, as if to confirm his identity and comes towards her with the faintest trace of a limp.

'You paint then?' He notes.

'Yes. Well, not for a long time. How's your leg?'

'Not too bad. I had the stitches out yesterday. The bike's taking longer. I'm picking it up at the weekend.'

'I was wondering when you would call about that.'

Around them painters and sketchers settle to their task. Twitch looks away from Luke to the scene in the room. Jess is in the centre with students spread round the room, standing sideways to their easels and staring at her in deep concentration. The model is leaning on her left elbow, with pendulous breasts hanging almost to the table, and her hips are draped with a satin sheet. The glow of the lights in the satin, and the more absorbent nature of the velvet will be a challenge to reproduce on paper.

Twitch notices Jess's feet. The toe nails have been carefully filed, and painted with pale pink varnish, and the soles look as if they are regularly scrubbed and moisturised.

Her attention returns to Luke. He has gone back to his easel but smiles across at her and mouths, 'We'll talk later.' His thumb jerks in the direction of the classroom door behind him. Twitch nods and smiles back. What on earth is he doing here? He lives near Oxford, doesn't he? Well, no doubt she'll find out soon enough. She studies Jess, whose impeccable feet are pointing straight at her, deciding instantly that she is not ready to use her paints. She begins sketching in rough shapes, struggling with the foreshortening, and is soon absorbed in her task. Anna jingles up behind her and after asking permission, takes the pencil from Twitch's hand. Bellowing in Twitch's ear she explains that the dainty feet need to be much larger. She holds the wooden pencil at arm's length, across Twitch's view, turning it from the perpendicular to the horizontal to demonstrate the size of Jess's feet in relation to the width of her shoulders beyond, and deftly sketches in new lines. Twitch is dismayed at how out of practice she has become.

'Don't rub out your lines yet,' Anna instructs. 'Just keep going. When you start blocking in the shadow, all this will disappear'. She sweeps her hand across the paper to indicate Twitch's attempts, and the gaudy bracelets fall across her thumb. 'You can tidy it up when you're happy with it'. She moves off, her skirt flowing behind her.

They take a short break to give Jess a rest. The model stretches her arms above her head and so does Twitch. While the woman covers up her chubby body, and rotates her head to ease aching muscles in her neck, Twitch finds Luke, waiting to catch her eye. He sets off ahead of her, and despite his injury, stays well in front, swinging a thermos flask in one hand. When Twitch reaches the refectory, he has vanished. She purchases mint tea in a thick white mug, sweeping her eyes round the smart room, but there's no sign of him, so she strolls between tables looking to left and right until she discovers him behind a pillar, at the back. He grins attractively as she takes her seat.

'You hid yourself away. I wondered where you'd gone.'

'Playing hard to get.' He smiles playfully, and Twitch is startled by the unexpectedly flirty remark.

She feels uncomfortable and sounding accusing, says, 'You're the last person I expected to see tonight.'

'I know.' Luke looks uncomfortable 'What a surprise. I knew you lived somewhere round here but I really didn't expect to see you.' I started coming over on my bike, you know, training. The countryside's glorious once you get out of town. I stopped for chewing gum in a corner shop up the road and saw the advert on the notice board. I thought, well, it'll give me a reason for the ride.

'Of course, I've had to come on my old bike.' He smiles to take the criticism out of his words.

'It's a very long evening for you!'

'Yes, but it's so great. The ride and the drawing, they help me unwind.' He pauses and then as though realising the unlikelihood of this scenario, adds quietly, 'sometimes it's difficult to let go of the stuff I have to deal with.'

Twitch nods. 'How long have you been painting?'

'I've been coming to Anna's classes for a few weeks – when I can get away. She's great, isn't she?' He is less shy today, enthusing about Anna and discussing art. 'I haven't painted since I was at school. I got an A' level but I never went to college, I've always regretted it.'

'I'm the same!' Twitch's eyebrows shoot up and her mouth forms an ah. 'I've been thinking about it lately, how I gave up everything to have my children, and that I should be doing something to make my life more fulfilled. That's why I'm here. Dipping my toe back into the water, so to speak.'

'Well, it's good to see you again.' Luke looks briefly into her face. 'I know we didn't meet in the best of circumstances, but,' he stops talking, then takes a breath and says in a rush, 'it'll be nice to get to know you better on these evenings.'

Twitch is horrified to find herself blushing. She stares into her pallid coffee. 'Yes, that might be good,' she mutters, then to change the subject, shares the fact that she has bought a bicycle. He's immediately interested, asking technical questions she can't answer. She tells him he'll have to come to the bike sheds to see it for himself, then tails off in further embarrassment. Luke misses, or maybe ignores, her unintended innuendo, and says he will definitely do that when he has his bike back, then he can show her the differences between their two models.

They make their way back to class, Twitch slopping her half empty cup into the black-lined bin and Luke screwing the lid onto his flask.

At the end of class Twitch is rather pleased with her efforts. She will come back, so hangs back to sign up for the rest of the term. Luke leaves without a wave, and a delighted Anna hands over a sheet of A4, detailing holiday dates, and a s receipt for Twitch's cheque with her flourishing signature at the bottom.

When Twitch emerges into the playground, night has fallen. Street-lights glow along the pavement and cars cruise by, their headlights scanning the hedges and fences of houses opposite, and washing over cars in sheltered driveways.

Twitch steps into the dense darkness of the bicycle shed, thinking of Luke. She isn't really in the market for a relationship but Millie is on her mind. What a waste of life. She fumbles to unlock her bike and decides it's time to give herself a break, there's nothing wrong with a cup a coffee and a chat.

She drops the bike padlock into her bag next to her rolled up efforts from tonight. Expertly mounting her bicycle, she switches on her cycle light and bumps onto the empty road. Fee will be waiting to hear how the evening has gone. Twitch will describe her fellow students, the amply proportioned model and of course Anna but there will be no mention of gentle Luke – yet.

Chapter 46

The dead heads of roses and hydrangeas lie in a yellow trug on the lawn, another sign of autumn's approach.

Twitch, her skirt tucked into her knickers, and bare legs thrust into Maurice's enormous wellington boots, brought inadvertently in the confusion of moving out, is energetically hoeing a flower bed at the end of the garden. Overnight rain means the morning earth now steams in the sunshine. Birdsong chatters and flutes all around, and the scent of the soil fills her nostrils. Perspiration bathes her back, and prickles on her face and she wipes the back of an arm across her upper lip.

The children have returned to school after the holidays, and Twitch is trying to catch up on house and garden. They've had an enjoyable time but she's glad it's over. It's been hard keeping them occupied, and Fee couldn't take more leave from work because she had so much time off after Millie. Twitch is looking forward to her art class starting again this week.

Her mobile ring-tone comes faintly from the house. Damn and blast, she hasn't brought it out with her. The handle of the hoe drops to the soil and she flops up the lawn, the enormous wellingtons smacking against her calves. By the time she's climbed out of the boots and shuffled into the hall in her socks, the ringing has stopped.

Disgruntled, she plods into the kitchen to run herself a glass of water, taking the telephone with her and placing it beside the sink while she swallows noisily.

There's no message, and the number is unknown - how very annoying. It rings again, making her jump.

'Hello?'

'Twitch?' She recognises his voice immediately.

'Hello Luke. Did you ring just now?'

'Yes, sorry, I don't like answer phones. Hope I'm not disturbing you.'

'Not at all, I needed a rest. I've been gardening. The weeds are growing faster than I can cope with.'

They make small talk, while Twitch wonders what Luke wants. Eventually, and with audible discomfort, he tells her that he has collected his bike from the repair shop. The price causes her to wince but she assures him she will bring the money to art class.

***

She pushes open the classroom door, with the folded cheque in a pocket of her art bag. Her eyes scan the other students but Luke is not here, and she feels a twinge of anti-climax. There are three other people besides herself: Jess, sitting at the front of the room drinking from a mug as usual, and chatting to Anna, and another woman unpacking paints and brushes near an ornate seat in the centre of the room.

Twitch positions her easel diagonally to the chair so she will be able to see part of Jess's face and left side. The Queen Ann style seat will be a challenge, with its complicated carving and strangely angled back, and she holds her pencil out, trying to get a sense of its proportions.

A tap on her shoulder startles her, and Luke is grinning behind her.

'You made me jump.'

'Sorry. How are you?'

'Fine thanks,' lies Twitch. Her heart pounds and her hands, holding the pencil are suddenly clumsy so that she drops it, breaking the lead. She bends to retrieve it and places it safely on the ledge of the easel, then fumbles in her bag. 'I've brought your cheque.'

He looks embarrassed but slides it into his top pocket. 'I've brought my bike with me. Have you got yours?'

She nods. 'Yes.'

'If you want, we could cycle down the road to the pub afterwards.' He shrugs his shoulders. 'It doesn't matter if you don't, I just thought...'

Twitch interrupts, 'That'd be lovely. You can educate me on the finer points of cycling.'

'Well, I suppose I could bore you with that, or maybe we can find other things to talk about.'

Twitch looks at him sharply but his face and body illustrate profound discomfort, not innuendo, and she relaxes. Other students begin to arrive and the room to fill. Luke retreats to another part of the room as Twitch smiles and nods to faces she recognises from last term.

Towards the end of the class everyone wanders round the room, to see what others have created. It's amazing how differently people approach the same object. She reaches Luke's easel with curiosity and is amazed and impressed by the intricate, almost photographic quality of the image he has produced.

At nine O'clock the two leave the college and make for their bicycles. Soon they are sitting in a window seat overlooking the garden at the Kings Head, their bikes padlocked to a fence. Neither is drinking alcohol, Twitch wants to keep her head this evening, and Luke needs to be sober when he cycles home along the busy night time roads. She asks about his job.

'Do you mind if we don't talk about work. Let's just say it's endless, frustrating, and very often a waste of time. Sorry, if that sounds rude.'

'No, not at all. I understand. You want to unwind.'

He looks relieved. 'Exactly. Do *you* work?'

Twitch tells him of her home life, Millie's death, and her longing to do something creative. 'That's why I'm here, I want to get my eye back in, and maybe, who knows, perhaps finish my degree one day.'

'So we're both fed up with our jobs then, we've found something in common already.'

'Can't we find something positive?'

The evening passes easily, and when Twitch looks at her watch is surprised to see that the time is 10.30.

'I should go. Fee'll wonder where I am.' She puts her drink on the table and rises to her feet. Luke follows suit, and they stare at one another for a long moment, then Twitch blinks and stoops to grab her rucksack.

'See you next week then.' Luke mutters, 'Unless…'

The word *gauche*, springs to mind as she straightens, swinging the bag over one shoulder. 'Yes?'

'Well… I enjoyed this evening. If you like, we could do it again before next week.'

'That would be nice.'

They leave the pub side by side, almost touching, and when they have unlocked the bikes, wondering to each other what the traffic will be like, and how much the temperature has dropped, they wheel them to the road, and part company in opposite directions. Luke swings a leg over his saddle with more grace than he has shown all evening, and Twitch pedals under the street lights, humming *A fine romance, with no kisses.*

Chapter 47

It is not a big hill, more a long slope, but the children shriek with a mixture of terror and excitement. Seated one behind the other, arms wrapped round waists and legs herring-boned along its edges, the long wooden trolley carries them over the bumpy grass and slows to a halt just before the fence.

Maurice, grinning at the top of the hill, watches Paul rummage between the front wheels for a rope. In the carpark beyond, Maurice's car is parked beside Paul's motorbike and sidecar. Paul flexes his body and begins to heave his small passengers back up and Maurice lopes towards them to share the load. The two men drop to the ground, breathing hard.

'Come on Daddy, do it again.' Kitty rocks the cart back and forth.

'Careful Pops.' Paul sticks a toe under one of the wheels.

A warm wind feathers Kitty's hair into her eyes and she brushes it back with two gloved hands. The boys are protected by woollen hats and Olivia's springy curls shiver round her head as the wind whips the grass sends white eels of sunlight across its surface.

Maurice and Paul have been labouring up and down this slope for about an hour now. Mick's children, Lucas and Olivia have come along to help test Paul's home-made vehicle. Judging by the sparkling eyes and beaming faces, the expedition has been an enormous success but Maurice has had enough.

'I think it's time we went home.'

'O-oh.' Chorused on two notes the small word conveys big disappointment.

'We'll come back another day, but you lot need to get back.' Maurice struggles to his feet. 'Come on, I'll pull you back to the cars. Hold tight.'

The two men heft the trolley into the back of Maurice's estate car then then Olivia, Lucas, Sam and Josh, scramble into the passenger seats, while Kitty settles, snug in the side-car.

Outside Crispin Road, Maurice herds his small passengers through the gate, and Kitty skips up to join them. Fee comes to the door.

'Hi Maurice.' She looks towards the curb and raises a hand to Paul, still astride his bike. He nods, then she drops her eyes to the troops. 'Hello everyone, have you had fun?' She smiles down at the children as they clamour to explain what they have been doing, then raises her eyes in bewilderment to Maurice.

'Paul's made a sort of giant go-cart,' he explains. 'All the kids sat on it, and we ran it down the slope at the foot of Little Callun Hill.'

Fee's puzzlement clears and she hustles the children into the hall to take off their coats and shoes. 'Come in a sec, could you, Maurice. I was hoping you could do me a favour.'

The children thud up the stairs leaving a heap of muddy shoes in the empty hall.

Maurice glances back at Paul, then steps inside. 'I can't stay long. Paul and I need to unload the trolley from the car.'

'I won't keep you a minute.'

She closes the front door and hugs her waist with crossed arms. 'I hate to ask this, but do you think you could have Sam and Josh tomorrow as well? It's just that Twitch is going out with her art group, and I'll be on my own with them all. It would be an immense help.'

Maurice thinks of Paul standing on the pavement, then of his ex-wife gadding about enjoying herself. 'I'm sorry Fee. You know I would if I could but I've got something important to do tomorrow. I'm not sure how long it will take or I'd offer to come for them afterwards.' He looks at her face, its pleading expression dropping to one of disappointment. 'Look, if I can manage it I'll call for them later, how's that?'

'Whatever you can manage, Maurice.'

'I'll text you.'

'OK. Thanks.'

Back at the bike Maurice says, 'I may as well leave this in the car for now. You get home and we'll unload it tomorrow.'

202

'OK mate.' Paul flexes his back. 'I'm bloody knackered. There's a lager in the fridge with my name on it. I'll see you tomorrow.'

'See yer.' Maurice cocks a leg into the car and nods towards the trolley. 'Looks like it's good and strong.'

'Yeah. It was good today.'

'Yes. Bye.'

Chapter 48

Twitch and Luke have arranged to meet on a Saturday at the viewpoint overlooking the Callun Valley, a local beauty-spot. The children are with their fathers so the entire day is at their disposal. She has concealed her plans from Fee.

A light, warm breeze blows fronds of hair across her eyes as she puffs up the final hill towards Luke whose eyes squint against the sun, his hair awash with gold.

Although they have dated a few times, the relationship has got no more physical than a brief hug and a peck on the cheek. Luke seems to sense Twitch's nervousness and up to now, hasn't as much as held her hand. Today, she feels, may be different.

'I thought we might cycle a bit further if you're not too tired,' he suggests when they have greeted one another.

'As long as it's downhill!'

'It is as a matter of fact. There's a piece of woodland - there.' He points to a spot a couple of miles along the valley. 'Can you see it? Most of it's closed off for repairs to the footpaths, and there are signs round it, saying, 'No Entry', but I found a bridleway they haven't taped off. It leads to the lake. There won't be a soul around so we can have our picnic in peace.'

'Sounds wonderful. Lead the way.'

Luke is riding a different bike today with fatter tyres and thicker framework. He explains that he has borrowed it from a friend as his own cycle is not suitable for this sort of terrain. As they ride along, side by side, Twitch feels a delicious anticipation.

As Luke predicted, the little woodland is deserted.

Luke flaps a tartan rug onto the earth and pulls food, then a bottle of wine, from his rucksack. The fact of their rule breaking adds a frisson to the increasingly charged atmosphere. Each movement, each brush of hand against hand, causes Twitch's heart to thud.

With fumbling fingers Luke opens the bottle and pours wine into two tumblers, presenting one to Twitch and wedging the bottle between the roots of a tree. He raises his glass, making no toast, and swallows. Twitch mirrors his action, then they dig into the food. She's hungry - it must be the exercise. Afterwards they sip their wine and stare at the water in silence. Luke sits, a few inches from her and still he doesn't make a move. When she has almost given up hope, he puts down his wine and turns his face to her. His kiss is tender, exploratory, just what Twitch had hoped for. Her confidence grows and she opens her mouth wide to his, her tongue snaking round his teeth and her body pressing against him. With only the birdsong to keep them company, they give rein to their passion.

Chapter 49

Fee looks at her watch for the third time - it's getting late. She goes to the hallway, and as is her habit on a Friday, winds the grandfather clock. If she left it to Twitch, the clock would never tick. She checks her wrist and adjusts the minute hand of the old timepiece a fraction. She peers through the bottle glass in the front door but sees no movement outside.

A fresh, crusty loaf sits on the table, its flaky surface gleaming under the soft glow of the dining room light. It will be served later with a salmon salad. They've promised themselves a healthy evening with no wine, as both have been hitting the bottle too much since Millie went. Only Kitty is at home, tucked up now and fast asleep. Maurice turned up mid-afternoon looking so flustered she felt guilty. Mick picked up Lucas and Olivia at lunch time, but Paul made some excuse that he had business elsewhere.

Aware of Twitch's fragile state of mind Fee has been trying to get home from work earlier and as a result, her meticulous attention to detail has slipped, causing raised eyebrows in the office. To add to complications, she has started seeing Will, and he wants more from their relationship than she is ready to give.

She glances at her watch again. What can have happened to Twitch? It's good that she is making a social life for herself, but it would be nice to get a call. Earlier she had dialled Twitch's mobile, to be greeted by its ring-tone, shrilling from the kitchen.

At eight o'clock, Fee gives up waiting and with rising indignation loads a plate and sits at the breakfast bar sipping fruit juice, resisting the temptation to change it for something stronger.

At nine o'clock she calls the hospital. Nobody matching Twitch's description has been admitted. If Twitch hasn't had an accident then what can be keeping her? One heard of people walking out on their families. Can Twitch have been sicker than Fee or the doctor had realised? On an impulse, she picks up the telephone again and dials a number from memory.

'Hello?' Will's warm and comforting voice comes through the ether, and she is dismayed to find tears erupting from her eyes.

'Fee, is that you?' Will's voice sounds far away. It is, she realises, somewhere in the North Sea.

'Will.'

'Has something happened?'

'I don't know. I suppose - probably not, but...'

'What's the matter?'

She blurts out her fears for Twitch's safety, the cycle ride with friends unknown, the missed meal, the dark night, the telephone left behind. There is a long silence.

'Hello. Will? Are you still there?'

His voice comes back. 'Yes. Sorry. I was just wondering what to say. I'm so far away I can't really help.'

He asks a few questions then says, 'She'll be back. I expect she's lost track of time, or decided to go for a meal. She can't call you, can she? Not without a phone. I'd go to bed. She'll come creeping in, in the early hours of the morning.' It is a comfort to hear his pragmatic advice.

'When will you be home?' She asks.

'Thursday evening. Don't worry, she'll come home. Text me when she gets in, to put my mind at rest.'

Fee ends the call and decides to take his advice. She washes and dries her plate and cutlery and puts them away, then wipes round the kitchen and turns off the light, switching on a table lamp to provide a hospitable warmth in the hall. Kitty lies, mouth open, her hair a blond froth on the pillow. Fee pulls the duvet over her slender shoulders and starts her own night time routine, her ears straining for sound from the street. Cars cruise by, and alcohol-noisy voices pass on the pavement but there is no clicking of the gate latch, or footstep on the path.

Not knowing is worse than hearing the worst of truths. Fee reclines onto her pillows and picks up a book, then turns it face down on the covers in front of her and stares at her empty room. After a long time, she floats into an edgy doze.

***

It is still dark when her eyes fly open. Something has woken her. Deluged with relief she swings her bare feet to the carpet. There's no light under Twitch's bedroom door, she must either be asleep or downstairs. Fee crosses the landing and opens Twitch's door with care. The flat outline of the bed is bathed in the light of a street lamp shining in through the unclosed curtains. The slow tick and tock of the grandfather clock percusses in the deep silence downstairs. It whirrs, and chimes, one, two and three. Time to call the police.

***

Two blue topped heads, bob beyond the thick glass. Fee pulls open the door, her head light and senses heightened. Two uniformed policemen stand before her in the watery dawn. One is young, with a smooth, lively face, and the other, older and more collected, with the ruddy visage and expanded girth of high blood pressure and a penchant for beer or doughnuts.

They sit, side by side on a settee like a comedy duo.

She offers, 'Coffee? Tea?' They decline, so she sits in an armchair facing them, and explains the situation to PCs Robins (older) and Porter. PC Robins, leans forwards, and the springs in the settee clamour their objection.

'I know this is worrying, Mrs Thomas,' he says, his sympathetic face bobbing up and down, 'but most people turn up unharmed within forty eight hours, so try to relax.'

'I hope you're right.' She wants to cry. 'It's hard not to worry.' She takes a steadying breath. 'What will you do if she doesn't come home?'

'If Mrs Roman doesn't return by tomorrow, I'll talk you through the procedures. As I said, it probably won't come to this'.

Fee fixes her attention on the older man as if the act of listening will contribute to Twitch's return.

'It depends on how seriously we view the risk to your, er, friend.' PC Robins' face takes on a deeper hue of red and the younger officer beside him, looks at the ceiling.

Fee ignores his discomfort and waits. He clears his throat and his manner becomes business-like. 'Perhaps you could explain more about your domestic arrangements.'

Fee describes their circumstances, and the policeman seems to relax. 'So Mrs Roman's husband may be able to shed some light on the situation?'

'Maurice? I suppose he might. He doesn't know about this yet.' Fee gives her head a hopeless shake, 'This is really unlike Twitch, that's why I'm so worried about her.'

PC Robins explains, 'If Mrs Roman hasn't turned up in twenty four hours we'll escalated enquiries, check her mobile and computer, and search the house and garden. We'll do a house to house, and CCTV footage of the area will be checked to see if we can work out her movements last evening.

The older policeman's face puckers. 'Do you have a photograph of Mrs Roman? Twitch, do you call her? If you could find one before we come back - if we come back - it will save time.'

'I'll have a look now.'

Fee runs upstairs to Twitch's room, feeling like an imposter. There is an air of waiting about the room, as if it's holding its breath. Feeling uncomfortable she opens the wardrobe, and the smell of Twitch's perfume wafts out. *Twitch, please be alright.* Fee slides her hand along the shelf above the rail, and finds slippers and scarves, but no box of pictures or photograph album. She stands on tiptoe in the middle of the room and cranes her neck to see the top of the cupboard - nothing up there at all. Under the bed, in the drawers, it's as though Twitch had no life before coming to Crispin Road.

Back in the lounge she drops into a chair and reaches for her phone to find a group photo, taken at the beach hut. She hasn't looked at it since Millie's death, afraid to see that vivacious face laughing out at her.

'I have this.' She hands over the mobile. 'I could email it to you if you think it'll help, otherwise you could try Maurice.'

PC Porter records Maurice's address, and takes a description of Twitch, along with the contact details or their doctor and dentist.

When the two men have taken their jingling leave, Fee closes the door and leans on it for a moment listening to the thick silence, then she picks up the telephone.

Chapter 50

Yesterday evening was fabulous even though Maurice was expecting a night in front of the television. He took the boys to the cinema, having first fed them on KFC. After the film, they indulged in outrageously priced ice cream in the foyer and Josh fell asleep as soon as he was strapped into his car seat and remained fast asleep, hanging like a hefty rag doll over Maurice's shoulder as he was hauled up the stairs, threaded into pyjamas and tucked under his duvet. Maurice and Sam sat in front of the television for half an hour before Sam too went to bed.

Now, at the breakfast table, Josh fills his mouth with toast and strawberry jam, dried daubs of the previous evening's chocolate ice cream still decorating his face. Sam pipes up, 'What shall we do today Dad? Can we go swimming?'

Swimming, especially at the weekend when the sultry building is crowded and noisy, is not an appealing prospect. The slimy floors of the cubicles will be littered with soggy tissues and lost sticking plasters, and the bins will be overflowing with used nappies. The last time Maurice took the boys to their local pool they were called from the water because a baby had defecated in it. They stood around waiting until two members staff appeared with a long-handled fishing net and simply scooped out the offending 'floater' before announcing that they could re-enter. The experience led Maurice to insist that future visits are limited to week-day evenings. This doesn't stop Sam trying to change his mind at every opportunity.

'Sorry son, you need to be back at Mum's this morning, apparently you need new shoes.' Josh stuffs the last piece of toast into his mouth and slides from his chair to the floor. Maurice grabs him by the arm, to prevent escape, and snatches the dishcloth from the sink to scrub at the chocolate and jam.

Josh splutters from its folds, indignant and breathless. 'Yuk Daddy. Smells yuk!' Maurice sniffs at the cloth, which does indeed stink. He lobs it towards the washing machine. 'Sorry Joshy. Let's go upstairs and do it properly. 'Come on Sam-boy, you could do with a clean too.'

The telephone trills from the kitchen and Maurice skips back to pick up the receiver leaving Sam to deal with matters of hygiene for both boys.

'Maurice, it's Fee.' Her voice sounds tense.

'Hi Fee. How are you?'

'Maurice, Twitch didn't come back last night. I was expecting her for dinner and she didn't turn up.' Fee's wobbling voice rises an octave. 'I don't know what's happened to her but can you keep the boys for now?' Maurice sits down on Josh's crumb covered chair and hunches over the receiver keeping his voice low. 'Do you think she's OK?'

'I don't know Maurice. I'm concerned.' With a wobbling voice, she tells him about the events of the previous day.

'Of course, I'll keep them here. Try and stay calm Fee, we don't know anything yet, and let me know when she turns up.'

There's a wet sound of Fee blowing her nose. 'Thanks Maurice. I'm about to call Mick and Paul. I rather hope they can have their children too, until I know what's what. It'll be difficult not to pass on my anxiety if they're here.'

Swimming is now unavoidable. Brushing the back of his trousers he goes to the foot of the stairs. 'Josh, Sam. Good news. Mummy's been held up so shoe shopping's cancelled. Let's go swimming.' The boys squeal, and hurtle off to find their trunks. Maurice checks the battery on his phone and sticks it in his pocket.

Once in the water, Sam, already a strong swimmer, strikes out towards the deep end and is soon cavorting with school friends. Anxious Josh clings to Maurice, nervously demanding to be towed around, and to ride on Maurice's slippery back. Maurice splashes Josh, trying to give him confidence, but his thoughts are on Twitch.

After a couple of hours, they all patter into the changing area. As the boys stand dripping and shivering, Maurice fumbles with the plastic-coated locker key, squinting with sore eyes. He loads himself up with a Crackerjack armful of bags, jackets and shoes, and directs the boys into a family cubicle. As soon as he's dumped the belongings, and wrapped his sons in towels, he looks at his phone. There's a message from Fee.

Twitch still not here. Going bike shop. F x

Going to the bike shop? Maurice stares at the screen.

In the cafe, the boys sip hot chocolate and pick at a pale heap of drooping chips in a polystyrene tray. Maurice watches, his gut in a knot.

At home, he parks the boys in front of a DVD, and creeps outside to dial Fee.

'Oh, Hi Maurice. No news I'm afraid.'

He hadn't expected news - she would have called him.

'I wanted to find out about the bike shop - why did you go?'

'I thought I'd save time by going to the shop where Twitch bought her bike. To find the make and model and so on. I'm so unobservant, I couldn't even remember what colour it is.'

'How did you know where to go?'

'I found the receipt in Twitch's bedside drawer. I'm at home now, having a look through the rest of her things,'

Maurice can hear papers and books being riffled, and Fee's laboured breathing. 'I'm looking for something about her friends, or the art course but I haven't come across anything yet. It's as though she doesn't want to be found. I think I showed her an advert in the local paper but I don't remember the details now. There's been so much more to think about.

'Maurice, the police need a photo of Twitch; do you have anything suitable?'

'I'll see what I can find.' He looks up as Sam appears at the back door. 'I have to go now Fee. Keep me informed though, won't you?' He hangs up and turns to his son.

'What's up Dad?'

'Nothing to worry about Sam-boy. Mummy's a bit tired, that's all. She needs a rest, so you two are to stay with me for a while. Isn't that great?'

Sam looks dubious but doesn't argue, turning instead to help Josh reach a bag of crisps from a wall cupboard.

The phone rings again, and this time it's Paul. Maurice lowers his voice to update Paul. His reaction is immediate. 'Come over here. I'm going to collect Kitty, now but I'll be back in half an hour or so. I've got pizza in the freezer and beer in the fridge.'

***

The cellophane wrappers from two frozen pizzas, squeak as Paul balls them and presses the pedal of the bin. Topsy's eyes follow his every movement round the kitchen, her wet nose quivering in the air. Maurice leans against the kitchen door frame, while in the small living room, the boys and Kitty are engrossed in a cartoon. They wait in silence for the pizzas. The dog sniffs round the skirtings, extending her pink tongue every now and again to clean up crumbs.

Paul puffs out his cheeks and blows a gentle breath. 'You think Mick's OK? He might need help with the kids if he's got work this w...' There is a shrill ring on the doorbell, and he heads along the hall, with Topsy wagging at his heels. 'Oh, Hi mate, that's a coincidence. *Down*, Topsy.' He nods at the children, 'Go on in with the others, guys,' and pushes open the door to the sitting room.

The smell of basil and dough seeps through the small flat, and Paul takes the food through to the children. Topsy follows the aroma into the sitting room and lowers her bottom to the carpet, her brown eyes tailing each biscuity slice as it heads for demolition between small teeth. 'Don't feed the dog.' Paul give them a fierce look. 'She'll get fat.'

In the kitchen, the three men pull the rings from beer cans.

'How you feeling man?' Mick speaks quietly to Maurice.

'I don't know. OK.'

Paul sits down at the kitchen table and stares at the two oven trays, side by side in front of him.

'Fuck me, this is hard.' He stacks the two baking trays and rubs the corners with his thumb.

'Watch your language, man.' Mick, swings his leather jacket off and drops it over the back of a chair. With a deft movement, he spins the chair and sits astride it, folding his arms along the heavy, brown leather. Paul shoves his hands into his armpits and turns his face to stare out of the window.

Mick is business-like. 'First thing we got to do is plan for the next, say, week. I'm working all hours, but I've been thinking about what to do with Luc and Livvie.' He pauses. 'I think I'll have to give my mum a call. Maybe they can go to her for a while.'

'Well, that won't help me and Maurice.' Paul stands and picks up the trays. 'No. We need to find someone to look after them all.'

'I could ask Ma to come up here.' Mick is pretty sure that Gloria will leap at the chance to help her only son - and interfere in the raising of her grandchildren. 'If she'd come, that would solve everything – well almost everything. Maybe she could stay with Fee.' Mick looks at Paul for confirmation, and his friend nods.

'I'll call her now.' Mick pulls out his phone. 'Hello Ma…' He goes back into the hall and out of the front door pulling it behind him until only a crack of light shows between it and the frame.

Paul passes Maurice another beer and they swig, and wait, listening to the laughter of the kids in the other room and the muffled tones of Mick's voice, rising and falling.

Mick returns with his thumb up. 'She's coming. I spoke to Fee, too. She said it'd be OK. She seems a bit out of it.

'Blimey, I've never known that happen before.' A look of satisfaction crosses Paul's face. 'What are we going to tell the kids? Maurice, what do you want to say to your two?'

The easiest option is to stick to Maurice's original tale: Twitch is tired and needs a rest so she is going away for a little while. Who's to say it isn't the truth, anyway?

Maurice's phone shrills in the little kitchen and they tense. 'Hello.'

'Mr Roman?'

'Yes?'

'This is Chelterton Valley Police, PC Porter speaking.'

'Oh, hello Constable.' Maurice looks at his friends and they raise their eyebrows. He straightens his back. 'Have you news about my wife – ex-wife?'

'No sir, I'm sorry there's no news as yet. We'd like to talk to you though, a matter of routine. May I ask where you are, Sir?'

Maurice offers to return to his house to meet them. 'I understand you need a photo. I can look one out while you're there.'

Paul signals that the kids can stay for a while, and Maurice nods and smiles his thanks.

When Maurice has left, Paul turns to Mick. 'And then there was one,' he murmurs.

Chapter 51

Gloria, driven by Mick, arrives at Crispin Road on the following Friday, with three huge bags. After hefting them into the hall Mick dashes back to work with a promise to collect the children from school and see them later.

The two women appraise one another in front of the clock.

'Hello Gloria.'

'Pleased to meet you Fee.'

Gloria's hand is hard and dry in Fee's, as she announces in a crisp voice, 'We need to get things straight from the start. I'm happy Mick asked me to come, and I'm very sorry for your troubles, but this arrangement is strictly on a trial basis.'

Fee goes to interject but Gloria ploughs on. 'We don't know each other. Don't know nothin' about one another, so let's just take it one day at a time.'

This is perfectly acceptable to Fee. Her overwhelming memory of Mick's mother is of the small and smartly clothed woman, glaring from under the fish net pelmet of a pill box hat at Millie's funeral. She decides that courtesy is the way forward. 'Would you like a cup of tea - or coffee?'

'Tea would be lovely. I'll hang my coat up here.' Gloria tucks her brightly coloured rayon scarf into the arm of her camel coat and strains to reach the high coat hook.

'Let me.' Fee takes it and hangs it among the rest of the family outer wear, which includes Twitch's knitted jacket, left in preference for a waterproof one on the evening of her outing.

'I can see I'm goin' to need a ladder round here.' There is a re-assuring twinkle in Gloria's eye.

They sit in the lounge and Gloria asks Fee how the children are coping with all the upheaval. 'I tried to ask Mick but you know what men are like, he just said they're not bad.'

'He's been really supportive, in fact they all have. They've helped with the practical things - like getting you up here. I'm so grateful Gloria.'

'Aww, don't feel like that. I bet I'm goin' to love bein' with the kiddies. It'll be like a holiday for me.' Fee is staggered at Gloria's speedy change of attitude.

There is something maternal and essentially comforting in Gloria's presence. The two women chat, and Fee learns that the person sipping daintily from her china mug of sweet tea, has received and returned many of life's knocks and blows. A kindred spirit? Maybe.

Once the tea has been drained they hoist Gloria's bags upstairs and drop them on the floor of Twitch's room. Lucas and Olivia have doubled up with Sam and Josh to make room for the new guest.

'I'll unpack later.' Gloria looks round approvingly. 'Very nice.' She pokes her head into Twitch's sparsely filled wardrobe. 'This will do me fine for now.'

At lunch time the women continue to weigh one another up over a chicken sandwich. Fee tries to tell Gloria about the children's routines and idiosyncrasies.

'I realise now how much Twitch did. I was so wrapped up in work. I keep wanting to ask her, "Where's this?" or "How do I do that?"'. She shakes her head, then stands to clear the table.

When the doorbell rings, Gloria is outside, exploring the garden and sticking her nose into the shed.

'Hi Mick. Hello, you lot' Fee smiles a welcome to the children as they mass into the hall. 'Have you time to come in this time, Mick? Your mum's settled in and I'm sure she'd like to see you.'

Lucas and Olivia dance out to the garden to hug Granny, dragging her in to meet the others. More tea is brewed but Fee notices that all the time he is drinking, Mick is checking his watch and tapping his fingers. Soon he is saying his goodbyes, telling Gloria that he will look in again when he can.

When he has gone the children escort Gloria back to her bedroom, and Fee loads plates and cups into the dishwasher before following. She stands in the doorway and watches as the children 'help' Gloria unpack.

Kitty takes great interest in Gloria's belongings: her sensible shoes and contrastingly flamboyant dresses, her blurry and amateurish photographs, one of Mick as a child in Regents Park, peeping from behind a tree, another of him sitting on a wall outside Southwark Cathedral, his feet dangling and his socks smart and straight. Last is a photo of her long dead husband, a big man with a strong resemblance to Mick. He stands proudly at the bottom of a staircase in some dingy hallway.

Lucas and Olivia look important as they bear Granny's belongings to the drawers and wardrobe, and struggle to hang dresses and cardigans on lop-sided hangers. Sam holds Josh's hand and quietly follows Kitty as she touches and fiddles where she should not. Eventually Gloria shoos them out to play.

Fee goes back to the kitchen to make a snack for the children. There are no biscuits or cakes, not even grubby and shapeless ones, so she spreads a few crackers with seedless raspberry jam. At her shout, they thunder from their rooms, taking the stairs in their individual ways. Sam waits at the bottom to help Josh, and when all the children are together in the hall, they huddle into the kitchen as one.

Minutes later Gloria, singing powerfully and tunefully, creaks along the landing, and they listen to the melody tail off and sedate footsteps mark her progress from tread to tread and into the kitchen. 'Well, what a lovely scene.' She moves across to the table and peers at the plate. 'Looks like we need to go shopping though, I should think you need some nice healthy fruit to be snackin' on.'

Fee accepts the criticism with grace. Of the two of them Gloria will make the better carer. Fee is out of the habit of catering, insofar as she ever did it. In the old days, there was always food in her freezer but it was more likely to have been from M & S, than home-made.

She puts two mugs of tea onto the work top, and Gloria mounts a stool with some difficulty. When she finally settles, with her back to the children, she seems in the wrong setting, like a princess taking tea in a caravan. Despite the stress of the situation Fee smiles to herself. Breakfast bars are unsuited to dignified, portly ladies, especially if their feet don't reach the foot rail.

Fee slides with ease onto the other stool, resisting the urge to suggest, as she watches Gloria shovel two heaped teaspoons of sugar into her tea, that she has fruit instead. The older woman leans across the granite surface and gives Fee's hand a squeeze.

'You leave it to me now dear. I can get a taxi to the town and do a bit of shoppin' you don't need to worry.' Although she speaks quietly, Fee can see the children pricking up their ears. Gloria raises her voice to include them. 'I'm goin' to need some help findin' my way around this place.' She speaks over her shoulder. 'Can you to show me around the town? We could all fit into one of those minibus taxis.'

Sunshine creeps into the window behind Gloria forcing Fee to squint at her silhouette. 'We'll all fit into the people carrier. I'll drive, there's no need for a taxi.'

They finish their tea, and Fee sends the children to do their homework. Gloria wastes no time starting a shopping list. Opening and closing cupboards she tuts and grumbles at the paucity of supplies and the sticky marks on shelves, in much the same way her son had done in Mo's kitchen.

On the journey to Watco, Gloria and Fee speak only of practicalities. It turns out that although she doesn't have a car in London, Gloria passed her driving test a few years ago. Fee decides that she must be added to the insurance for this car but Gloria is worried about driving such a big vehicle. Fee scans the roadside and fields as she drives, hoping to catch a glimpse of Twitch but it seems a waste of time. Then something catches her eye. She drives on without comment.

They cruise along Chelteton's High Street, and Fee points out the superstore, the market place, and various shops, including the deli. 'The church is up there.' She indicates the spire but turns right at the lights so they don't have to pass the workmen dealing with the blackened remains of Feast. They cause a small traffic queue at the front of Watco, while Fee chivvies them out, promising to pick them up in three quarters of an hour, then, alone in the car, she swings round the parking lot to retrace her journey.

About half a mile out of town she slows to a crawl. The car behind swerves round her and accelerates away with a loud blast of his horn. Fee's pulse accelerates with it. Edging along the road she cranes her neck, convinced she had seen something in a field on her right, but which field? Then she sees it.

The car bounces off the road and settles at an angle in a dry tractor rut. Fee steps out and sticks her phone into the back pocket of her jeans. Cars whoosh past behind her, and the air resonates with the sounds of birds and flies. Fee places a flat shoe onto the bottom rung of a metal gate. Horses graze in the middle of the meadow, and on the far side, beyond their swishing tails and stooping heads, something under the hedge is catching the light. She cocks her leg over the gate and picks her way among heaps of dung and grassy tussocks. When she reaches the object, she pulls out her phone.

Chapter 52

The back wheel of a push-bike projects from under the hedge, its electric-blue frame gleaming in the late afternoon sunlight. The front wheel has been shoved between dock leaves and nettles into a ditch. Fee looks about, squinting into the setting sun. Behind the hedge, a narrow track, leads from the road and round two sides of the field, to climb the hill beyond.

The sound of a vehicle manoeuvring in low gear attracts her attention. A police car has pulled up next to the people carrier, and she watches a uniformed officer unfold himself from the driver's seat and hold his hand above his eyes, sweeping his gaze round the field.

She waves, and he grasps the gate, flinging his body over the top bar in an athletic leap. Fee watches stride across the field. As he gets close he extends his hand.

'Mrs Thomas? I'm P.C. Allen.' Fee shakes the large, moist hand and wipes her palm on the back of her jeans.

Standing side by side, she and PC Allen observe the bicycle. 'Do you recognise the bike Mrs Thomas?'

'Well, it could be Twitch's but to be honest I'm not a great bike rider and I'm afraid I didn't pay much attention when she showed her bike to me. I wish I had now'. She looks at PC Allen. 'I have got the receipt at home though; I could let you have it later. I went to the bike shop yesterday and the lady told me the make and model. I can't see the writing on this one from here and I didn't want to disturb anything'.

PC Allen excuses himself and walks a few paces away, pulling out his radio. Fee strains to hear his murmured conversation as she stares at the bike. Her heart tells her it belongs to Twitch, and her body begins to shake.

The policeman raises his voice. 'Affirmative,' then, 'Roger, out.'

Fee takes a deep breath and puts on her calm mask.

The officer strolls back, and nods in the direction of the bike. 'It shouldn't take too long to identify this, once you've given us details.' He gives Fee permission to leave the scene but says she should make herself available later when a member of CID will come to the house to take finger prints, collect the information about the bicycle, and take another statement.

As she crosses the field towards her car she glances at her watch. Gloria and the children will be waiting for her. Stepping onto the gate she looks back at PC Allen, who has his back to her and is facing a tree. He appears to be zipping his flies with a little policeman bob of the knees, and with the vestige of humour she can muster, Fee hopes he isn't contaminating a crime scene.

In the supermarket car park, Gloria's eyes are alternating between her watch and the entrance to the car park. An expression of relief crosses her face when she catches sight of the car.

On the way home, Fee, her eyes on the road, listens to the children telling her what they have bought. Like Millie, Gloria's tastes err towards the exotic, and the children seem excited to try something spicy and fruity.

'We'll cook it together,' Gloria promises the children as the car cruises past the farm gate.

'Why is there a policeman standing in a field?' Sam shouts suddenly, then bursts out laughing at the absurdity of the scene.

'P'raps he's guarding the horses,' suggests Kitty.

Fee puts her foot hard on the accelerator, and glances meaningfully at Gloria, who raises her eyebrows. 'I'll tell you later,' she murmurs.

Home again, Fee tells Gloria of the afternoon's events and the proposed police visit. Gloria pauses in the middle of loading a litre of semi-skimmed into the refrigerator. 'I'll take the kiddies upstairs when they get here. The big ones can help me get the little ones ready for bed'.

They finish unpacking the shopping in a silence.

Gloria and the children cook the evening meal, and Fee keeps out of the crowded kitchen. She paces through upstairs rooms, putting away toys and straightening pictures, then sits on her bed and stares out of the window. The repeated banging of the dinner gong jolts her back to reality.

The rice, fried plantain, vegetables and chicken are fragrant and tasty, but Fee coerces her throat to swallow. The children clear the table, and supervised by Gloria, Sam, Olivia, and Kitty wash and dry up, while Fee takes the little ones into the garden.

With Lucas on her hip Fee pushes the wooden baby swing, and Josh gives an untroubled hoot of pleasure.

'Higher, higher.'

'Not too high Josh, you might be sick after that big dinner.'

The doorbell shrills through the house, and hauling Josh's small legs from between the rungs of the swing seat Fee dangles him awkwardly to the grass, grabs him by the hand and they hurry inside to find Gloria standing at the open front door appraising a tall, attractive man in plain clothes. The man clasps a laptop bag and presents his identification to Gloria like a flash card. Fee hurries forwards and passes Josh to Gloria, who smiles into Josh's face, touching her nose to his. 'OK. Time to get ready for bed, young man.' She raises her voice to call the others. 'Everyone follow me.' Her tone brooks no argument and the children troop upstairs, the older ones glancing back curiously at the man on the step.

'Sorry about that. We're trying to protect the children until we know more.' Fee follows him into the sitting room. The policeman hitches up sharply creased suit trousers, and lowers himself onto the sofa, dumping the laptop bag on the floor beside him.

She offers tea, knowing from experience that he'll probably say no, and when he refuses she closes the lounge door and crosses the room, collecting an upright, wooden chair from a corner to sit on.

The man stands up.

'Mrs Thomas...'

'Ms.' She too rises.

'Sorry - Ms Thomas. I'm D.S. Bailey.' He takes a step towards her and gives an engaging grin. 'I understand you found a bike in a field on the outskirts of Chelterton today.'

'Yes.'

'Well done. Would you mind telling me how you managed that? It was quite a way from the main road.'

Is he doubting her? 'I've got into the habit of looking for Twitch - Ms Roman – when I'm out. In the past she's suffered from depression, and I'm worried about her. She could be wandering anywhere. I saw the metal glinting in the sunshine and decided to look.'

Upstairs Gloria calls the children to their baths. Music starts up in a bedroom, footsteps thump and the ceiling groans.

'I have the make and model of the cycle now.' Fee picks up the shop receipt.

The officer flips open a note book.' I have the details of the one in the field.'

'It was a Claud Butler, Cambridge, Hybrid, Classic,' she reads from notes in her own hand, on the reverse of the slip of paper.

Bailey raises his eyes. 'That's what I've got written here.' They stare at each other, then D.S. Bailey clears his throat. 'This could be a coincidence of course, but your friend has been missing some time now, and the bike turning up makes the circumstances suspicious, so I think it's time to escalate enquiries. Did the other officers explain to you what will happen now?'

Fee nods, 'Searches, house to house enquiries and following up leads.'

'Exactly.' The officer nods. 'We'll need to collect finger prints from here – to eliminate you all from our enquiries. Do you mind?'

Eliminate you from our enquiries? Policemen really say that? Fee agrees, and from then on, the similarity to a police drama fades. The detective extracts a brush, and a bag of black dust from his pocket and proceeds to dab the dust over door handles, windows and anything shiny in the room without the aid of a single forensic expert. Fee watches with interest as prints are revealed in the powder, and he uses sticky tape to collect them.

She is anxious that he won't go upstairs.

'I should think I'll get all the prints I need from down here.' He slips the pieces of sticky tape into envelopes and pops them in his pocket. In the living room, he stoops to pick up his laptop, unzipping it deftly. 'I have to fill in this blooming form.' He looks up at her and screws up his nose. 'Computers!' he flips his eyes upwards, 'I spend half my time on one these days. Now...'

Fee sits back on her wooden chair, and watches him hike up the trouser legs again. He draws a pair of reading glasses from his breast pocket, and squints at the open machine on his knees.

'Sorry about this. I have to log on...' Fee waits, her hands clasped on her knees.

'OK, here we go. Right. I have to ask you all these questions, then when we have everything completed it'll go onto the main police computer and can be used by Interpol and so on.'

He asks about Twitch's appearance, her frame of mind. 'Did you say she was depressed? '

'Well, she *was*. She has a history of depression but I thought she was getting better. She'd been to the doctor and was taking tablets, and I've been trying to give her some time for herself, you know, to do her art and go to galleries. She seemed happier, but...'

D.S. Bailey notes down the contact details of Twitch's doctor and dentist again, places she might have visited, and details of friends and family.

As Fee speaks, the saliva in her mouth evaporates. 'Are you sure you won't have that drink. I'm going to have one myself.'

'No thank you Ms Thomas, but you go ahead. I can come out to the kitchen if you like.' He clicks the laptop closed.

In the kitchen Fee glances at the detective sitting at her breakfast bar, and is startled to see a marked change in his demeanour. His back is straight, and the friendly eyes have become hard and business-like.

'May I ask a few questions about *your* movements yesterday, when Mrs Roman went missing?'

'Me?' She pauses. 'I was here, in the house when she went out. We were going to have supper when she got back. Salmon. Sorry, I don't suppose you want to know what was on the menu.'

The detective is silent, gazing at her with an unreadable expression. She continues to describe her evening and then her disturbed night.

The officer asks about times, television programmes and conversations with Twitch, then he says, 'And your other friend, Millie, was it? What were you doing the night, when *she* died?'

'When Millie died?' Fee's mind goes blank, and sweat prickles under her arms. 'I, I can't remember. Just a minute, let me think.' She rubs her cheeks, dragging her hands past the corners of her mouth.

After careful probing, the policeman drags from her the painful events of the morning of the explosion, and the night before. His fingers fly over the keys of the computer, and when Fee can think of nothing more to tell him, he says, 'Thank you Ms Thomas.' He slides the laptop back into its sleeve. 'I think I have everything I need now so I'll get out of your way. Some uniformed officers will be here later. They'll need access to the house and garden, to look round in case they can find any

224

clue to what might have happened.' He pauses, looks at her with a serious expression. 'One more thing. If we were to ask you to be part of a television appeal, would you be prepared to do it?'

Fee's eyes widen. Isn't the person weeping on the television, the one who turns out to be the kidnapper? Then there would be the speculation - *I bet she's a dyke. Ooh, I've seen her in town, right stuck up.*

'I don't really want the children to see anything on the news unless it's absolutely necessary. As I said, I haven't told them yet. Once I have, I suppose I would, if you thought it would help. Or perhaps Maurice would do it.'

When he has left Fee glances at her watch and goes to the telephone.

***

Fee relates the latest news to a shocked Maurice. In the background is a deep, familiar voice and after telling Maurice all she knows, she asks to speak to Mick.

'Hey Fee; what's going on?'

'I found a bike in a field outside the town this morning. Mick, we don't know yet if it's Twitch's so tell Maurice to keep calm. It's a good thing you're there with him.'

'Yeah.'

'Mick?'

"Yeah?'

Fee takes a slug of cold coffee. 'Your mum's being a fantastic help. I don't know how I'd have managed without her this morning. Are you happy for me to invite her to stay longer?'

Mick's voice goes up a surprised semi-tone. 'It's up to her. I'd be surprised if she didn't want to stay. I expect you can tell how much she loves kids.'

Fee nods, 'Yes. If she does stay I was wondering if you'd help her get used to the car. She says she's passed her test but she's never driven. It would be most helpful if she could drive the children to various places. Would you mind?'

Mick is uneasy about trying to teach his mother anything, but says he'll give it a try.

'And, sorry to keep asking favours but I've bought her a mobile phone. While you're with her, could you help her get used to it?'

Mick explodes with mirth. 'Talk about dragging her into the 21st century - she hates those things. Are you going to get her a hands-free thing so she can drive and talk at the same time? Only joking.'

Several pairs of feet pound on the stairs. 'I have to go Mick; the children are coming. I'll leave that with you if I may?'
'OK Fee. Take care, and keep us posted.'

Chapter 53

'Mr Thomas, thank you for seeing us, sir.'

The three plain clothes officers struggle past Topsy's joyful welcome and huddle into Paul's small living room. The one who has spoken looks to be the older, although that may be because he is almost bald. He carries an air of authority. The other man is, Paul guesses, in his early forties with thick, wavy black hair. His suit is better quality and less creased than that of his companion.

They stand, surrounded by open cupboards and stacked boxes and while Topsy pokes her nose into each policeman's crutch, they introduce themselves as D.S. Bailey - baldy, and D.C. Parks - curly. They decline offers of seats and hot drinks.

'Mr Thomas,' Baldy is in control. 'We need to ask your movements on the day Mrs Roman went missing.'

Paul doesn't think about an answer. 'Why would you want to know that?'

'Simply eliminating people from our enquiries sir. Would you please answer the question?'

Curly takes a notebook from his pocket.

Paul pauses to consider his answer. 'Sorry mate, no idea. Can you remember what you were doing?'

'Mr Thomas, please think. As I said, we want to *eliminate* you from our enquiries.'

'Is Twitch dead then?'

'We haven't found Mrs Roman, Sir.'

'What enquiries are you eliminating me from?' Paul's former high spirits are waning, in fact he finds himself feeling quite stroppy, and this drives him to push between the two men and haul open the front door. 'I'd like you to leave.' He stares hard at them, his hand on the door catch. 'I'll have a think about where I was, and if I remember I'll let you know. I have a lot to do. I'm moving house as you can see by all these boxes.' He nods at the packing cases strewn round the flat. 'So, if you'd like to get on with your job of finding Twitch then I can get on with my packing.'

The policemen look back at him calmly. 'Only a couple more things, Mr Thomas.' D.S. Bailey's tone is friendly.

'About what?' Paul stands by the front door with his chin jutting out.

'About your relationship with Mrs – Ms Thomas, and the other ladies in that household.'

'The other ladies. You mean Millie and Twitch. Why would I have anything to do with them?' Fear creeps into his voice.

'Please stay calm Mr Thomas. We're simply trying to build a picture of the situation between you all. If you'd be kind enough to come back into the room we'll get this sorted out and be on our way.'

By the door, Topsy leans her body against Paul's leg. He gives her a stroke, 'Good girl,' and pushes the door shut, then pats his thigh. 'Come on Tops.' The dog, now large, lollops after him to the armchair and puts her chin on his knee. He rubs the warm head to still his shaking fingers.

Parks stands by the wall, while Baldy sits down in another chair. 'You must have felt very frustrated when Ms Thomas left you so suddenly.'

'Well it was a long time ago. I was upset at the time but I'm OK now. As you can see I'm making plans to move into a bigger place for the dog – and my kid.'

'Very nice Sir,' DS Bailey shows little interest, 'but I'm sure you were angry, perhaps you even wanted revenge?'

Paul's glares at the policeman in silence. Topsy pushes her muzzle under Paul's stilled hand but he ignores her. She licks it and he pulls it away, so with a swift movement, the dog leaps onto his lap and licks his face.

Paul bobs his head to one side to look round her huge body. 'Sorry officer, my dog seems to want to protect me.' He grins and his anger evaporates.

DS Baldy responds with a quick up and down of the corners of his mouth, and Paul pushes Topsy to the floor. With one hand holding the dog's collar he meets the officer's eyes. 'Look, I'm sorry I can't help you more. I've told you the truth. I can't remember what I was doing on that date but if I do remember I'll let you know. No problem.'

The policeman looks unconvinced, so Paul continues, 'I was upset when Fee left but so what? If I wanted to punish her I'd have done something long ago and anyway it would have cost me my kid. I may be stupid but I wouldn't risk that for anything.' He hopes he sounds sincere, hopes Topsy hasn't ruined his 'street cred.'.

When the policemen have left, letting themselves out, Paul remains in the arm chair with Topsy's collar trapped in his fist and murmurs, 'thanks Tops. I really needed to be sat on right then.' He releases her and stands up. Sod the packing, he needs a pint. He goes to the phone.

'Maurice?'

'Hi Paul, how goes it?'

Paul tells of the police visit.

'They've been here too, gave me a bit of a start actually. I felt as if I was a suspect.'

'Well, there's no body so I don't understand what all the fuss is about.' Maurice sounds less sure, 'Fee found Twitch's bike. Apparently, the police are escalating their enquiries, as the saying goes...' There's a pause then he goes on, 'I've done something a bit daft, I think.'

'What? What have you done Maurice?' What could he have done? The man's a disaster but he couldn't make things much worse.

'Sam asked me about Twitch, you know, where she was, and when she would come home and I…. Well… I told him.'

'Told him what?' Paul's voice is hard.

'That Twitch has disappeared. He went berserk. He thought Twitch had left because he was naughty.' Maurice rushes this latter part of his sentence into Paul's silence.

Paul looks at the ceiling.

'Bloody hell Maurice, what were you thinking of?'

'Well, he's got a right to know, hasn't he?'

'Yeah, but I thought we agreed.'

Maurice is gloomy, 'I know. You don't need to tell me. We were in the car when he asked. I told him and he started to screech. I had to mount the curb and stop to calm him down. The pavement was packed

- mums and bloody kids everywhere. Josh woke up with all the shouting and started to bellow too.'

Paul almost smiles at the mental picture of his inept friend coping with two squawking kids in the school rush hour. He relents.

'I could do with a pint, Mate. How are you fixed?'

'I'm up for that. I need one after the day I've had. I'm just going to take the children back to Fee. I don't think she's going to be too pleased with me either.'

'Oh well, it'll be OK in the end.' Paul adds a silent addendum: I bloody well hope so anyway!

Chapter 54

Fee has spent most of her time at work worrying about that police visit. She tidies papers on her desk and files some documents. At lunch time her boss, John, calls her into his office.

'Fee, forgive me for saying this but you're not really managing very well, are you?'

She takes a breath to speak but he holds up a hand.

'I quite understand. Don't worry, I'm not firing you. You're an excellent member of my team, and I'd hate to lose you.' He leans on the desk in his rolled-up shirt sleeves, and the scent of his aftershave wafts over. 'I'm worried about you Fee. This isn't like you, so I know things must be pretty dire.' He leans back again, and the back of his chair reclines under his weight. 'If you wouldn't mind, for my peace of mind, would you please go home and stay there until your family life is back to a something like normality?'

Fee looks at her hands, resting on her knees, and nods. She lifts her eyes to meet his. They are too sympathetic and she looks away.

At her desk, she gathers papers and walks round to Nick. 'I think you're going to need these.' She drops them in an empty space and grabs a pen. 'This is the password for my emails. I have to go home.' Nick picks up the heap, and the password. Does she detect triumph in his manner? Forget it. She turns away.

At the lift she waits, her back to the room, and jumps at the loud 'ping'. The doors open loudly, and behind her a murmur of voices begins to crescendo. Inside the lift she leans wearily against the wall, while the doors meet behind her like final curtains.

The drive home is speedy, the roads almost empty. When she pulls up in the drive Maurice's car is parked against the curb. Slamming the car door, she rushes up the steps.

Maurice is in the kitchen with Sam and Josh. The boys are wailing and Gloria is cuddling Josh to her bosom.

'What's happened? Is there news?'

Gloria looks over Josh's head and frowns slightly, shaking her head.

'Maurice?' Fee looks at him.

'Fee, can we go in there?' Maurice points towards the lounge door opposite.

In the empty room Fee shuts the door. 'What's going on Maurice? Is there news?'

'No Fee; nothing like that.' He hangs his head, exposing the beginnings of a bald patch. 'I'm afraid I've done something stupid. I didn't think it through.'

She waits.

'Sam asked me when Twitch would be back. I'm really sorry, but I told him the truth.'

She plops into a chair, and presses her palms to her eyes. 'He's upset. Of course he's upset.' She looks at her watch. 'The others will be back soon, I'll explain the truth to them, as I'm here.'

'Why are you home, anyway?'

'Oh, you know. There's a lot to do in the house. Work can manage without me for a while.'

'You've got a good job there. I couldn't have done that when Twitch left *me*.'

Fee pierces Maurice with a look.

'I'm only saying.' Maurice folds his arms across his chest.

'Well I need to get on now.' Fee rises to open the lounge door and holds it for him. 'Gloria and I will handle everything. Don't worry.' A lifetime of practice prevents her scorn from showing.

Sam and Josh have calmed down and are sitting at the kitchen table, each holding a mug of warm milk.

'Good for the nerves,' Gloria explains. 'So,' she looks at Fee, 'to what do we owe this unexpected pleasure?'

Before Fee can explain her presence, the doorbell rings. Paul hands Kitty in, and the child plants a peck on Fee's cheek and runs off to play.

'How are they?' asks Paul. 'Sam and Josh, I mean.'

'OK. I'll have to tell Kitty now though.'
'Yeah, I thought that. I think she'll be OK; it's the other two…'
'We'll cope.' Fee shutters her dry eyes with hot lids.
Paul nods and turns away. 'See you soon.'
'Yes.'

***

The children are all in bed and Fee can't erase the picture of their shocked faces when she told them the truth about Twitch. She hasn't eaten since breakfast but refuses Gloria's barrage of offers of food and advice, and dashes to her car with an urgency verging on hysteria.
'I have to be somewhere, Gloria. You'll be OK on your own, won't you?'
'Of course I will dear, but …'
The area at the front of the flats where Will lives was once a garden but has been compressed over years into parking space. She noses her car between posts, their gates long gone, and reverses at a haphazard angle into a space between a Fiesta and a shabby old Beetle.
Grabbing her bag and shoving herself from her seat she stabs Will's door bell and waits for his voice at the intercom. She climbs the worn, wooden stairs from the cool vestibule, taking deep drafts of air to control her tears.
Will stands at the top, and when he sees her face, gallops down to meet her. Taking her hand, and relieving her of her handbag, he draws her up the remaining stairs and into the flat, in silence.
Seating her on his sofa Will places a large glass of red wine into her hand, and sits beside her, scooping an arm round her shoulders. She can feel his breath, warm on her cheek but she stares at the wall opposite with its rather Avant-garde, russet coloured paint and huge and ornately framed bronze mirror above a traditional Georgian fireplace.
Will has been working hard on his flat since Fee first met him in the supermarket. True to his word he would accept no help. He said it was therapy; it kept him occupied during the long days when she was unable to get away because of one crisis after another. He's achieved a masculine but cosy space.
She takes a sip of the wine and puts it down on a side table and they sit in silence. Fee settles more comfortably into the crook of Will's arm and he strokes some hair from her forehead and kisses the top of her head.

'Thank you,' is all she can say.

'For what?' He's smiling, she can tell from his voice.

'For not clamouring; for giving me space and peace.'

'Me? Clamour?' He sounds mock affronted.

'Everything and everyone has been clamouring since Twitch went missing. You seem to know exactly what I need, so thank you.'

'It is,' he kisses the top of her head again, 'an absolute pleasure, ma'am. If you don't want to talk then it's fine with me. We can sit here all night if you wish.'

Abruptly Fee knows what she does wish. Ignoring her weariness, she reaches across, takes Will's face in her hands and kisses him on the lips. Her need grows and she rises to her knees on the settee and wraps her arms around his neck.

Will responds with passion and, after fumbling with her clothing for a while, gives a grunt of frustration, picks her up and carries her into the bedroom. They undress quickly and dive into bed to make desperate, urgent love. When they have fallen, shattered onto the pillows, and lain there for some minutes, Will reaches across and begins to explore Fee's body more slowly and thoroughly.

Later, she gazes at the ceiling from the comfort of Will's arm, and begins to talk in a low voice. Everything hitherto unsaid, flows from her lips: Her fears for the future, her childhood, her mother's death and her marriage break-down. When she has run out of words, she becomes aware that Will is still and unresponsive. She rolls onto her side to look at his face and meets a tense stare.

'Is there anything wrong?'

Will looks away. 'This sounds mad.' He seems to be addressing himself then he draws his eyes to her face. 'I just wondered if you would… Will you…?' He hesitates. 'Do you think you can…'

'What?' *Please, not that.*

'Marry me?'

Fee is silent, searching for adequate words

'Will…'

Will pulls his arm from her shoulders and twists away. 'I know. It's mad. Forget I asked. I shouldn't have put pressure on you, you've got enough on your plate. I thought it might help. We could look after the children between us. I could take some of the worries from your shoulders.' He turns to face her again and cups his palms over her naked shoulders.

234

Fee puts up her hand and strokes his fingers. 'No, don't blame yourself. I wasn't expecting it, that's all. I've been so preoccupied with everything that's going on...'

'I know. You don't need to explain, but I can't get you out of my head, and all this: Millie, and then Twitch, it's made me realise that you have to seize your chance when you can.' He pulls her to him. 'I love you Fee and I want to be with you. I don't want to spend my time in this flat, waiting for you to slip away from home as though we were having an affair.

'Look, forget marriage for now and look at this.' He leans over the side of the bed and picks up something from the floor - holiday brochures, thumbed and gaudy. 'Come away with me to Mauritius. You don't need to do anything except say yes. I'll do everything, book the hotel buy the tickets, get your new passport...'

'You *have* thought about this.'

He dumps the pile of magazines heavily onto her lap and they unfurl along the valley between her outstretched legs.

'How did you know I need a new passport?'

Will shrugs, looking a bit bashful. 'You mentioned it on our first date.' He shuffles towards her in bed and picks up one of her limp hands, laying it onto the stream of brochures. 'Don't answer me now; think about it. I was planning to go in September, after the school holidays. I know that will be harder, with the children, but you'll have Gloria, and Twitch might be back by then, and I suppose the children's fathers can help.

She remains silent. Up until tonight Will has avoided putting any pressure on her but now…

'I can't leave the children, or Gloria.' She blocks any objection by holding her hands in front of her face with the palms facing Will. 'I can't deal with this,' and she pulls away and swings her feet to the floor. 'I might love you too Will, but I can't think about it. Give it a week or two to see whether Twitch comes home. Let Gloria get more established, and then I'll give it some thought.' She looks at him sadly, 'I'm sorry. I'm not much company at the moment. I'm not saying no – to anything, just,' she hesitates, 'give me time.'

She pulls on clothes, while Will watches with obvious regret.

'You will come back?'

'Yes, yes of course. I won't run away, don't think that, but I need time to sort out everything else. You do understand, don't you?'

'I wish I'd kept my mouth shut. I've made things worse for you.'
'Well, maybe a bit more complicated.' Fee gives him a small smile, and sees him relax. He beams back and swings out of bed and into the bathroom.

She dresses quickly and gathers up her bag, keys and phone, overcome by a powerful need to be at home. As soon as he comes out she stretches an arm round his neck and kisses him on the lips. He tastes of toothpaste, and smells of soap. She's in a hurry, but something in his dejection pulls at her and on impulse, she raises her phone and takes his picture.

Outside, there's a chill to the darkness, and the car park is uneven beneath her feet. The noise of the engine is shocking in the night time peace, but when she peers up at Will's window, his curtains are still. She presses her foot on the accelerator, and directs the car between the gate posts. Her brain is already on home, and the car speeds up, too fast. She forces herself to slow down.

Chapter 55

Gloria has gone home for a couple of days to sort out something or other, and the children are at school. The house breathes quietly, with the grandfather clock at its heart. Although she often looks at the photo of Will on her phone, Fee has let a week pass before ringing him.

Standing in the empty hallway, Fee clears her throat and counts the rings, one, two, three ... There's a click and Will answers.

'Fee?' His voice sounds strained.

She keeps her tone light as she asks,

'How are you?'

'Feeling a bit worried - about you. Are you OK?'

'Yes, fine,' she pokes with her toe at a bit of fluff on the carpet then bends to pluck it up, and wanders into the kitchen holding the ear piece. She watches the feathery white stuff float into the bin and disappear into the darkness - like Twitch. 'I've been busy. I thought I'd call now to say goodbye.' She drags out a kitchen stool and lifts her hip onto it.

There's a pause, a heartbeat before he replies, 'Goodbye?'

'Yes, you're going back to your rig, aren't you?' She shuffles her behind more comfortably onto the seat and rubs the shiny worktop with her sleeve, to remove an imaginary smear.

Another short silence, then, 'Yes. Yes I am - on Thursday.' His voice takes on an eagerness. 'Can we meet before that? I'd like to see you before I leave, if you can make it.'

Fee pretends to look at her diary, then says, 'Yes, tomorrow looks fine,' and they decide to meet at Will's flat.

'I'll cook you a meal you won't forget. Maybe the way to a woman's heart is through her stomach.'

Fee is silent.

'I'm only joking Fee.'

'I know, sorry. You know food isn't high on my list of priorities. Eggs and chocolate, remember?'

There is a smile in his voice.

'I'll never forget. It'll be omelette with chocolate frosting then. See you later.'

She puts the phone down and it rings again.

'Good morning Ms Thomas, this is Chelterton Valley police.' The man's even voice is polite and business-like. 'We have some news about the bike, and other matters.'

'Oh?'

'We've been making enquiries about Mrs Roman's movements on the day she disappeared.'

'Well there must be plenty of people who can tell you about that evening. After all she was with a crowd...'

'Mrs Thomas.'

'Ms.'

'It seems Mrs Roman didn't meet a crowd of friends that evening. We need to talk to you about our findings and look at her room if we may?'

'Yes, yes of course. I'm here now if you want to come.'

She hangs up and lowers the phone. Twitch lied to her. The small piece of information that Fee had known, was a fabrication. She stares at the telephone in her hand.

***

The officers make themselves comfortable at the kitchen table, accepting this time the offer of a cup of tea. When Fee has dealt with the business of tea bags and coasters she joins them. D.S. Bailey and D.C. Parks introduce themselves and then Bailey clears his throat while Parks flips open his notebook.

'We've had confirmation that the bike you found belongs to your friend.' Bailey's voice is gentle.

Fee looks and waits.

'The fingerprints on the bike match those taken here, so there can be no doubt. As you know the bike is the same model and colour that Sabrina...'

'Twitch.' Fee interjects.

'...Twitch - bought from the bicycle shop.'

Fee's mind churns over the implications of this news. She's still taking in the news that Twitch wasn't out with her art friends. Could she have been lured away? Kidnapped? Killed? Or has she faked her own disappearance? Through all her worrying Fee has been convinced that Twitch disappeared on purpose. Perhaps the pressure got too much for her and she decided to walk away. You do hear of people who do that, then they turn up, maybe years later. The bike in the ditch changes everything. Twitch didn't take her car that evening, she would hardly have gone to the trouble of dumping her bike in a ditch so far from the school. Then again, she may not have gone to the school. She lied to Fee about her plans so anything could have happened. Fee shakes her head. 'What else have you discovered?'

'Well,' D.S. Bailey consults his notes, 'we went to the school where you told us the art class was held and interviewed Twitch's fellow students, and the art teacher, 'he refers again to his notes, 'Mrs Coombs.'

Fee waits for him to get to the point.

'It seems that there was no outing, in fact most of the students hardly remembered Sab..., er, Twitch.'

'The teacher must have remembered her though.' It seems important that someone remembers her lost friend.

'Well yes, she did, sort of...' She seemed to remember more about Twitch's art though, she thinks your friend has a notable talent.' The police officer looks at Fee with an unreadable expression. 'Mrs Roman seems to have gone to some trouble to keep her movements secret. Can you think of any reason why she would do that?'

'No, none. As I've said before Twitch used to suffer from depression, and she certainly kept that to herself, but once it was out in the open we dealt with it and I was keen for her to go out and enjoy herself. You know, meet some outsiders with a similar interest, and be free to be creative. That's supposed to help with depression, isn't it?'

D.S. Bailey shrugs. 'Could Mrs Roman have met somebody at another location? Perhaps she's come across a person somewhere else.'

Fee thinks. 'Well, there's the school. I didn't think she'd made any friends there but I suppose she may have done.'

'We've already been to the school gate. Mrs Roman seems to have kept to herself while waiting for the children.'

The questions go on for a while before the two officers ask to see Twitch's room, and Fee leads them upstairs.

'You can leave us to it, Ms Thomas.' She is dismissed. In the kitchen, she picks up a cloth and starts wiping. In the hallway, she pokes her fingers into the pockets of Twitch's crazily coloured woollen jacket and pulls out tissues, sweet papers, and a shopping list. She wanders into the lounge and straightens a cushion, listening for sounds of movement from above but all is quiet. After a while, the two men lope down the stairs and take to the garden. Fee watches them squint into the shed, cupping their hands round their eyes. They stoop over flower beds, paying particular attention to the partially dug vegetable patch. Twitch was trying to get it back under control, and Gloria has already had a stab at planting something or other.

At last they stamp their feet on the decking, and heave open the sliding door.

'Thank you, Ms Thomas.' There's no hint of their findings. 'We'll talk to the neighbours now. Do you mind if we leave our car outside?'

They take their leave, shaking Fee's hand at the front door, and promising to be in touch if anything arises. A curtain moves in the house opposite.

An hour later, Fee looks out of the lounge window to the road. The police car has gone. In the lonely room, she forces her mind to more practical matters: dinner, laundry and picking up the children.

She and Gloria have already fallen into a routine, and Fee is missing the help, and comforting strength of Mick's mother. There is a lot to do without her. Fee thinks ahead to the conversation they must have on Sunday. Not only must she tell of the latest events concerning Twitch, but also break the news that the following day, Gloria will have her first driving lesson with her son.

Chapter 56

Mick stands at the bottom of the stairs at Fee's. 'Right Ma, are you ready?'

'OK, just give me a minute, Son,' Gloria lowers herself onto a squat bedroom chair, and with fumbling fingers pulls on flat shoes. She had hoped that with all the distractions at home, Mick and Fee might forget about her blessed driving lessons. Oh well, better get this over with. She rises, wincing at the pain in her back and hips, and heads for the landing. Standing below her in the hall, her son is holding something flat and blue. It looks a bit like a plastic brief case. Gloria is too nervous to think about it.

'Come on Ma. It's going to be fine. I won't let anything go wrong.'

'I know son. I know.'

He holds open the front door. The large silver coloured car is parked on the road, and as they approach, Mick dangles the keys in front of her like a bit of bait on the end of a fishing line.

'Here Ma,' He gives them a shake, waiting for her to bite, 'you unlock it.' She takes the large black key from him and studies it. Mick points out a button depicting an open padlock and Gloria presses it. Lights flicker on the car and she hears a clunk.

'Well, I got that right anyhow.' Gloria smiles to herself. She's not feeling confident at all but you have to look on the bright side. It's only a car, a lump of metal with four wheels. She's been through far more traumatic things in her life than trundling along a few streets.

Hauling her tightly corseted body into this car has always been a struggle but when Gloria has tugged open the driver's door, Mick unfolds the mysterious, blue, plastic object, and places it, a folding stool, on the ground.

'There you are Ma. Service with a smile.'

She climbs in with ease. 'That's an excellent idea son but I don't think I can pick it up once I'm in here so unless you come with me every time I drive we need to think of another solution.'

'We'll work on that, but it'll do for now. OK, let's get on with the lesson.' He gathers up the step stool and climbs in beside her.

'Now,' his gaze moves to the controls of the car, 'how much do you remember?'

Gloria studies the dash board, and looks under the steering wheel at her feet. 'ABC.' she says

'ABC?'

Yes. Accelerator, brake, clutch.' Gloria has another look round the car. 'This is the gear lever, you got to check it's in neutral before you start the engine.' She gives the knob a wiggle. 'That's in neutral.'

'Good. See, it's all coming back.'

It is. She looks at the road. 'I can't see very well son. I think this car is too big for me.'

Mick stretches across her. 'I think we can change the height,' he grunts.

'Yes. Is that better?'

Gloria feels the seat rising. 'That's better, can you do it a bit more.'

The tarmac comes into view above the steering wheel, and Gloria feels like the Queen of the Road. 'Stop there. I can see now. Ooh I feel better already.' She reaches under the seat and slides it forward until her feet connect with the pedals. 'Much better.' She wiggles in her seat, getting a feel for things. 'So, let's see. Key in the ignition, check for neutral, adjust the mirror, check the wing mirrors. Turn on.'

'Seat belt.' Mick interjects

'Oh yes.' She reaches behind her and pulls it across her body.

The engine is running and Gloria looks over her shoulder. 'Look behind, nothin' coming so, into first, let out the clutch and...'

With a juddering leap, the car takes off. Gloria grips the steering wheel and leans towards the windscreen in concentration. 'Where we goin' son?'

Mick's astonished voice directs her to turn left at the next junction.

'The indicator is that lever there Ma.'

'Thanks son. I should have used that before, shouldn't I?'

The car clips the curb slightly as they negotiate the corner.

242

'Slow down Ma. We're not in a hurry.' Mick's voice sounds strange. 'OK let's turn into this industrial estate. Indicate. OK, slow down.' Mick's hand hovers between the handbrake and the steering wheel. 'Slow down! Good… and… turn.

They make the turn without incident and Gloria finds herself looking at a small business park. To right and left there are units with cars drawn up in bays, but no traffic travels along the concrete road they now follow. Soon the buildings peter out like the last notes of a song, and they reach an area not yet developed. There are car parks but no units.

'Now Ma, turn in here.' Mick points to a concrete space surrounded by scrub. 'Do you remember how to stop?'

Good Lord - I have to stop! Don't panic girl, think. Oh yes. 'Declutch and brake of course,' she announces with pride. They jerk to a halt, both pitching forward into the constraints. Gloria looks triumphantly at her son. 'There. I did it!'

Mick looks a bit sick. 'You did Ma, you did. Hand-brake on and engine off.'

Gloria obeys. 'You weren't afraid, were you?'

'*No.* Of course not.' He smiles. 'I think you did brilliantly. Don't forget to put it into neutral.'

Mick suggests they practise doing some manoeuvres here, 'You know? To be sure you have full control.'

Gloria is indignant. 'Course I got control.'

'OK, so, can you do a three-point turn, so we are facing the entrance again?'

'No problem. Er, where's reverse?'

They manoeuvre the car round the space, practising clutch control and steering. After half an hour Mick tells Gloria to stop, and from the rear of the car pulls traffic cones, borrowed from the car park at work, and sets them up in a rectangle.

'Right Ma, these are the back of a parked car, and these are the front of another car. He points to two pairs of cones. 'All you need to do is park between them without hitting them, or the curb here.' He indicates the edge of the concrete.

Gloria fails time and again.

'You have to get this right, Ma.'

'I know that. You think I'm stupid.' Gloria grips the steering wheel. 'Right.'

'You've done it!' Mick leans across and plants a loud kiss on Gloria's cheek. 'Come on Mother, if you can do it one more time you can take me for a cup of coffee. I'll even treat you to a slice of cake.'

Gloria manages to park the car again. With pride, she eases out of the business park, and they cruise through residential streets towards the town.

Looking in her mirrors she indicates right and then left, and they join the main road and pass the spot where Fee found the bike. They reach the High Street just as a car pulls from a space up ahead, and Gloria, all attention, reverses into the spot.

'Hey, not bad.' Mick climbs out of the passenger side and comes into the road to open the door for his mother. She slides to the ground without the aid of the step.

It is mid-morning and tables in the tea room are filling up fast. Gloria sits at one in the middle of the room, and watches as Mick orders their refreshments. She observes his tall, broad body, considering, as she often does, how much he resembles his tall and attractive father.

How did she ever manage to deliver that huge baby? It wasn't much fun that's for sure. She hadn't considered that aspect when she agreed to marry a big man, that his baby might be equally huge. It was only as Mick was growing inside her, kicking and struggling to be born as if he was ready long before she was, that she had begun to worry about his size. Her small body was still slim back then and her front stuck out like Mount Afadjato. You tried to hide pregnancy in those days; not like now when young girls expose bare stomachs under tight tee-shirts. In those days, at home in Ghana, you didn't even mention that you were expecting. That would mean acknowledging what had gone on before it. Gloria had stayed inside for most of her later pregnancy. It was a confinement for sure.

She feels a sudden empathy with Millie, also petite and bearing Mick's children. Did she have the same worries during her pregnancy? Gloria apologises to the Lord for her prior lack of thought.

Mick advances between tables bearing a tray with two cups, and a couple of cream buns on plates. The tea is good enough, and the cream cake - mmm! She licks the icing from her fingers and wishes she hadn't worn such a tight girdle.

When they have finished Mick picks up the keys. Would you like me to drive you home Ma?

'Thanks Son. That would be nice.'

244

She sits in the passenger seat and waits as Mick struggles into the car and moves the seat to something like a fit.

'Don't forget to indicate.'

Mick raises his eyebrows at her, 'Are you going to be a backseat driver Ma?'

'Sorry Son.' She clamps her lips shut. They turn into a side road, down the side of the park and a blink of movement catches Gloria's eye.

'There's Paul.'

Emerging from a gate Paul crosses the pavement to his bike. He looks up as they pass and Gloria could swear he looks afraid.

Outside the house Mick parks by the curb. 'I'll leave you here Ma, if you don't mind. I need to get back to work.'

'Yes, OK Son. I can lock the car. You get off. Thank you for helpin' me. I feel much happier about drivin' now.' Gloria leans across to receive a kiss on her cheek, and they both climb out. While Mick strides to his vehicle, Gloria collects the step stool from the door pocket and locks the car expertly then trots up the path to the front door.

Chapter 57

He no longer perches on the wooden carver. The shapely sides of a
wing chair provide the cocoon-like booth in which Paul now shrinks,
peering at Max from a shadowed corner.
'I couldn't resist it. I needed to see what they were up to, to know if
anything was going wrong. I suppose I wanted them to be unhappy.'
'So why tell me this now, after so long?'
Paul blinks a couple of times and scratches his head.
'Kitty saw me once, but she doesn't seem to have said anything. Then
the other day Mick and his mum saw me coming out of the park. I
thought then, it's time to stop. I felt ridiculous. Imagine if they'd asked
me what I was doing in the park. What would I say? Would I lie some
more, or tell the truth, which would seem even more stupid?'
From his usual cock-kneed, flop-haired position, Max's mouth curves,
and his eyes gleam as though Paul has handed him a gift.
'I'm glad you've decided to stop. It's a sign you're coming to terms
with the break up. From what you've told me, Kitty is quite open about
her home life. Fee keeps you informed about school and holidays and
so on, I imagine.'
Paul wriggles into the corner his seat and sticks his legs out in front of
him. 'Well, I find out about school from Kitty. Since you mentioned
her reading and home-work and so on, I've been taking quite an
interest. She's a bright little thing. There's a parents' evening coming up
and I'm going to suggest to Fee that we both go. She does belong to us
both after all.' His brow bounces in and out of a brief frown. 'Fee

hasn't been on holiday for ages though, well apart from a quick trip to Whitstable a while back.'

Max pokes his pen behind his ear, then pulls it out again and places it on the table.

'Did Kitty tell you about that?'

Paul cocks one leg over the other. 'I suppose she must have done.'

There's a short silence.

'I still feel annoyed with Fee, sometimes. I wish I could see more of Kitty. You've no idea how many nights I spend turning everything over in my head, planning ridiculous kidnaps or hoping something bad will happen.'

Max is staring hard at Paul.

'Sad things have happened to them though Paul. Is there anything you want to tell me about that?'

Paul shrugs his shoulders and pulls his water glass towards him.

'Course not.' He takes a sip and looks straight at Max.

Chapter 58

Fee steps into the calm hallway of Will's home, and the enticing aroma of Moules Mariniere stimulates her saliva glands. Will hugs her. In the lounge, holiday brochures are stacked on the coffee table but he ignores them, enquiring about her day and concentrating on her responses. She tells of the police visit.

'Well, they seem to be taking it seriously. That's good, isn't it?'

'I'm scared, though. What if Twitch doesn't come back? Where can she be? Is she hurt somewhere? Oh *God*.' She hugs her body and feels the ribs dig into her forearms.

'Fee, darling. There's nothing you can do, so try and forget it for now. Think about this evening, our last hours together before I go away - and the divine meal I've cooked.' He smirks. 'In fact, it's about ready. Come and eat it, and have a glass of Chablis.' He rises from his seat and leads the way to his compact kitchen, where wine glasses and cutlery are arranged with military precision.

With an effort, she pushes Twitch from her mind. 'Pour me a glass of that wine then.'

The mussels are delicious, and Fee mops up the garlicky liquor with crusty bread. Soon the warmth of the food and crisp coolness of the wine impose their influences. She holds her glass in both hands, elbows on the table, 'What have you been doing with yourself since I last saw you?'

'Worrying. I was worried you'd run away. I know you said it was OK, but then you didn't call me and I thought I'd blown it.' He hurries on as she tries to compose an answer. 'You were right. I can't expect you to think about anything long term right now. I've been looking at holidays.' He flaps his hand at her to intercept her objection. 'On my own. I don't expect you to come with me this time but, maybe some other time.' His voice drops at the end of the last sentence. A statement rather than a question.

They share fruit and cheese, then Will makes espresso coffees, which they carry back into the lounge leaving the dirty dishes on the table. They sit side by side in the dints they left in the sofa cushions, earlier. Gloria would have plumped them up. Will leans forwards and grabs a brochure from the top of the heap.

'I'm thinking I might go here.' A strip of paper marks his place, and he flips the glossy magazine open, laying its cool cover across her knees. 'It looks pretty nice. What do you think?' She lifts the book. There are the usual royal blue seas and perfect models on white beaches, but the sumptuous hotel with every possible luxury is fabulous.

'It looks lovely.' She drops it back quickly. 'I'm sure you'll have a lovely time there. You deserve a rest after working so hard on this place,' she indicates her surroundings, 'and trailing back and forth across the North Sea.'

Will's voice is soft. 'Don't you think you deserve a break too?' He squeezes her shoulders. 'My life is a doddle compared to everything you've been through.'

'Will, I'm still going through it. How can I go on holiday now?'

'Not now. September, or October, or even November if you prefer. Surely Twitch will be back by then, and if not I think you can assume she's not coming.'

'Maybe that's true …' Fee thinks of that hotel, a temporary escape from her stomach twisting anxiety, time to get to know Will better, to decide about his proposal of marriage. 'Maybe…' She pauses.

'Maybe? You mean you might come?' Will's face lights up and he doesn't give her a chance to say that she meant perhaps he was right about Twitch coming back.

Will is full of plans. 'I've made enquiries and we can have a suite, with a deck outside. It overlooks the sea.' He wraps his arms about her, pulling her closer and Fee senses his desire. He speaks softly into her hair. 'We can sip cocktails and make love all night.' His hand moves to her breast and he begins to undo her buttons. He kisses her eyes, her ears then her neck, then his lips move to one of her breasts, while his hand caresses the other. Very softly, his incisors nibble her erect nipple making her body arch, and her need for him prevents thoughts of anything else. His mouth moves over her body, and he pulls her down the settee, putting his head between her thighs. Nothing is more important than this.

They make long slow love, and when she climaxes Fee screams out, her head back, in an abandon she has never before experienced. Tears course from her eyes and into her ears. Will pulls her to his naked chest and holds her tightly until she has cried herself empty.

Later they dress, and Will makes coffee. Two hours have passed in this place of safety, without a thought of home. Fee decides Will is right: wherever Twitch is, she will have turned up by November.

'We could catch fish, and cook them on the beach.'

Will's head snaps up, a look of delight on his face. 'You mean you'll really come?'

'Well, I seem to have agreed to it without realising.' She smiles.

Chapter 59

The house at Crispin Road is becoming tatty. It's not Gloria's fault; she is doing her best, but she's not a young woman. She is, however, brilliant with the children. Although bossy, she exudes a quality of security, with her old-fashioned views, and motherly way of enforcing them.

In the kitchen, the two women are catching up with the cleaning. Fee is on her hands and knees scrubbing round the floor at the edge of the cooker. 'We ought to pull this out really.'

'Hmm, I think we need a man to help with that.' Gloria, is kneeling on the work top, her breath coming out in puffs and grunts as she polishes the panes of the big sash windows. She pauses to study the stove. 'It's a big thing that cooker.'

'Yes,' Fee looks at Millie's substantial gas range, 'perhaps you're right.' Fee has something else on her mind. 'Gloria?'

'Mm?' Gloria leans back on her haunches to check for smears.

Fee continues, 'How are you enjoying your stay here?'

Gloria looks over her shoulder. 'Enjoyin'? I love it. I'd forgotten how wonderful little ones are. I feel useful, and I can see my Mick and Lucas and Olivia as much as I like. Why? You want me to go?'

'Go? No. *No.* That's the last thing I want. I love having you here. I don't want you to go at all. I'm worried that I'm keeping you from your home and your friends.'

'Well, my house is just fine. My neighbour's lookin' after it. I haven't got much garden, not like here, so he hasn't got a lot to do, really.' She dips her cloth in a bowl of water and squeezes it. 'I love this garden.

Wait till I have that vegetable patch planted up with onions and chillies - and potatoes and carrots and maybe some soft fruit. Ooh, I can make jam and pies for you all. We could even have one of them urban chicken run things - have fresh eggs.'

Fee lets out a breath that she didn't know she was holding. 'Oh Gloria, you don't know how happy that makes me. Come down from there and let me give you a hug.'

Gloria looks embarrassed. 'You don't have to do that. I'm happy to be of help. You're helpin' me too you know? I was OK down there in Fulham, but I never realised how much better it is to have your family right under your roof with you. She stops and pulls a pained face. 'These knees are hurtin' a bit, I might come down for a while after all. Let's have a cup of tea and one of the kiddies' cakes.' She struggles into a sitting position, her legs dangling over the front of a cupboard, and Fee moves a chair for her to climb down, then goes to fill the kettle.

'I'm not goin' to use that dratted phone though.' Gloria nods at the new mobile on the work top. 'Don't know why you bought me such a thing.'

'It will be useful if I need to contact you while you're out.'

'But it does so much! What do I want with somethin' that tells me the weather in New York, and lets me look at the internet? I keep pressin' three buttons at once. And when it rings it makes me jump.'

'Well, if you break down in the car, you can call the AA, or Mick or me, to rescue you. I'm positive you'll be glad of it one day. It's another kind of insurance really.'

Fee wonders if she should mention her holiday with Will. Now she's agreed to go she feels awkward about asking Gloria to hold the fort. Gloria carries the tea tray to the table, and pulls the lid off the cake tin to study its contents. 'Bit on the brown side,' she observes, and takes a healthy bite from a muffin, chewing analytically. 'Not too bad though. They're getting' quite good at cakes, those kiddies.'

'Thanks to you Gloria. Millie and Twitch used to cook with them regularly. They were missing it. Think how lovely it'll be to put home-made jam into sandwich cakes next summer. They'll love that…'

They look at one another, and Gloria puts down her cake. 'She'll be back by then, makin' her own jam.'

'Yes.'

Chapter 60

House to house enquiries have turned up nothing. One or two people saw Twitch leaving home on her bike that evening but nobody saw her en route to the school where her art classes were held. They found no helpful CCTV footage in the town and there were no cameras on the country roads, so the police have pulled back, apparently now it's a waiting game. With no clue to where Twitch went, a television appeal would be pointless.

Josh and Sam are the main concern. They've stayed with Maurice most weekends and although the other children miss them, it's the best arrangement. When the two boys are here they are withdrawn. Both have lost weight and Fee is worried about them. Apart from Gloria gossiping and laughing, the house is subdued.

Fee pulls her car out of the drive. As she enters the town a figure catches her eye. It looks like Will, but it's someone with a similar walk. She keeps doing this - she's seen Twitch a few times too. It's amazing how many women look like her.

The car stops and starts, crawling past the wine bar where she and Will met on that first lunch date. Her office comes in to sight on the left, and she turns hard into the little car park. It's chock-a-block - she hadn't expected that. In the normal course of events Fee would be first in and last out, so the capacity of the car park never crossed her mind. She backs and fills to turn the long car round in the cramped space, and pulls back into the traffic. After cruising slowly along side streets, she pulls into a spot, and marches back down two long roads to the building.

The code for the door has changed, so she buzzes for access. She looks at the security camera so they can see who she is and is startled when an unfamiliar voice comes from the speaker. 'Can I help you?'

'Fee Thomas, I'm here to see John Simpson.'

The door buzzes and she pushes it. In the foyer, she's relieved that nothing has changed. The low seats, polished plants and gleaming lift evoke in Fee the same resigned familiarity that she once felt on returning home to her parents from university.

She steps out of the lift to a familiar view. Ranks of programmers arranged in rows on a powder blue carpet. Each industrious worker in a bee hive pod. At the end of the room, in a glass office, she can see John tipped back in his wide chair, looking at the ceiling with a phone clamped to his ear. She walks up the aisle between the cubicles feeling eyes turn towards her, and passes Nick, his shirt sleeves hitched up. His fingers pause on his keyboard and he looks at her. She nods a greeting.

'Hi Fee, how are you?'

'Fine thanks Nick. You?'

'Good thanks.'

She moves on and meets the eyes of her boss through the glass partition. As soon as he sees her his body straightens, his elbow pokes out in readiness to end his call. Then he is at the door.

'Fee, how great to see you!' He gives her a hug and ushers her to a chair opposite his own. 'Would you like a coffee or tea?'

She could be a guest. 'No thanks John.' She settles into the chair and crosses her ankles. 'It's good to see you. How are things going here?'

'Well, they've been better to be honest. We heard last week that we've lost the Hampton contract.'

Hampton's has been the main source of business for the company for the past ten years or so. Losing the contract will be a big blow.

'I'm sorry to hear that but actually, it makes it easier for me to tell you this.' She's decided.

John cocks his head on one side. 'Out with it Fee, I hope it's not what I think it is.'

'I've decided to leave, John. All this business with Millie and Twitch has knocked us all for six. I'm not really ready to come back to work and the children need me at home. I don't think it's feasible for me to stay. I'm sorry.'

Her boss pokes out his bottom lip like a thwarted child, but Fee has a suspicion he is relieved. 'You had a brilliant future here,' he meets her eyes briefly, 'but I do understand. I hope things work out for you.' He clears his throat and glances through the glass of his office, at the ranks of pods.

Fee nods her head silently, trying not to weep.

He pushes back his chair and rises to his feet to open the door for her. 'I wish you every success in the future, and if there's ever anything I can do to help you please let me know.'

'Thanks John, you never know I may take you up on that, one day.' Fee smiles sadly wondering if either of them is being genuine.

On her final journey through the room she stops occasionally at a desk to bid farewell to a colleague. She'll miss it here, but her thoughts are already moving to the day ahead.

Chapter 61

Monday morning in Maurice's house. Ugh! School and work.

The phone rings while he's cleaning his teeth and shouting foamily to Sam to get Josh moving. He drops the toothbrush into the sink, quickly scoops some water into his mouth, spits and leaps through to the bedroom before his voice-mail kicks in.

'Hello?'

'Mr Roman?'

'Yes?'

'This is Lymeshire police.'

***

The children are at school and Maurice sits at a scratched table in a bare room. Twitch's body has turned up in a lake, spotted by a couple of walkers. Maurice knows no more than this. Twitch was a good swimmer - years ago she swam for her school.

A round faced WPC opens the door and enters the small room, carrying some paperwork on a clip-board. She sits down opposite him with a smile on her face.

'Sorry to have kept you waiting Mr Roman,' her accent is northern - Yorkshire maybe. 'I have to get a few details from you then another officer will have a word with you.'

The details are mainly personal: name, address, relationship with Twitch, then about Twitch: identifying features, hair, shoe size, dress size, name of her dentist. He does his best to help. Her hair of course, is easy to describe but he doesn't feel qualified to comment on the clothes and shoes, and she might have changed her dentist. 'You should ask Fee about that.'

'Don't worry sir, we already have. We just like to check everything.'

A male officer arrives, in plain clothes. The WPC rises, and hands over the clip-board, then stands by the door, while he sits in her place, and introduces himself as DI Collins. He is investigating the death of a woman, found in the lake in Callun Woods. He looks hard at Maurice before telling him that the information he has given them will be used to check whether the person is Mrs Roman. They will also check her dental records but that she will not be easy to identify visually as decomposition is advanced. Maurice is revolted, at the same time he has a faint sense of unease at the way the DI Collins is staring at him. 'How long before they know?' He asks.

A few days. They will be in touch.

'Oh, and by the way, we are treating the death as suspicious.'

Maurice blinks his eyes, and raises them to find the policeman watching him.

***

The body in the lake belongs to Twitch. There was never any doubt in Maurice's mind but the news still has the power to shock. From his position in an armchair, he stares with dry eyes at nothing.

Murder. Such a blunt word, and so out of place here, in middle England. Thank God, he didn't have to identify her. The police took DNA samples from the children, and matched them to Twitch's body. The children, they're another thing to cope with. Gloria is fantastic, comforting and everything but of course Josh and Sam want to be with Maurice as much as possible. They are missing their mother. He's useless in emotional situations. He doesn't know what to say to make them feel secure. And the cooking! He may be adept by now at a few things, but he can't match what Gloria's been conjuring up for them. Yesterday they asked for fish stew. Good grief!

Maurice pulls himself together. They'll need collecting from school soon.

During the journey to school, words scud through his mind, phrases to soften the news he is about to deliver. Of course, he's imagined this moment before, has prepared, psychologically. At the school, he is disgusted by the crush of badly parked cars, across gateways and double parked. *Women!* After parking his car at the curb some distance away, he strides to the school gate and positions himself awkwardly among groups of gossiping mothers. Across their heads he notices another lone man, a stay-at-home father possibly, with his right hand resting on a push chair. Their eyes meet and Maurice nods at him but is in no mood for small talk. The two men remain silent amid the gaggle and complaint.

A muffled bell from inside the school, and a few minutes later children filter out. Mothers, eyes only for their beloved children, start to leave, asking loud, proud questions about the events of their children's day.

'Hello Dad.' Sam is surprised to see his father today.

'Hello Sam-boy. Have you had a good day?'

'The boy searches his father's face. 'What's wrong Dad?'

Maurice doesn't want to say anything yet. He needs to get them home and tell them together. 'Something's happened love. I'll tell you when we get home.'

'Daddy!' Josh rushes up looking delighted to see his father on this unexpected afternoon. He holds his arms up for a hug and Maurice stoops down to squeeze him tightly.

'Careful Daddy, I can't breathe.'

Sam interjects, 'Can we go on the waggon again, Dad?' The boys haven't forgotten their brilliant day on Callun Hill.

'Sorry son.' Maurice lifts Josh onto his shoulders, and holds out his hand to Sam. 'Someone stole it from the garden.'

'Is that the thing you wanted to tell us?

'No, Sam. Something else.'

They trail back to the car ignoring disapproving whispers,

'He's spoiling that child.'

'He'll never walk if he's carried everywhere.'

***

The children are weeping and Maurice, sitting once again in his armchair, holds them awkwardly, worrying what to do next. He needs help here, he's not equipped for this. In fairness, nobody is equipped for it but some would deal with it better than he. Gloria for instance, or his mother. Women in fact are better at the hugging, comforting stuff. Maurice's instinct is more practical. What can he provide to help here? Nothing. Can he work harder to make things better? No. He sits and waits for the kids to calm down then pushes them gently to one side and squeezes to his feet saying brightly, 'OK, who's for a McDonalds?' He doesn't get the response he is hoping for. The boys remain huddled together in the chair. Sam shuffles towards his small brother and wraps his arms round him. Josh has his thumb poked deep beyond his lips and is sucking hard. His eyes are beginning to close, a mercy in the circumstances.

Maurice's heart constricts. Poor boy, poor sweet little love. He's been through too much in his short life. 'Come on Sam. Let's take him to bed then you and I can snuggle up and watch something on television.'

'No Dad, keep him here with us. He might wake up and be scared.'

Such a wise boy. Maurice gathers up the sleepy Josh while Sam finds something on the television, then the three of them settle onto the settee.

Chapter 62

'It's murder,' announces Gloria from the driver's seat.

Fee's stomach lurches. 'What is?'

'Keepin' the house clean.' Gloria turns her eyes from the road, and looks aghast. 'Oh Lord. Sorry Fee. I wasn't thinkin'.'

'Don't worry, Gloria. I'm a bit on edge.'

'Of course you are dear. Is there any news?'

'Not yet. They're doing the post mortem today.'

Fee shifts her aching hand on the grab handle, her eyes riveted to the road.

'Gloria?'

'Yes?' Gloria frowns at the windscreen, her hands at ten to two on the steering wheel.

'I want to tell you something.'

The engine whines as the car drops a gear and comes to rest in front of a red traffic signal.

'I've met a man.'

Gloria's head twists to the left, a beam stretched between her ears. 'I thought you were goin' to tell me to leave.'

'Gosh no. I told you before, I need you.'

'I'm happy for you Fee. Tell me all about him.' Gloria is as inquisitive as her late daughter-in-law was.

There's a horn behind. The lights have turned green. With a hand raised in apology Gloria leaps off in the direction of Watco.

Fee describes Will in vague terms. 'He works on the oil rigs. He's a good cook and he keeps his flat clean, and he's just finished decorating.

It looks nice.' She knows what Gloria will be interested in. 'The thing is,' she takes a breath, 'he's asked me to go away with him for a couple of weeks in November. Do you think I should go?'
'Do you love him?'
'Perhaps.' She's being disingenuous. 'Yes, I do.'
'Then go. You don't get chances like that too often. You got to grab them. I'll be fine here with the kiddies. They'll be at school most of the time and their dads can help, can't they?'
'I hope so.' Fee turns her eyes to the side window. She's uneasy about the whole idea of a holiday now that Twitch's body has turned up. Thank goodness it's a couple of months off.

***

It is the following weekend and Gloria has gone home again, 'Just to check things are all OK. I might rent it out, what do you think of that?' The men have decided to have their children, and Kitty is the last to go – and the slowest.
'Kitty, come on, Daddy's waiting for you.'
'Where are my trainers Mummy?'
'Where you left them, I expect.' Fee looks apologetically at Paul as they stand at the bottom of the stairs.
'Don't worry. I'm not in a hurry.' His body language contradicts his words but that can't be helped. Fee gestures to the kitchen.
'I wanted to have a word with you anyway.'
There are thuds from upstairs. Kitty seems to be emptying things onto her bedroom floor.
'Mummy.' She appears at the top of the stairs. 'Come and help me'.
'You'll find them darling. You should put things away then you'll always know where they are.'
'Yeah, yeah,' smirks Paul, and Fee flashes a wry smile.
'I know it falls on deaf ears but I can't help saying it. Coffee?'
He nods.
She shouts up the stairs, 'Keep looking Kitty, Daddy's going to have a drink,' and leads her ex into the kitchen. He settles at the breakfast bar.
'How's things?' There is genuine concern in his voice. Fee reaches for two mugs and places them in front of him, then turns away to grind the beans.
'Oh, you know.' The grinder roars. When the noise has died away, she taps clinging grounds into a jug. 'I don't know what I'd do without Gloria. She runs the house like clockwork, and the kids love her.

'Paul?'

Her eyes remain on the boiling water, that slops into the coffee jug. When she meets his eyes he's all attention. She looks away and presses the shining plunger through the black sludge in the jug.

'I've met someone.' She pours coffee into the mugs. 'I haven't told Kitty yet. I thought you ought to know first.' She sides a mug across the counter. 'Still black with no sugar?'

'How long?' Paul's voice is strangled.

'Oh, a while now. The thing is,' she drizzles milk into her mug, 'we want to go on holiday, and I may need to call on you to have Kitty while I'm away. Just in case of emergency.'

'Holiday?' His tone is as she had expected.

'Not until November. Hopefully all this investigation will be finished by then. I know what you're thinking,' she meets his eyes for the first time since she told him, 'and I don't blame you, but I need a break. The pressure of the last few weeks has been huge. And the police...' She tails off, bowing her head and looking at the coffee again.

'What about the police?'

She glances up. 'I think they suspect me.'

'You?' Paul barks out a laugh. 'Don't be ridiculous. What do they think you did, lure Twitch away on her bicycle and poke a stick between the spokes?'

'I suppose, because of Millie - it is a bit of a coincidence.' She falters.

'So you're going to run away.' Paul's statement conveys his disapproval.

'No, not at all. Will has been asking me for ages. Until Gloria was established, I couldn't - wouldn't go, but now, I know it doesn't look great but I need something to look forward to. It's only for a couple of weeks.'

'Two weeks? *Two weeks.*' Paul launches onto his feet, and his stool rocks.

'You're going to leave Kitty, not to mention Josh and Sam, who have just lost their mother, for a fortnight?' He raises a clenched fist to shoulder height and brings it down. The edges of his curled fingers halt about a centimetre above the shiny worktop and bounce silently up again like a bungee jumper.

Fee starts to close down. 'Paul, please be quiet, Kitty will hear you.'

'Oh, here we go.' Paul thrusts his face towards hers, his top lip raised to expose teeth the colour of ancient piano keys. 'Mzzz Perfect. Never flustered, never out of control.'

If he only knew.

'We're not married any longer, Paul.' Her voice is low. 'Please don't talk to me like that. I'm telling you as a matter of courtesy, not asking your permission.'

He compresses his lips, and his eyes drill into her, but the sound of Kitty thumping down the stairs prevents further debate.

'Are you shouting about something Daddy?' Kitty looks at her father with a face so like her mother's, it's scary.

'Who me? I'm Mr Tickle, he never shouts.' He grabs her and probes fingers into her ribs, while she screams with laughter.

When they have left, Fee sits back on her stool and raises her coffee mug to her lips with shaking fingers.

***

The ringtone of Gloria's mobile sounds in her handbag, and she runs to fetch it from the hall. It hasn't rung before, possibly because Gloria has just discovered that it was set to silent. She rummages between her purse and make up bag, eager to fish it out before it stops ringing.

'Hello, who is this please?' She holds the gadget in both hands, breathing fast.

'Hello, is that Mrs Adu?' A male voice she doesn't recognise floats down the line to her.

'Yes?'

'I'm glad I've caught you, I've been trying for a while.'

'Who is this?' She's not about to buy anything over the telephone from one of those scammers or telephone selling people.

'You don't know me. My name is Will.'

***

'Mr Ro…, this is Lym…er p…lice.' Maurice holds the phone to his ear, and ducks into a passage between two shops to block the rumble of the traffic on the main road. He covers the other ear with his palm.

'I'm sorry, this isn't a good signal. You're breaking up.'

The flow of dialogue stammers on, and the words Post Mor… emerge for a second, like an English word in a Welsh sentence.

'Excuse me.' Maurice shouts, trying to stem the unintelligible stream. 'I can't hear you. Give me a few minutes and I'll come into the station, I'm only round the corner. OK?'

Who knows if she can hear him?

The voice stutters some more and Maurice hangs up on it. Bursting from his shelter he runs along the pavement, dodging shoppers and jumping over obstacles.

***

He recognises the policeman - a balding fellow who came to the house when Twitch first went missing. The man's expression in the pallid light from a small metal-framed window, fills Maurice with foreboding. The officer switches on a tape recorder and reaches for a pen and bound note book from the grimy window ledge.

'Detective Sergeant Bailey interviewing Mr Maurice Roman.' He gives the date and time.

'Mr Roman, we have completed the post mortem on your ex-wife and as we expected, her death was by drowning.'

Maurice waits in silence. What can he say?'

'Given some other injuries to her body, we are treating her death as murder.'

'Murder?' Maurice stares at the officer.

'I'm afraid it's hard to reach any other conclusion.'

Maurice presses his straightened fingers to his mouth, and his chin into his palm. His neck is too weak to support his head. The man in front of him continues talking, words winging past. Maurice interrupts.

'Sorry. I know you're telling me things but I can't take this in. Why would she be murdered? Was she raped or attacked in any way?'

'I can't tell you any more than that now Sir; I'm sure you understand. This is a murder enquiry. I'm afraid we won't be able to release the body for a while.'

'Could you not call her 'The Body'? She is – was a person.'

We're searching the area round the lake for any clue to the identity of the murderer, and there will be a press release, appealing for witnesses.

Maurice's mind turns to his children. 'Will it be on television?'

'Very probably. We'll let you know when it's going to happen. I imagine it will be done quite soon to avoid unnecessary scaremongering.

'I understand you are friendly with Mr Paul Thomas.'

Maurice is still absorbing the word "scaremongering", but he pulls his attention back to the question.

'Paul? Yes. We got friendly when our wives left us. Mick too. The girls all lived together at that house in Crispin Road so it was natural we should join forces as well.'

'Join forces?

'Well. You know. Mutual support. I didn't know how to cook. Mick taught me to do some basics so I could feed my kids...'

The policeman interrupts. 'Mick. That would be Mr Michael Adu.'

'Yes. And Paul helped me put up shelves and mend cupboards. We go for the occasional pint together. Nothing ominous.'

D.S. Bailey continues to take an interest in Paul, and after answering some simple questions, Maurice becomes reticent at the mention his friend's outbursts of temper.

'He's a good man, and I can't imagine him as a murderer if that's what you're getting at. Why would he kill Twitch anyway?'

'He does have a temper though, doesn't he?'

The feet of Maurice's wooden chair screech on the floor and he finds himself glaring down at the detective. 'Everyone has a temper, if provoked enough.' His voice echoes back to him from the walls and he drops back into his chair.

When he has settled, Bailey asks, 'Can you tell me your movements on the day your ex-wife went missing?'

'I took the boys swimming. Fee rang to say Twitch hadn't come home and so we went to the pool in Chelterton.'

'So Ms Thomas rang you in the morning?'

'Yes. No – hang on, that was the Sunday, she went missing on the Saturday, didn't she?'

'Indeed, sir.'

OK. Let me think.' He pauses to gather his thoughts. 'Yes, I remember, Fee wanted me to have the kids but I had some shopping to do. I went to Watco, then to the Post Office - the card bit, to buy a birthday card for my Mother.'

'Do you have the receipt?'

'I doubt it, it's not the kind of thing you keep, is it? I'll check when I get home though. It might be in a pocket.'

'Thank you, sir.' The officer hunches his shoulders over his pen. 'So, when you had finished shopping?'

'I went home, made a sandwich then picked up Josh and Sam at, I suppose about 3-ish. We went to the pictures – Despicable Me, then home. I kept the boys overnight and then Fee rang while we were having breakfast.'

'Thank you, sir. That's most helpful.' D.S. Bailey signs off from the tape 'Interview terminated at...'

***

Boxes are packed. Removals begin tomorrow. Paul has not lived in the flat long but even so rectangular ghosts hint at where his motor prints were hung. In his bedroom, the wardrobe and drawers stand empty, and across the hall the kitchen is bereft of clutter. A loaf and a jar of coffee sit lonely on the counter with a mug, a teaspoon and a plate, ready for breakfast tomorrow. In the fridge, apart from butter and milk, several bottles of beer pledge reward for the labours of the day. Topsy is at the kennels. He left her looking mournful inside her pen, and felt guilty all the way home. It had to be done though, for everyone's safety.

When the doorbell shrills he jumps. On the threshold, the bloody police again. He leads them into the living room, and they regard him across a packing case full of unidentifiable, wrapped objects.

'Sorry to trouble you again Mr Thomas, we are still trying to confirm your movements when Mrs Roman disappeared.'

'I told you last time, I can't remember. If I could I'd look in my diary but as you can see, everything is packed. I'm moving tomorrow.'

D.S. Bailey makes a note of Paul's new address. 'It seems then, Sir, that you have no alibi?'

'Alibi for what? There hasn't been a crime.'

'I'm afraid there has. A forensic examination of Mrs Roman's body suggests that she was murdered.'

'Jesus.'

'Well sir, I don't think he can help you at the moment. The balding officer's face is impassive and his eyes meet Paul's sharp look.

'Am I under arrest?'

Bailey shakes his head. 'No Mr Thomas, but your interests will be better served if you co-operate. Perhaps you would search your boxes for the diary you mentioned.'

Paul knows exactly where to find his appointment diary, he also knows there is nothing noted in it for the Saturday when Twitch went missing. He now makes a convincing show of ripping open boxes until he 'finds' the box with his paper work inside.

'OK, here it is.' He waves the diary above his shoulder at Tweedle Dum and Tweedle Dee, his back still toward them. 'Now,' he straightens up, feeling a twinge in his back from hours of lifting and wrapping, 'what was that date?'

266

There follows more play-acting as he flaps through annotated pages until he is staring at the blank Saturday in question. 'Apparently I did nothing special on that date. You're right, I have no alibi.' He raises his eyes again to the policemen.

'Perhaps we can jog your memory Sir. I believe your wife asked you to look after your daughter for the day and you refused.'

Paul slits his eyes. 'I'm not sure I refused. I had something on already.'

'I see Sir, I'm glad I've helped you to remember.'

'You did. Thank you.' Paul folds his arms. 'I suppose you want to know what this amazing thing was that I had already booked.'

'Yes Sir. That would be very helpful.'

'A hang-over.'

'Sir?'

'I had a hangover to nurse. I knew I was going to have it because I was planning to get pissed the night before.'

'I see. And where did you go for this drink?'

'Nowhere. I was right here with a bottle of Scotch and a crate of beer.'

The officer looks sceptical. 'Was there some reason to plan this binge of yours?'

'None of your bloody business. If I choose to drown my sorrows occasionally, it's up to me.'

When they have left, Paul flips the cap from one of his beers, and sits for a long time among the remnants of his home, staring at nothing.

***

Fee fights to stay calm.

'Will. I'm sorry. We need to cancel our holiday. You haven't booked it yet, have you?' His voice is tinny, as it reaches her from across the North Sea. There are other voices in the back ground.

'Hang on Fee, I'll just go back to my cabin.' He gives her a running commentary as he walks along passages and through doors, while she swallows and takes deep breaths. After a faint clunk the background noise is silenced and in the quiet of his quarters he asks, 'OK. What were you saying?'

'Twitch was murdered.' She drops into a chair and unleashes her tears.

'Fee? Are you alright?' He sounds worried. She shudders,

'Not really.'

'Look I'll be home in a few days. Shall I come over?'

'No, I'll come to you.' She's not ready to deal with introductions yet. The children have enough to come to terms with. 'What am I going to tell the children?'

'Talk it over with the men and Gloria. I'm sorry Fee, I can't help you with that one. I wish I could.'

'You need to cancel the holiday, Will. I can't possibly go now.' There's silence. 'Hello? Will?'

'I've paid in full, Fee. I got a good deal for paying early. I can't cancel now. Look. Wait and see what happens, November's still a long way off. You're going to need the holiday more than ever after all this.'

The holiday is the least important of an extensive list of worries, and Fee inhales a lungful of air. 'I suppose you're right.' She breathes out. All she wants to do is sleep.

'Take care my lovely Fee. I'll see you very soon.'

'OK.' She hangs up and drags herself to the kitchen where Gloria sits staring at a crumpled tissue, her nostrils red.

'What are we goin' to tell the kiddies?' She peeks at Fee through swollen eyes and Fee slumps into another chair.

'I don't know Gloria. The thing is we can't hide it once it's in the papers, they're going to find out from someone at school. And the press will be round here with cameras. It might be better to come clean, and then face the media before they become a nuisance.'

A look of horror traverses Gloria's face. 'I hadn't thought about reporters. You see them on the telly, crowdin' round people when they come out of their houses. That's goin' to be awful.'

'Maurice will be here soon, we can talk it through together.'

***

This must be someone else's life. Fee stands on the pavement outside the police station, shoulder to shoulder with Maurice, amid the locust-clicks of a plague of cameras, and the snake heads of microphones jabbing at their faces.

Projecting an air of authority, the Chief Constable, immaculate in dark serge, his large feet planted in shoes bright enough to dazzle, steps forward. His intake of breath brings silence to the waiting crowd.

'The body of a woman has been found in Downham Lake, in Little Callum Woods. She has been identified as Ms Sabrina Roman, a resident of Chelterton, and mother of two young children. The police are treating her death as suspicious, and would ask anyone who was in the area of Chelterton, or the lake, or anywhere in between, on the afternoon or evening of 12th May to come and talk to us. We are particularly interested to find the route of a woman riding a bright blue bicycle, but if you saw anything out of the ordinary please give us a call. 'We would also like to know how the bicycle ended up in a ditch at the far side of a field on the A243, outside Chelterton, at some time during the following week.

'Ms Roman leaves her ex-husband and father of her children, Maurice Roman. And house-mate, in loco parentis, Fee Thomas.' The cameras clatter into life as the officer continues. 'Mr Roman and Ms Thomas ask that members of the press keep their distance at this sad time, for the benefit of the children.

'There is uproar.

'Ms Thomas, can you tell us about your relationship with Ms Roman?'

'Maurice, look this way.'

'How are the children taking the news?'

'Fee. Over here.'

They dive back into the police station and wait while two uniformed officers clear the area.

Chapter 63

The shriek of his electric drill is deafening and Paul screws up his eyes to avoid iron coloured dust that flies from a hole in the wall of the garage. He pushes in a plastic plug and offers up the body of a wall phone, 'won' on eBay. This morning has been passed, connecting the phone to the telephone system inside his new house.

With a concluding turn of the screwdriver, he blows dust from the receiver and picks it up. The dial tone purrs, strong and clear. *Excellent.* Metal shelves stretch behind him down the breeze-block walls, and rows of tools hang from brackets above a work bench. The garage is in better shape than the house, where bare rooms await pictures and in one room, curtains. Still, he, Kitty and the dog have everything they need.

Kitty has pranced back into his life, happy that he has moved away from the unpleasant, former neighbours.

The investigation into Twitch's death seems to have stalled. He hasn't spoken to a policeman for weeks. After Twitch was found, the press engaged in a frenzy of speculation. Newspaper headlines changed daily, ranging from TRAGIC DEATH OF LESBIAN MOTHER, to EX-HUSBANDS IN MURDER MYSTERY. This latter carried pictures of himself, Mick and Maurice with the question, 'Guilty?'

The gutter press has other victims to torture now.

Paul twists the drill chuck and pokes the bit into its clip on the wall, then cocks his head. From outside, at the front of the house he hears several male voices through the metal door up and over door. In the hallway, his doorbell rings. He pushes the bottom of the door and ducks out.

'Hello?'

From the concealed area beside the garage, several uniformed men barge past him into the workshop, milling past his motor bike and through the door into the hallway.

'Hey. What do you think you're doing?'

There are footfalls on the staircase, and a male voice issues orders. One officer stops in the garage to restrain Paul.

'Mr Paul Thomas, I have a warrant to search these premises. Please remain with me until my officers have finished.'

'What are you looking for?'

'I'm not at liberty to say, Sir but if you stay calm we'll soon be out of your hair.' Agitation whelms up in Paul. With his pulse belting in his ears he clenches his fists, preparing to lash out at the officer. At that moment, like Jiminy Cricket, Max's face floats through his ruby haze, and with enormous effort he draws a shuddering breath, *1, 2, 3, 4…* He unclamps his fingers.

Conscious thought returns and he scans through what might be in the house to throw suspicion on him? He tries to control his shaking hands and legs, and strains his ears for a clue to what is going on inside.

'Would you please turn out your pockets?' The police officer, whose name he's been told but can't remember, is polite, although his tone is imperative.

Paul unloads an oily rag and a couple of brass screws onto his workbench.

The two men stand, side by side, mainly in silence, and after about an hour, the front door opens and closes, and footsteps approach the open garage. One of the group seems to be in control. He gives the officer beside Paul a small shake of his head, and hands him a sheet of flimsy paper. The officer glances at it and folds it before Paul can get a look.

'Thank you for your time Mr Thomas. There's a receipt inside the house for any items we have removed. Your belongings will be returned to you as soon as possible.'

'Is that it then?' Paul jerks away from the officer, and stuffs the oil covered rag back into his trousers. 'No explanation?'

'Sir, we have removed some items from the house to help with our investigations. We'll be in touch if we need you again, but in the meantime, please let us know if you plan to be away from home, and, to coin a phrase,' he grins to himself, 'don't leave the country.'

Inside the house, on the arm of a chair a flimsy, pink sheet of paper bears a faint copy of things they have removed. A shoe, a toothbrush, cigarette ends, mobile phone and a business card. Paul stares in bafflement at the list.

Chapter 64

As she folds flimsy fabric into her suitcase Fee's emotions bounce between extremes. Her longing to escape to paradise versus profound guilt. Going through the routine of packing she consults her list, and adds perfume and jewellery to the bag. Most of her clothes will probably hang on her like flapping laundry. She should have tried them on before now. She could have done, it's not as if she's been rushing off to work every day. She has some outfits that fit. She knows because she's bought them specially, thanks to Gloria.

Gloria must be worried about her. She has stretched her repertoire of dishes to the limit in a vain attempt to make Fee eat, and taken an avid interest in Fee's trip, especially her packing, suggesting outfits, 'in case you go somewhere *very* romantic.'

Last Saturday they all went shopping. Kitty and Josh needed new shoes again. In the shop, they squeezed between parents and children, and waited in resignation. A young assistant on black woollen knees, smoothed the tops, and squeezed the sides of sturdy school footwear. When they escaped onto the High Street, Gloria peered into the window of the lingerie shop next door. 'You ought to buy somethin' special. Get some new underwear and a negligee.'

'A negligee?' Fee laughed it off but now she wonders if perhaps Gloria was right. She might nip into town and get a sexy little number. She's not sure what Will's underwear predilections are but there's only one way to find out.

She stands up and surveys the open case then flapping the lid loosely over the clothes, stretches her back, and heads downstairs towards the sound of the Hoover.

Gloria's raised voice is talking to Kitty. The two have become good friends. Paul's parents have moved to the coast so Kitty no longer has a grandmother nearby. Gloria is a perfect substitute. Fee can't hear what she is saying, but her tone implies that she is imparting advice - in other words delivering a lecture. Gloria knows just how the world should be run, how children should behave – and their mothers. It can be irritating, but at the same time reassuring.

The roar of the machine stops as Fee reaches the hall, and she hears Kitty and Gloria whispering behind a half open door. She pushes it open.

'What's all this?' She smiles. 'What are you two 'children' up to?'

Kitty and Gloria leap apart, looking guilty.

'Oh, nothin' dear.' Gloria is not convincing. 'We were just talking about Christmas.'

Kitty's face is a picture of innocence.

'What would you like Mummy?'

Fee is touched.

'Ooh, I don't know, a kiss maybe.'

'Oh Mummy, you always say that!'

'Well, I can't think of anything I'd like more, apart from a hug.'

Kitty runs up and wraps her small arms round Fee's waist.

'I'm going to need lots of hugs now. One for each day I'm away. That means fourteen.'

A fortnight is a long time, and she hopes she has made the necessary arrangements? Will the children's fathers come when they should and will they feed them properly?

Gloria looks at her as if reading her mind.

'We'll be fine without you. It's only a couple of weeks after all. What can go wrong in such a brief time?'

Fee pulls herself together. 'You're right, of course you are.' Her tone becomes brisk, 'I'm just going to pop into town.

'Goin' to that underwear shop?' Gloria winks.

'Gloria, you should be ashamed. I thought you were a well brought up lady. I'm not sure I should leave you with my daughter.'

Gloria lets out a bellow of laughter.

'I'm only human you know dear.' Fee can still hear her cackling as she closes the front door.

Chapter 65

The car tyres swish on the wet motorway and Fee tries to relax. Her mind is running over things, again and again: did she tell Paul how to contact the doctor? Does Gloria know about all the children's after school activities? Locations of stop cocks and the fuse box.

Will is silent, concentrating on driving through the clouds of spray kicked up by thundering waggons.

Signs for the airport loom through the murky air, and before long Will signals his intention to leave the motorway. The blinkers click in counterpoint to the slurp, slurp of the windscreen wipers. He pulls into the near side lane, then as he is about to take the feeder road the car gives a jolt and the tyre noise changes to a rumble. Will's knuckles whiten on the steering wheel, and the car heads off course on the wet road. Fee's hand flies to the grab handle above her door, but Will regains control and pulls onto the hard shoulder, just beyond the junction. Cars squirt past, throwing up swathes of spray.

They climb out to investigate, shielding themselves from the spewing water. A long nail protrudes from the wall of the front, nearside tyre. A faint hissing is discernible over the noise of the traffic, and as they watch, the tyre spreads on the tarmac.

Undaunted, Will sets to work extracting the spare wheel, a task that requires the unloading of their cases from the boot. He sends Fee to sit inside, and she watches him kneel on the grimy tarmac as he deftly undoes wheel nuts and jacks her up. The car rocks as he heaves on the spare and tightens the nuts. When he stands up, his hair is stuck to his skull, and his hands and knees sodden and filthy.

He climbs into the driver's seat, a roar of wet traffic following him for a moment before the door slams shut.

'Oh no, you're in such a state.'

'I can change in the gents. My hair will soon dry, and my hands will wash.' He wipes them on his thighs leaving a gritty streak.

They cruise along the hard shoulder until a brief gap in the traffic enables them to accelerate back onto the slip road. The mishap and its potential for disaster have distracted Fee from her troubles. Suddenly her spirits lift and she is overcome with relief that they will make it on time.

***

Mick is on his own trip – for work. He and his manager are to view a hotel in Belgium to consider its suitability as the hotel chain's first European venue. Mick is to look at the catering side of the business and talk to staff and possibly customers, while Jack, his manager will view the hospitality rooms, and examine the accounts.

As they cruise along the motorway Mick reflects on how pleasant it is to be a passenger, especially in this foul weather. He watches the raindrops racing and merging on the side window and then peers through it at the distant scenery, thinking, as he often does, of the background in a cartoon. The far distance passing slower than the foreground to create the illusion of movement.

Jack is quiet, they have both had a busy morning and Jack will be mentally reviewing his task list, as indeed is Mick.

The motorway is busy here and huge aeroplanes bear down on them as if they will land on the roof.

They are passing the exit road for terminal B, not the one they want. A small tableau at the side of the road catches Micks eye. He screws up his eyes to see through the blurry glass. It looks like Fee, standing beside a car that Mick doesn't recognise. She is trying to keep her hair from her eyes with one hand while gripping together the open neck of her coat with the other. Beside her is a man, squatting to study a wheel. The weather and spray rip at their clothes, and Mick is wondering whether to ask Jack to pull over. Jack's car has slowed down, and they are now in the nearside lane, ready to exit at the next junction. Mick presses his face to the side window. That must be the new man in Fee's life. Mick keeps his eyes on them, craning his neck as they pass. The man seems vaguely familiar. It looks as though they have a puncture but judging from the calm look on his face, all is under control. Mick decides with relief that he can let them get on with it.

Where has he seen that fellow before? He searches his memory. He has a good memory for faces – can't remember names, but faces, he's good at. Jack's voice interrupts his pondering and Mick is distracted. Never mind, it will come to him.

Chapter 66

Fee kicks of her shoes, pulls the vertical blind to one side. The glass door glides easily along its metal channel at her touch. Outside, the smooth honey-coloured deck warms the soles of her feet and the scent of flowers fills her head. Shiny leaves in shades of green and yellow, interspersed with outrageously coloured blooms, burgeon from gardens and tumble over rails to right and left. In front of her, beyond a set of deeply cushioned chairs and a rectangular void in the deck, is a gate, and beyond it the beach and sea. She crosses to the edge of the rectangular cut-out, and stands with her toes hooked over the edge. Coloured fish weave a graceful ballet in shaded water beneath the wooden slats of the entire deck. She stares for a moment at the beautiful creatures, then raises her eyes to the ocean. Skirting the hole, she crosses to the gate, and places her hand on the scalding catch. Two steps lead down to white, sizzling sand, exactly like the brochure, and beyond the beach, about twenty metres away, the sea smacks gently. 'Well my darling, how do you like it so far?' Will is at her side, smiling down at her.

She wraps her arms around his body and with eyes closed, leans her head on his chest. 'It's perfect.'

With his arm around her shoulders he draws her back to their cool, marbled room and lifts a champagne bottle from a tumble of ice in a silver bucket. 'Just as I promised?' He grins.

'Just as you promised.' She nods, watching as he polishes two flutes, and wraps the white cloth round the neck of the bottle. There's a muffled pop and golden liquid flows into the glasses, in a mist of vapour. He hands her a glass and raises his own. 'To us.'

'To us.'

They sit outside for a long time, until the ruddy face of the sun dips into the pillow of the sea. The tension begins to leave Fee's shoulders. Will describes his plans for them for the following day. 'I've done a bit of research. There's a walk along the cliffs. You can't see it from here because of all this greenery, but it's round there.' He hooks his fingers in a curve to indicate the area behind and to the left of where they are sitting. 'Apparently there's a little restaurant up there where they sell fresh mussels.' He winks at her. 'I know how much you like mussels!'

Fee laughs. The sound catches her by surprise, and she wonders when she last laughed out loud.

'There's a private bay just over the headland. I've hired a sailing boat so we can get to it. Apparently, it's the only way in but then we'll have the place to ourselves. I thought we could do some diving.'

Fee widens her eyes. 'It's been a long time since I scuba dived, I'm not sure I can remember how.'

Will shrugs, 'You'll be fine, it's like riding a bike, well, without the pedals of course.' He grins like a boy. 'Anyway, I've hired the kit now.'

'I didn't know you could sail.' There is so much to learn about this amazing man.

'Aah, I have many talents.' He winks at her. 'Would you like me to show you another one?'

'And what might that be?'

'Follow me and I'll show you.' He stands and takes her hand.

'Oh, by the way, I've organised a surprise for you tomorrow afternoon'.

Fee tilts her head at him.

'What is it?'

'Well,' They reach the bed and he puts his arms round her, 'I could tell you,' He kisses her tenderly, 'but then I'd have to kill you.'

***

She is wearing a rather dressy affair of gauzy layers that exposes shoulders, already pink from the morning's walk. Will is in a dashing dark suit and tie.

'We look like a couple of guests at a wedding.' She smiles, and he fires her an enigmatic look. The telephone rings in their room and Will rushes to answer it.

'The car's here, come on.' He hustles her from the room and down to the foyer.

A shining black limousine stands outside, with a uniformed chauffeur holding open the rear door. Fee slides inside, across the smooth, warmth of the leather seat, and waits for Will to join her.

'Will, what...?'

He lifts a finger to her lips.

'Shhh, just wait and see.'

The car pulls away and cruises along the coast road, its wheels sending up sandy dust that fogs out the view behind. Fee sits in silence beside Will, trying to guess what lies ahead. She becomes aware that he is looking at her, and turns to meet his gaze. He is holding something out to her - a small box. She knows what it will hold, and is in no doubt now, that she will accept this engagement ring with all her heart. Smiling, she watches as he drops to one knee, on the floor of the car and opens the small casket, then he takes her hand, and her eyes move to the box. Nestled in the satin is not an engagement ring but a plain golden band.

'Will!' she stares at the ring in bafflement. 'I don't know...'

'Fee, please. Don't make me wait any longer.'

The car pulls up outside a tiny, white church.

'Don't say a word yet.' Will snaps the box shut and pockets it. 'Come inside and have a look. Take your time.'

He leaps from the car, and the chauffeur opens Fee's door.

Hand in hand, they step into a miniature chapel. Outside in the dazzling light the driver waits to be summoned. Will watches her face as she looks around her. His own conveys a mixture of love and fear. Music plays faintly in the background and, although feeling duped Fee is captivated by the trouble he's taken. She looks around her at the small coloured window and the stone floor. What will she do? Does she love Will? Yes, of that she is sure. Would she have married him eventually? Yes, that too. If in the future then why not now?

'But there's Kitty, I want her to know you too, and to be at our wedding.'

'She is.' Will grins at her and jerks his head towards the back of the chapel. To Fee's amazement her daughter stands alone and beaming in the doorway, wearing a pretty, lilac dress, and clutching a posy of freesias.

'Hello Mummy,' she calls. Her eyes sparkle with excitement.

'Gloria took her to the airport, and she travelled as an unaccompanied minor. Gloria really loves a conspiracy,' Will tells her.

'So, what do you think?'

Fee feels her throat constrict. She nods her head slowly, then more decisively.

'Yes, I will marry you.'

Kitty comes flying up the aisle, her curls bouncing under a small floral band,

'Mummy, you look beautiful. Come on.' She grabs Fee's hand and pulls her towards the altar. 'Have you got the ring, Will?'

Will pats his pocket,

'Right here little lady,' he reassures in an American accent. Kitty giggles. A minister arrives from a door at the back, and behind Fee the chauffeur and an unknown lady slide through the entrance.

'That's Maria, she's been looking after me.' Kitty is jigging with excitement. 'Were you surprised Mummy?'

'That doesn't go anywhere near describing how I feel you little monkey.' Fee hugs her daughter to her then turns to Will. 'OK, let's do this.'

***

Leaving the beaming taxi driver to drive Maria home, they climb the shining white steps to the hotel. A quiet cheer rises from behind the reception desk and staff begin to clap. Soon guests, clad in sandals and swim suits, are joining in.

In the restaurant their table is unmistakable, strewn as it is with fragrant Frangipane, Amaryllis and Orchid flowers. Once their glasses have been charged, Will raises his flute.

'Thank you, my lovely Fee. You had me worried there for a moment.'

'Well, you took a bit of a risk, husband,' Fee leans towards Kitty, 'and as for you young lady, how on earth did you manage to keep such a huge secret?'

'Gloria helped, but Will organised it all. He got my passport and visa - you signed the forms you know.'

'I did?'

Will looks sheepish,

'I'm afraid I tricked you a bit. All those forms I gave you to sign, some of them were for your passport and visa, one was a marriage form and one was for Kitty's passport.'

'I can't believe I was so stupid.'

'You were distracted. I took advantage.'

Fee punches him lightly on his suited arm. 'I'm not sure I'll ever be able to trust you again.'

Dishes of food begin to arrive: lobster, langoustines, caviar, salads, cheeses and fruit. After their meal, sated and exhausted, the little family climb aboard the gleaming lift, and are fired off to the cool peace of their bedroom. A small bed has been erected for Kitty, who will spend one night with them. In the morning Maria will collect her and put her on a plane back to London.

Chapter 67

'Hi Gloria, it's Paul.'

Gloria stands in the empty hall holding the telephone, and her heart drops to her boots.

'Hello, Paul, how are you?'

'I'm round the corner. I thought I'd come and see Kitty?'

'Well, er, she's not here. She went to tea with a friend.' Gloria prays silently for forgiveness.

'That's OK. Tell me where, and I'll pick her up afterwards. I expect she could do with some parent time, with Fee being away.'

Gloria is hopeless at lying.

'Paul, you'd better come round, I've got somethin' to tell you.'

In the lounge, she sits opposite Paul, wearing an expression of profound discomfort.

'Kitty went to Mauritius.'

He frowns, not understanding.

'They took her with them?'

'No. I drove her to the airport and put her on a plane. The thing is, it's not Fee's fault.' Gloria dries up and gives her head a small shake. Placing her hands on the arms of her chair she gets ready to push herself upright. 'Would you like a cup of tea?'

'No. Just tell me what's going on.'

She subsides into the cushions and meets Paul's baffled gaze.

'They're getting' married. - Fee and Will. It's a surprise.' She rushes on. 'Fee doesn't know anythin' about it. Will arranged it all, and Kitty and I kept it a secret. Kitty went this mornin', to be a bridesmaid.'

Paul wonders if things could get any worse. Being raided by the police should top the list but this overshadows everything. He stares at Gloria as she stands up,

'I'll make that tea.' She scuttles from the room.

Kitty didn't tell him, her own father, that Mummy was about to re-marry. Tears rise to blur his vision, and he pats his pockets for a tissue. Gloria comes in with the tray, and her expression softens when she sees him blowing his nose. 'I'm sorry Paul. I didn't know how to tell you.

'Here.' She hands him a cup, and he takes a sip.

She explains about the telephone call, and her conspiracy with Kitty, buying an outfit and handing her over to a stewardess at the airport.

'And you don't know if Fee went through with it?'

'Not yet.'

Paul sits blowing his tea.

'What's he like?'

'I'm not sure. I haven't met him. He seemed nice enough on the phone. Well spoken, and he smiled a lot.'

'I thought you said you hadn't met him.'

Gloria puts down her cup. 'I haven't but you can hear someone smilin' in their voice, can't you?'

'Never thought about it.' Paul shrugs.

The phone in his pocket starts to vibrate and he digs it out and answers it. 'Oh, hi mate. Good trip?'

Gloria hears her son's voice speaking faintly into Paul's ear, and beams.

'What?' Paul stands up suddenly. 'OK. I'm at Fee's with your mum. Yes. See you in about an hour.' He lowers the phone slowly, a look of disbelief on his face.

Gloria reaches over to touch his arm.

'What's happened Paul? Are they alright? There hasn't been another accident has there?'

'No.' He puts his hands to his temples, blinkering his eyes. 'I need to think.' His mind focusses on what Mick has just told him. He needs proof.

'Gloria, is Fee's phone at home?'

'Yes. It's in her room. She got one of them pay as you go ones to use over there.'

Flying upstairs he realises he doesn't know which room is Fee's, but after a brief search, her room is obvious. It has her smell, and the compulsive neatness he had almost forgotten.

The mobile is in the bedside table, and he switches it on. Thankfully it has some battery power, and when it comes to life he stares at the screen, then without a word he gallops down the stairs and out of the front door.

Chapter 68

The hall phone rings beside Gloria and she gives a lurch. 'Hello?'
'Gloria, it's me.' Fee's voice is joyful.
'Fee. Can you forgive me?'
'Yes, I forgive you. I do. What a time I've had, thanks to Will, and you and Kitty.'
Gloria's knees buckle, and she sits on the bottom stair, dropping the duster that was clutched in her hand. 'I'm so relieved. Tell me all about it.'
When Fee has given Gloria a brief account of her wedding day, she confirms that Kitty will be on her return journey as planned.
Gloria takes a breath. 'I had to tell Paul about the weddin'. He wanted to take Kitty out for the evening.'
'Oh.' There's a pause. 'Well he had to know some time. I'm sorry you had to tell him, it should have come from me. How did he take it?'
'Not too bad.'
'I must go, my battery's low. Let me know when Kitty gets home. You can text if you like.'
'OK.' She has no idea how to send a text.

***

Paul sits at the departure gate. He had to pay nearly a thousand pounds for a last-minute flight, plus the cost of a rail journey to London for an emergency visa and the taxi to get here.
His phone rings from an unknown number.
'Is that you, Paul?' Paul pulls the receiver a short distance from his ear.

'Yes Gloria. Is everything alright?' He keeps his voice low in the public space.
'I didn't think I'd get you with this silly phone, but it works.'
'Yes, it works. You can speak normally, no need to shout. What's up?' Gloria moderates her voice. 'I just wanted to see if you were OK. You ran away, and I was worried about you? I couldn't get hold of you at home, then I remembered that Mick had put your number in the phone for me.'
'Sorry about that, Gloria. I had to meet Mick about something.' He puts his bag between his feet and pats his coat for his cigarettes before realising that he can't smoke in here. 'Have you heard from Fee?'
Gloria introduces sympathy to her voice. 'Yes. They got married Paul. She sounded happy.'
He bites his lip.
'You OK Paul?'
'Yeah, fine. I've been called away on business. When Kitty gets back, give her a kiss from me and tell her I'll see her in a few days. Mick's feeding Topsy, so she needn't worry about that.'
People around him stir, and a queue begins to form at the desk.
'I have to go Gloria. I've told Mick and Maurice I'm away. You can call them if you need anything. Will you be OK with the kids?'
'Yes, we'll be fine. I'll get Mick to collect Kitty if necessary. Don't worry.'

***

Gloria presses the red button to end her call with a sense that something odd is going on.

***

The sun burns Paul's neck and cooks his shoulders as he pays the Asian taxi driver, with currency obtained from a cash machine at the airport. He should have worn something lighter but it had been cool at home. The car drives off, and he turns to stare at a flight of white steps leading up to a low, wood and glass hotel. Behind him cars, scooters, bicycles and horse drawn tourist carriages vie for space on the road, but in front, to either side of the steps, lush trees and heavy flowers flop over tightly cropped squares of grass. He picks up his small bag, and climbs to the entrance. Familiar smells: sun screen and expensive perfume, pervade the cooled atmosphere of the foyer. He approaches the reception desk and drops his case on the floor. A small, dark skinned man raise his eyebrows in expectation.

288

'Good morning sir, do you have a reservation?'

'No, I'm afraid I left home in a bit of a hurry. I'm here to find someone.'

'I'll help if I can, sir.' The man pulls the immaculate cuffs of his shirt from inside the sleeves of his navy jacket, and places his fingers on the edge of the smooth wooden counter. His badge advertises his role as Manager, and his name, Francois Bernier.

'I'm looking for a couple,' says Paul, 'a man and woman who married here recently. I'm afraid I don't know their surname, but the woman's name, before, was Fiona Thomas.

The manager's expression becomes suspicious.

'May I ask your business with them sir?'

Paul thrusts his face at the bloke. 'Look, I need to see Fee. I don't have to explain my reasons to you.'

Bernier pulls himself up, and points the end of his nose in Paul's direction.

'Well Mr Thomas, I'm afraid she and her husband are out. Perhaps you'd like a cold drink while you wait. There is a bar through there or we can bring something out here if you prefer. He indicates low chairs not far away.

'No thanks. Do you know where they went?

'Sorry sir. I can't tell you that, but please feel free to stay as long as you need.' He is polite to the point of offensiveness. 'Perhaps you'd like to book a room?'

A sign behind the desk exhibits prices well beyond Paul's pocket and he declines, deciding to venture back onto the street in search of either the happy couple, or a cheaper place to stay.

Heat blasts his face as he leaves the air conditioning. On a whim, he drops into a 'trash for trippers' shop next door, and comes out half an hour later sporting a cheap tee shirt with a picture of a Dodo plodding across its chest, a pair of khaki coloured knee-length shorts and a pair of rubber flip flops. He feels less out of place.

Holding a parcel of his cast-off clothing in one hand, and his travel bag in the other, he looks up the street, undecided which way to go. At the sight of a sign blinking out the word: HOTEL, he shuffles towards it, the flip flops uncomfortable between his toes.

Once checked into a simple room, he returns to the street enjoying the release from carrying his heavy belongings. In the absence of any sign of Fee he decides to park himself strategically in a pavement café, and chooses a shady spot under a canopy, half hidden behind some plants in tubs. He can see the entrance to Fee's hotel on the opposite side of the road.

A waiter appears with a promptness unknown at home, and takes his order for beer. Moments later a chilled glass arrives, along with a ticket, stabbed onto a spike. Very pleasant. A person could get used to this type of life; Max was right. Yeah, his mind remains in contemplation of Max, he certainly is a very clever bloke.

He finishes his drink and orders another, watching tourists and traffic, his eyes drooping after his long flight. There is movement over the road and his eyes fly open. A familiar figure runs up the steps of the hotel. She's lost weight. He downs the second beer, and prepares to leave. When Fee comes back through the glass doors wearing a jacket, and carrying a white shoulder-bag, Paul digs out a handful of notes, and stabs them onto the spike with the chits, then squeezes between metal tables, and crosses the road, dodging between taxis and bicycles. Fee is walking purposefully, and soon rounds a corner. Paul hops along in his unsuitable footwear and when he gets to the junction, peers round the wall in time to see his ex-wife climbing a pathway that, according to a white, painted sign, leads to the cliff top. Keeping his distance, he follows, and watches as the woman he still loves, reaches the top of the rough path, and climbs a short distance further onto a black rock that juts like a claw towards the translucent, blue sky, higher than any other visible point. Paul can hear the sea crashing below as she lowers herself to the ground, and dangles her legs over the edge. With her hands on the volcanic surface, she leans forward gingerly to stare at the breakers far below.

In the distance stands a restaurant. Covered verandas skirt its wooden sides, and indistinct figures move on them. Is this where Fee is headed, to meet her new spouse, to chink romantic glasses and taste each other's food? Perhaps he is already in there, waiting for her. Paul ducks out of sight to watch.

Before long a shape steps from the restaurant and strides towards them.

***

Although Gloria urged Fee to go away with Will, home life alone with the children is far from easy. Since the news of Twitch's murder, Sam has become morose, spending too much time in his room, and screaming at Josh when he tries to come in. Little Josh doesn't understand where his mother has gone. He is clingy, and cries for her or Maurice, especially at night. Gloria has spent many an evening cuddling the little boy to sleep.

Lucas and Olivia had been getting used to losing their own mother, but the discovery of Twitch's body and attending another funeral, has upset them. Gloria has changed a few wet sheets and pants for her grandchildren. It's to be expected of course, the poor kiddies, but Gloria, capable and efficient, and experienced in matters of bereavement, is still out of her depth and looking forward to Fee's return.

This evening they are waiting for Kitty in the muted grandeur of the airport. Mick couldn't come because he is on a late shift, and Maurice, well she didn't ask him. Why should she expect the poor man to drag himself out? He's got enough on his plate. She stands among the waiting crowd with Josh in her arms.

People trickle through the gate wearing travel-weary expressions. All round them, excited families, their voices swallowed by the cavernous space, crane to spot loved ones. On the periphery, thick necked chauffeurs in straining suits, gossip together, holding scrawled notices to attract emerging clients.

Kitty's flight is late, but it has landed. Gloria watches the display board, and eventually sees that Kitty is collecting her luggage. The child will be tired and tetchy after a journey half way round the world in little more than a weekend.

It's Josh who spots Kitty hand in hand with an air hostess. 'Kitty, Kitty, Kitty,' he cries, and leans towards the girl, his arms outstretched. Gloria puts him down and grasps his hand, shoving through the crowd to the end of the barrier.

While she signs a discharge form, the children hug Kitty, demanding to know about her adventure, but Kitty is half-asleep and can hardly talk, so they straggle back to the car in silence.

Gloria stares alertly at the monotonous motorway, wondering how many fellow road users are suffering from jet lag. She's longing to know from Kitty how everything went, but it will have to wait until the morning. She looks through the mirror at the children, nodding in the back seats, and decides to keep them off school tomorrow. One day won't hurt, and Sam and Josh will benefit from hearing something happy.

***

Sirens split the scorching air and a police car, its blue light ablaze, weaves between vehicles, which pull over to let it pass. Another siren, then another. People stop and turn, murmuring questions:

'Que'est'ce'qui ce pass?'

'Something's happened, I can't see anything?'

Two police cars skid around the corner and up a gritty pathway, unsuitable though it is for vehicles. Behind them an ambulance and a fire truck. The vehicles slew to different sides on the grassy cliff top, and Paul strides to meet them.

'God, I'm glad you're here.' His voice breaks with emotion. 'My wife is at the bottom of the cliff and that man, he raises a stabbing finger, Max Rutherford, pushed her.' He is suddenly overwhelmed with the enormity of the situation and lets his knees buckle until he is sitting on the ground between an ambulance and a police car.

Men rush from vehicles. One concerned officer helps Paul to his feet and encourages him into his car. Paul watches another pull Max towards the second police vehicle. He peers through the windscreen trying to make out what is going on with Max, but grey dust on the glass makes it impossible.

He gives his statement: Max must have tapped him for information about his wife during their counselling sessions, and then insinuated himself into her life. Paul had followed Fee out here to warn her, and had watched her climb to the cliff top on her own. He had hidden behind a bush to get a feel for the situation, and to be sure he was right about his theory. Max came out of the restaurant and climbed up the peak, then, instead of joining his wife, he had put his arms out and shoved her over the edge her death.

Motive? Who knew? He was very secretive about his private life. Money perhaps?

Was Fee well off? Quite comfortable, and her father was wealthy. When Paul had seen what was about to happen, he had rushed out but was too late. Max saw him appear and simply froze on the spot, and that's where he still was when the police turned up. He didn't know who had called the police, maybe someone from the restaurant?

The copper excuses himself and leaves Paul sweating in the sun-beaten car. Paul watches as he walks to the other car and confers with the second policeman. They compare notes, gesticulating and shrugging, then Paul's officer returns and asks Paul to step from the car.

He's pleased to obey, there is a slight breeze out here on the cliff top.

When the policeman speaks it is in a serious voice. 'Mr Thomas? I must inform you that you are under arrest for the murder of Mrs Fiona Owen.'

Paul's head is buzzing as his rights are read and he is handcuffed, and pushed back into the sweltering car. As they swing in a circle to return to the town, Paul catches a glimpse of Max, looking at him, his backside rests on the wing of the car and his arms are folded. There is a faint smirk on his face as he watches the car turn, and leave the scene.

Chapter 69

'It must have been hard knowing your ex-wife was marrying another man. Perhaps you were hoping she would come back to you.' The policeman, who bears the unlikely name of Kipling, sits opposite Paul at a wooden table, his heavy French accent giving the room the feel of a cheap 'B' movie. It's an effect emphasised by the stuffy little room. Outside the open window, the sea slaps and sucks against rocks, and happy voices contrast with the stern tone of Paul's interrogator.
Paul glares. 'Do you think I travelled half way round the world to confront a man on a cliff top, and murder my wife?'
'*His* wife, sir. She was his wife.' The policeman pauses to watch Paul sweat. 'And jealousy is a powerful emotion.'
'No, you don't understand.'
The man, olive skinned and attractive in a white shirt, open at the neck, cocks his head to one side.
'I think you need to do some talking Monsieur Thomas. You are in a lot of trouble, and I'm fascinated to understand exactly why you found it necessary to threaten a man, and push his wife over a cliff to her death.'
'I did not threaten him. We hardly spoke.' Paul can hear his voice rising and pulls it back down. 'I simply watched, out of sight, as he pushed the woman I love, to her death.'
'Well Mr Owen has another tale to tell, and believe me, from our enquiries, it is far more convincing.'
Paul gulps in some air and wills himself to breathe evenly. 'I can't imagine what Max has told you. He does know things about me

294

nobody else does, and some of them are not things I'm proud of, but I repeat, I am innocent. He is guilty.

The officer crosses his arms across his chest and settles back on his chair. 'The floor is yours, Mr Thomas. Explain yourself.'

Paul's mind searches for a place to start.

'Years ago, two or three, I forget now, I was having a tough time accepting that Fee had left me. I was angry and hurting - myself and others - so I went to counselling. My counsellor was *him*.' He jerks his thumb over his shoulder as though Max were in the hallway.

'Monsieur Owen?'

'Yes. He told me his name was Max Rutherford, so when Fee said she was coming out here with someone called Will, I thought nothing of it. I didn't know they were going to get married.'

The policeman sits forward and leans his folded arms on the table.

Paul thinks back to his sessions with Max. 'He helped me a lot.

'When I heard that he was taking Fee to Mauritius I was hit with a powerful feeling that she was in danger. I felt uneasy. Max had given the impression that he was totally ethical, but all the time he was using the information I gave him to get into bed with Fee.'

Paul starts to tell what he can remember about his sessions with Max, but the inspector stops him with an upward sweep of his hand.

'Monsieur Owen has told us all this. We know he counselled you, and also that you have a volatile temper.'

Paul slumps into his chair and stares at Kipling.

'He told you that?'

'Yes sir. Also, we have been in touch with the police in your local area,' he glances at his piece of paper. 'Lee-may-shire.'

'Lymeshire.'

'Ah,' the man smiles, 'Thank you Monsieur, my English can always be improved.' His face grows serious. 'These *Lymeshire* Police tell us that you are suspected of the murder of your wife's friend, Mrs Sabrina Roman.'

Paul drops his head forwards. His palms smell of institutional soap.

'I haven't killed anyone.'

'And the rape?'

The question comes like a thump in the chest. Paul raises his eyes slowly to meet those of the officer.

'Rape?'

Yes. Mr Owen told me that you raped Ms Roman.

'He told you that? Why would he say such a thing? I did not rape Twitch. I liked her.'

'And now she is dead.'

'Yes, that's true.' His body sags.

***

'Thank you for coming in Mr Owen. I know this is a trying time for you.' Kipling is all sympathy and Max dips his head.

'I'm very sorry we have to ask you these questions, when you must be suffering greatly from your loss.'

Max looks dully at Inspector Kipling.

'I don't feel anything, really.'

'Could you tell me, please, exactly what happened this afternoon?'

'My wife and I decided to go for a walk along the cliff top. We had found a restaurant up there, "Le Chamarel", we'd been there before.' Max stops speaking, his face quivering, shoulders shaking with suppressed emotion. 'Sorry.'

'That's alright Sir. Would you like a glass of water?'

When Max nods, Kipling fills a tumbler. He watches Max take a gulp and fumble in his pocket for a handkerchief.

'So, you walked up the path to the top?'

'Well, I went up first, Fee was having her nails done so I brought a book and sat on the veranda reading. Fee said she'd follow, and she did. I was only there half an hour before I looked up and saw her in the distance, sitting on the edge of the cliff. I knew it must be her. She loved it there. Said it felt like the prow of a ship.'

The inspector's face is full of sympathy. He reaches a hand towards Max, not quite making contact. 'Go on Sir.'

'I decided to go up and join her. We've sat there before, it's such a beautiful spot. I ordered two glasses of wine and carried them along the cliff path. It's a bit of a trek but I knew she'd love the gesture.' Max blinks, and wipes his palm across his eyes.

'I'd only gone a little way when a figure came out of the shrubs at the side of the path that leads up from the town. A man ran up the slope towards Fee and I could see what he was going to do. I dropped the glasses and ran towards them but I was too late.'

Max sobs out the last words and covers his face with both hands. His shoulders heave and Kipling looks on, waiting for the emotion to subside.

'Why do you think he would do this thing?' The policeman frowns.

296

'I suppose he'd found out about our marriage. Perhaps Gloria told him, Gloria looks after the children. She knew I'd planned to surprise Fee. I needed to confide in her to get Kitty out here.'

'Kitty is Fee's daughter, is that right?'

'Yes.' Max jerks his head up, a look of realisation dawning on his face. 'Has anyone told her?'

'Kipling shakes his head. 'Non, Monsieur. Do you think you will be able to do that?'

Max nods.

Max is subjected to a multitude more questions.

How long has he known Paul?

About a year.

How does Paul's anger manifest itself?

Anything to do with Fee, or antisocial behaviour and he loses control He has beaten people up.

Does Max have notes relating to his consultations with Paul?

Yes. Only relevant to his anger, though.

Max repeats in a monotone, details of Paul's attacks on Twitch, his neighbours, and the yobs in the chip shop. By the end of the interview his face is pale. Deep lines descend from his nose to the corners of his mouth and his eyes are red rimmed and darkly circled.

Detective Kipling pushes his chair from the table. With his hands still resting on the edge he contemplates the man opposite. He looks exhausted.

'I think that will be all for now, Mr Owen. Thank you very much for your time.'

***

Children, no matter how sad or tired, must be kept occupied. After lunch Kitty and the others troop along the canal with Gloria, their destination, a village with a tea room beside a small playground.

Gloria wears a tightly fitting emerald green dress under her camel coat. Her feet, in brown support tights, are laced into stalwart shoes, which keep her upright despite the uneven surface of the path. Over her arm bounces a patent leather handbag containing the necessary accessories for the outing: Tissues, wipes, plasters, money, lipstick and more.

As they trudge, Gloria explains to the children about the history of the canals.

'Children used to travel with their families you know. Helpin' their mums and dads. They had to go to school at a different place each day, and sometimes the school would come to them, and the church.'

'Where did they live?' Kitty was more interested than the others, walking beside Gloria with Josh's hand gripped tightly in her own.

'In those long narrow boats. There's not much room inside. They would have had to be very tidy.'

They stop to look at some ducks, and Gloria pulls bread from her bottomless bag. The *wack, wack* laughter from the birds, diminishes to quiet muttering as they scoop pieces of bread from the surface of the water with their greedy beaks.

'Keep hold of that child, Kitty.' Gloria checks on Josh, and grabs Lucas's hand before he follows his bread into the water amid the hungry flock.

In the park, the children run straight to the equipment. The vigorous walk has warmed Gloria and she slips off her coat and drapes it over the back of a bench. Her phone trills, and still standing she grabs it from her bag. A familiar voice hails her.

'Hello Gloria.'

'Will. It's lovely to hear from you. Congratulations.'

'Gloria…'

'What is it? Is somethin' wrong?' His silence scares her. 'Will. Is Fee OK?' There's a long stillness and Gloria's hand reaches for the back of the seat.

'No. Gloria, she's dead.'

The phone clatters from Gloria's grasp and she doubles over and vomits on the grass.

***

Maurice, Mick and Gloria sit round the kitchen table. They have put the children to bed, trying to appear normal. Nobody has yet told Kitty what happened.

'Have you got anything to drink, Gloria?' Maurice looks vaguely around the kitchen.

'In the other room, in the cupboard.' Gloria doesn't move, and Maurice rises slowly, pads out, and returns with a whisky bottle. 'Glasses?'

Gloria points and Maurice fetches three tumblers, the kind the children would drink squash from. They each take a slug of neat liquor. The harsh liquid jolts Gloria to life.

'How are we goin' to tell them?'

Mick raises his eyes from the honey coloured fluid at the bottom of his glass.

'We just have to say it. Probably best to tell the school that they won't be in for a while. We'll do it together.'

Gloria looks at him with a feeble smile. 'I'm so glad you said that, Son. I don't think I could do it on my own.'

Maurice is shaking his head slowly from side to side.

'I can't believe they've arrested Paul. That's almost the worst bit. Kitty's got no mum or dad to lean on.'

'She's got a granddad. Fee's father's not far away.' Gloria looks dubious. 'I don' think they get on – got on, very well. Fee didn't talk about her father much.'

'What about Paul's parents, anyone know about them? Maurice looks from one to the other.

'Moved away I think he said, but alive as far as I know.' Mick shrugs his shoulders. 'Poor little kid. She ought to be able to stay here with you Ma.'

Gloria's face grows grim. 'I'll do everythin' in my power to make sure she does. That little kiddy's had enough upset without havin' to leave her home again.'

'You can't bring up all the children on your own, though, Ma.'

'Well you'll just have to help me.' The two men look at one another in silence.

Mick revolves his head to relieve tension in his neck. He stops, his eyes on the ceiling and says,

'I don't trust that Will. Bit of a coincidence him being Paul's neighbour and ending up with Fee. Paul was incredibly angry when I told him I'd seen him.'

'Paul came here to look at Fee's phone.' Gloria stands up. 'Let's have a look at it.' She trots from the room and returns with the mobile device in her hand. 'The battery's flat.'

They plug in the charger and find Will's picture, and a couple of text messages, nothing incriminating, just *I'm on my way* and *Can't wait to see you tonight.*

'Well, we've got his number. Let's see if we can find him on the internet. Maurice grabs Fee's lap top from a shelf and opens it. He taps away for a while, and the others wait, sipping their drinks.

'It's weird that they didn't email each other. I can't find a single reference to Will on here.' He clicks to open the browser and types in the mobile telephone number from Fee's phone.

'Ah. Here's something.' Maurice puts his face closer to the screen. 'Max Rutherford. Counsellor. There's an address in Chelterton, and a landline number.' He raises his eyes to the others. 'Did Fee say anything to you about his job, Gloria?'

'Yes. She said he worked on the rigs. You sure you put in the right number? Max isn't even his name.'

***

After a lot of paperwork - bloody bureaucracy according to DI Bailey – and weeks of finger tapping, Paul arrives at Chelterton Police Station in a black van. Thank God, thinks Bailey, that there is an extradition treaty between the UK and Mauritius. He regards the familiar face across the table. He's not quite so cocky now. Caught in the act, the policeman thinks. He isn't even trying to deny his guilt. The look on the Paul's face is one familiar to Bailey, he calls it the 'fair-cop-guvnor' look. Villains get it when they realise there's no way out. Meticulous police investigation has left no room for doubt. He murdered his ex-wife, and most likely, her house mates as well.

Little Kitty, Mr Thomas's own daughter, told them her father had hidden behind the bushes opposite her house, and several cigarette butts bearing the man's DNA were found there, on the soil. A woman in Baker Avenue identified him as the man she had seen on several occasions, mounting his motor bike outside her house, and once, coming out of the park.

Thomas has denied the rape of Mrs Roman, but Mr Rutherford's records state that he admitted the offence. They are awaiting DNA evidence from the house. If semen samples are found then Thomas is well and truly stuffed.

'You were told not to leave the country, Mr Thomas.' The suggestion of a triumphant smile plays on his lips.

'Yeah, well I disobeyed. No law against that is there?'

'You would do well to co-operate. Being difficult will do you no favours, especially when this goes to court, which I can assure you it will.

'If you say so.' Anger and frustration make Paul's voice almost inaudible, but Bailey resists the temptation to ask him to repeat his words.

There is a brisk knock, and a uniformed constable shows in Paul's solicitor, the same one who had been so impressed by Paul's attendance at Max's clinic.

'I think my client has said enough for now Detective.' The lawyer beams down at Paul. 'He and I need to talk, while you decide whether you plan to charge him.'

***

In a bedroom in Crispin Road, Maurice curls his body round his children. He stares into the darkness and thinks about Twitch, and the way she died.

***

Gloria is alone on the sofa. Kitty lies in her arms, sobbing, as she has done for most of the last 24 hours. Gloria doesn't know what the others are doing but for now she doesn't care.

***

Mick walks along the hotel corridor to the night kitchen, and sticks his head in. The young chef is on the iPad again.

'You'll get square eyes, as my mother used to say. Well, she probably still says it, but not to me.'

'Mothers eh?' The young chef glances up from his game.

'Yeah, mothers.' Mick thinks of Gloria. 'Couldn't be without mine, she's a star.'

'Mm.' The chef's lanky legs stick out like clothes props from the chair, and his eyes remain riveted to the screen.

'See ya.' Mick calls as he leaves.

***

Max sits in his consulting room and stares into the flames. His receptionist went home hours ago, after weeping and wailing all over him for about half an hour. Alone at last he pulls some papers from his pocket and one by one, throws them into the fire. He watches as the edges glow and blacken until they are nothing but ash and soot.

COURT

Chapter 70

Posters offering legal advice, monetary support and counselling services move in and out of focus on the institutional grey of the wall in the room where Paul waits for his turn in the dock.

Elsewhere in the court building, witnesses for the defence and the prosecution lurk, awaiting their five minutes of fame: the bloke he hit in the chip shop, the druggie across the hall, the woman who witnessed him coming from the park, and of course Max.

For the defence, Maurice and Mick, people from work, Mr and Mrs Hun Po, Julie: Max's receptionist, Penny, Max's ex-girlfriend, Iris, the woman from work, who gave him Max's card, and Gloria. Not much of a show.

His solicitor has employed the services of a barrister, David Porterhouse. He's costing a fortune, but Paul has some hope that the man may be worth it. The bespectacled lawyer is tiny, possibly 4ft 3 or 4 at most, but what he lacks in stature is compensated for by the sharpness of his mind. As he questioned Paul and the solicitor before this case, Paul felt his confidence grow. Perhaps things would be alright. Now however, in this lonely room, his mind is playing negative tricks.

***

The public gallery is full. After the sensational press coverage, there is much curiosity.

'All rise.' The Clerk to the Court, a young woman in a dark grey suit, and wearing flat black pumps, stands to expose horizontal creases and shining mounds in the back of her over-snug skirt. The courtroom rises to its feet and the Judge, Lord William Cannon, stalks onto a platform and moves to stand behind a chair at the centre of a dark-wood table. He faces the courtroom his legs hidden from view, nods and sits. The room subsides and settles with a scraping of chairs, a low murmur of voices and rustling of papers.

The Clerk rises again and reads out the indictment that Paul pushed Fee to her death, then the lawyer for the prosecution, David Fitzsimons, steps forward. 'My Lord, members of the jury.' Seven women and five men, sit upright, their eyes following the gaunt, robed figure of the Prosecutor with avid attention. 'We are here to show that Paul James Thomas of …' He gives Paul's new address, 'pushed his ex-wife, newly married to Mr Maximus James William Owen-Rutherford, from a clifftop in Mauritius, where she was enjoying her honeymoon. 'I will show that Mr Thomas,' he indicates Paul, sitting in his enclosure, 'has a violent temper, was obsessed with his ex-wife's movements and lied to his friends. Furthermore, I will demonstrate that he had the opportunity and the motive to murder her.'

Paul pleads 'Not Guilty', and proceedings commence. After a few legal statements regarding facts that both parties agree, such as where the incident took place and who was present, the prosecutor calls his first witness.

'State your name and address.'

'Lee Duggan. Flat 26b, High Street, Longforth.'

'And how do you know Mr Paul Thomas?'

'He was my neighbour and he beat the shit out of me.'

David Porterhouse, the tiny but affable-looking Rottweiler for the defence, stands and leans towards the judge.

'Objection my Lord.'

'Sustained. Mr Duggan, kindly moderate your language.'

'Sorry.' Lee Duggan's pallid face darkens to a deep plum colour.

The jury listens as Duggan describes how Paul broke down the door of his flat and threw his music player down the stairs, causing damage to it and the stair-well. How he had feared for his life and has been suffering from insomnia since the event.

When Fitzsimons has finished, David Porterhouse launches onto his feet:

'What were you doing, Mr Duggan, when the defendant broke down your door?'

'I was playing music with me mate.'

'Just sitting there, minding your own business, listening to a bit of music? The defence lawyer smiles, friendly, warm.

'Yeah. Then this bloke comes barging in, all threats, and thumps me.'

'I wonder, Mr Duggan, if you can explain why the walls and floor of Mr Thomas's flat were vibrating so much that his little girl was unable to hear the television?'

Duggan shrugs, 'Dunno.'

'You don't know? Could it have been because your music was turned up so high that despite being asked to turn it down, you returned the music to full volume when Mr Thomas had returned to his flat next door?'

'Might've. I can't remember now.'

'Perhaps, Mr Duggan, that is because you were, at the same time as "listening",' the barrister wiggles double fingers above both ears, 'to the music, you were also using heroine?'

David Porterhouse looks up at the Judge. 'May I draw your attention to exhibits 3P and 4P, my Lord, the Lymchester Police report on the arrest of Mr Lee Duggan and the subsequent decision to drop charges against Mr Thomas.

Mr Duggan is dismissed, his humiliation complete.

***

Max's casual good looks are strained, and his knuckles on the edge of the witness box, are like eight pearls, gleaming in the fluorescent light. He faces the jury, and they stare back at him with expectant eyes.

'Mr Owen, would you please tell us your relationship to the defendant, Paul Thomas?'

Max nods. 'Of course. He was my client. He came to me for anger management and counselling, after his wife left him.'

'Thank you, Mr Owen. Now, on the subject of Mr Thomas's ex-wife, is it true that you married her recently?'

'Yes. Fee and I met quite by accident in a supermarket, and struck up a conversation. It was only when I was talking to her in the coffee shop that it dawned on me that she might have been married to Paul. Then she gave me her business card and I was almost sure.'

'Did you say anything to her?'

Max shrugs his shoulders, holding out his palms. 'How could I? I would have been breaking client confidentiality. Anyway, it was a brief meeting, and I wasn't sure at that time that things would progress. What would have been the point?

306

The barrister smiles and crosses to his table to pick up a sheaf of papers. He peruses the top one then out loud, intones, 'Today Paul described a violent incident in a take-away shop.' He looks up at the stand. 'Is this a quote from your notes, Mr Owen?'

'Max nods. 'Yes. Paul told me that he had broken a man's foot and kneed him in the testicles.'

'Would you say that Mr Thomas is a danger to society, Mr Owen?'

David Porterhouse bounces to his feet.

'Objection. Speculation.'

'The judge cocks his head a few degrees.

'I'll allow it as Mr Owen could be viewed as an expert witness.'

Porterhouse raises his eyebrows. May I remind you My Lord that Mr Owen is also the only witness to the actual crime under examination in this court?

'The judge's head tilts a few more degrees and his jaw muscles clench as he glares at David Porterhouse.

'Thank you, Mr Porterhouse.' He swivels his eyes across the jury, then on to Counsel for the prosecution. 'Objection sustained. Please choose another route of questioning, Mr Fitzsimons.'

'Very well My Lord.

'Mr Owen, is this also from your notes?' He holds the sheets of paper high in front of his face like a script, and declaims, 'Paul told me that he has committed a rape.' On the word 'rape', Fitzsimons slaps the back of his hand on the papers and fixes his eyes on Max.

There is a murmur from the public gallery and some press members hunch their bodies to write. A couple leave the room, fumbling mobile phones from their pockets as they go.

'Max looks at the jury and raises his voice a little. 'Yes. Those are my notes. Paul came to me in some distress after he had forced himself onto one of my wife's house-mates. This was before Fee, my wife, and I were married.' Max drops his eyes and digs into his pocket for a handkerchief.

'Would you like a glass of water, Mr Owen?'

Max nods and wipes his eyes.

***

David Porterhouse adjusts his glasses, and advances on the witness stand where Max waits, his eyes drifting in blank dispassion, over the courtroom.

'Mr Rutherford, or should I call you Mr Owen?'

Max's mouth forms a smile. 'Either will do. My name is Owen-Rutherford.'

'But you made a point of using a different name with your late wife, from the one you assumed with Mr Thomas when he came to you for help. Is that not so?'

'My business cards say Max Rutherford. My whole name is a bit of a mouthful, so I tend to use Max. When I found that Fee was married to Paul, I'm afraid I was a bit disingenuous. It wasn't ethical to have a relationship with her, given that her husband at the time, was a client, so I used the name Will.'

The lawyer stares hard at the witness, and Max looks back into his eyes. 'But you told her eventually?' Porterhouse puts his hands behind his back and raises his eyebrows in Max's direction.

'No. I never told her. She never knew about Paul's visits to me. I'm not that unscrupulous.'

'Well, you were unscrupulous enough to get her to sign forms without her knowledge, and obtain a consent to marriage without her permission.'

Max gives another small smile. 'Yes, I admit I did that. I was trying to surprise her. I was desperate to marry her.'

'Desperate, why? If she wasn't ready, surely it would have been kinder to wait until she didn't feel pushed into a corner.'

'I knew she wanted to marry me. She was just afraid of the commitment.' Max nods, an expression of absolute certainty on his face.

The lawyer nods and consults his notes. 'Going back to your meeting with Fee. You say you knew she was Mr Thomas's wife on the day that you met her.'

'We bumped into each other in the supermarket. I asked her for a coffee. I didn't realise at first, then she handed me her business card and the penny dropped.

'And is it true that you told her that you worked on the oil rigs, on shift work?'

Max's features stiffen and he swallows. 'Yes. That is true. The fact is, I had another girlfriend at the time, and I wanted to spend time with her too. No point in complicating things until I was sure of my feelings.'

'It seems *very* complicated, to lie so completely about your profession. Why not simply tell the truth about your circumstances?'

Max's upper lip pushes out almost imperceptibly, and the inner ends of his eyebrows draw up. 'I wish I had. If I'd been more honest with them both then she might be alive today.'

'By "them both", I assume you mean Mr Thomas and your wife.'

'Yes.' Max drops his head and squeezes his eyes closed. 'I wove a very tangled web.'

'In fact Mr Owen-Rutherford, it would be true to say that you are a complete liar.'

The barrister for the defence picks up the exhibit envelope containing Max's notes about Paul. He directs a chill stare at Max. 'There is no proof that you wrote these notes at the time you say you did. Isn't it perfectly possible that you wrote them recently, to destroy my client's reputation?'

'I certainly did write them at the time.'

'And then you murdered your wife.' The barrister glares up at Max, in the witness box. 'You killed her and tried to blame Mr Thomas.'

Philip Fitzsimons' voice rings through the court room. 'Ob-jection!'

Judge William Cannon leans over his table and regards the lawyer for the defence. 'May we know where this line of questioning is heading, Mr Porterhouse?'

'Sorry, My Lord. It goes to throwing doubt on the balance of the police investigation.'

'I'll allow it then but please get to the point.'

Max leans over the barrier in front of the witness box. 'Why would I do that? I loved her.' Max points his finger Paul. 'He's the one with anger issues. He's the one who pushed her over the cliff, after thumping people on two separate occ…'

'That's enough Mr Rutherford. Kindly answer only the questions you are asked.'

Porterhouse turns his back on Max and strolls towards the jury. They stare back at him, transfixed. When he reaches the barrier he swings back, and calls across the court.

'Tell me what you know about Mrs Sabrina Roman.'

'I knew she was another one.' Max is clearly agitated, his cool façade lost.

'Another one?'

'Yes, another woman who had abandoned her husband.'

'Ms Roman shared a house with your wife, did she not?'

Max is now shuffling his feet, and scraping his palm repeatedly through his hair, his elbow jabbing the air as if to nudge away some invisible irritant. 'Yes.'

'And you thought of her in those terms? As a deserter of her husband. Is this also how you viewed your wife, and perhaps their other companion Ms Adu?'

'The world is full of such women. I deal daily with men who find it difficult to cope with life after their wives have left them.' Max forces his hands back to the edge of the witness box and fixes his eyes on the floor in front of the witness stand.

'And you blame them for the damage they do?'

'No. Not blame. They have become the regular fodder of my business, I suppose you could say.'

The barrister pulls back a little, allowing pause for thought and a change of tack.

'Tell the court about your childhood, Mr Owen-Rutherford.'

'Objection!' The members of the jury flinch in unison at the volume of the Counsel for the Prosecution's words.

'Sustained.' The judge glares at Porterhouse.

Porterhouse looks beseeching.

'May I have a word in private My Lord?'

'Very well. My Chambers.'

The court waits while Mr Justice William Cannon and David Porterhouse and Philip Fitzsimons leave the room.

Ten minutes later they return, filing through a high wooden door and back to their respective places.

Porterhouse stands in front of his witness once more and poses his question again.

'Tell the court about your upbringing, Mr Owen-Rutherford.'

Max's elbow stabs the air again and his eyes dart round the room.'

'You want me to tell you about my mother, I suppose. Well, she left us, my father and me. I haven't seen her since I was seven - apart from one other occasion when she made it perfectly plain that she had no interest in me.'

'And how was life with your father?'

Max's shoulders slump. 'He beat me. It's the reason I became a counsellor. Anger, violence, resentment, I know about these things first hand. I wanted to…'

'Tell me. What are your hobbies?'

310

'Objection.' Fitzsimons' voice reports like a gunshot, across the court room.

'Over ruled.'

'I don't have much spare time. I like to eat out.

'Did you eat out at the restaurant called Feast, in Chelterton High Street?'

Max stares at the lawyer and says nothing.

'Mr Owen-Rutherford, did you eat at Feast?'

'Yes, I did.'

And was the restaurant, Feast run by Ms Millicent Adu?'

'I'm not sure.'

'Not sure Mr Owen-Rutherford. That seems unlikely, as Ms Adu was a housemate of the defendant's ex-wife, and shared a house with her. A bit of a co-incidence, don't you agree?'

Max mutters something inaudible.

'I'm sorry Mr Owen-Rutherford, would you repeat that for the benefit of the jury, please?'

Max straightens up. 'It does seem a coincidence. I didn't know she was a housemate of my wife.'

'Surely we can't believe that. Surely she would have talked to you about Millie, who ran a restaurant, and Twitch, who suffered from depression. I imagine, Mr Owen-Rutherford, that between them, Mr and Mrs Thomas fed you much information about the goings on at that house in Crispin Road.

'Do you have any other hobbies, Mr Rutherford?'

'I don't get much time for a social life.'

'How about gambling? Do you like a flutter now and then?'

Max takes a sip of his water, and lowers the glass slowly onto the ledge beside him, then he lifts his eyes. 'I do occasionally have a bet, yes.'

'Indeed. Is it not true to say that you have lost thousands of pounds, and that you are in debt to the tune of approximately £150,000?'

'Yes.'

'Thank you, Mr Owen-Rutherford. That will be all.'

***

'The prosecution calls Detective Colin Robins

DI Robins takes the stand and swears to tell the truth. His handsome face is sombre and business like.

Philip Fitzsimons advances towards the stand, his expression, as usual, banal. 'Are you in charge of the investigation into Mrs Fiona Rutherford?'

'I am.'

I believe that the matter was passed to you by the Mauritian police. Is that correct?'

The officer pulls out his notebook. 'Indeed. I received a telephone call from an Inspector Kipling on 15th November, 2002'

'And did you get the impression from Inspector Kipling that Mr Thomas was guilty?'

'He gave no such impression, although he did reveal that Mr and Mrs Rutherford had come to Mauritius to marry, and that they were on their honeymoon. Apparently, they had made themselves very popular in their hotel, and were regular visitors at the restaurant, where they had booked a table when the murder occurred.'

The barrister angles his head. 'But of course, there were no witnesses so you had to investigate Mr Rutherford and Mr Thomas, did you not?'

'We knew Mr Rutherford had been accused repeatedly by Mr Thomas, but we could find no indication that Mr Rutherford had ever behaved in a dangerous or violent way. He had no criminal record. He had bought the glasses of wine, and had thrown them to the ground exactly as he claimed, when he started to run towards the crag.

'He did admit to hiding his identity from Mrs Rutherford, but we were happy with his explanation that this was to protect his professional reputation.

'Mr Thomas on the other hand, was already known to us as a violent man so we concentrated our resources on his movements. We interviewed his young daughter, Kitty, who advised us that Mr Thomas had been seen hiding in the bushes opposite the house, where she and Mrs Rutherford, then Thomas, lived.

'Further investigation revealed cigarette ends containing Mr Thomas's DNA in those bushes. Three further witnesses,' he pauses to consult his notes, 'Mrs Margaret Stonier of 22 Gressingham Avenue, the road that runs down the side of Gressingham playing field, Mrs Gloria Adu and Mr Michael Adu, both known to the defendant, witnessed him on other occasions emerging from the park into Gressingham Road.'

The defendant has a history of violence, and Mr Rutherford's notes from their sessions together revealed that he was obsessed with his wife. He would become angry at the mention of her name. He blamed her for their break up, and as soon as he found she was re-marrying, booked a highly expensive flight to pursue her.

'When he arrived at the hotel in Mauritius where the Rutherfords were staying, he spoke to the manager rudely and displayed aggressive behaviour.'

The barrister turns his eyes to the jury to note that a broad, round shouldered woman with orange hair, is shaking her head and making a note on her pad. Others mutter and shuffle, and a young woman, pregnant by the looks of it, bites her bottom lip. The nail of victory is being driven in, and he raises the hammer once more.

Thank you, inspector. Now if we may, we will hear a little more about Mr Thomas's violence.'

Every scowl and punch is pulled apart until the jury begins to yawn. Fitzsimons recognises that his job is done, and sits down.

Court will resume tomorrow with cross examination by the defence.

***

You say that Mr Thomas committed rape on Mrs Sabrina Roman, of 63 Crispin Road.'

The officer nods, 'That's correct.'

'At any time, did the police receive a complaint from Ms Roman to that effect?'

'No. Mrs Roman never reported the incident.'

'Was there any subsequent DNA evidence?'

'We found finger prints at the house, but no semen.'

'And Mrs Roman is now deceased?'

'Yes. She was murdered. We were already investigating Mr Paul Thomas for her murder when he was arrested in Mauritius.'

'Any evidence of rape on the corpse?'

'Ms Roman drowned and spent some considerable time in the water. Her body was badly damaged.'

'Not so badly that you couldn't tell she had been forcibly drowned.'

The tiny barrister pushes back the sides of his jacket with his wrists, and shoves his hands into the pockets of his impeccable trousers. 'The arrest in Mauritius was just what you needed then. A very convenient corroboration of what you already suspected.'

DI Robins does battle with his face. 'We carried out a thorough investigation into Mr Thomas's movements, as I've already stated.'

The barrister raises a hand. 'Ah yes, indeed you did, into the movements of Mr Thomas, but did you check on Mr Rutherford's movements? Was *his* DNA behind the bushes opposite that house in Crispin Road? Were his notes made at the time of his interviews with my client, or later? Did you investigate any of *those* things Detective Inspector?'

Robins forces his words out. 'No, we did not, but...'

'So, in fact, you have no evidence that my client committed rape, no evidence that he pushed Mrs Owen-Rutherford over that cliff, and no evidence that Mr Owen-Rutherford wrote his notes at the time of his consultation with Mr Thomas. I think it is safe to say that you have no case against my client.'

Up in his enclosure, Paul's face beams. One might imagine him clapping and cheering but he restrains himself.

'No further questions My Lord.' David Porterhouse sweeps back to his chair with an air of contented competence.

***

'The prosecution calls Paul Thomas.'

Standing in position, Paul's face is calm and his body relaxed.

The prosecutor walks towards him wearing a grim expression. 'Would you tell the court why you consulted Mr Owen Rutherford, Mr Thomas?'

Paul assumes a position, a bit like a policeman. His hands are cupped over his genitals and his chin is firm and sure. He looks straight at the barrister. 'I was angry. I blamed Fee – my ex-wife for our break up and the cold-hearted way she walked out with Kitty, my daughter. I was bad tempered at work, and Iris, a colleague, told me to go and get help with the anger.'

'You certainly were angry, weren't you? You beat up two men, frightened your daughter with your violence, raped a woman...'

'I didn't rape anyone.'

'Well, Mr Thomas, according to the notes made by Mr Rutherford at the time of your consultation with him, you admitted to the rape, denying responsibility and insisting that she led you on.'

Paul holds his stance and remains calm. 'I did not rape Twitch.'

'Well I suppose you would say that, knowing there is no evidence to prove it.'

'I did not rape her.' His voice remains steady.

'Do you deny that you broke a man's foot in a brawl?'

Paul looks at the jury 'I don't deny that. I was defend…'

'Thank you, Mr Thomas.'

'And how about your neighbour, whose music player was ruined, did you hit him?'

'I'm afraid I did. He was making so much noi…'

'Thank you, Mr Thomas.'

'You saw Mr Owen-Rutherford in Chelterton one day, when you were with your friends Mr Adu and Mr Roman, is that correct?'

'Yes.'

'But you lied to them, didn't you? You told them he was a neighbour.'

'I did but…'

'Thank you.

'Now, moving onto Mauritius if I may.' The lawyer doesn't wait for permission. 'You discovered that Mr Owen-Rutherford was in a relationship with your ex-wife and that they were going on holiday together, so in fury, you purchased a highly priced ticket and followed her out there with the express purpose of murdering her.'

Paul grips his balls and swallows, but doesn't let his posture slip. 'I did not have any intention of murdering her.'

'But you couldn't help yourself.'

'I did not murder Fee,' Paul meets the eyes of his aggressor with as much composure as he can muster.

The barrister continues his attack, his aim to incur fury, to enable the jury to experience first-hand the anger and violence of this person on the stand, but Paul has been primed by Porterhouse and he stands firm, the only hint of his feelings, a slight tensing of the jaw.

When Porterhouse bounces to his feet, Paul's shoulders and face muscles drop, just a little.

'When you began your sessions with Mr Owen-Rutherford, did you find him helpful?'

Paul nods three times. 'Yes. It took a while but eventually I realised that I was as much at fault as Fee. He showed me how to manage my anger. I'm a better man because of Max.'

'That's very magnanimous of you, considering you tell us that the man murdered your wife.'

'You asked me the question and I am telling you the truth.' Paul's breath speeds up, 'If you asked me how I feel about him now I'd…'

'Thank you, Mr Thomas, just answer my questions if you would.'

Paul pulls his head up and resumes his stance.

There's a short pause as Porterhouse strolls across the court and consults his notes. Paul takes slow, deep breaths.

'What did you talk about?'

'To start with I was so mad with Fee, I think I ranted and raved quite a bit. Max kept asking me questions, trying to get me to think about our relationship from Fee's point of view, and eventually I got what he meant.'

'And what was that.'

'I was a selfish ba…, idiot and did nothing much to contribute to our marriage.'

'He told you that?'

'No. I worked it out for myself.'

Questions are served and answers returned in the court where no tennis ball is ever seen. The lawyer draws from Paul, a picture of his trust in Max, and Max's unreasonable interest in Fee and her home life. Paul's attack on the neighbour is revisited. Yes, Paul admits, he was stupid but he was protecting his small daughter and dog, who were frightened.

In mitigation of his attack on the youths in the Chinese restaurant, they were being rude and threatening to the very likeable proprietor and his wife. Paul was defending them, and the owners seemed grateful. They gave him his meal without charge.

'Why did you follow Fee to Mauritius, Paul?'

'I was worried about her. At first, I thought I was being over dramatic, but the more I thought about it, the more I realised how much Max knew about her, through me. I don't know what made me think she was in danger. Probably the way Max had used a different name, and lied about his job. It didn't feel right so I hot-footed it over there to see for myself.

'That was very foolhardy, and expensive wasn't it Mr Thomas?'

'I didn't think about that. Something in my gut told me she was in danger.'

'How did you feel about your ex-wife Mr Thomas?'

Paul relaxes his stance and puts his palm to the back of his neck, dropping his eyes to the edge of the witness box.

'I loved her.'

***

The defence case begins.

'No. I never saw him lose his temper.' Gloria stands upright in the box, one hand resting on the wooden edge, the other hanging at her hip still in the position she assumed while she swore to tell the truth.

David Porterhouse strolls to the edge of the box and considers her. 'But surely you knew what he was capable of. Mrs Thomas must have confided in you about his behaviour.'

Gloria stands tall and shakes her head. 'She was a very private person. She didn't really confide anythin' about Paul to me. And I didn't ask her. You have to respect people's feelin's.'

'But Kitty was very upset by a particular incident was she not? When her father was violent towards his neighbours.'

'Yes, she was for a while, but not for long because she loves her father. It was a storm in a teacup, that.'

The lawyer scans his notes. 'We've heard evidence from the police that Mr Thomas hid in the bushes and spied on you all. Did you ever see him?'

'No never. I think he had trouble adjustin' to bein' on his own. He isn't the type to kill anyone.'

'Please restrict yourself to answering the questions Mrs Adu.'

'Sorry.'

'He is accused of raping Mrs Roman. Did you get any impression that this happened?

'None at all. Twitch was a depressive. She had her ups and downs, but I never thought there was any reason for that. I know she suffered from post-natal depression in the past.'

'And Kitty was happy to go off with her father?'

'Oh yes. She loved her Daddy. He bought a dog, just for her, and they walked it and trained it together. He was a good Dad.'

The lawyer changes his tone to one of gentle enquiry. 'Mrs Adu, was Fee wealthy?'

Gloria frowns. 'I don't know. She had savin's I think, because there was never any problem buyin' what was needed. Her father has lots of money, and helped her with a deposit when she first moved into that house. I got the feelin' she would come into quite a bit when he died, and she had a well-paid job, until all this dyin' started. She gave that up to help me look after the kiddies.'

'Did she make any provision for the children's futures in the event of her death?'

Gloria nods. 'Yes. She showed me where her will was, and life insurance certificates. The children will be fine, financially, thank God.' Gloria touches her crucifix. 'She left everything to her next of kin. That's the kiddies, right?'

'Thank you Mrs Adu.'

The prosecution has no questions.

***

Maurice's fists are clenched and moisture slithers between his fingers. He opens his hands and moves them slightly in the cool air.

'I've known Mr Thomas for a couple of years. We met when our wives deserted us.'

'And did you have a smooth relationship?'

'Yes. No fights if that's what you mean. In fact, I can't even remember a heated discussion.'

'But you knew he had a temper.'

'He has a powerful sense of justice. His hackles rise if someone is thoughtless, but he's never been anything but loving with Kitty, his daughter. I think her happiness is a priority for him.'

'And with his ex-wife? Did he get angry with her?'

Maurice pauses and presses his fingers into the nape of his neck, tipping back his head to stare at the ceiling. 'He did get frustrated at first. I think he felt he was being excluded from decisions about Kitty's future. But he and Fee came to an understanding eventually.'

***

'Yeah, he raised his voice once or twice. At the beginning, he found it difficult to get to grips with the way Fee had walked out on him. We all felt the same about our relationships, it's why we got together. Mutual support.' Mick shrugs.

'It's a bit of a coincidence don't you think, Mr Adu, that your wives are all dead?'

'Unbelievable.' Mick sweeps his head from side to side. 'Millie was the first. A terrible accident. Paul and Maurice were there for me every step of the way. If they hadn't been, I would have cracked up.' He frowns. 'Of course, we didn't know Twitch was dead. She went missing and everyone thought she might have run away because of the pressure. She was a depressive, but we thought that if she'd killed herself she would have made it easier to find her, and left a note.'

The barrister for the prosecution rises.

318

You saw Mr Owen-Rutherford with the defendant's ex-wife, on your way to the airport, did you not.'

Yeah. I didn't know who he was, although I recognised him from somewhere. It was only later that I realised it was the guy we'd seen when we were in the deli. I thought he was Paul's neighbour. I told Paul as soon as I got home.

The lawyer stops pacing the floor and searches Mick's face. 'And now Mrs Owen-Rutherford is dead too.'

'Yes. What do you want me to say? It's terrible, but I don't see how Paul could be responsible.'

***

'You are Mr Rutherford's receptionist, I believe. May we know your name?'

Max's receptionist kneads her hands together.

'Julie Glover.'

'And how long have you worked for Mr Rutherford, Julie.' The defence barrister makes his voice sympathetic.

'About six years.'

'Six years. You must know him well after all that time.'

'Yes, I suppose so.'

'Were you responsible for filing his notes?'

'No. Mr Rutherford kept those in a cabinet in his office. He was very security conscious.'

'And in all the time you worked for him, did he give any indication that he was having a relationship with anyone?'

Julie relaxes. 'I guessed he'd met someone a year or two ago. Not that he said anything to me about it, but I could tell. He took more trouble over his appearance, and once, he took a bunch of flowers out to lunch with him.'

'But before that, no signs of romance?'

Julie gives her head a quick shake. 'No.'

'But you might not have known. If he'd had another girlfriend.'

'I might not, but he did ask *me* out, once. I said no of course, I'm happily married.'

'Did Mr Rutherford know that you were married?'

'Yes.' She tightens her lips.

The prosecutor rises. 'You didn't do his filing? Surely as a receptionist and administrator that would be something in the job description.'

'Well, I did some filing, correspondence, bills and so on.'

'So, you would have seen letters going out to clients confirming their appointments, for example.'

'Yes.'

'And Mr Thomas there.' Fitzsimons nods in Paul's direction, 'did you confirm his appointments?'

'Yes, although there was one occasion when he rang asking for an emergency consultation.'

'Would you tell the court when that was, please, Mrs Glover?'

'It was 2nd March.'

'Do you remember Mr Thomas arriving at the practice on that occasion?'

Julie's voice drops to a whisper. 'Yes, I do.'

'You do? And how did he seem?'

Objection. The witness is being asked to speculate.'

'Sustained.'

'Sorry My Lord.'

'Julie, would you describe to the court, the way Mr Thomas behaved on that day.'

'He looked stiff. He hardly spoke to me while he sat and waited for Mr Rutherford to come out and collect him.'

'Thank you, Mrs Glover. No further questions.'

***

In his summing up, the barrister for the prosecution struts back and forth before the jury. The twelve men and women lean back in their seats, withdrawing from his considerable presence.

'The defence has tried to distract you from the facts by throwing suspicion on the counsellor, Mr Owen-Rutherford, a man of good reputation, who took to his career because he wanted to help people who had suffered at the hands of deserting spouses. Who better to understand violence than a man who had it inflicted upon him as a child, and how worthy of him to use that experience to help others? Members of the jury, you have heard in the evidence that this man,' Fitzsimons indicates Paul with an outstretched arm, his finger jabbing in accusation, '*this* man, has lied and fought his way through life since his wife left him. We have heard witnesses state that he caused GBH, frightened his daughter so much that she refused to see him, and raped a woman, not any woman but a close friend of his ex-wife's. He has caused hurt at work, lied to his friends, and spied on his wife. He had the motives of jealousy, and anger at being duped.

As he takes his seat the jury members stare at Paul. Are their faces speculative, or accusing? Paul is afraid to contemplate. He hopes his own barrister will make as convincing an argument in his defence. The lawyer for the defence rises, and walks confidently towards the jurors. The twelve members lean towards him. Again, Paul wonders if he can read anything into their body language, so different for the defence from their apparent revulsion of the prosecutor.

'On the one hand we have Paul Thomas, loving and passionate, who rushed to his ex-wife's side at great expense in concern that she had been misled. A man who cares deeply for his daughter and is a faithful and reliable friend. A man who admits to still loving his wife despite the way she treated him.

On the other we have a lying, scheming and unethical counsellor. Max Owen-Rutherford pumped his client, Mr Thomas far more than was necessary, about his ex-wife. He then became everything she looked for in a man. He lied to her, talked her into a holiday and duped her and Mrs Adu, and Fee's small and innocent daughter, Kitty, into taking part in a marriage. He had a motive - two motives even. First, from his own experience, his dislike of women who desert their husbands, and second, money. He was in terrible debt, and Fee Thomas was comfortably off with a rich father. Max Rutherford, or William Owen, or whatever name you choose to call him, married Fee to become her next of kin, and so inherit her savings and her life insurance.

Mr Owen-Rutherford, pretended to be someone he was not. He lied about his career on the oil rigs, used a false name and tricked this unsuspecting woman, Fee Thomas, into marrying him. Then he pushed her from a cliff-top to a violent death. He wanted revenge for all the pain of his childhood. He needed money to pay off his debt.

'There can be no doubt that Mr Thomas is prone to anger, but this, historically, has been a knee-jerk re-action to anti-social behaviour. He took the expensive step of attending counselling sessions because he recognised the impact of his anger on himself and those around him. His motives for going all that way to Mauritius were not, as the prosecution suggests, in order to kill Fee, but to protect her.

'You have heard that despite Mr Owen-Rutherford being at the top of that same cliff where his wife died, the police did not investigate him as fully as they should have done, instead concentrating their efforts on poor Mr Thomas. If they had checked, they would have found that Mr

Owen-Rutherford had considerable motivation to commit this murder, and Mr Thomas would not be standing before you today.

When both lawyers are seated and the court has returned to silence, the judge has the final word, reminding the jury of the evidence they have heard. He sums up by saying, 'There appear to be two suspects in this case, and they are also the only witnesses to the events that unfolded on that fateful afternoon. The law demands that you must be in *no doubt* if you are to pronounce the defendant guilty. If you are satisfied that the police procedures were carried out properly and that Mr Owen-Rutherford could not possibly have murdered his new wife, then you should return a guilty plea, but if there is doubt in your mind, you must find Paul Thomas not guilty.

***

Paul looks down at the courtroom from the witness stand. Below him, members of the public, the press, his friends, his parents and Gloria, sit with their eyes riveted on the returning jury. The men and women file into their places and their leader, the woman with the orange hair, rises to her feet.

The judge clears his throat.

'Members of the jury, have you reached a verdict upon which you all agree?'

'We have.'

'Do you find the defendant guilty, or not guilty?'

Paul stiffens, his breath shallow and his pulse fast.

The woman looks at Paul and smiles, then turns to the judge. 'Not guilty.'

Paul inhales, plonks onto the seat behind him and covers his face with both hands. Tears spurt from his eyes and between his fingers.

An officer of the court touches him on the shoulder.

'Mr Thomas, you're free to go.'

'Yes.' He pulls out a tissue. 'Thank you.'

As he steps down, Mick and Maurice rush to his side. Mick grasps his friend in a huge bear-hug and Paul can feel the rough fabric of his jacket against his face and the banging of Maurice's fists on his back. Across the room, police officers are heading towards Max.

Chapter 71

'Thank God that's over.' Paul stands with Mick and Maurice on the pavement outside the Crown Court, watching Max being helped into the back seat of a police car. People troop up and down the steps of the building, glancing at the three men and whispering to one another. Mick bangs Paul on the back. 'It's over man. You did it!'

Paul shakes his head, humping his shoulders to slide his fingers into the snug pockets of his jeans. 'I thought I'd blown it for a while. They haven't come after me for Twitch's murder either. I suppose they could pin that on him as well.'

'Let's get out of here.' Mick jerks his thumb at a pub a short way along the road, its sign, a picture of a bewigged and bespectacled elderly man with a bulbous nose, and its name, *The Judge and Jury*. 'Fancy a pint?'

Paul grins at his friends, then punches Mick on the upper arm. 'Your round, Mate. I've done my bit.'

In the back of the police car, Max's pale face looms from the dark interior staring in bleak amazement at the three men, dodging through the crowd towards *The Judge and Jury*. The indicator of the unmarked vehicle blinks, and its bumper nudges into the traffic. Soon he is lost among the flickering hips and bonnets of the rush-hour.

The End...

or is it?